BY CHRISTIE GOLDEN

WORLD OF WARCRAFT

Lord of the Clans
Rise of the Horde
Beyond the Dark Portal
  (with Aaron S. Rosenberg)
Arthas: Rise of the Lich King
The Shattering: Prelude to Cataclysm
Thrall: Twilight of the Aspects

Jaina Proudmoore: Tides of War
War Crimes
Warcraft: Durotan: The Official Movie
  Prequel
Warcraft: The Official Movie Novelization
Before the Storm

STARCRAFT

The Dark Templar Saga, Book One:
  Firstborn
The Dark Templar Saga, Book Two:
  Shadow Hunters

The Dark Templar Saga, Book Three:
  Twilight
StarCraft II: Devils' Due
StarCraft II: Flashpoint

STAR WARS

Star Wars: Fate of the Jedi: *Omen*
Star Wars: Fate of the Jedi: *Allies*
Star Wars: Fate of the Jedi: *Ascension*

Star Wars: Dark Disciple
Star Wars: Battlefront II: Inferno Squad

ORIGINAL NOVELS

On Fire's Wings
In Stone's Clasp
Under Sea's Shadow

Instrument of Fate
King's Man & Thief
A.D. 999 (as Jadrien Bell)

STAR TREK

Star Trek Voyager: The Murdered Sun
Star Trek Voyager: Marooned
Star Trek Voyager: Seven of Nine
Star Trek: Voyager: The Dark Matters
  Trilogy, Book 1: Cloak and Dagger
Star Trek: Voyager: The Dark Matters
  Trilogy, Book 2: Ghost Dance
Star Trek: Voyager: The Dark Matters
  Trilogy, Book 3: Shadow of Heaven
Star Trek Voyager: No Man's Land
Star Trek Voyager: What Lay Beyond

Star Trek Voyager: Homecoming
Star Trek Voyager: The Farther Shore
Star Trek Voyager: Spirit Walk, Book 1:
  Old Wounds
Star Trek Voyager: Spirit Walk, Book 2:
  Enemy of My Enemy
Star Trek The Next Generation:
  Double Helix: The First Virtue
  (with Michael Jan Friedman)
Star Trek: Hard Crash (short story)
Star Trek: The Last Roundup

WORLD OF WARCRAFT

Before the Storm

BEFORE THE STORM

Christie Golden

DEL REY · NEW YORK

Published in the United States by Del Rey, an imprint of Random House, a division of Penguin Random House LLC, New York.

DEL REY and the HOUSE colophon are registered trademarks of Penguin Random House LLC.

WARCRAFT, WORLD OF WARCRAFT, and BLIZZARD ENTERTAINMENT are trademarks and/or registered trademarks of Blizzard Entertainment, Inc., in the U.S. and/or other countries. All other trademark references herein are the properties of their respective owners.

Hardback ISBN 978-0-399-59409-0
Ebook ISBN 978-0-399-59410-6

Printed in the United States of America on acid-free paper

randomhousebooks.com

4 6 8 9 7 5

Book design by Mary Wirth

This book is dedicated to three who have
championed it and striven to make it even better:

Tom Hoeler, my editor at Del Rey, Cate Gary, my editor
a few steps away, here at Blizzard, and Alex Afrasiabi,
creative director of World of Warcraft.

Thank you all so very much for your love for the characters
and the world, for your attention to both little details
and the big picture, for exploring this path with me,
and for wanting to make *Before the Storm*
the best book it could possibly be.

LORDAERON

UNDERCITY

EASTERN ARATHI
HIGHLANDS

KINGDOMS

IRONFORGE

STORMWIND
CITY

DARNASSUS

AZSHARA

ORGRIMMAR

KALIMDOR

THUNDER BLUFF

SILITHUS   TANARIS

WORLD OF WARCRAFT

Before the Storm

Silithus

Kezzig Klackwhistle straightened from where he'd been kneeling for what felt like at least a decade, placing his big green hands on the small of his back and grimacing at the ensuing cascade of pops. He licked his dry lips and looked around, squinting against the blinding sunlight and mopping his bald head with a sweat-stiff kerchief. Here and there were tightly clustered swirling swarms of insects. And of course the sand, everywhere, and most of it probably going to end up inside his underclothes. Just as it had yesterday. And the day before.

Man, Silithus was an ugly place.

Its appearance had not been improved in the slightest by the gargantuan sword an angry titan had shoved into it.

The thing was massive. Ginormous. Colossal. All the grand and fancy and multisyllabic words goblins smarter than he could possibly throw at it. It had been plunged deep into the heart of the world, right here in scenic Silithus. The bright side, of course, was that the enormous artifact provided a great deal of what he and the other hundred or so goblins were searching for right this very moment.

"Jixil?" he said to his companion, who was analyzing a hovering rock with the Spect-o-Matic 4000.

"Yeah?" The other goblin peered at the reading, shook his head, and tried again.

"I hate this place."

"Ya do? Huh. It speaks well of you." Glaring at the piece of equipment, the smaller, squatter goblin smacked it soundly.

"Ha ha, very funny," Kezzig grumbled. "No, I mean it."

Jixil sighed, trudged to another rock, and began to scan it. "We *all* hate this place, Kezzig."

"No, I really mean it. I'm not cut out for this environment. I used to work in Winterspring. I'm a snow-loving, snuggle-by-the-fire, holly-jolly kinda goblin."

Jixil threw him a withering glance. "So what happened to bring you here instead of staying there, where you weren't annoying me?"

Kezzig grimaced, rubbing the back of his neck. "Little Miss Lunnix Sprocketslip happened. See, I was working in her mining supply shop. I'd go out as a guide for the occasional visitor to our cozy little hamlet of Everlook. Lunny and I kinda . . . yeah." He smiled nostalgically for a moment, then scowled. "Then she goes and gets her nose out of joint when she caught me hanging around Gogo."

"Gogo," Jixil repeated in a flat voice. "Gee. I wonder why Lunnix would get upset with you hanging around a girl named *Gogo*."

"I know! Gimme a break. It gets *cold* up there. A guy has to snuggle by the fire now and then or he'll freeze, am I right? Anyway, that place suddenly got hotter than here at midday."

"We got nothing here," Jixil said. He'd obviously stopped paying attention to Kezzig's description of his Winterspring plight. Sighing, Kezzig picked up the huge pack of equipment, slung it easily over his shoulders, and lugged it over to where Jixil still was hoping for positive results. Kezzig let the bundle drop to the earth, and there came the sound of delicate pieces of equipment clanking perilously against one another.

"I hate sand," he continued. "I hate the sun. And oh boy, do I really, *really* hate bugs. I hate the little bugs, because they like to crawl into your ears and up your nose. I hate the big bugs because, well, they're big bugs. I mean, who doesn't hate that? It's kind of a universal hate. But my particular hate burns with the light of a thousand suns."

"I thought you hated suns."

"I do, but I—"

Jixil suddenly stiffened. His magenta eyes widened as he stared at his Spect-o-Matic.

"What I meant was—"

"Shut up, you idiot!" Jixil snapped. Now Kezzig was staring at the instrument, too.

It was going insane.

Its little needle flipped back and forth. The small light at the top flashed an urgent, excited red.

The two goblins looked at each other. "Do you know what this means?" Jixil said in a voice that trembled.

Kezzig's lips curved in a grin that revealed almost all of his jagged yellow teeth. He curled one hand into a fist and smacked it firmly into the palm of the other.

"It means," he said, "we get to eliminate the competition."

CHAPTER ONE

Stormwind

R ain fell on the somber throngs making their way to Lion's Rest as if even the sky wept for those who had sacrificed their lives to defeat the Burning Legion. Anduin Wrynn, king of Stormwind, stood a few steps back from the podium where he soon would be addressing mourners of all the Alliance races. He watched them silently as they arrived, moved to see them, loath to speak to them. He suspected that this service honoring the fallen would be the most difficult he had endured in his relatively short life not just for the other mourners but for himself; it would be held in the shadow of his father's empty tomb.

Anduin had attended far, far too many ceremonies honoring the casualties of war. As he did each time—as, he believed, every good leader did—he hoped and prayed that this one would be the last.

But it never was.

Somehow there was always another enemy. Sometimes the enemy was new, a group springing up seemingly out of nowhere. Or something ancient and long-chained or buried, supposedly neutralized, rising after eons of silence to terrorize and destroy innocents. Other times the enemy was bleakly familiar but no less a threat for the intimacy of the knowledge.

How had his father met those challenges time after time? Anduin wondered. How had his grandfather? Now was a time of relative quiet, but the next enemy, the next challenge, doubtless would arrive all too soon.

It had not been all that long since Varian Wrynn's death, but for the great man's son it felt like a lifetime. Varian had fallen in the first real push of this latest war against the Legion, apparently slain as much by betrayal from a supposed ally, Sylvanas Windrunner, as by the monstrous, fel-fueled creatures vomited forth from the Twisting Nether. Another account, from someone Anduin trusted, contested that version, suggesting that Sylvanas had had no other choice. Anduin was not sure what to believe. Thoughts of the cunning and treacherous leader of the Horde made Anduin angry, as they always did. And, as always, he called on the Holy Light for calmness. It did not serve to harbor hatred in his heart even for such a deserving enemy. And it would not bring back his father. Anduin took comfort in knowing that the legendary warrior had died fighting and that his sacrifice had saved many lives.

And in that fraction of a second, Prince Anduin Wrynn had become king.

In many ways, Anduin had been preparing for this position all his life. Even so, he was keenly aware that in other, very important, ways, he hadn't truly been ready. Maybe still wasn't. His father had loomed so large not just in the eyes of his youthful son but in the eyes of Varian's people—even in the eyes of his enemies.

Dubbed Lo'Gosh, or "ghost wolf," for his ferocity in battle, Varian had been more than a powerful warrior superbly skilled at combat. He had been an extraordinary leader. In the first few weeks after his father's shocking death, Anduin had done his best to comfort a grieving, stunned populace reeling from the loss, while denying himself a proper chance to mourn.

They grieved for the Wolf. Anduin grieved for the man.

And when he lay awake at night, unable to sleep, he would wonder just how many demons in the end it had taken to murder King Varian Wrynn.

Once he had voiced this thought to Genn Greymane, king of the fallen realm of Gilneas, who had stepped in to counsel the fledgling monarch. The old man had smiled even though sorrow haunted his eyes.

"All I can tell you, my boy, is that before they got to your father, he had single-handedly killed the largest fel reaver I ever saw, in order to save an airship full of retreating soldiers. I know for certain that Varian Wrynn made the Legion pay dearly for taking him."

Anduin did not doubt that. It wasn't enough, but it had to be.

Although there were plenty of armed guards in attendance, Anduin had put on no armor on this day when the dead were remembered. He was dressed in a white silk shirt, lambskin gloves, dark blue breeches, and a heavy formal coat trimmed in gold. His only weapon was an instrument of peace as much as war: the mace Fearbreaker, which he wore at his side. When he had gifted the young prince with it, the former dwarf king Magni Bronzebeard had said that Fearbreaker was a weapon that had known the taste of blood in some hands and had stanched blood in others.

Anduin wanted to meet and thank as many as he could among the bereaved today. He wished he could console everyone, but the cold truth was that such a thing was impossible. He took comfort in the certainty that the Light shone upon them all . . . even a tired young king.

He lifted his face, knowing the sun was behind the clouds and letting the gentle drops fall like a benediction. He recalled that it also had rained a few years ago during a similar ceremony honoring those who had made the final, greatest sacrifice in the campaign to halt the mighty Lich King.

Two whom Anduin loved had been in attendance then who were not here today. One, of course, was his father. The second was the woman he had fondly called Aunt Jaina: Lady Jaina Proudmoore. Once, the lady of Theramore and the prince of Stormwind had been in agreement regarding the desire for peace between the Alliance and the Horde.

And once there had *been* a Theramore.

But Jaina's city had been destroyed by the Horde in the most horrific manner possible, and its bereft lady had never been able to ease the pain of that terrible moment fully. Anduin had watched her try repeatedly, only to have some fresh torment reinjure her wounded heart. Finally, unable to bear the thought of working alongside the Horde even against so dread a foe as the demonic Legion, Jaina had walked out on the Kirin Tor, which she led, on the blue dragon Kalecgos, whom she loved, and on Anduin, whom she had inspired his whole life.

"May I?" The voice was warm and kind, as was the woman who asked the question.

Anduin smiled down at High Priestess Laurena. She was asking if he wished her blessing. He nodded and inclined his head and felt the tightness in his chest ease and his soul settle. He then stood respectfully to the side while she spoke to the crowd, awaiting his own turn.

He had not been able to speak formally at his father's memorial service. The grief had been too raw, too overwhelming. It had shifted shape in his heart over time, becoming less immediate but no less great, and so he had agreed to say a few words today.

Anduin stepped beside his father's tomb. It was empty; what the Legion had done to Varian had ensured that his body could not be recovered. Anduin regarded the stone face on the tomb. It was a good likeness and a comfort to look upon. But even the skilled stonecrafters could not capture Varian's fire, his quick temper, his easy laugh, his *motion*. In a way, Anduin was glad the tomb was empty; he would always, in his heart, see his father as alive and vibrant.

His mind went back to when he first had ventured to the place where his father had fallen. Where Shalamayne, gifted to Varian by the lady Jaina, had lain, dormant without Varian's touch. Awaiting the touch of another to which it would respond.

The touch of the great warrior's son.

As he held it, he had almost felt Varian's presence. It was then, when Anduin truly accepted the duties of a king, that light had again begun to swirl in the sword—not the orange-red hue of the warrior but the warm, golden glow of the priest. At that moment, Anduin had begun to heal.

Genn Greymane would be the last person to call himself eloquent, but Anduin would never forget the words the older man had said: *Your father's actions were indeed heroic. They were his challenge to us, his people, to never let fear prevail . . . even at the very gates of hell.*

Genn wisely had not said they were never to fear. They were only not to let it win.

I will not, Father. And Shalamayne knows that.

Anduin forced himself to return to the present. He nodded to Laurena, then turned to look at the crowd. The rain was slowing but hadn't stopped, yet no one seemed inclined to leave. Anduin's gaze swept over the widows and widowers, the childless parents, the orphans, and the veterans. He was proud of the soldiers who had died on the battlefield. He hoped their spirits would rest easily, knowing their loved ones were heroes, too.

Because there was no one assembled at Lion's Rest today who had let fear prevail.

He spotted Greymane, hanging back beside a lamppost. Their eyes met, and the older man nodded a brief acknowledgment. Anduin allowed his gaze to roam over the faces, those he knew and those he did not. A little pandaren girl was struggling not to cry; he gave her a reassuring smile. She gulped and smiled back shakily.

"Like many of you, I know firsthand the pain of loss," he said. His voice rang clear and strong, carrying to those who stood in the farthest rows. "You all know that my fath—"

He paused, clearing his throat, and continued. "King Varian Wrynn . . . fell during the first major battle at the Broken Isles, when the Legion invaded Azeroth yet again. He died to save his soldiers— the brave men and women who faced unspeakable horrors to protect us, our lands, our world. He knew that no one—not even a king—is more important than the Alliance. Each of you has lost your own king or queen. Your father or mother, brother or sister, son or daughter.

"And because he and so many others had the courage to make that sacrifice, we did the impossible." Anduin looked from face to face, saw how hungry they were for comfort. "We *defeated* the Burning Legion. And now we honor those who sacrificed all. We honor them not by dying . . . but by living. By healing our wounds and helping others heal. By laughing and feeling the sun on our faces. By holding our loved ones close and letting them know every hour, every minute of every day, *that they matter.*"

The rain had stopped. The clouds began to clear, and bits of bright blue peeked through.

"Neither we nor our world escaped unscathed," Anduin continued. "We are scarred. A defeated titan has pierced our beloved Azeroth with a terrible sword crafted from hatred made manifest, and we do not yet know what toll it will take. Places in our hearts will forever remain empty. But if you would serve one king who grieves with you today, if you would honor the memory of another king who died for you, then I urge you—live. For our lives, our joy, our world, these are the gifts of the fallen. And we must cherish them. For the Alliance!"

The crowd cheered, some through their tears. Now it was others' turn to speak. Anduin stepped to the side, allowing them to come up and address the crowd. As he did so, his gaze flitted back to Greymane, and his heart sank.

Mathias Shaw, master of spies and head of Stormwind's intelligence service, SI:7, stood beside the deposed king of Gilneas. And both men looked as grim as Anduin had ever seen them.

He was not overly fond of Shaw, though the spymaster had served Varian and now Anduin loyally and well. The king was intelligent enough to understand and value the service SI:7 agents performed for their kingdom. Indeed, he would never know exactly how many agents had lost their lives in this recent war. Unlike warriors, those who operated in the shadows lived, served, and died with few ever knowing of their deeds. No, it wasn't the spymaster himself Anduin disliked. It was the need for men and women like him that he regretted.

Laurena had followed his gaze and stepped in without a word as Anduin nodded to Genn and Shaw, moving his head to indicate that they should speak away from the throngs of mourners who would not depart for some time. Some lingered, kneeling in prayer. Some would go home and continue to grieve in private. Others would go to taverns to remind themselves that they were still among the living and could yet enjoy food and drink and laughter. To celebrate life, as Anduin had urged them.

But a king's tasks were never done.

The three men walked quietly behind the memorial. The clouds were almost gone, and the rays of the setting sun sparkled on the water of the harbor that spread out below.

Anduin went to the carved stone wall and placed his hands on it, breathing deeply of the sea air and listening to the cry of the gulls. Taking a moment to steady himself before hearing whatever dark words Shaw had to utter.

As soon as word of the great sword in Silithus had reached him, Anduin had ordered Shaw to investigate and report. He needed boots on the ground there, not the wild rumors that had been circulating. It sounded impossible, and terrifying, and the worst part of it was that it was all true. The final act of a corrupted being, the very last and most devastating blow struck in the war against the Legion, had all but obliterated much of Silithus. The only thing that had mitigated the scope of the disaster had been that mercifully, in his random, angry blow, Sargeras had not thrust the sword into a more populated part of the world than the nearly empty desert land. Had he struck here, in the Eastern Kingdoms, a continent away from Silithus . . . Anduin could not permit himself to go down that path. He would be grateful for what little he could be.

Shaw had hitherto sent missives with information. Anduin had not expected the man himself to return quite so soon.

"Tell me," was all the king said.

"Goblins, sir. A whole mess of the unsavory creatures. It seems they began arriving within a day of—"

He broke off. No one had come up with a vocabulary to describe the sword that felt comfortable. "Of the sword-strike," Mathias continued.

"That fast?" Anduin was startled. He kept his expression neutral as he continued to gaze out over the water. *The ships and their crews look so small from here,* he thought. *Like toys. So breakable.*

"That fast," Shaw confirmed.

"Goblins aren't the most charming, but they are cunning. And they do things for a reason," Anduin said.

"And those reasons usually involve money."

Only one group could gather and finance so many goblins so quickly: the Bilgewater Cartel, which had the support of the Horde. This had the oily fingerprints of the unctuous and morally deficient Jastor Gallywix all over it.

Anduin pressed his lips together for a moment before speaking. "So. The Horde has found something valuable in Silithus. What is it this time? Another ancient city to scavenge?"

"No, Your Majesty. They found . . . this."

The king turned around. In Shaw's palm was a dirty white handkerchief. Wordlessly, he unfolded it.

In the center was a small pebble of some golden substance. It looked like honey and ice, warm and inviting, yet also cool and comforting. And . . . it was glowing. Anduin eyed it skeptically. It was appealing, yes, but no more so than other gems. It didn't look like anything to warrant a huge influx of goblins.

Anduin was confused, and he glanced over at Genn, an eyebrow raised in query. He knew little of spycraft, and Shaw, though well regarded by all, was still largely an enigma that Anduin was only beginning to decipher.

Genn nodded, acknowledging that Shaw's gesture was odd and the object odder but indicating that however Shaw wished to proceed, Anduin could trust him. The king removed his glove and held out his hand.

The stone tumbled gently into Anduin's palm.

And he gasped.

The heaviness of grief vanished as if it were physical armor that had been seized and yanked off. Weariness fled, replaced by surging, almost crackling energy and insight. Strategies raced through his head, each one of them sound and successful, each one of them engendering a shift in comprehension and ensuring a lasting peace that benefited every being on Azeroth.

Not only his mind but also his body seemed to ascend abruptly and shockingly, rocketing in an instant to whole new levels of strength, dexterity, and control. Anduin felt like he could not only climb mountains . . . he could *move* them. He could end war, channel the Light into every dark corner. He was exultant and also perfectly, wholly calm and completely certain as to how to channel this rushing river—no, tsunami—of energy and power. Not even the Light affected him as this . . . *this* did. The sensation was similar but less spiritual, more physical.

More alarming.

For a long moment, Anduin couldn't speak, could only stare in wonder at the infinitely precious thing he cupped in his palm. At last he found his voice.

"What . . . what *is* this?" he managed.

"We don't know." Shaw's voice was blunt.

What could be done with this! Anduin thought. *How many could it heal? How many could it strengthen, soothe, invigorate, inspire?*

How many could it kill?

The thought was a gut punch, and he felt the elation inspired by the gemstone retreat.

When he spoke again, Anduin's voice was strong and determined. "It would seem the Horde *does* know . . . and we must find out more." This could not be allowed to fall into the wrong hands.

Into Sylvanas's hands . . .

So much power . . .

He closed his fingers carefully around the small nugget of limitless possibility and turned again to the west.

"Agreed," Shaw replied. "We have eyes on it."

They stood for a moment while Anduin considered his next words. He knew that both Shaw and Greymane—the latter uncharacteristically silent but looking on approvingly—were awaiting his orders, and he was grateful to have such staunch individuals in his service. A lesser man than Shaw would have pocketed this sample.

"Get your best people on it, Shaw. Pull them off other assignments if need be. We must learn more about this. I'll be calling a meeting of my advisers shortly." Anduin extended his hand for Shaw's handkerchief and carefully rewrapped the small chunk of this unknown, unbelievable material. He tucked it into a pocket. The sensation was less intense, but he still could feel it.

Anduin already had intended to travel, to visit the lands of Stormwind's allies. To thank them and help them recover from the ravages of war.

His schedule had just been accelerated drastically.

CHAPTER TWO

Orgrimmar

Sylvanas Windrunner, former ranger-general of Silvermoon, the Dark Lady of the Forsaken, and present warchief of the mighty Horde, had resented being told to come to Orgrimmar like a dog that needed to perform all its tricks. She had wanted to return to the Undercity. She missed its shadows, its dampness, its restful quietude. *Rest in peace,* she thought grimly, and felt the tug of an amused smile. It faded almost at once as she continued pacing impatiently in the small chamber behind the warchief's throne in Grommash Hold.

She paused, her sharp ears picking up the sound of familiar footsteps. The tanned hide that served as a nod to privacy was drawn aside, and the newcomer entered.

"You are late. Another quarter of an hour and I would have been forced to ride without my champion beside me."

He bowed. "Forgive me, my queen. I have been about your business, and it took longer than expected."

She was unarmed, but he carried a bow and bore a quiver full of arrows. The only human ever to become a ranger, he was a superlative marksman. It was one reason he was the best bodyguard Sylvanas could possibly have. There were other reasons, too, reasons that had their roots in the distant past, when the two had connected under a bright and beautiful sun and had fought for bright and beautiful things.

Death had claimed them both, human and elf alike. Little now was bright and beautiful, and much of the past they had shared had grown dim and hazy.

But not all of it.

Although Sylvanas had left behind most warmer emotions the moment she had risen from the dead as a banshee, anger somehow had retained its heat. But she felt it subside to embers now. She seldom stayed angry for long at Nathanos Marris, known now as Blightcaller. And he had indeed been about her business, visiting the Undercity, while she had been saddled with duties that had kept her here in Orgrimmar.

She wanted to reach for his hand but contented herself with smiling benevolently at him. "You are forgiven," she said. "Now. Tell me of our home."

Sylvanas expected a brief recitation of modest concerns, a reaffirmation of the Forsaken's loyalty to their Dark Lady. Instead, Nathanos frowned. "The situation . . . is complicated, my queen."

Her smile faded. What could possibly be "complicated" about it? The Undercity belonged to the Forsaken, and they were her people.

"Your presence has been sorely missed," he said. "While many are proud that at last the Horde has a Forsaken as its warchief, there are some who feel that you have perchance forgotten those who have been more loyal to you than any other."

She laughed sharply and without humor. "Baine and Saurfang and the others say I have not been giving them enough attention. My people say I have been giving them *too* much. Whatever I do, someone objects. How can anyone rule like this?" She shook her pale head. "A curse upon Vol'jin and his loa. I should have stayed in the shadows, where I could be effective without being interrogated."

Where I could do as I truly wished.

She'd never wanted this. Not really. As she had told the troll Vol'jin before, during the trial of the late and greatly unlamented Garrosh Hellscream, she liked her power, her control, on the subtle side. But with quite literally his dying breath, Vol'jin, the Horde's leader, had commanded that she do the opposite. He had claimed he had been granted a vision by the loa he honored.

You must step out of da shadows and lead.

You must be warchief.

Vol'jin had been someone she respected, although they had clashed on occasion. He lacked the abrasiveness that so often characterized orc leadership. And she had been genuinely sorry he had fallen—and not just because of the responsibility he had placed on her head.

She had opened her mouth to ask Nathanos to continue when she heard the *thump-thump* of a spear butt on the stone floor outside the small room. Sylvanas closed her eyes, trying to gather patience. "Enter," she growled.

One of the Kor'kron, the elite orc guards of the hold, obeyed and stood at attention, his green face unreadable. "Warchief," he said, "it is time. Your people await you."

Your people. No. Her people were back in the Undercity, missing her and feeling slighted, unaware that she would like nothing more than to return and be among them once more.

"I will be out momentarily," Sylvanas said, adding, in case the guard did not understand what was behind the words, "Leave us."

The orc saluted and withdrew, letting the skin flap fall into place.

"We will continue this as we ride," she told Nathanos. "And I have other things I wish to discuss with you as well."

"As my queen wishes," Nathanos replied.

A few years earlier, Garrosh Hellscream had pushed to have a massive celebration in Orgrimmar to commemorate the end of the Northrend campaign. He wasn't warchief—not then. There had been a parade of every veteran who wished to participate, their path strewn with imported pine boughs, and a gigantic feast awaited them at the end of the route.

It had been extravagant, and expensive, and Sylvanas had no intention of following in the footsteps of Hellscream, not just in this situation but in any. He had been arrogant, brutal, impulsive. His decision to attack Theramore with a devastating mana bomb had the softer races wrestling with their consciences, although the only thing that had truly troubled Sylvanas about it was the orc's timing. Sylvanas had loathed him and had secretly conspired—regrettably without success—to kill him even after he had been arrested and charged with war crimes. When, inevitably, Garrosh *had* been killed, Sylvanas had been immensely pleased.

Varok Saurfang, the leader of the orcs, and Baine Bloodhoof, high chieftain of the tauren, had borne no love for Garrosh either. But they had pushed Sylvanas to make a public appearance in Orgrimmar and at least some kind of gesture to mark the end of the war. *Brave members of this Horde you lead fought and died to make sure the Legion did not destroy this world, as the demons have so many others,* the young bull had intoned. He had been but one step away from openly rebuking her.

Sylvanas recalled Saurfang's thinly veiled . . . warning? Threat? *You are the leader of* all *the Horde—orcs, tauren, trolls, blood elves, pandaren, goblins—as well as the Forsaken. You must never forget that, or else* they *might.*

What I will not forget, orc, she thought, ire rising in her anew, *are those words.*

So now, instead of returning home and addressing the Forsaken's concerns, Sylvanas sat astride one of her bony skeletal horses, waving to the throngs of celebrants who crowded the streets of Orgrimmar. The march—she had taken care that no one referred to it as a "parade"—officially began at the entrance to the Horde capital. On one side of the gargantuan gates were clusters of the blood elves and Forsaken who inhabited the city.

The blood elves were all dressed splendidly in their predictable colors of red and gold. At their head was Lor'themar Theron. He rode a red-plumed hawkstrider and met her gaze evenly.

Friends, they had been. Theron had served under a living Sylvanas when she was ranger-general of the high elves. They had been comrades in arms, much like the one who rode beside her as her champion. But whereas Nathanos, a mortal human in years past and now Forsaken, had kept his unswerving loyalty to her, Sylvanas knew that Theron's was to his people.

People who had been just like her once.

They were just like her no more.

Theron inclined his head. He would serve, at least for the moment. Not one for speeches, Sylvanas merely nodded back and turned to the group of Forsaken.

They stood patiently, as always, and she was proud of them for that. But she could not show favoritism, not here. So she gave them the same greeting she had given Lor'themar and the sin'dorei, then nudged her steed to move through the gate. The blood elves and the Forsaken fell in line, riding behind so as not to crowd her. That had been her stipulation, and she had stood firm on it. She wanted to be able to snatch at least a few moments of privacy. There were things meant for her champion's ears alone.

"Tell me more about the thoughts of my people," she ordered.

"From their perspective," the dark ranger resumed, "you were a fixture in the Undercity. You made them, you worked to prolong their existence, you were everything to them. Your ascension to warchief was so sudden, the threat so great and so immediate, that you left no one behind to care for them."

Sylvanas nodded. She supposed she could understand that.

"You left a great hole. And holes in power tend to be filled."

Her red eyes widened. Was he speaking of a coup? The queen's mind flashed back a few years to the betrayal of Varimathras, a demon she had thought would obey her. He had joined with the ungrateful wretch Putress, a Forsaken apothecary who had created a plague against both the living and the undead and who had nearly killed Sylvanas herself. Retaking the Undercity had been a bloody endeavor. But no. Even as the thought occurred to her, she knew that her loyal champion would not be speaking in so casual a manner if something so terrible had happened.

Reading her expression perfectly, as he so often did, Nathanos hastened to reassure her. "All is calm there, my queen. But in the absence of a single powerful leader, the inhabitants of your city have formed a governing body to tend to the population's needs."

"Ah, I see. An interim organization. That is . . . not unreasonable."

The warchief's path through the city would take her first through an alley lined with shops called the Drag and then to the Valley of

Honor. The Drag had once been an apt name for the area, which had abutted a canyon wall in a less than savory part of the city before the Cataclysm. With that terrible event, the Drag, like so much of beleaguered Azeroth, had physically shifted. Like Sylvanas Windrunner herself, it had emerged from the shadows. Sunlight now illuminated the winding, hard-packed dirt of the streets. More reputable establishments, such as clothing shops and ink supply stores, seemed to be springing up as well.

"They are calling themselves the Desolate Council," Nathanos continued.

"A rather self-pitying name," Sylvanas murmured.

"Perhaps," Nathanos agreed. "But it is a clear indicator of their feelings." He glanced over at her as they rode. "My queen, there are rumors about things that you have done in this war. Some of those rumors are even true."

"What kind of rumors?" she asked, perhaps too quickly. Sylvanas had plans upon plans, and wondered which of them had seeped into the realm of rumor among her people.

"Word has reached them of some of your more extreme efforts to continue their existence," Nathanos said.

Ah. That. "I assume that word has also reached them that Genn Greymane destroyed their hope," Sylvanas replied bitterly.

She had taken her flagship, the *Windrunner,* to Stormheim in the Broken Isles in search of more Val'kyr to resurrect the fallen. It was, thus far, the only way Sylvanas had found to create more Forsaken.

"I was almost able to enslave the great Eyir. She would have given me the Val'kyr for all eternity. None of my people would have ever died again." She paused. "I would have saved them."

"That . . . is the concern."

"Do not dance around this, Nathanos. Speak plainly."

"Not all of them desire for themselves what you desire for them, my queen. Many on the Desolate Council harbor deep reservations." His face, still that of a dead man but better preserved because of an elaborate ritual she had ordered performed, twisted in a smile. "This is the peril you created when you gave them free will. They are now free to disagree."

Her pale brows drew together in a terrible frown. "Do they *want* extinction, then?" she hissed, anger flaring brightly inside her. "Do they want to be *rotting* in the earth?"

"I do not know what they want," Nathanos replied calmly. "They wish to speak with you, not with me."

Sylvanas growled softly under her breath. Nathanos, ever patient, waited. He would obey her in all things, she knew. She could, right now, order a group of any combination of non-Forsaken Horde warriors to march on the Undercity and seize the members of this ungrateful council. But even as she had that satisfying thought, she knew it would be unwise. She needed to know more—much more—before she could act. She would prefer to dissuade Forsaken—any Forsaken—than destroy them.

"I . . . will consider their request. But for now I have something else I wish to discuss. We need to increase what is in the Horde's coffers," Sylvanas murmured quietly to her champion. "We will need the funds, and we will need *them*."

She waved at a family of orcs. Both the male and the female bore battle scars, but they were smiling, and the child they lifted over their heads to see her warchief was plump and healthy-looking. Clearly, some of the Horde loved their warchief.

"I'm not sure I understand, my queen," Nathanos said. "Of course, the Horde needs funds and its members."

"It is not the members that concern me. It is the army. I have decided I will not dissolve it."

He turned to look at her. "They think they've come home," he said. "Is this not the case?"

"It is, for the moment," she said. "Injuries need time to heal. Crops need to be planted. But soon I will call upon the brave fighters of the Horde for another battle. The one you and I have both longed for."

Nathanos was silent. She did not take that for disagreement or disapproval. He was often silent. That he did not press her for more details meant that he understood what she wanted.

Stormwind.

CHAPTER THREE

Orgrimmar

The peace-hungry boy-king Anduin Wrynn had lost his father and by all accounts had taken it badly. There were rumors that he had recovered Shalamayne and was now fighting with cold steel as well as with the Light. Sylvanas was dubious. She had difficulty imagining the sensitive child doing such things. She had respected Varian. She had even liked him. And the specter of the Legion had been so dreadful that she had been willing to put aside the hatred that fueled her now as food and drink had fueled her in life.

But the Wolf was gone, and the young lion was still a cub, really, and the humans had taken tremendous losses. They were weak.

Vulnerable. *Prey.*

And Sylvanas was a hunter.

The Horde was tough. Strong. Battle-hardened. Its members would recover far more swiftly than the Alliance races. They would need less time for the things she had cited; crops, healing, a chance to pause and restore themselves. Soon enough, they would thirst for blood, and she would offer the red life-fluid of Stormwind's humans, the oldest enemies of the Horde, to slake that thirst.

And in the bargain she would increase the population of the Forsaken. For all the humans who fell with their city would be reborn to serve her. Would that be so terrible, really? They would be with their loved ones for all time. They would not suffer the daggers of passion or loss any longer. They would need no sleep. They could pursue their interests in death as well as in life. There would at last be unity.

If the humans only understood how terribly life and all its attendant suffering dealt with them, Sylvanas thought, they would leap at the chance. The Forsaken understood . . . at least, she had thought they did, until the Desolate Council had inexplicably concluded otherwise.

Baine Bloodhoof, Varok Saurfang, Lor'themar Theron, and Jastor Gallywix would no doubt consider that Sylvanas had a certain interest in creating human corpses. They had not become leaders of their people by being stupid, after all. But they also would be fighting against the hated humans and claiming their shining white city, with its neighboring forested land and bountiful fields, for their own. They would not begrudge her the bodies, not when she handed them such a victory—one both practical and highly symbolic.

There was no longer a human hero to stand and rally the Alliance against them. No Anduin Lothar, who was slain by Orgrim Doomhammer, and no Llane or Varian Wrynn. The only one by those names was Anduin Wrynn, and he was nothing.

Sylvanas, Nathanos, and her entourage of veterans had gone all the way through the Valley of Honor and looped back, heading into the Valley of Wisdom. There Baine awaited her. He stood in full traditional tauren regalia, only his ears and tail moving as they flicked off the flies that buzzed in the summer air. Many of his braves were gathered around him. Mounted, Sylvanas was tall enough to look even the males in the eye, and she did so steadily. Baine stared calmly back.

Except for those pandaren who had chosen to ally with the Horde, Sylvanas had the least in common with the tauren. They were a deeply spiritual people, calm and steady. They craved the tranquillity of nature and honored ancient ways. Sylvanas once had understood those sentiments but no longer could relate to any of them.

What irked her the most about Baine was that despite the murder of his father and wrong upon wrong being heaped upon his horned head, the young bull still cherished peace above all pursuits: peace between races and in one's own heart.

Baine's honor obligated him to serve her, and he would not tarnish it. Not unless he was pushed to limits that Sylvanas still hadn't reached.

He placed his hand on his broad chest, over his heart, and stamped his hoof in a tauren version of a salute. The braves followed suit, and the ground of Orgrimmar trembled ever so slightly. Then Sylvanas continued, and the tauren fell in line behind the cluster of Forsaken and Theron's blood elves.

Still Nathanos remained silent. They followed the twining road toward the Valley of Spirits, the long-standing seat of the trolls. They were so proud of themselves, these "first" few races. Sylvanas believed that they never truly accepted the later races—the blood elves, the goblins, and her own people—as "true" Horde members. It amused her that, since the goblins had joined the Horde, they had oozed into the Valley of Spirits and had nearly ruined their allotted area.

Like the tauren, the trolls were among the first friends to the orcs. The orc leader Thrall had named the land Durotar for his father, Durotan. Orgrimmar was so named to honor an early warchief of the Horde, Orgrim Doomhammer. In fact, until Vol'jin, *all* warchiefs had been orcs. And until Sylvanas, they all had been members of the original founding races. And male.

Sylvanas had changed all that, and she was proud of it.

Like her, Vol'jin had left his people leaderless upon his ascension to warchief. The trolls stood today with no public face to represent them, save potentially Rokhan; at least the Forsaken had her in the role of warchief. Sylvanas reminded herself to appoint someone head of the trolls as swiftly as possible. Someone she could work with. Could control. The last thing she needed was for the trolls to choose someone who might want to challenge her position.

Although many today had greeted her with cheers and smiles, Sylvanas did not fool herself that she was universally beloved. She had led the Horde to a seemingly impossible victory, and for now, at least, it appeared that its members were solidly with her.

Good.

She nodded courteously to the trolls, then braced herself to meet the next group.

Sylvanas did not much care for goblins. Although her own sense of honor was somewhat fluid, she could appreciate honor in others. It was, like many things, an echo of something she once had heard. But the goblins were little better than squat, ugly money-grubbing parasites as far as she was concerned. Oh, they were intelligent. Sometimes dangerously so—to themselves and others. That they were creative and inventive there was no doubt. But she preferred the days when the only relationship one had with them was purely financial. Now they were full-fledged members of the Horde, and she had to pretend that they mattered.

They, of course, were not without their leader: the multi-chinned, waistband-straining green lump of greed that was Trade Prince Jastor Gallywix. He stood in the front of his motley gaggle of goblins, all of them grinning and showing their sharp yellow teeth. His spindly legs seemed already too tired to bear his frame, and he sported his favorite top hat and cane. At her approach, he bowed as deeply as his midsection would permit.

"Warchief," he said in that unctuous voice, "I hope you might find some time for me later. I have something that might interest you a very great deal."

No one else had dared try to insert their own agenda this day. Trust a goblin to do so. She frowned at him and opened her mouth to speak. Then she looked carefully at his expression.

Sylvanas had lived a very long life before Arthas Menethil had cut her down. And now she lived, after a fashion, again. She had spent much of that time looking into faces, judging the character behind them and the words that were spoken.

Gallywix often had that sort of hail-fellow-well-met artificial cheer that she so despised, but not today. There was no desperate push from him. He was . . . calm. He looked like a player who knew he was going to win. That he so boldly addressed her here, now, meant that he was serious about speaking with her. But his body language—he wasn't hunching obsequiously but stood straight for perhaps the first time she'd ever seen—told her even more clearly that this was someone willing to walk away from the table without undue disappointment.

This time he meant it. He *did* have something that would interest her a very great deal.

"Speak with me at the feast," she said.

"As my warchief commands," the goblin said, and doffed his top hat to her.

Sylvanas turned away to complete the route.

"I do not trust that goblin." Nathanos, who had remained so silent for so long, spoke with distaste.

"Nor do I," Sylvanas replied. "But one thing goblins understand is profit. I can listen without promising anything."

Nathanos nodded. "Of course, Warchief."

The goblins and the trolls had fallen in line behind her. Gallywix was riding in a litter behind Sylvanas's own guards. How he had finagled that position, she didn't know. He met her gaze and grinned, giving her a thumbs-up and a wink. Sylvanas fought to keep her lip from curling in disgust. She already was regretting her decision to talk with Gallywix later, so she focused on something else.

"We do still agree, do we not?" she said to Nathanos. "Stormwind must fall, and the victims of the battle will become Forsaken."

"All is as you would wish it, my queen," he said, "but I do not think mine is the opinion with which you need to concern yourself. Have you broached this with the other leaders? They may have something to say about the idea. I do not think we have seen a peace more dearly bought, nor more appreciated. They may not want to upend the cart just yet."

"While our enemies remain, peace is not victory." Not when vulnerable prey yet remained to be hunted. And not when the continued existence of her Forsaken was so uncertain.

"For the warchief!" a tauren bellowed, his oversized lungs enabling the cry to carry far.

"Warchief! Warchief! Warchief!"

The long "victory march" was nearing its end. Now Sylvanas approached Grommash Hold. Only one more leader awaited her—one to whom she gave grudging respect.

Varok Saurfang was intelligent, strong, fierce, and, like Baine, loyal. But there was something in the orc's eyes that always put her on alert when she gazed into them. The knowledge that if she misstepped too badly, he might well challenge, or even outright oppose, her.

That look was in his eyes now as he stepped forward. He met Sylvanas stare for stare, not breaking eye contact even as he executed a brief bow and stepped aside to let her pass before he fell in line behind her.

As all the others would do.

Warchief Sylvanas dismounted and entered Grommash Hold with her head held high.

Nathanos was concerned that the other leaders wouldn't support her plan.

I will tell them what they will do . . . when the time is right.

A heavy, rough-hewn wooden table and benches had been brought into Grommash Hold. A celebratory feast would be served for the leaders of each group and a select few of their guards or companions. Sylvanas herself would sit at the head of the table, as befitted her position.

Now, as Sylvanas regarded her tablemates, she reflected that none of them had family of any sort. Her champion was the closest thing to a formal consort or even companion present. And their relationship was complicated, even to themselves.

Each of the races had been encouraged to present a ritual celebrating victory or honoring its veterans. Sylvanas was willing to indulge this request; it would appease many, and the funds for such an event would come not from Horde coffers but from those of each race. The idea had been suggested by Baine, of course, whose people had practiced such rituals as part of their culture for . . . well, as long as there had been tauren, Sylvanas assumed.

The trolls, too, had agreed to participate, as well as the Horde's pandaren. They had a unique position among the Horde in that they were a collection of individuals who felt a connection to the Horde's ideals. Their leader, and their land, was far away, but they had proven their worth to the Horde. They had nodded their furry round heads at the prospect of presenting a ritual, promising beauty and spectacle to uplift the spirits. Sylvanas had smiled pleasantly and told them that such would be welcomed.

Sylvanas recalled that once, Quel'Thalas used to host magnificent, bright, shining ceremonies with mock battles and pomp and pageantry. But in more recent times the former high elves, wrestling with betrayal and addiction, had turned much grimmer. Quel'Thalas was recovering, and the blood elves still loved their luxuries and comforts, but they now found such ostentatious displays distasteful in the light of so much unrelenting tragedy for their people. Their contribution, Theron had told her, would be brief and to the point. They were bitter now. Bitter as the Forsaken still were; Sylvanas had flatly refused to participate in what she perceived as a waste of time and gold.

In this, the goblins were on her side. It was a darkly amusing thought.

She waited as several shaman of all races opened the ceremonies with a ritual. The tauren offered a re-creation of one of the great battles of the war. And finally, the pandaren stepped into the center of Grommash Hold. They wore silk outfits—tunics and breeches and dresses—in hues of jade green, sky blue, and nauseating pink. Sylvanas had to admit, for as large and soft and round as the pandaren appeared, they were startlingly graceful as they danced, tumbled, and staged mock battles.

Baine rose to close the events. Slowly, his gaze roamed the hall, taking in not just the leaders at the table but others who sat on rugs and hides on the hard-packed dirt floor.

"It is with both pain and pride that we gather here today," he rumbled. "Pain, for many brave heroes of the Horde fell in honorable and terrible battle. Vol'jin, warchief of the Horde, led the vanguard against the Legion. He fought with courage. He fought for the Horde."

"For the Horde," came the solemn murmur. Baine turned to look at something. Sylvanas followed his gaze and saw Vol'jin's weapons and ritual mask hanging in a place of honor. Others, too, bowed their heads. Sylvanas inclined her own.

"But we do not forget the pride we hold in those battles—and their outcome. For against all odds, we have vanquished the Legion. Our victory was bought with blood, but it *was* bought. We bled. Now we heal. We mourned. Now we celebrate! For the Horde!"

The response was no hushed, respectful one this time but a full-throated, openhearted cheer that all but shook the rafters of the hold. *"For the Horde!"*

Roasted boar and root vegetables were served, with ale, wine, or harder liquor to wash it down. Sylvanas observed while others partook. Shortly after the first course was cleared, she noticed a red and purple top hat splotched with stars heading toward her end of the table.

"Oh, Warchief? A moment of your time."

"*One* moment," Sylvanas told the grinning goblin. He halted beside her chair. "You have my attention. Do not waste it."

"I'm certain you'll agree that I'm not, Warchief," he said again with that air of complete confidence. "But first a little background. I'm sure you're aware of the tragedies and challenges the Bilgewater Cartel faced before we were invited to join the Horde."

"Yes. Your island was destroyed by an erupting volcano," Sylvanas said.

Gallywix looked unconvincingly sad. He touched a gloved finger to his eye to wipe away a nonexistent tear. "So many lost," he sighed. "So much kaja'mite *gone*, just like that."

Sylvanas amended her thought. Perhaps the tears *were* genuine.

"Kaja'Cola." The goblin sniffled nostalgically. "'It gives you ideas.'"

"Yes, I am aware there is no more kaja'mite," Sylvanas said flatly. "Get to the point, assuming you have one." Her conversation with the goblin was drawing undue attention from Baine and Saurfang, among others.

"Oh, yes indeed, I most certainly do. You know," he said, laughing a little, "it's kind of funny. There's a distinct possibility that that volcano . . . might *not* have been caused by Deathwing or the Cataclysm."

Her glowing eyes widened slightly. Was he really saying what she thought he was? She waited with an impatience that was not usually associated with the dead.

"You see, hmm . . . how to put this?" He drummed his fingers against his first chin. "We were mining rather deeply on Kezan. We had to keep our customers happy, now, didn't we? Kaja'Cola being the delicious, brain-boosting beverage that—"

"Do not push me, goblin."

"Gotcha. So. Back to my tale. We were digging deep. Very deep. And we found something unexpected. A hitherto unknown substance. Something truly phenomenal. Unique! Only a small vein of liquid that turned solid and changed color once exposed to the air. One of my smarter miners, ah . . . *recovered* a chunk of it privately and brought it to me as a token of his esteem."

"In other words, he stole it and tried to bribe you with it."

"That's one way of looking at it. But that's not the point. The point is that while that awful Deathwing certainly had a lot to do with triggering the volcano, digging that deep may—*may*, I repeat, I'm not at all certain of it—have contributed."

Sylvanas regarded the trade prince with newfound awe at the depths of his avarice and selfishness. If Gallywix was right, he'd cheerfully destroyed his own island and a goodly number of innocent—well, comparatively innocent—goblins along with it. All for a piece of some kind of marvelous ore.

"I did not know you had it in you," she said almost in a tone of admiration.

He seemed about to thank her, then thought better of it. "Well. It was a very *special* mineral, I must say."

"And I imagine you keep it locked away in a very secure location."

Gallywix opened his mouth, then slitted his eyes and looked mistrustfully at Nathanos. Sylvanas almost laughed. "My champion Nathanos is a dour sort. He barely speaks, even to me. Any secrets you have to share with me are more than safe with him."

"As my warchief says," Gallywix replied slowly, clearly unconvinced but seeing no other option. "You are incorrect, Dark Lady. I do not keep it hidden away. I keep it in plain sight, literally close at hand."

He used the golden-hued tip of his cane to push back his hideous top hat in a casual gesture. Sylvanas waited for an answer. When a moment passed and she received none, she started to frown. The goblin's tiny eyes moved, flickering to the top of his cane and then back to Sylvanas.

The cane? She looked at it again, more closely this time. She'd never paid it much attention. She never paid much attention to anything Gallywix wore, carried, or said. But something was nagging at her.

Then she knew what it was. "It used to be red."

"It *used* to be," he agreed. "It isn't now."

Sylvanas realized that the small orb, only about the size of an apple, was not actually made of gold. It was made of something that looked like . . . like . . .

Amber. Tree sap that over the centuries had hardened to become something that could be crafted into jewelry. Sometimes ancient insects had gotten caught in the flowing fluid, forever enveloped by it. This one had that same warmth to it. It was pretty. But she was skeptical that this harmless-looking decoration was as all-powerful as Gallywix would have her believe.

"Let me see it," she demanded.

"I will happily do so, but not in front of prying eyes. Can we go someplace a little less public?" At her irritated glance, he said in the sincerest voice she had ever heard from him, "Look. You are gonna want to keep this information close. Trust me on this."

Oddly, she did. "If you are exaggerating, you will suffer."

"Oh, I know that. And I also know you're going to like what you find out."

Sylvanas leaned over and murmured to Nathanos. "I will be back momentarily. He had best be right."

Aware of the eyes on her, she rose and indicated that Gallywix might follow her back to the room behind the throne. He did so, and as the skin flap dropped closed, he said, "Huh. I never knew this place was here."

Sylvanas did not reply, instead simply extending her hand for the cane. With a little bow, he handed it to her. Her hand closed around it.

Nothing.

The decoration was garish, but Sylvanas could see now that it was of fine craftsmanship. She was rapidly tiring of the goblin's game. She frowned slightly and slipped one hand up the cane's shaft to the gem that was perched atop it.

Her eyes flew wide, and she sucked in a soft gasp of astonishment.

Once she had mourned the life denied to her. She had contented herself with the gifts of her undeath: her devastating banshee wail, the freedom from hunger and exhaustion, and the other shackles that tethered mortals. But this sensation dwarfed them both.

She felt not merely strong but *mighty*. As if her grip could crush a skull, as if a single stride could cover a league and more. Energy coiled inside each muscle, straining like a beast of pure precision and power against a leash. Thoughts raced through her brain, not simply her usual calculating, cunning, clever thoughts but shining, frighteningly brilliant ones. Innovative. Creative.

She was no longer a dark lady or even a queen. She was a goddess of destruction and creation, and she was stunned that she had never understood how deeply the two were intertwined. Armies, cities, entire cultures—she could raise them.

And fell them. Stormwind would be among the first, yielding its people to swell the numbers of her own.

She could deal death on a scale that—

Sylvanas released the orb as if it had burned her.

"This . . . will change *everything*." Her voice was shaking. She summoned her usual icy calm. "Why have you not used this ere now?"

"It was gold when it was liquid, see, and it was *amazing*. Then it became solid and red, and it was pretty but ordinary. I always held out hope I'd find more of the stuff one day. And then . . . one day, boom, the top of the cane turned gold and amazing again. Who knew?"

Sylvanas needed to get back to the feast. The other leaders doubtless were talking already. She didn't intend to give them more fodder by lingering here.

"You see the possibilities," the goblin said as they reentered the hold. As if he were talking about something mundane and pragmatic, not something that had shaken Sylvanas Windrunner to her very core with a taste of power hitherto unimaginable.

"I do," she said, her voice under control again, though inside she still trembled. "Once this feast is finished, you and I will talk at length. This will serve the Horde well."

Only the Horde.

"The Alliance knows nothing of this?"

"Don't worry, Warchief," he said, his old glib self again. "I got people on it."

CHAPTER FOUR

Stormwind

Anduin summoned his counselors to join him in Stormwind Keep's map room. They inclined their heads as he entered; he had long ago bidden them not to bow.

Greymane and Shaw were there, of course. So was Prophet Velen, the ancient draenei who had tutored Anduin in the ways of the Light. Of all of them, it could be said that perhaps the draenei Prophet had lost the most in this war. Genn had lost his son to violence in years past, and of course this war had claimed Varian Wrynn. But Velen had witnessed the death not only of his son but of his entire *world*—quite literally.

And yet, Anduin mused as he regarded the lavender-skinned being, *though I can sense his sorrow, he remains the most serene of us all.*

Sky Admiral Catherine Rogers was also present. Anduin had similar sentiments toward her as he did toward Spymaster Shaw. Anduin respected both individuals, but his relationship with them wasn't comfortable. Rogers was too thirsty for Horde blood for his liking. He had forcefully rebuked both her and Greymane for taking a recent assignment much further than he had ordered. But the Alliance had needed Rogers's hawkishness in the war, and Mathias protected the innocent in his own way.

"It has been a difficult day," Anduin said. "But it was more difficult for those we addressed. In the end, the war is over, the Legion is defeated, and we can bury the dead knowing that tomorrow will not contribute to the numbers of those slain in battle. And for this I am grateful.

"However, it does not mean that we can cease our efforts toward making this world better. Instead of slaying our enemies, we must heal and restore our people—and a world that is dreadfully wounded. And," Anduin added, "we must protect and study a precious resource that has come to my attention just today. All these things pose a fresh set of challenges."

Anduin could sense the small golden-blue stone in his pocket, nestled there quietly and benevolently. He knew very little about it yet, but one thing he did know: it was not evil, though he understood full well that it certainly could be turned to dark purposes. Even the naaru could.

Anduin withdrew the handkerchief. "This morning, Spymaster Shaw reported to me about what he has observed in Silithus. Not only are there great fissures that have erupted, spreading out from where the sword of Sargeras impaled the world, but those fissures have revealed a hitherto unknown substance. It's . . . unique. It's easier to show you how rather than tell you."

He handed the handkerchief to Velen, who reacted as Anduin had. The draenei took in a startled breath. Almost before Anduin's eyes, years—decades—of suffering seemed to be lifted. As profound as it had been to experience it himself, it was almost more moving for Anduin to witness the material's effect on another.

"For a moment, I thought it a piece of a naaru," Velen breathed. "It is not, but the sensation is . . . similar."

The naaru were benevolent beings made of holy energy. Nothing was closer to the Light than they. When Anduin had studied under the draenei at the *Exodar*, he had spent much time in the presence of the naaru O'ros. The beautiful, benevolent being had been another casualty of the war, and the memory of that time was now tinged with pain. Even so, Anduin recalled the emotions O'ros had engendered, and he agreed with Velen's assessment.

"Although," Velen added, "there is the potential for great harm here, as well as great good."

Greymane took it next. He seemed stunned by what he experienced, almost confused by it, as if some deep, firmly held belief had been shattered. Then he frowned, the lines around his eyes deepening, and he thrust the honey-hued stone toward Shaw.

"I admit," he said in a rough voice, directing his words to both the king and the spymaster, "I thought perhaps you were exaggerating. You weren't. This stuff is powerful—and dangerous."

Shaw waved the stone away; he seemed to have no desire to handle it more than was necessary. Anduin respected that. Rogers took it next. She stumbled, reaching out to grasp the side of the large map table for balance, gazing raptly at the tiny piece of stone. Then her expression turned to one of anger and hope commingled. "Is there more of this?"

Shaw gave Velen and Rogers an edited version of what he'd told Genn and Anduin earlier. The two listened intently. When he had finished, Rogers said, "If we can find a way to use this . . . we could crush the Horde."

"The thought of Sylvanas with this sickens me," Genn said, not mincing words.

Why must we bend everything to violence? Anduin thought with his own hint of anger. Instead he said, answering Rogers's first question, "I told Spymaster Shaw we must obtain more of this and study it. I believe there are far better things we can do with this substance than create methods to kill more efficiently."

"Sylvanas wouldn't think so, and neither must we."

Anduin leveled his blue-eyed gaze at Greymane. "I would say that what makes us better than her is that we *do* think so." As Genn started to protest, Anduin lifted a hand. "But I would *never* leave the Alliance vulnerable. With enough information, we can apply our skills to more than one task." He squared his shoulders and turned his attention to the map of Azeroth spread before him, his blue eyes roaming the image of a world that had become newly precious to him. His gaze lingered on the home of Stormwind's nearest ally, the dwarven lands and their capital city of Ironforge.

"Humans did not stand alone against the Legion," Anduin reminded those assembled. "We were joined in that fight by the draenei and those pandaren who had chosen the Alliance. Your people, too, Genn: worgen and human refugees who have more than earned their place in the Alliance by standing shoulder to shoulder first with my father and then with me to face that awful peril. The dwarves and the gnomes also stood with us."

"If not *quite* shoulder to shoulder," Genn said. Anduin had discovered that the softer emotions tended to make the gruff king uncomfortable. Genn wore rage and stubbornness better than warmth or gratitude. So, too, had Varian for many years.

"Perhaps not," Anduin said, smiling a little; the joke was one at which the dwarves themselves probably would guffaw. He envisioned their former king, Magni Bronzebeard, retorting with something like *Nae worries, lad, we'll cut ye down tae size.*

"But they have always been there for us, as sturdy and undefeatable as stone." Affection for these strong, hardheaded people, who had been the ones to start him along both his path to the priesthood as well as toward proper fighting technique, swept through Anduin. "We should take this to the Explorers' League. They might have some insight that we lack. And they are all over the world. That's a lot of extra eyes and ears for you, Shaw."

Shaw nodded his reddish-brown head. Anduin continued.

"The night elves might also be of assistance. As ancient as their race is, perhaps they have encountered something like this before. They, too, lost many in this war, and I believe a pledge of aid and support would be welcome. And the draenei—" Anduin reached to touch the arm of his old friend Velen. "You have lost more than any of us can fully comprehend. And as you say, this . . . material . . . evokes the naaru. Perhaps there is some kind of connection."

He returned his attention to the group. "All came when we called. And now their veterans have returned to fields too long neglected, to supplies dangerously depleted. We remember what happened after the battle for Northrend. When resources are depleted, sparks of resentment can turn to a conflagration—even among races on the same side. Let us make sure that none of our allies regret having offered aid to Stormwind."

They were looking at one another, nodding in agreement.

"I intend to travel to the lands of our steadfast friends," Anduin informed them. "To thank them in person for their sacrifices, to offer what we can so their economic recovery will be swift, and to enlist their aid as well."

He had expected Greymane to protest, and the older man did not disappoint. "Your people are in Stormwind," Genn reminded the king unnecessarily. "They need you here. And Gilneas, at least, needs no royal visit."

No. Gilneas did not. It never had. In years past, by the order of Greymane himself, Gilneas had cut itself off from all contact with anything outside its massive stone walls. The kingdom had not come to the aid of others when they were in need, and that isolation had evoked anger and resentment toward the Gilneans, at least at the outset, when they at last had been forced to abandon their self-imposed seclusion. But now there was nothing left of the once great realm but ruins, shades, and sorrow.

"You were angry with me, as I recall, when I ventured into the Broken Isles to see the place where my father fell," Anduin replied mildly.

"Of course I was. You left Stormwind and told no one," Greymane retorted. "You hadn't even named a successor. *Still* haven't, by the way. What would have happened if you'd been killed?"

"But I wasn't," Anduin countered. "And my leaving was the right thing to do." More gently, he continued. "Genn, you told me I didn't need to see that place. But I did. To me, my father's sacrifice has made it hallowed ground. It is where I found Shalamayne—or perhaps I should say, where it found me. It is where I . . ." He paused. He was not yet ready to tell anyone what he had experienced, not even Velen, the Prophet, who would have understood.

"Where I truly accepted the mantle of my kingship," he said instead. He cleared his throat; his voice was too thick. "Where I was able to lead the Alliance to a hard-won victory. Yes. Stormwind's people need me. But so do those in Ironforge and Darnassus. This is how we use peace. To lay the groundwork for unity and prosperity so that perhaps war might one day be relegated to the history books."

It was a noble goal, but perhaps an unattainable one. Most of those

around the table seemed to think the latter. But Anduin was determined to try.

"Ol' Emma" was what most people in Stormwind knew her as. She
was all right with that nickname; she *was* old, after all, and it was usually spoken with friendliness. But she had a real name—Felstone—
and a past, just like everyone else. She had loved and been loved once,
and if sometimes she got lost in the past because, well, that was where
everyone was, then so be it.

First it was her husband, Jem, who had died in the First War. But
people died in war, didn't they? And they were honored and remembered in ceremonies like the ones that sweet boy-king had led.

Anduin Wrynn reminded her so much of her own bright boys.
Three of them there had been: Little Jem, named for his father; Jack,
named for his uncle John; and Jake. They, too, had died in a war, just
like her sister, Janice. Except that war was worse than the one that had
just ended, in a way. Her sons had perished because of Arthas Menethil and his war on the living. They'd been warriors of Lordaeron,
given places of honor as King Terenas's guards. They'd fallen along
with their king and their kingdom.

But no one honored their names with a formal ceremony. No one
thought of them as war heroes. They'd been turned into mindless undead monstrosities. They were still in that brutally cruel state, were
dead, or had become one of the Banshee Queen's Forsaken.

Whatever her beautiful sons' final fate, they were lost to her, and
the living world of humans spoke of such horrors only in whispers.

She gripped the handle of the bucket she carried and focused on
her task: drawing water from the well. Thinking of Jem, Jack, and Jake
was never a good thing. The places it dragged her mind and heart—

Emma gripped the handle of her bucket more tightly as she approached the well. *Focus on what the living need*, she told herself. *Not
the dead.*

Or the undead.

CHAPTER FIVE

Stormwind

"I heard that you spoke most eloquently at the service today, Your Majesty."

Anduin smiled tiredly at the elderly servant. He was quite capable of preparing for bed himself, but Wyll Benton had taken care of him since he was a little boy and would be offended if his service was refused.

"Princes and kings have so much to worry about," he had said once, the first time Anduin had tried to decrease his duties. "The last thing they need is to bother themselves with things like candlewick trimming and hanging their clothes properly."

He was tall and heavyset, though Anduin noted that he'd slimmed down some recently. His mild, somewhat detached demeanor disguised a stubborn will and fierce devotion to the house of Wrynn. *So much has changed, and most of it not for the better,* Anduin thought. *But at least Wyll is a constant.*

"If indeed I was eloquent, it was the Light speaking through me to comfort those in need of it," Anduin replied.

"You underestimate yourself, Your Majesty. You've always had a way with words."

Wyll removed Anduin's belt, hanging the mace Fearbreaker reverently from a hook on the wall near the king's bed. The servant himself had mounted the hook there, where Anduin could reach it at any moment. *Just in case,* he had said. The prince Anduin had been at the time had rolled his eyes at that, but the man he had become felt his heart warm at the unspoken expression of concern of a man who was more than a servant—Wyll was an old friend.

"You're too kind," Anduin said.

"Oh, sir," Wyll sighed, "I'm *never* that, as you well know."

Anduin pressed his lips together to keep from smiling outright. His spirits lifted, and he couldn't resist teasing Wyll.

"You'll be pleased to hear we're going back to Ironforge soon. Unless you'd rather not?"

"Why, Your Majesty, why would I not? There's nothing like the constant heat and clanging of a continuously running giant forge to make certain one rests well. Besides, surely nothing bad ever happens in Ironforge. No one gets turned to diamond, or is buried beneath rubble, or taken hostage, or forced to flee for his life," the old servant continued in a voice just shy of sarcastic.

Wyll had accompanied Anduin on his last visit to Ironforge, shortly before the Cataclysm had forever altered the face of Azeroth. All the things the servant had just mentioned, along with many others, had occurred on that eventful trip, and two of them had happened to Anduin.

The words, meant as a joke—at least as much of a joke as Wyll could manage—caused another wave of sorrow to flow over the young king. This one, though, was different; the loss was older. Time had mellowed the pain, though it would never completely leave him. At his king's silence, Wyll looked at him as he hung up the coat.

"Your pardon, Your Majesty," he said, his voice heavy with remorse. "I didn't mean to make light of your loss."

"Of Khaz Modan's loss," Anduin said. The earthquake in Dun Morogh, its tremors felt even in Ironforge, had marked the first indication that the unhappy world was in true peril. Anduin had gone to Dun Morogh to assist with the rescue efforts. He had not yet embraced the path of priesthood, but he knew first aid and desperately wanted to help. The round of aftershocks claimed the life of Aerin Stonehand, the young dwarf woman who had been assigned to train him.

It was the first time Anduin had lost anyone close to his age. And, if he was being honest with himself, he had begun to feel more than simple friendship toward the bright-eyed, lively warrior.

"It's all right," he reassured Wyll. "Things are better there now. Magni's awoken from his . . . ah, communing with the earth, I'm just fine, and the Three Hammers are working together like a well-oiled gnomish machine."

Magni Bronzebeard, who had been king of Ironforge at the time, had participated in a ritual that would "make him one with the earth." All had hoped the rite would give some insight into the distressed world, but the ritual had been quite literal, not metaphorical. It had turned Magni into diamond. At the time, the already beleaguered city had grieved deeply. Thank the Light, it transpired that Magni had not been killed . . . but he had been changed. Now, Anduin had been told that the former king spoke with—and for—Azeroth herself. No one was sure where or how to find him; he wandered the world and came when needed.

Anduin wondered if he would ever see Magni again. He hoped so.

"Even so, sir," Wyll said. "Of course I'll come with you."

Of course he would. As far as Anduin knew, the devoted servant had no family of his own, and he had served the Wrynns for most of his life. Anduin didn't need Wyll's tending—he was quite capable of hanging up a coat by himself and removing his own boots—but as increasing age prohibited Wyll from doing many things, Anduin knew his childhood servant still wanted to feel that he was of use. Anduin cherished Wyll not for what he did but for who he was.

"I'll be glad of your company," Anduin said, and he was. "That will be all for now, though. Good night, Wyll."

The old man bowed. "Good night, Your Majesty."

Anduin watched him close the door, smiling affectionately after him. When the door snicked shut, he turned back to his dressing table. The amber-hued stone, still wrapped in the handkerchief, sat beside two items that held great personal meaning for Anduin. One was a small carved box that contained Queen Tiffin's engagement and wedding rings. The other was the compass Anduin once had given his father.

He looked at the white piece of fabric for a moment, but it was the compass he reached for, the same one that had been recovered and returned to him by an adventurer who had helped the distraught new king on his first steps toward healing his grief.

He opened the compass now and regarded the portrait of a little boy painted within, cheeks still round with childhood's softness. After all he had beheld and experienced in the last few months, Anduin wondered if he had ever truly been as young as the artist had depicted him.

A compass. Something to keep you on the right path.

There had been a clear compass in fighting the Burning Legion. Clear, good, true, and powerful. Anduin knew the immediate next step in his path. To meet with his allies, help them aid their own people, and demonstrate how valuable he considered those ties. To ask for their assistance in learning more about this strange mineral—and keep it from being misused. After that . . .

He closed his eyes. *Light*, he prayed, *you have given me good advisers and true who have helped me lead well thus far. I trust in you to show me the next steps in their proper time. I have always longed for peace, and now peace of a sort is upon us. And this material . . . it could be used to further that peace in ways we can't even begin to imagine.*

Give me the guidance to lead well now, too.

He placed the compass down gently, blew out the single candle Wyll had left burning on the nightstand, and had no dreams.

In the morning, Anduin called for a less formal gathering in the receiving room outside his private quarters. He had spent many a night there, dining alone with his father. He still had difficulty thinking of the room as belonging to him now.

"I had almost forgotten we were heading into summer," Greymane said as he helped himself to a sweet-smelling, perfectly ripe peach.

Amberseed buns, Stromgarde cheese, herbed eggs, ham, bacon, fresh sunfruit, and pastries also had been laid out, and milk, coffee, tea, and a selection of juices were provided to wash it down.

As a worgen, Greymane had hunted for food in a way that the rest of the Alliance could not, and could feed upon things others could not. Worgen were, in many ways, the strongest and best suited to war, for the adage that an army marched on its stomach was a true one. But clearly the king of Gilneas still relished the taste of summer's first fruits.

It seemed most of them had slept well, as had the young king. He wondered if it was an effect of the stone. After a few pleasantries about the meal, the king steered the conversation to practicalities.

"Genn," he said, helping himself to a second serving of eggs, "I would like to ask you to look after my kingdom while I am away. I can't think of anyone better to tend to it than someone already familiar with what that entails. Don't worry," he added, smiling, "I promise I'll formalize it before I leave this time."

Slowly, Genn put down his fork. "Your Majesty," he said, "I am honored. I will serve Stormwind as I have served two of its kings. But I am an old man. You might do well to begin looking for a way to have someone younger rule should anything happen to you."

Inwardly Anduin sighed. This was not the first time the subject of an heir had been brought up. He chose to ignore it, but he was almost certain that Genn would reference it at least once more before he left for Ironforge even though Anduin had made his opinion quite clear. He was *not* going to marry a woman he didn't love.

"I'm pleased you accept," Anduin said, dodging the entire issue and turning to Velen before Genn could pursue it. "Prophet, I hope you will accompany me on my journey both to Ironforge and overseas. I have not forgotten the draenei who still guard the *Exodar*. I would see them and thank them."

The white-bearded draenei inclined his head, moved. "It is an honor to accompany you, Your Majesty. It will mean so much to my people."

"It will mean much to me as well," Anduin replied, buttering his toast. *Butter*, he thought. Something he took for granted when so many didn't have so much as a slice of bread. "What can Stormwind offer the draenei to show our deep appreciation for their aid against our mutual enemy?"

"That Your Majesty cares enough to even inquire after all that you have endured will surely warm their hearts."

The young king placed the butter knife down and regarded his old friend. "You know more of endurance than any of us," he said quietly. "Of suffering, of loss."

Liam Greymane was not the only son who had left behind a loving father. More than even this deeply personal loss was the one that Velen's people had suffered. Argus, their beloved homeworld, not only had become overrun with corrupted eredar but had been deliberately tortured for eons by the fallen titan Sargeras. The very soul of that broken world had risen to turn on anyone and everyone, even those who had liberated it and sought to help it. Even now, Anduin could hardly bear to think of it, and he prayed to the Light that their own world, their beautiful Azeroth, which had sustained such varied and marvelous forms of life, would not suffer the same fate.

Velen's face softened with sorrow that would never, *could* never, be assuaged, but his voice was warm as he spoke. "It is precisely because we know so much of the darkness of this universe that we focus instead on that which is good and kind and true. I say again, your presence in the violet halls of our city will soothe our spirits more than you yet understand."

There was no arguing with a draenei, Anduin thought. A smile quirked his lips. "It's as you wish, my old friend. But I ask that you set your mind to thinking of something more tangible we can bring as well."

The ancient being's own lips curved in a smile that was eternally youthful. "I will see what I can come up with."

"Good. More pressing is what we need to bring to Ironforge, as it's the first city I intend to visit. What can we offer the dwarves as a gift that they would most appreciate?"

For a moment, brows were furrowed in contemplation. And then, as one, all of them, even the great Prophet Velen, began to laugh.

CHAPTER SIX

Tanaris

Grizzek Fizzwrench stepped outside his simple ramshackle hut into the lazy, slowly fading heat of the late afternoon. He smiled at the familiar sound of the ocean lapping against the shore, the rustle of the palm trees. The nostrils on his large, long nose flared and his narrow chest expanded as he breathed in the salty air.

"Another beautiful day all to myself," he said aloud, cracking his neck, knuckles, and toes in a lovely long stretch. Then, with a cackle of anticipation, he plunged into the surf.

Once he'd been an ordinary goblin. Just like all the others, he'd lived in cramped, less than hygienic slums and shantytowns, performing unsavory deeds for even more unsavory people. It had been fine when he was on Kezan, but when that island . . . well, *exploded*—which islands were really not supposed to do—and the refugees of the Bilgewater Cartel moved to Azshara, things changed.

He didn't like Azshara, for one thing. It was too autumnal for his summer spirit. All those orange and red and brown colors. He liked the blue of sky and sea and that bright yellow sand and the soothing waving of green-fronded palm trees. Then, when the shredders began tearing up the land, rendering it ugly, he disliked Azshara even more.

The idea of wasting both time and money—which were kind of one and the same—reshaping a part of Azshara to make a symbol of the Horde seemed like the worst brownnosing Grizzek had ever seen—and he'd seen a lot.

And all those other races in the Horde: they just didn't seem to understand the goblin mentality. The "deaders," as he thought of the Forsaken, gave him the creeps, and the only thing they seemed to enjoy tinkering with was poisons. The orcs thought they were better than everyone else. "Original Horde" and all that claptrap. The tauren were too in love with the land to make any reasonable person comfortable, and the whole thing the trolls had going on with the loa scared the crap out of him. Pandaren were just too ... well ... nice. He'd met a blood elf or two he could share a beer with, but the race as a whole was *way* too pretty, and they liked pretty things, and goblins and their culture most definitely did not qualify as pretty things.

But the very worst part of joining the Horde was that the union had elevated Jastor Gallywix from a simple slimy trade prince to the powerful slimy leader of an entire Horde faction. And then one day, quite suddenly, as if a switch had been flipped, Grizzek had had enough.

He had taken everything he owned—all of his laboratory knickknacks, books filled with years of painstakingly detailed notes on experiments, and a small warehouse full of supplies—and moved here, to a deserted beach in Tanaris.

Working alone in the sweltering sun, which turned his pale yellow-green skin to a rich forest-emerald hue, he had constructed a small, modest domicile and a not so small, not very modest laboratory. Grizzek found that he flourished in solitude and sunlight. He rose in the late afternoon, went for a swim, and broke his fast, then headed in to work during the cooler evening and night hours. Over the years, he'd constructed a bristling defense system composed of robots, alarums, whistles, and other warning devices.

His favorite such device was Feathers, the unimaginatively named robotic parrot who provided what passed for company. Feathers flew reconnaissance several times a day, using its mechanical eyes to scan for anything out of the ordinary. It would immediately alert Grizzek to trouble. And then . . . well, depending on the nature of the intruder, they would be sent off with a gruff warning or else a blast of the Goblin Dragon Gun Mark II he always kept handy.

It was a beautiful life. And he had made many beautiful things. Well, beautiful might not be the right word. He'd made things that blew other things up in a spectacular fashion and practical gizmos that made it possible for him not to worry about cooking, cleaning, or, really, anything other than creating more gadgets and explosive devices.

And so of course, when Feathers suddenly appeared while he was lying on his back, floating lazily, and squawked loudly, "Intruder alert, west side entrance!" it meant that his beautiful life was probably about to implode.

Grizzek grimaced, listening to Feathers's report. When it came to a single name, though, his eyes snapped open.

He swore long, loudly, and colorfully, and swam back to shore.

"Trade Prince," Grizzek said a few moments later, standing at the main gate, dripping and wearing nothing but a towel. "I thought we had a deal. You got to keep all my inventions, I got to leave the cartel with supplies and peace of mind."

Trade Prince Jastor Gallywix, garishly dressed as always, his round bulging tummy preceding him by almost two full paces, merely smiled. He had brought with him several bruisers, including the muscle-bound Druz, his chief enforcer.

"Hey, Druz," Grizzek added.

"Yo, Grizzek," Druz replied.

"Is this how you greet an old friend?" Gallywix boomed.

Grizzek stared at him flatly.

"Traditional goblin etiquette demands that you invite in a trade prince!"

"Actually, no," Grizzek shot back. "It don't, and anyway, I ain't never been much for etiquette." Druz leaned against the doorway, cleaning his nails with a knife. The thought of being stabbed with a knife coated with what was under Druz's fingernails was horrifying.

Gallywix's smile didn't falter. "Twelve extremely strong goblins, many of them with guns trained on you, demand that you invite in a trade prince."

Grizzek drooped. He sighed heavily. "Okay, okay. What's this all about, Gallywix?" he asked, not bothering with the Horde leader's title.

"What's it always about?"

"Creative expression, intellectual stimulation, and sound sleep at night?" Grizzek offered.

"Of course not! This is business. A, shall we say, *golden* opportunity." Gallywix gestured with his cane.

Grizzek's eyes automatically went to the orb perched atop it. He'd seen it a thousand times, that bright red—

He blinked.

"It's gold," he said.

"Not *gold* gold, but yes."

"Ah. So that's the pun."

Gallywix's smile faded somewhat, and Grizzek relished the fact that he was getting underneath the trade prince's skin. "Yes," he said. "That's the pun."

"It used to be red."

Gallywix frowned, and his chins jiggled with irritation. "It did. Same adornment, different color. C'mon, Grizzy, you gotta be intrigued by *that* at least!"

Damn the goblin, Grizzek *was* intrigued. Curiosity, as it always did, got the better of him. Besides, he could stand having his supplies replenished.

I'm gonna regret this, he thought, then opened the gate to admit Gallywix. "Just you," he said as Druz tried to step in. "I only got one chair."

"S'okay. I'll stand," Druz said.

What passed for the kitchen was cramped with three goblins crammed into it, and there was indeed only one chair. While Gallywix tried to maneuver his bulk into it, Grizzek excused himself to put on a pair of pants and a linen shirt, then stood and listened. Gallywix spoke of delving too deeply into the heart of Kezan, of the single golden glorious vein they had found that had petered out, of how the power of this substance had surged, then seemingly died as time passed, turning from a warm honey hue to red as a drop of human blood.

His eyes initially were fixed on the trade prince, but his gaze wandered toward the cane as the story grew ever more fantastic.

"And then," Gallywix was saying, "along comes this giant, titan-whipped-up sword, plunged right into Silithus. The earth opened up, and there were veins and veins of the stuff, flowing like a beautiful river of pure honey. Of course, *I* and I alone truly understood what it was, so I jumped right on it. Right now, we got lots of people mining it and making sure only the *right* people get it."

"I am deeply skeptical that this stuff is the wonder you think it is, Trade Prince." Grizzek glanced over at Druz for confirmation of the story. Oddly, he and the chief muscle Gallywix employed had always gotten along pretty well. Druz shrugged his massive shoulders.

Gallywix's ugly smile deepened, and the small eyes twinkled. "The proof is in the pudding."

Grizzek blinked. "What does that even *mean*?"

"No idea, but it sounds good. Look, I'll make a deal with you. Take the cane, touch the top, and see what happens. If you don't want to be involved in working with this stuff, just say the word. I'll be out of your hair."

"I'm bald."

"Figure of speech."

"Okay, but how's about we take it a step further. If you want my help, I get to dictate what I do, what I make, and how it's used."

That did not sit well with the top-hatted trade prince. The smile froze as if Gallywix had run afoul of an angry frost mage. "You're not the only engineer in the world, you know."

"True enough. But I know you wouldn't have tracked me down after all this time if you didn't need my help."

"Grizzek," Gallywix said, sighing, "you are too smart for your own good."

Grizzek waited, arms crossed. "All right, all right," the goblin leader said crossly. "But you only get paid a small percentage."

"We'll negotiate my hourly fee and benefits after I decide."

Again, Gallywix stuck out the cane. Grizzek grasped it. He closed his other hand over the top.

Everything in the room suddenly came into hyperfocus. The color amplified. The lines were sharp, clean. He heard layers in the sound of the ocean, could almost feel the vibrations of birdsong.

And his mind—

It raced, tumbled pell-mell, analyzing and calculating what percentage of his hand was in contact with the orb, to what degree a callus or the sheen of sweat on his suddenly damp palm inhibited contact, to what uses this could be put—

Grizzek snatched his hand away as if it had been burned. It was glorious—almost too much.

"Holy mackerel," he muttered.

"See?"

The engineer's body was still vibrating from the experience, his heart racing, his hands trembling. He knew he had a brilliant mind. He knew he was a genius. It was why Gallywix had sought him out. And the trade prince had been right to do so, because the things that could be created with this stuff . . .

"I, uh . . . Okay. I'll work on it. Run experiments, design some prototypes."

Gallywix's smile was cruelly happy now. "I thought you'd come around."

"My demand still stands," Grizzek insisted. "I want full autonomy on this." He'd betrayed himself earlier with his reaction, he knew, but it wasn't too late to salvage something. He'd been startled, that was all, and now he brought his best poker face to bear.

"You're dying to get your hands on it, and you know it."

Grizzek shrugged, trying to imitate Druz's utter lack of interest.

"Bah, all right," Gallywix huffed. "But I'm going to have some of my people out here from now on."

"Go right ahead," Grizzek said. He knew full well that he wouldn't be venturing far from this stuff anyway. "But before we get started, I'm going to write up a list of supplies. And top of that list"—he nodded at the cane tip—"is a sample of that."

"You'll get plenty of this. Provided that plenty of new things created with it start leaving here on a regular basis."

"Of course, of course. And . . ." Oh, how he hated to say this. "I have one more request. I'm gonna need my former lab partner to work with me on this."

"Sure, sure." Gallywix had gotten what he wanted and clearly was feeling generous. "Gimme a name; I'll get 'em right to you."

Grizzek told him.

Gallywix almost exploded, but a quarter of an hour later he had relented.

It was with both relief and reluctance that Grizzek closed the door of his little hut. He wiped off the chair in which Gallywix had sat, just because, and plopped down into it.

This was either the best idea of his life . . . or the worst.

Grizzek suspected the latter.

CHAPTER SEVEN

Ironforge

Anduin had performed all his kingly obligations, observing the proper protocol upon arriving at the massive gates of Ironforge and later during the lengthy formal meal. He'd had to pace himself. Dwarves loved to eat and they loved to drink, and although Anduin was larger than any of them, he was well aware that even the slightest dwarf could drink him under the table if he wasn't careful.

Moira Thaurissan, the daughter of Magni Bronzebeard and the leader of the Dark Iron dwarf clan by marriage, was one of the Three Hammers who governed Ironforge. She personally preferred wine to the beloved beer of most dwarves, and she ensured the visiting king was served one of Ironforge's finest reds as they dined on braised boar meat with plenty of hearty brown bread to sop the juices, vegetables roasted with honey, and a mountain of pastries with which to end the meal.

Anduin had wanted to convene a meeting with the Three Hammers right away, but they had told him one needed time to digest such a hearty meal. Unless it was a matter of immediate life or death, a pipe, brandy, or more desserts were required first.

Moira, observing Anduin's reaction to the option of any of the three, suggested an hourlong amble around Ironforge instead to help them digest. Anduin gratefully accepted. He invited the draenei to accompany them, but Velen demurred, saying, "You two have much to discuss, I am certain. I will stay here and converse with Muradin and Falstad." Muradin Bronzebeard, the middle brother of the three Bronzebeards, represented his family's clan in the Council of Three Hammers. (The youngest of the famous brothers, Brann, had founded the Explorers' League and had too much wanderlust in him to stay in Ironforge.) Falstad Wildhammer, the third Hammer and the leader of the famed Wildhammer clan, raised a stein to the draenei.

"Pipe, brandy, or dessert?" Anduin quipped.

"Dessert, I think," Velen replied. "It seems the most innocuous choice."

"Have my share. If I eat another bite, I'll burst."

"Mind if we have a bit of company?" Moira asked as they rose and left the table.

"Of course; anyone you like."

The queen spoke quietly with one of the guards, who nodded and stepped out. A few minutes later, he returned, escorting a little dwarf boy. The child's skin was an unusual but appealingly warm shade of gray. His eyes were large and green, holding no hint of the red glow common to the Dark Iron dwarves, and his hair was white. Anduin knew at once who it had to be: Moira's son, Magni Bronzebeard's grandson, and the heir to the throne, Prince Dagran.

"I know we've met before, Your Majesty, but I'm afraid I don't remember it," the young prince said with perfect politeness and little more than a trace of the local dwarven accent. How old was he? Six, seven? Anduin recalled that he, too, had been schooled in etiquette and courtesies appropriate to the child of a king when he was even younger than this lad.

"I'd be astonished if you did. Let us consider this our first meeting." Anduin leaned forward and extended his hand in a formal manner, and the boy shook it solemnly. "I'm glad you could join us on our walk today. So . . . what's your favorite place in Ironforge?"

The boy's eyes lit up. "Th' Hall o' Explorers!"

Anduin shot Moira a pleased look as he replied, "Mine, too. Let's go!" Once they had reached the hall and had enjoyed looking around it, he would ask Moira to summon Falstad, Muradin, and Velen. Then Anduin would reveal the second reason why he had come to Iron-forge.

As they made their leisurely way toward their destination, human and dwarf guards following at a discreet yet expedient distance, Anduin indulged himself in nostalgia. Heat buffeted him as they passed the Great Forge that gave the ancient city its name. The distinctive smell of molten metal transported him back to his last visit a few years earlier.

"It's been too long since I've been here," he said to Moira.

Moira's green eyes were on her son as she replied, "Aye, it has. The years go by faster than we think."

Regarding the boy who was clearly struggling not to race ahead of his mother and the human king, Anduin said to Moira, "It was good of the Three Hammers to come to Stormwind to honor my father. Especially given the fact that the last time I was here, he tried to kill you."

Moira chuckled. "Oh, lad, you know he and I made our peace over that long ago. By the time we lost him, we'd come to admire and respect each other. Your father was angry at me for keeping you here. He was worried for your safety. As Dagran's grown, impossible as it seems, that boy has become more precious to me by the day. Big as Varian Wrynn was, I'd have torn him apart with my bare hands had he kidnapped my wee one." A fierce expression flickered across her face.

"I believe you," Anduin said, and he did. "Dwarves are fighters, that's for sure."

"He was proud of you," Moira said quietly. "Even when he didn't understand you. Don't think he only loved you in the later years, Your Majesty."

"I don't. I knew. And please," Anduin said, "just call me Anduin. I'm more used to friendship than formality here. When I came to visit, your father asked me to call him Uncle Magni, and Aerin called me 'li'l lion.'"

"Aerin?"

"A young woman who was the first female in your father's guard. You'd have liked her. She was trying to improve my abilities with sword and shield before she died at Kharanos."

"Ah," Moira said, regarding him speculatively. "Lost your first friend, did you? I'm sorry." She brightened a little. "But at least from what I hear, her teaching wasn't wasted. You're not the warrior your father was, but there's no shame in that, and I understand your swordsmanship isn't half bad these days."

He gave her a wry smile. "Surprising everyone, no doubt."

"Well, maybe just a wee bit."

Anduin chuckled. "I'm definitely not the warrior Father was. Never will be. No one will." *I can't be the hero you were,* he had said, kneeling where his father had died. *I can't be the king you were.* He turned to her, deciding to confide in her.

"But I will tell you something. Before I met Aerin, I hated heavy weapons training. I avoided it as much as possible, and I became extremely creative with my excuses. But after she died, I began training in earnest. I didn't shirk it anymore. I wanted to become, if not a superior swordsman, a good one at least. The Light has blessed me with other gifts. I trust in it to aid me even if I have no weapon in my hand at all. Aerin promised to 'dwarf-temper' me, and she did."

Moira laughed out loud at that. "That's as good a term as I've ever heard! Dwarf-tempered, eh? Well. You're a fine specimen, Anduin Wrynn, and I'm proud my people have contributed to the man you've grown up to be."

"Thank you. I'm honored to have such a strong personal friendship with the dwarves—all of them." He hesitated. "You all do seem to be getting along."

"We're dwarves," she said, shrugging. "Words fly. Sometimes so do beer steins. Although I'm thinking that the latter will happen less often when they're full. We're most grateful for your gift."

"I could tell." When Anduin had made his formal entrance to Ironforge a few hours earlier, he'd been greeted by the Three Hammers and an honor guard. They'd made him welcome in this, his first visit as a ruling king. And he knew that welcome was genuine.

But when the ten wagons bearing Stormwind's gift rolled up and the protective covering was whisked off the first one, thunderous applause and cheers rang out.

The gift, of course, was barley, the key ingredient in what was arguably Ironforge's best-loved export.

"Think of it as Stormwind's contribution to peace and goodwill in Ironforge," Anduin said.

"Once you're done with your travels, hurry back and we'll toast you with the first batch," Moira promised. "I've heard the brewmasters are going to call it Anduin's Amber Ale."

That got a full-fledged laugh out of him. She joined in. "I can't remember the last time I laughed like that," he said. "It feels . . . good."

"Aye, it does. To answer your question before we got sidetracked on the extremely important topic of beer, the Hammers have been able to work through things, yes."

"And . . . how is your father?"

"Well," she said, "he's diamond, now, and Light knows where he is from day to day. Would you like to see where he was?"

"Yes. I would."

Dagran paused. Up ahead, Anduin could glimpse the shape of the familiar winged skeleton through the archways that marked the Hall of Explorers. The boy looked longingly at it and said, "As long as you *promise* we come back t' the pteradon!"

Magni had become one with the earth in Old Ironforge, a chamber deep below the High Seat. The three descended, and Anduin could almost feel the press of tons of stone and earth above him. The dwarves, of course, had no such unease as their path took them deeper still.

Anduin knew that the dais where Magni had been turned to diamond would be empty. He knew. Even so, actually seeing it was a shock.

He had been present on that day when King Magni Bronzebeard had performed the ancient ritual. Now he stood, wordless, as Dagran ascended the steps nimbly before his mother and the visiting ruler, bypassing translucent blue-tinted chunks that once had formed the diamond encasement of the diamond king. The boy went straight for a scroll that had been safely mounted behind glass and began to read aloud. The hairs at the back of Anduin's neck prickled as he heard again the words that had been spoken by Advisor Belgrum, now uttered in the treble tones of Magni's grandchild.

"'And here are the why and th' how, to again become one wi' the mountain. For behold, we are earthen, o' the land, an' its soul is ours, its pain is ours, its heartbeat is ours. We sing its song an' weep for its beauty. For who would not wish t' return home? That is the why, O children o' the earth.'" Dagran looked up. "Should I keep going?"

"No, sweet boy," Moira said.

Anduin bent and picked up one of the shards. "It was a terrible thing to behold," he said quietly, turning over the diamond chunk in his hands. "It happened so quickly and so completely. I thought he was dead."

"And why would you not?" Moira said. "Even we dwarves thought so."

"That had to have been a tremendous shock when he awoke."

"That phrase," Moira said, "does not *begin* to capture it. All I can say is it's a good thing dwarven hearts are almost as strong as stone."

Anduin hesitated. "I'm so glad. Not just for me and my friendship with him but for you. There was a time I thought my father and I would never become a real family, but we did."

Moira was quiet for a while. Her bright, bookish son was busying himself with another ancient tome, his green eyes flicking over ancient words. When she spoke, she pitched her voice low.

"It's for that child that I'd want that more than for myself," she said. "It's . . . a lot to undo, Anduin. But he said he wanted to try."

"Will you?" Anduin asked, speaking quietly so the boy could not hear.

"I think my people and my son would be best served by having good relationships with a being who speaks directly to Azeroth." It was an attempt at lightness, but it fell flat.

"But what about you?"

Again Moira was silent. She had just opened her mouth to speak when a voice interrupted her.

"Yer Highness, Yer Majesty, come quickly!" It was one of the guards usually stationed at the High Seat. He was flushed and out of breath.

"What is it?" Moira demanded.

"It's yer father! He's here! And he needs tae see you two right away!"

CHAPTER EIGHT

Ironforge

Magni Bronzebeard awaited them in the Hall of Explorers.

Anduin, who once had looked on, helpless to intervene, as the king was agonizingly transformed into gleaming stone, had thought he would be prepared to meet the awakened Magni.

He was not.

Magni stood beneath the pteradon skeleton with his back to the entrance, deep in conversation with Velen and High Explorer Muninn Magellas. Falstad and Muradin stood beside them, listening intently, their bushy eyebrows drawn together in concern.

High Tinker Gelbin Mekkatorque, the white-bearded leader of the gnomes whose cheerful demeanor belied his deep, quiet wisdom, also had been summoned. Anduin had scheduled a meeting with him for the next day. The gnomes had been invaluable against the Legion, and he wanted to make sure he had a chance to thank the physically smallest but perhaps intellectually greatest members of the Alliance. The presence of the high tinker's adviser, the gruff warrior Captain Tread Sparknozzle, whose black eye patch was testimony to his years of battlefield experience, indicated that this was no mere diplomatic visit on Magni's part.

When the glittering shape turned to Anduin, the young king felt as if he had been punched in the gut. A thing made of stone should not move so gracefully, nor should its diamond beard flutter with that movement. Magni was neither the dwarf he had been nor the statue he had become; he was both and neither, and the juxtaposition struck Anduin on a profound level. A heartbeat later, though, gratitude and joy flooded him at Magni's words.

"Anduin! My, ye've grown!"

The phrase loathed by children everywhere was transformed by the power of nostalgia and the inexorable arrival of adulthood. It was so ordinary a phrase, so *real*, that the illusion of "other" was as shattered as Magni's diamond prison had been. The voice was warm, living, and very definitely Magni's. Anduin wondered whether the diamond "flesh" would be warm, too, if he were to touch the being who now strode toward him. But the spurs and shards that dotted the dwarf-shaped form precluded the enthusiastic handshakes and crushing hugs that Magni had been so prone to in his former incarnation.

Had Moira or Dagran found a way around that? Did Magni even wish to bestow the gestures he'd been so free with during his life as a being of flesh and blood? For the sake of all of them, Anduin hoped so. Moira had asked Belgrum to take care of Dagran, who had protested that he wanted to meet his grandfather. *We'll see,* she said. Her face wasn't hard exactly, but it was concerned.

"Magni," Anduin said. "It is so good to see you."

"And ye and me daughter." Magni turned his stone eyes to Moira. "I dare tae hope that once me duty's done here, I might be able tae meet me grandson. But sadly, a visit's nae what I've come about."

Of course not. Magni spoke for Azeroth now, and that was a great and solemn duty. Anduin's gaze flickered to the draenei. Velen was not a maudlin soul. He smiled easily and warmly and often laughed. But he had known so much pain that it was those lines his ancient face remembered, cutting through his visage as if they had been chiseled, and they were set in a grim expression now.

Magni regarded Moira, Anduin, and Velen seriously. "I've sought the three o' ye out nae because all o' ye are leaders o' yer people but because ye are priests."

Moira and Anduin exchanged surprised glances. Anduin was aware of this commonality, of course, but for some reason he hadn't given much thought to it.

"She's in terrible pain," he said, his diamond face, seemingly so hard, furrowing easily into an empathetic wince. Anduin wondered if the rite that had so transformed Magni meant that he could now literally sense Azeroth's pain. Anduin thought of the destruction of Silithus, of the almost inconceivable size of the sword now towering over the landscape. If Sargeras's last attempt to destroy Azeroth had come close to succeeding, it was a terrifying thought.

"She needs healin'. An' that's what priests do. She made it clear that all must heal her or all will perish."

Velen and Moira turned to each other. "I believe that the words your father has spoken are true," the draenei said. "If we do not tend to our wounded world—as many of us as possible—then most assuredly we all *will* perish. There are others who must hear this message."

"Aye," Moira said, "and I think it's time that the lad met the rest of us."

And as one, the two turned to look directly at Anduin.

Anduin's brow furrowed in confusion. "The rest of whom?"

"Other priests," Moira said. "The Prophet and I have been working with a group you're long overdue to get to know."

And then Anduin understood. "The Conclave. In the Netherlight Temple."

The very name seemed to set calm upon Anduin's soul, almost in defiance of the temple's history as the prison for Saraka, a void lord and a fallen naaru, and its location in the heart of the Twisting Nether. For eons, the draenei had studied the creature. Only recently had they been able to purify it. Now, as its true self, Saa'ra, the naaru lingered, embracing its former prison as a sanctuary it offered to others.

Anduin had heard about the struggle that had unfolded in the early days of the Legion's invasion. And he knew that many who now walked its hallowed halls were, like the naaru itself, those who had fallen into darkness but had been brought back into the Light. These priests, known as the Conclave, had reached out to others on Azeroth so they would join together to help stand against the onslaught of the

Legion. Although the threat had ended, the Conclave still existed, offering help and compassion to all who would seek the Light.

"What the Conclave did and continues to do is so important," Anduin said. During the war, they had roamed Azeroth, recruiting priests to tend to those who were on the front lines against the Legion. Now they still tended to those courageous fighters as they dealt with lasting injuries to body, mind, and spirit. Not all scars were physical. "I wish I could have assisted their efforts during the war."

"Dear boy," Velen said, "you have always been right where you needed to be. We have our own paths, our own struggles. My son's fate was mine. Moira's path is overcoming prejudice and championing the Dark Irons who believe in her. Yours was succeeding a great king and governing the people who have loved you since your birth. It is time to let go of regrets. There is no place for them in the Netherlight Temple. It is a site filled with only hope and determination to follow where the Light leads us and bring it into the dark places that so need its blessing."

"The Prophet, as he usually is, is dead right," Moira said. "Though I admit I'm pleased to finally be able to share this place with you. Despite the dire nature behind this visit now, I know you'll find some balm for your soul there. It's impossible not to."

She spoke as one who herself had found such a balm. Anduin thought of the strange material safely inside his pocket. He had planned to show it to the Three Hammers after what was supposed to have been a pleasant walk. Now he realized that no one would be better able to identify the stone than Magni, who was still one with the earth.

"We will go, but not yet. I thank you for your message, Magni. And . . . there's something I need to show you. All of you." Briefly he summarized what he knew about the amber material, realizing as he spoke that it was precious little.

"We don't know much," he finished, "but I believe you can tell us more."

He withdrew the handkerchief and folded it open. The little gem glowed its warm amber and blue hues.

Magni's eyes filled with diamond tears. "Azerite," he breathed.

Azerite. They had a name for it at last. "What is it?" Moira asked.

"Och," Magni said softly, sadly, "I told ye she was hurtin'. Now ye can see it fer yerselves. This . . . is *part* o' her. It's . . . bah, 'tis so hard tae describe in words. Her essence, I suppose will do. More an' more o' it is comin' tae th' surface."

"Can she not heal herself?" Mekkatorque wanted to know.

"Aye, she can and has," Magni replied. "Ye've nae forgotten th' Cataclysm, have ye? But that fel thing that bastard stuck her wi' . . ." He shook his head, looking like someone who was losing his beloved. Anduin supposed he was.

" 'Tis a good an' noble effort she's made, but one that's destined tae fail. Azeroth canna do it by hersel'. Nae this time. That's why she's beggin' fer our help!"

It all made sense. Perfect, devastating sense. Anduin passed the small sample of Azerite to Moira. As all did, she went wide-eyed with wonder at what she was feeling.

"We hear you," he said to Magni, looking deep into the diamond eyes. "We will do all we can. But we also need to make sure that this . . . Azerite . . . isn't used by the Horde."

The Azerite pebble now rested in Muradin's hands. He glowered. "Enough o' this and ye could take down a whole city."

"Enough o' this," Falstad said, "an' we could shatter th' Horde."

"We're not at war," Anduin said. "For now, our task is twofold— and it's clear. We need to heal Azeroth, and we need to keep this"— and he accepted the Azerite—"safely away from the Horde."

He regarded Mekkatorque. "If anyone can figure out how to put this . . . this essence to good use for a worthy purpose, it's your people. Magni has told us that Azeroth is producing increasing amounts of this substance. We will send you samples when we have obtained them."

Gelbin nodded. "I'll get my best minds on it. I think I know just the person."

"An' I'll talk tae the other members of th' Explorers' League an' send a team down tae Silithus," Magellas said.

"All that's grand," Magni said even as he shook his head in sorrow.

To Anduin he said, "Aye, I ken that all this was a shocker tae ye, lad. Off wi' ye three. Go tae yer priest hall an' let them know a whole world might be dyin'." He cleared his throat and straightened. "Right, then. Me job's done. I'll be off."

"Father," Moira said. "If you aren't called away by . . . by her . . . then I'd ask you to stay for a bit." She took a deep breath. "There's a wee lad who's been pestering me about meeting you for some time now."

THE NETHERLIGHT TEMPLE

Anduin stepped through a portal into a realm of wonder so beautiful, so Light-filled, his heart seemed to break even as it swelled with joy.

He had spent much time in the *Exodar* and was accustomed to the soothing purple light and the sense of peace that pervaded the place. But this . . . this had the *Exodar*'s essence writ large, but with a different touch.

The massive carved statues of draenei should have been intimidating, towering over visitors as they did. Instead, they felt like protective benevolent presences. The melodic sound of flowing water came from both sides of the ramp that Anduin descended; sparks of light floated up gently, as if created by the soft splashing.

He took a deep breath of the clean, sweet air as if he'd never truly expanded his lungs before. Farther into the temple, down the long, gentle incline, was a cluster of people. He knew who they were or, rather, what they represented, and the knowledge filled him with quiet anticipatory joy.

Velen laid a hand on the king's shoulder as he had done so many times over the last years and smiled.

"Yes," he affirmed, seeing Anduin's unspoken question. "They are all here."

"When you said priests," Anduin said, "I assumed you meant . . ."

"Priests just like us," Moira finished. She gestured to the various individuals milling around them. Among their number Anduin saw not only humans, gnomes, dwarves, draenei, and worgen—those who would be at home in Stormwind's Cathedral of Light—but also night elves, who worshipped their moon goddess, Elune; tauren, who followed their sun god, An'she; and . . .

"Forsaken," he whispered as the hair along his arms and the back of his neck lifted.

One of them stood, her stooped back toward him, cheerfully talking with a draenei and a dwarf. There was another group heading toward one of the hall's alcoves, carefully bearing piles of no doubt ancient tomes. This one consisted of a Forsaken, a night elf, and a worgen.

Words would not come. Anduin found himself staring openly, hardly daring to blink lest it all turn out to be a dream. In Azeroth, these groups would be killing one another—or, at the very least, they would be suspicious, hate-filled, and fearful. The musical sound of a night elf's throaty laugh wafted to him.

Velen looked completely content, but Moira was eyeing him carefully. "You all right, Anduin?"

He nodded. "Yes," he said, his voice husky. "I can honestly say I've never felt better. This . . . all this. . . ." He shook his head, smiling. "It's what I've dreamed of seeing all my life."

"We are priests before all else," came a voice. It was masculine, warm, and jovial, though it had a peculiar timbre to it, and as Anduin turned, he fully expected to greet a human priest of the Light.

He found himself face-to-face with a Forsaken.

Anduin, schooled since childhood not to let his emotions show, hoped he recovered sufficiently, but inwardly he was reeling. "So it seems," he said, his voice betraying his astonishment despite himself. "And I am glad for it."

"Your Majesty," said Velen, "may I present Archbishop Alonsus Faol."

The Forsaken's eyes glowed an eerie yellow. They couldn't possibly twinkle with amusement as a living man's would, but somehow they did.

"Don't fret about not recognizing me," the archbishop said. "I know I don't look like my portrait." He lifted a bony hand and stroked his chin. "I've lost the beard, you see. Slimmed down quite a bit, too."

Oh, yes, those undead eyes were twinkling.

Anduin gave up any hope of behaving in a typically regal manner here. *We are priests before all else,* the undead being had told him, and he discovered it was a relief to put away the burden of royalty at least temporarily. He smiled and bowed.

"You are a man out of history, sir," Anduin told the archbishop in a voice of awe. "You founded the paladin order—the Silver Hand. Uther Lightbringer was your first apprentice. And Stormwind might not be standing today were it not for your diligent efforts. To say it is an honor to meet you doesn't begin to describe it. You were . . . you *are* one of my heroes."

Anduin was utterly sincere. He'd pored through all the thick tomes about the benevolent, Greatfather Winter–like priest. The words on those pages painted a picture of a man who was quick to laugh but stood as strong as stone. Historians, usually content with simply recording dry facts, had waxed eloquent about Faol's warmth and kindliness. Portraits depicted him as a short, stout man with a bushy white beard. The undead being who stood before the king of Stormwind was still shorter than average but otherwise unrecognizable. The beard was gone. Cut? Rotted away? And the hair was dark with dried blood and ichor. He smelled like old vellum: dusty but not unpleasant. Faol had died when Anduin was a child, and the boy had never gotten to meet him.

Faol sighed. "I have done and been those things you have cited, true. I have also been a mindless minion of the Scourge." He lifted his bony arms, indicating the glorious temple and those who tended it. "But here the only thing that matters is that I am a priest first."

"I've been working with the archbishop for some time now," Moira said. "He's been helping me and the Dark Irons find and gather priests for the temple. We needed to do that in order to stand against the Legion, but even now that the crisis has passed, I still keep coming here. The archbishop's fine company. Considering he is, after all . . . *you* know." She paused. "A man with no beard."

Anduin chuckled. He felt a familiar, welcome warmth in his chest as he looked around, trying to be more evaluating in his assessment of the place. Could this be a template for the future? Surely if gnome and tauren, human and blood elf, Forsaken and dwarf, could bond together for the common good, this could be re-created on a larger scale on Azeroth.

The problem was that the priests, at least, had a common point they all agreed on even if each saw the Light through a different lens, as it were.

"There is another notable person I think you'd like to meet," Faol said to Anduin. "She, too, is from Lordaeron. But do not fear; she yet breathes, though she faced many dangers with courage and the Light's aid. Come here, my dear." His voice grew fond as he beckoned to a smiling blond woman. She stepped forward, taking the archbishop's desiccated hand without hesitation, then turned to regard Anduin.

"Hello, Your Majesty," she said. She was, he guessed, a little bit older than Jaina, tall and slender with long golden hair and arresting blue-green eyes. She looked familiar somehow, though Anduin knew he had never met her before. "Please let me offer my condolences on the death of your father. Stormwind and the Alliance lost a truly great man. Your family has always been so kind to mine, and I regret that I wasn't able to pay my respects."

"Thank you," Anduin said. He was trying and failing to place her. "You'll have to pardon me, but . . . have we met?"

The woman smiled a little sadly. "No, we've not," she said, "but you've probably seen a family resemblance in some portraits. You see . . . I'm Calia Menethil. Arthas was my brother."

CHAPTER NINE

The Netherlight Temple

C alia Menethil. Hers was another name straight out of the history books. Calia, like the archbishop, had been thought lost. The older sister of the ill-fated Arthas Menethil, she was believed to have perished on the day when the heir to Lordaeron, who was by then a servant of the terrifying Lich King, had marched into the throne room, murdered his father in cold blood, and unleashed the undead Scourge upon the city. But his sister had survived, and she was here in the Netherlight Temple. The Light had found her.

Moved in a way he couldn't quite describe, Anduin closed the distance between him and Calia in three quick, long-legged strides and extended his hand mutely.

Calia hesitated, then took it. Anduin squeezed her hand and smiled. "I am gladder than I can say to find you still alive, my lady. After so long with no word, we assumed the worst."

"Thank you. There were moments, I assure you, when I thought the worst was upon me."

"What happened?"

"It is . . . a long story," she said, clearly unwilling to share it.

"And we have no time for a long tale this day." It was Velen. Anduin was filled with questions for both the archbishop and the queen of Lordaeron, for such, now, she was. But Velen was completely right. Despite the pleasant shocks he'd received in the last few moments, Anduin, Moira, and Velen were here with a grim purpose.

He smiled at Calia and, releasing her hand, turned to regard the assembled priests.

There were so many. As if reading his mind, Faol said, "It seems like a lot of us, doesn't it? But this is only a handful compared to the numbers we could have. There is plenty of room for all of us."

Anduin couldn't even wrap his mind around it. "What an amazing thing you've achieved here," he said to Faol. "All of you. I knew you were working toward this, but to truly see it with my own eyes is something else again. I wish this were nothing more than a visit to a place I've longed to behold, but we have received some dire news."

He nodded to Moira. She was the daughter of Magni, "the Speaker," who had brought the warning to them. She was also well known and well regarded here, whereas he was a newcomer—a king, to be sure, but in a place where that was not seen as the highest authority. The dwarf queen squared her shoulders and addressed the group.

"We're servants of the Light, but we live on Azeroth," she said. "And my father has now become the Speaker for our world. He came to Ironforge, where the Prophet and the king of Stormwind were visiting, with terrible news."

Her blunt, steady speech faltered slightly. And for a moment Anduin saw in her the face of the girl she had once been, lost and uncertain. She recovered quickly, though, and continued.

"Lads, lasses . . . our world's hurt badly. She's in trouble. In horrible pain. My father told us that she needs healing; she can't do it by herself."

Soft gasps rippled through the assembled crowd of priests.

"It is that monstrous sword!" a tauren rumbled, his deep voice reminding Anduin sharply of Baine Bloodhoof, the tauren high chieftain—and his friend.

"How can we possibly heal the world itself?" a draenei said, a note of despair making her melodious voice crack.

It was a valid question. How indeed? Priests healed, but their patients were flesh. They mended wounds, cured illnesses and curses, and sometimes, if the Light willed, brought the dead back to life. What could they do with a wound to the world?

He knew where they could start. He could feel the answer inside his coat, next to his heart, where he had placed the small, precious piece of Azerite. For a moment he hesitated, looking at the Forsaken, troll, and tauren faces turned toward them. Horde faces. Could they be trusted?

He asked the question of the Light—and his own body.

Anduin had been gravely injured when Garrosh Hellscream had caused an enormous artifact known as the Divine Bell to come crashing down upon him in Pandaria. Since that moment, his bones ached whenever he was on the wrong path—when he was being cruel, or thoughtless, or courting danger.

There was no ache in his body now. Indeed, he felt better than he had in a long time. Was it the Netherlight Temple or the piece of Azerite that placed this calm upon him?

He did not know. But he knew that both were benevolent influences.

Besides, Azeroth herself had asked for their aid.

Anduin stepped forward, lifting his hands for silence as the crowd began to grow increasingly anxious. "Brothers and sisters, listen to me, please!"

They quieted, their oh so different faces turned to him with exquisite, beautifully similar expressions of concern and a desire to help. And so he trusted them, these priests whose people owed allegiance to the Horde. He let them hold the Azerite, watching their reactions.

"Magni was once a dwarf, the father of a priestess," Anduin said as each of them held the small item. "It makes sense that he would turn first to our order. I feel certain that there is something we ourselves can do at some point, but first we'll need to do research. Ask questions. And in the meantime, we need to reach out to other types of healers. Shaman. Druids. Those who have closer ties to the earth and its living things than we do."

Anduin paused, looking around at the great hall. He wondered what the druidic equivalent looked like, or the shamanic. No doubt beautiful and perfectly right for them, as this temple was for the Conclave.

"I will be traveling to Teldrassil myself very shortly." He corrected himself. "No. Not shortly—on the morrow." He wished he had been able to spend more time in Ironforge. He had wanted to meet with Mekkatorque and his people and thank them for their contribution of gnomish brains and gnomish technology that had helped turn back an enemy so dire that there had been true doubt they would ever succeed. But events had overtaken them all. Mekkatorque would understand.

"You have been out in the world, finding your fellow priests," the king of Stormwind continued. "Now we need to broaden that outstretched hand of aid. We need to extend it to those who have a better chance of helping right away. This will not be easy. So I would ask the Horde and Alliance members present to seek out the druids and shaman on their own sides."

They began nodding, calmer now, and Anduin realized what he had just done. He had come, an invited guest, into this hall and had assumed he had the right to instruct members of the Conclave on their next actions.

Chagrined, he turned to Faol.

"My apologies, Archbishop. These are your people."

"They are people who serve the Light," the undead priest reminded him. "As are you." His head cocked to one side, and he smiled slightly. "You remind me of Calia's brother when he was younger, when he still followed the Light. You have a gift for ruling, my young friend. People will follow where you lead them."

Anduin understood that the comparison was meant as a compliment. He had heard it before, most memorably from Garrosh Hellscream.

While the former warchief of the Horde had been imprisoned below the Temple of the White Tiger during his trial, he had asked for

Anduin to visit him. Garrosh had brought up the specter of the man who had become the Lich King. *There was another golden-haired, beloved human prince once. He was a paladin, and yet he turned his back on the Light.*

Not an unexpected comparison at all, given their outward similarities, yet it was an uncomfortable one. Anduin found he glanced at Calia, who was smiling in agreement, nostalgia sharpening the premature lines on her face. Not even Jaina could smile when thinking of Arthas. No one could except the few left who remembered Arthas Menethil as an innocent child.

"Thank you," Anduin told Faol. "But I shan't insert myself again unless invited to do so. I respect the Conclave and its leadership."

Faol shrugged. A tiny piece of mummified skin fell off and wafted to the floor at the gesture. It should have been repellent, but Anduin found himself regarding it in much the same way as he would a feather falling from a trimmed cape. He was learning to see the person, not the body.

In a way, we are all trapped in a shell, he thought. *Theirs is just held together differently.*

"All voices are listened to here," Faol said. "Even the youngest acolyte may have something useful to say. Your voice is welcome here too, King Anduin Wrynn. As is your presence."

"I would like to return soon," Anduin said. He looked at Calia and Faol. "There is much I see here that I think I can learn from."

And much, he thought but did not say, *I need to learn about.* An idea was beginning to form, daring and audacious and unexpected. He would have to speak with Shaw.

Faol chuckled, a raspy but not unpleasant sound. "Admitting you do not know something is the beginning of wisdom. Of course. Any time . . . priest."

He inclined his head. Anduin looked at Moira and Velen. "I must return to Stormwind shortly and prepare for my trip. It has a fresh urgency." He handed Moira the Azerite sample. "Would you please deliver this to Mekkatorque for me? Tell him I'm sorry I can't deliver it in person."

"Aye," Moira said. "I'll share anything he learns, of course. My father will no doubt have some suggestions for us as well."

"I'm certain he will," Anduin said. The import of the task settled again upon his heart and mind, chasing away the peace of this place and his curiosity about Calia . . . and about the Forsaken.

CHAPTER TEN

Dalaran

When he was feeling restless, Kalecgos, the former blue Dragon Aspect and present member of the Kirin Tor's Council of Six, liked to walk through the streets of his adopted city. He addressed, reliably and responsibly, the concerns and troubles for the daylight hours—when he needed to be present to help tackle a thorny problem or suggest ancient methods that the current council might not have investigated. In the evenings, though, his concerns and troubles were his own.

Dragons often took on the forms of members of the younger races. Alexstrasza the Life-Binder appeared as a high elf. Chronormu, one of the most important of the time-warding bronze dragons, favored the guise of a gnome known as "Chromie." Kalecgos had long ago settled upon the face and body of a half-human, half-elf male. He'd never been sure why. Certainly not because it allowed him to pass unnoticed: there weren't a lot of half-elves running around.

He had decided that the form appealed to him because it represented a melding of two worlds. Because he, "Kalec," also felt that he was a blend of two worlds: that of dragon and that of human.

Kalec had always felt drawn to and protective of the younger races.

Like the great red dragon Korialstrasz, who had given his life to save others, he liked humans. And unlike Korialstrasz, who until his last breath had been loyal only to his adored Alexstrasza, Kalec had loved humans.

Two, in fact. Two strong, kind, and brave women. Loved and lost them both. Anveena Teague—who in the end realized she was not a true human at all—had sacrificed herself so that a monstrous, devastatingly powerful demon would be denied entry into Azeroth. And Lady Jaina Proudmoore—she was gone, too, sinking ever deeper into a dark pit of pain and hatred that he feared would consume her.

She used to join him on these rambles. They would walk together, hand in hand, often to pause and watch Windle Sparkshine light Dalaran's lamps at nine o'clock sharp. Windle's daughter, Kinndy, had been Jaina's apprentice and was one of the many casualties of Garrosh Hellscream's attack. *No,* Kalec thought, *call it what it was: destruction of Theramore.* Windle had gotten permission to nightly create a memorial to his little girl; her image, drawn in magical golden light, appeared when Windle used his wand to light each lamp.

But Jaina had left, wrapped in anger and frustration as if in a cloak. Left the organization of magi known as the Kirin Tor and her position as its leader; left him, too, with only a few angry words spoken between them. She had been pushed farther than she could bear, and now she was gone.

Kalec could have followed her, could have forced her to confront him, demanded an explanation as to why she had left so abruptly. But he didn't. He loved her, and he respected her. And although every day that passed made it less and less likely that she would return, he still held out hope.

In the meantime, he had been appointed to fill the vacancy left by Jaina's exodus, and the Kirin Tor had been busy indeed during the war against the Legion. He had a purpose. He had friends. He was making his way in the world.

He had thought about visiting his good friend, Kirygosa, who had quietly taken up residence in Stranglethorn. After a life spent in a part of the world that knew mostly winter, Kiry was enjoying a permanent summer. It might be nice to join her for a while. But somehow he never did. If Jaina was ever to seek him out, it would be here. And so he stayed.

Tonight, his feet brought him to the statue of one of Dalaran's greatest magi, Antonidas, who had been Jaina's tutor. It had been she who had commissioned the statue, which hovered a few feet off the green grass thanks to a spell. And it had been she who had written the inscription:

ARCHMAGE ANTONIDAS, GRAND MAGUS OF THE KIRIN TOR

THE GREAT CITY OF DALARAN STANDS ONCE AGAIN—

A TESTAMENT TO THE TENACITY AND WILL

OF ITS GREATEST SON.

YOUR SACRIFICES WILL NOT HAVE

BEEN IN VAIN, DEAREST FRIEND.

WITH LOVE AND HONOR, JAINA PROUDMOORE

It was here that he and Jaina once had a terrible argument. Devastated by the brutal obliteration of her city, Jaina had desired vengeance. When the Kirin Tor would not help her strike against the Horde, she had turned to him. Her words, first pleading, then scathing in their hurt-fueled anger, lingered with him still.

You once said you would fight for me—for the lady of Theramore. Theramore's gone. But I'm still here. Help me. Please. We have to destroy the Horde.

He had refused her. *This implacable . . . well, hatred—it's not you.*

You're wrong. This is *me. This is who the Horde* made *me.*

In so many ways, Jaina was as much a casualty of Theramore as Kinndy was. It had been the Kirin Tor's decision to again allow members of the Horde among their number. Azeroth was too vulnerable to the Legion to turn down aid out of fear and hatred. Kalec had wanted to speak with Jaina, but she had disappeared without a word.

And then—his skin prickled, and a sudden knowing filled his brain.

Lady Jaina Proudmoore had returned to Dalaran. He sensed her, and she was right—

"I thought I might find you here," came a soft voice behind him.

His heart leaping, Kalec swung around.

She was every bit as beautiful as he remembered as she slipped off the hood of her cloak. Moonlight shone upon her white hair with its single golden streak, and it looked like she was crowned with luminous silver. She wore it differently, in a braid this time. Her face was pale, her eyes pools of shadow.

"Jaina," Kalec breathed. "I—I'm so glad you're all right. It's so good to see you."

"Rumor has it you're now a member of the council." She was smiling as she said it. "Congratulations."

"Rumor is correct, and thank you," Kalec replied. "Though I'd vacate it more than happily . . . if you are back to stay."

The smile faded, turned sad. "No."

He nodded. It was what he had feared, and his heart hurt, but it would do no good to say that. She knew.

"Where will you go?" he said instead.

The light was bright enough to catch the little furrow between her brows that was so uniquely hers. It affected Kalec even more than the smile had.

"I don't know, actually. But I don't belong here anymore." Her voice sharpened slightly with anger. "I can't agree with what—" She caught herself and took a deep breath. "Well. I don't agree."

This is who the Horde made me.

They gazed at each other for a long moment. Then, to Kalec's surprise, Jaina stepped forward and took his hands in hers. The touch, so sweetly familiar, moved him even more than he expected it to. "You were right about something. I wanted you to know that."

"What?" he asked, trying to keep his voice steady.

"About how dangerous, how damaging, hate is. I don't like what it's done to me, but I don't know that I can change it now. I know what I'm against. I know what angers me. What I hate. What I don't want. But I don't know what calms me, or what I love, or what I do want." Her voice was pitched softly, but it trembled with emotion. Kalec gripped her hands tightly.

"Everything I've felt or done since Theramore has been a reaction *against* something. I feel . . . I feel like I'm in a pit and every time I try to climb out of it, I just tumble back down."

"I know," Kalec said gently. Her hands were so warm in his. He didn't want to ever let go. "I've watched you struggle so hard for so long. And I couldn't help."

"No one could," Jaina said. "This is something I have to do for my-self."

He looked down, running his thumb over her fingers. "I know that, too."

"I'm not leaving because of the vote."

Kalec, surprised, glanced up sharply at that. "You're not?"

"No. Not this time. People must be true to their own natures, as must I." She laughed softly, self-deprecatingly. "I just . . . have to figure out what that is."

"You will. And I believe it won't be anything ugly or cruel."

She eyed him. "I'm not sure *I* believe that."

"I do. And . . . I admire you. For having the courage to face this."

"I knew you'd understand. You always have."

"Peace is a noble goal for the world," Kalec said, "but it is also a noble goal for oneself." He realized he was smiling despite the ache in his human-shaped chest. "You'll find your way, Jaina Proudmoore. I have faith in you."

She said wryly, "You may be the only person in the world who does."

He lifted her hands and pressed a kiss on each of them. "Travel safely, my lady. And *never* forget: if you have need of me, I will be there."

She looked up at him for a moment, stepping closer. Now he could see her eyes catching the moonlight. He had missed her. Would miss her. He had a terrible feeling they wouldn't see each other again, and he hoped he was wrong.

Jaina let go of his hands, but only to bring hers up to cup his face. She stood on her toes as he bent. Their lips met—so familiar, so sweet, in a kiss so tender that it shook Kalec to his core. *Jaina . . .*

He wanted to kiss her forever. But all too soon, that precious warmth pulled back. He swallowed hard.

"Good-bye, Kalec," she whispered, and now he saw tears glistening in her eyes.

"Farewell, Jaina. I hope you find what you seek."

She gave him a tremulous smile, then retreated a few paces. Magic swirled as she conjured a portal. She stepped into it and was gone.

Farewell, beloved.

Kalec stood for a long time, his only company the statue of the great archmage.

CHAPTER ELEVEN

Stormwind

The Ironforge trip had been cut short, and Wyll had been running himself ragged trying to get everything together in time for the next leg of Anduin's journey. Anduin had, after much effort, managed to persuade Wyll to stay in Stormwind and have some well-deserved rest.

Once Wyll had retired, Anduin reached for the candelabra on the dressing table. He lit one of its three candles and placed it in the window before heading to the dining room for a very late supper. Tonight, as on certain previous occasions, the candelabra had a purpose other than providing illumination.

As Anduin eyed the roasted chicken, vegetables, and crisp Dalaran apples he had no appetite. The news from Shaw and Magni was too unsettling. He would have left for Teldrassil immediately, but it had taken this long to get everything prepared. First light couldn't come soon enough for him.

"Eat something," came a gruff voice. "Even priests and kings need to eat."

Anduin clapped a hand to his forehead. "Genn," he said, "I'm so sorry. Please, join me. We still have things to settle before I leave, don't we?"

"First thing is food," Greymane said, and he pulled up a chair and speared some chicken.

"You and Wyll are colluding against me," Anduin sighed. "The sad thing is, I'm glad of it."

Genn grunted in amusement as Anduin filled his own plate. "I've got the papers drawn up," Genn said.

"Thank you for handling that. I'll sign them right away."

"Read them first. Doesn't matter who wrote it. There's a free piece of advice for you."

Anduin smiled tiredly. "You've given me quite a bit of free advice."

"And some you're even grateful for, I imagine," Genn said.

"All of it. Even what I disagree with and choose to ignore."

"Ah, now there speaks a wise king." Greymane reached for the bottle of wine on the table and filled his glass.

"No coup planned, then?" Anduin found himself reaching for another helping of chicken. His body was hungry, it would seem, even if his mind was distracted.

"Not this visit."

"That's good. Save your plotting efforts for another time."

"There *is* one thing I'd like to discuss before you depart," Greymane said, turning serious. There was something in his body language that alerted Anduin, who put down his knife and fork and regarded the other king.

"Of course," Anduin said, concerned.

Now that he had the full attention of the king of Stormwind, Genn looked a bit uncomfortable. He took a drink of the wine, then faced Anduin squarely.

"You honor me with your trust," he said. "And I'll do everything I can to govern your people with care and diligence if, Light forbid, something should happen to you."

"I know you will," Anduin assured him.

"But I'm an old man. I won't be around forever."

Anduin sighed. He knew where this was heading. "It's been a long and challenging day. I'm too tired to have this discussion with you."

"You've always been too something or other every time I've brought it up," Genn pointed out. Anduin knew it was true. He toyed with his food. "We're on the eve of your departure to visit several different lands," Greymane continued. "Fresh dangers are cropping up. When *will* be a good time? Because I don't relish the thought of trying to sort through gaggles of nobility each pushing their best claim forward."

The image made Anduin smile in spite of himself, but it faded at Genn's next words.

"This isn't a game. If the wrong person is given the kingdom, Stormwind could find itself looking at a very dire situation indeed. Your mother was a horrible casualty of an angry mob furious at what the nobility was doing to the people. And you are old enough to re-member how unstable things were when your father went missing."

Anduin was. He'd been the nominal king during his father's disap-pearance, but he'd had Bolvar Fordragon standing by his side to offer advice. Varian had gone missing, and the black dragon Onyxia had replaced him with an impostor, ruling the kingdom through that pup-pet. Stormwind was unsettled and tumultuous until Onyxia was de-feated and the real Varian Wrynn again sat upon the throne.

The young king took a sip of his wine. "I remember, Genn," he said quietly.

Genn gazed down at his half-eaten meal. "When I lost my boy," he said softly, his voice intense, "I lost a piece of my soul. I didn't just love Liam. I admired him. I respected him. He would have been a tremen-dous king."

Anduin listened.

"And when he fell—when that heartless, undead banshee killed him with an arrow meant for *me*—so much died with him. I thought I would never recover. And I didn't . . . not completely. But I had my wife, Mia. I had my daughter, Tess, every bit as strong and smart as her brother."

Anduin did not interrupt. Genn had never been so open with him before. Now the Gilnean king lifted his blue eyes. In the candlelight, they shimmered, and his voice was husky with emotion.

"I moved on. But I had a hole in my heart where he used to be. A hole I tried to fill with my hatred for Sylvanas Windrunner."

Gently, Anduin said, "That kind of hole can't be filled with hate."

"No. It can't. But I met another young man who loved his people as Liam did. Who believed in things that were good, and just, and true. I found *you*, my boy. You're not my Liam. You're yourself. But I do catch myself trying to guide you."

"You can't replace my father, and I know you know that," Anduin said, deeply moved by Genn's words. "But you're a king and a father both. You understand being both. And it helps."

Genn cleared his throat. Emotions were no stranger to him, Anduin knew, but they were usually the hot, angry, violent ones. It was part of the worgen curse, yes, but Anduin knew it was also an intrinsic part of the man. Genn was not used to the softer emotions and almost always, as he did now, chased them away.

"I'd be saying the same thing to Liam right now if he were here. Life is too short. Too unpredictable. For anyone in this world, especially for a king. If you love Stormwind, you need to make sure it'll go into hands that will care for it."

He paused. *Here it comes*, Anduin thought.

"Anduin, is there anyone you've considered as a possible queen? Someone to rule in your stead should you fall in battle, bear a child to carry on the Wrynn bloodline?"

Anduin abruptly grew keenly interested in the food before him.

Genn sighed, but it came out as more of a growl. "Times of peace are rare in this world. And they're always too brief. You need to use this time to at least start the search. If you're traveling to all these places, couldn't you have a few formal dances, or theater visits, or something?"

"Believe it or not, I understand I need to do that," Anduin admitted. Genn did not know about the small box with Queen Tiffin's rings that Anduin kept close, and the younger man wasn't about to volunteer that information. "And the answer is no, I've not met anyone yet that I've felt that way about. There's time. I'm only eighteen."

"It's not uncommon for royal betrothals to occur when the participants are still in the cradle," Genn pressed. "I'm a bit of a stranger to Stormwind society, but surely there are others who could compile a list."

Genn meant well, Anduin knew. But he was weary and worried, and his focus was on what to do with a wounded world, not on an arranged marriage.

"Genn, I appreciate your concern," he said, choosing his words with care. "This is not an unimportant matter. I've told you I understand that. But the idea of an arranged marriage—agreeing to spend my life with someone I may not even know before making that commitment—it's abhorrent to me. Besides," he added, "you didn't have one."

Genn scowled. "Just because it's not a path I chose doesn't mean it's not a sound one. I know it's not the most romantic thing in the world, but it doesn't have to be some stranger. My daughter, Tess, is close to your age. She would make—"

"Quite the protest were she here at this moment," Anduin interrupted. "From the little I've seen of her, it's clear she's a remarkable woman. But she certainly has her own life, and I'm going to take a wild guess and say that I don't think queen of Stormwind is high on her list of what she wants for it."

Tess Greymane, a few years his senior, was by all accounts a strong-willed woman. There had been all kinds of rumors about her actions, implying that she had taken a page or two from Mathias Shaw. He had not asked Genn about it, and now that the man had put forth his daughter as a potential queen, he wasn't about to.

Genn's white brows drew together in a frown. "Anduin—"

"We will revisit this topic, I promise. But for now, there's another argument I'd like to get into with you."

Despite himself, Genn chuckled. "You know I'll argue with you any time, Your Majesty."

"I do indeed," Anduin said, "and especially about this. After Magni's visit, Moira, Velen, and I went to the Netherlight Temple. I don't think it would surprise you one whit to tell you that I found it to be . . ." He shook his head. "Truthfully, words fail me. It was serene and beautiful, and simply being there made me feel so peaceful. So focused."

"The only surprise I have about your visit was how long it took you to get there," Genn said. "But then again, a king has little time for serenity and peace."

"While I was there, I met two people who surprised me," he said. He took a breath. *Here we go,* he thought. "One of them was Calia Menethil."

Genn stared. "Are you certain? Not an impostor?"

"She looks a great deal like her brother. And I trust the priests of the temple have made sure her claim is true."

"You place a lot of faith in the priests' goodwill."

Anduin smiled. "Yes, I do."

"Well, out with it. What did you learn? How did she escape? Does she still lay claim to the throne of Lordaeron, provided we can one day evict those rotting squatters who currently defile it?"

Anduin smiled a bit ruefully. "I didn't press. I'll return and speak with her later. I got the impression that it wasn't a happy story."

"Light knows it couldn't be," Genn said. "That poor family. What the girl must have been through. Probably escaped those wretches by the skin of her teeth. How she must despise the undead after that!"

"Actually, that's the next thing I wanted to tell you. The Netherlight Temple is a hall for Azeroth's priests. *All* of its priests. Including Horde." He paused. "Including Forsaken."

Anduin had braced himself for an angry bellow of protest. Instead, Genn calmly put down his fork and spoke in a carefully controlled voice.

"Anduin," he said, "I understand that you always want to see the best in people."

"It's not—"

Genn held up a hand. "Please, Your Majesty. Hear me out."

Anduin frowned but nodded.

"It's an admirable trait. Especially in a ruler. But a ruler must be careful that he's not played for a fool. I know you met and respected Thrall. And I know you consider Baine a friend, and he has acted with honor. Even your father negotiated with Lor'themar Theron and held Vol'jin in high esteem. But the Forsaken are . . . different. They don't feel things like we do anymore. They're . . . abominations."

Anduin's voice was mild. "A current leader of the Conclave is Archbishop Faol."

Genn swore and sprang to his feet. Silverware clattered to the floor.

"Impossible!" His face had flushed, and a vein stood out on his neck. "That's *worse* than an abomination. That's blasphemy! How can you tolerate this, Anduin? Doesn't it sicken you?"

Anduin thought about the impish good humor the late Alonsus Faol had displayed. The kindness, the concern. *We are priests before all else.* And he was.

"No," Anduin said, smiling. "Quite the opposite. Seeing them there, in that place of Light . . . it gave me hope, Genn. The Forsaken aren't mindless Scourge. They're people. They have free will. And yes, some of them have been changed for the worse. Those have moved on in their new existence with hate and fear. But not all of them. I saw Forsaken priests speaking not only with tauren and trolls but with dwarves and draenei. They remembered the good. Moira's worked with Faol for some time now, and—"

Genn swore. "Moira, too? I thought dwarves had sense! I've heard enough." He turned, about to stalk out of the room.

"No, you haven't." Anduin's voice was soft but brooked no disagreement. He held out a hand and indicated the chair the other had vacated. "You'll stay, and you'll listen."

Genn eyed him, surprised, then nodded in approval as he sat back down, albeit with obvious reluctance. He took a deep breath.

"I will," he said. "Though I won't like it."

Anduin leaned forward intently. "There's an opportunity here if we're bold enough to take it. Sylvanas gave the Forsaken life. Of course they follow her. But the Alliance turned away from them. All we had to offer them were names—'deaders,' 'rotters.' We viewed them with fear. Disgust. We couldn't even fathom that they were people."

"*Were,*" Genn said. "They *were* people. Once. They're not any longer."

"We've chosen to see them that way."

Genn tried another tactic. "All right." He leaned back in his chair, eyes narrowed. "Let's say that you saw a few decent Forsaken, an extremely small handful, all of whom happened to be priests. Have you encountered any others like that?"

There was another Anduin recalled who had most definitely not been a priest. At the trial of Garrosh Hellscream, the bronze dragons had offered both the defense and the prosecution the ability to show scenes of the past through an artifact known as the Vision of Time. In one such vision, Anduin had witnessed a conversation between a Forsaken and a blood elf in a tavern shortly before that tavern had been destroyed by those too devoted to Hellscream.

The two soldiers had been against the violence and cruelty that Garrosh had personified. And they had died for their beliefs. Oh, what was the name . . . It began with an "F." "Farley," Anduin said. "Frandis Farley."

"Who?"

"A Forsaken captain who turned against Garrosh. He was outraged by the violence of Theramore. He lived right here, in Stormwind, when he was alive."

Genn looked as though he couldn't even comprehend what Anduin had just said.

"Frandis Farley wasn't a priest. Just a soldier who still had enough humanity left in him to understand evil when he saw it." The more Anduin worked it out, the more certain he became.

"Anomalies," Greymane said.

"I don't accept that," Anduin said, leaning forward. "We have *no* idea what the average citizen of the Undercity thinks or feels. And one thing you cannot argue with me: Sylvanas cares about her people. They matter to her. And that may be something we can use to our advantage."

"To bring her down?"

"To *bring* her to the negotiating table." The two men regarded each other, Anduin calm and focused, Genn struggling to suppress his anger.

"Her goal is to turn more of *us* into more of *them*," Genn said.

"Her *goal* is to protect her people," Anduin insisted. "If we let her know we understand that motivation, if we can assure her that those who already exist would never be in danger from the Alliance, she's going to be a lot less likely to use Azerite to create weapons to kill us. Even better, we might actually be able to work with the Horde to save a world we both have to live in."

Genn looked at him for a long moment. "You sure you didn't catch something in Ironforge?"

Anduin held up a placating hand. "I know it sounds like madness. But we've never tried to understand the Forsaken. Now could be the perfect chance. Archbishop Faol and the others could help open negotiations. Each side has something the other just might want."

"What do we have that the Forsaken want? And what do the Forsaken have that *we* could possibly want?"

Anduin smiled, gently. His heart was full as he answered, "Family."

His quarters were dark as he entered them, illuminated only by the light of the moons. "You got my message," Anduin said aloud as he lit a single candle and looked around.

The room appeared empty, but of course it wasn't. A shadow that had seemed perfectly ordinary a moment earlier shimmered, and a familiar lithe frame stepped into the faint light.

"I always do," said Valeera Sanguinar.

"One of these days I'm going to ask you to show me how you get in."

She smiled. "I think you might be a little too heavy to manage it."

Anduin chuckled. He counted himself fortunate that there were many people he trusted. Not all kings, he knew, could say the same thing. But Valeera was on an entirely different level from even Velen or Genn Greymane. She and Varian had fought alongside each other in the gladiator pits, and Anduin had met her years ago. She had saved both his and his father's lives on more than one occasion and had pledged her loyalty to the Wrynn line. And what was almost as important was that she was able to move in circles denied to Anduin and his advisers.

Valeera was a blood elf, and she was the king's personal spy.

She had served Varian in that capacity during his reign, and she had aided the prince when he needed messages delivered that he asked be kept secret even from his father. Although he trusted Spymaster Shaw to do what was best for the kingdom, Anduin didn't know the man well enough to trust that he would do what was best for the king. Certainly he would not have approved of the correspondence Anduin had been carrying on for the last few years.

"I assume you know about Azerite," he said.

Valeera nodded her golden head, perching on a chair without waiting to be asked. "I do," she said. "I hear it can build kingdoms, bring them down, and possibly doom the world."

"All that is true," Anduin confirmed. He poured them each a cup of wine and handed one to her. "I've never embraced the idea that Horde and Alliance must always be against each other. And it seems to me that now, more than ever, we have to have cooperation and trust on both sides. This new material . . ." He shook his head. "Far too dangerous in the hands of any enemy. And the best way to defeat an enemy is to make them a friend."

The blood elf sipped her wine. "I serve you, King Anduin. I believe in you. And I am most certainly your friend and always will be. I would like to live in this world that you see. But I don't think it's possible."

"Improbable," Anduin said, "but I *do* think it's possible. And you know better than anyone that I'm not alone in that sentiment."

He handed her a letter. It was written in a personal code understood by only a handful of individuals. Valeera took it and read. Her expression soured, but she nodded as she carefully tucked it into a pocket close to her heart. As always, she would memorize the contents in case the letter was lost or destroyed.

"I will see that his surrogate receives it," Valeera promised. She did not look happy.

"Be careful," she added. "No one will support this. It's doomed to failure."

"But what if it works?" Anduin pressed.

Valeera peered into the ruby depths of her cup, then lifted her glowing eyes to his. "Then," she said slowly and with deep reluctance, "I think I might have to stop using the word 'impossible.'"

CHAPTER TWELVE

Thunder Bluff

Sylvanas Windrunner reclined on a tanned hide in the large tepee on Spirit Rise. Nathanos sat beside her. He looked uncomfortable sitting cross-legged on the ground, but if she was not allowed to sit in a chair or stand, she wouldn't let him do it, either. A blood elf mage, Arandis Sunfire, had accompanied her as well so that she could make a quick exit if things grew too dull or if an emergency called her away. He stood stiffly to the left of the pair, looking as if he wished he were anywhere but here. On Sylvanas's right was one of her rangers, Cyndia, whose perfect stillness made Arandis's rigidity look energetic.

Sylvanas leaned over to Nathanos and whispered in his ear, "I am so weary of drums." To her, it was the unifying sound of the "old Horde"—the orcs, the trolls, and the tauren, of course, seemed to be willing to happily bang on the drums at any time. Now, at least, they were not the thuddingly loud war drums of the orcs but soft, steady drumming as Archdruid Hamuul Runetotem droned on about the "tragedy of Silithus."

As far as Sylvanas was concerned, what had happened wasn't really tragic at all. In her opinion, a crazed titan plunging a sword into the world had been a gift. She was keeping Gallywix's discovery quiet until she was certain about how the peculiar material could be properly utilized for maximum benefit to the Horde. Gallywix had told her he had "people on that, too."

Also, what was in Silithus, really, but giant bugs and Twilight cultists, both of which the world was better without? But the tauren in particular, whose people had given the Horde its original druids and who had lost several members of the Cenarion Circle, had been devastated at the loss of life.

Sylvanas had graciously sat through a ritual to honor and soothe their troubled spirits. And now she was listening to—and expected to approve—plans to send more shaman and druids to Silithus to investigate, all because Hamuul Runetotem had had a terrible dream.

"The spirits cry out," Hamuul was saying. "They died in an effort to protect the land, and now only death inhabits that place. Death and pain. We must not fail our Earth Mother. We must re-create the Cenarion Hold."

Baine was watching her closely. Some days she wished he would just follow his big, bleeding heart and turn the tauren to the Alliance. But her disdain for the tauren's gentleness did not eclipse her need of them. As long as Baine remained loyal—and thus far he was, where it counted—she would use him and his people to the Horde's advantage.

With Baine was a troll representative, the elderly Master Gadrin. The warchief wasn't looking forward to that conversation, either. There was a power vacuum in the troll hierarchy right now, and the trolls were a chaotic people. Only now, belatedly, had she realized just how calm and centered an individual Vol'jin had been. Certainly, she hadn't realized how effortless he made leading the Horde appear. The trolls would demand a visit, too, no doubt, so they could put forth their various suggestions for a leader.

Runetotem had finished his appeal. They were all looking at her now, all those furry, horned heads turned in her direction.

As she was pondering her answer, one of Baine's Longwalkers, Perith Stormhoof, arrived. He was panting heavily as he bent and whispered into his high chieftain's ear. Baine's eyes widened slightly, and his tail swished. He asked a question in Taur-ahe, to which the runner nodded. Everyone's attention was now on the tauren leader.

Solemn-visaged, he rose to speak. "I have just been informed that we will soon be having a guest. He wishes to speak with you, Warchief, of what has happened in Silithus."

Sylvanas tensed slightly but was outwardly calm. "Who is this visitor?"

Baine was quiet for a moment, then replied, "Magni Bronzebeard. The Speaker for Azeroth. He asks that you send a mage; he is too heavy for the lift to bear him safely."

Everyone started talking at once except for Sylvanas. She and Nathanos exchanged glances. Her mind was racing a thousand leagues a second. Magni couldn't have anything to say that she would appreciate hearing. He was the world's champion, and right now, the deep fissures in that world were yielding a spectacular treasure. She had to stop this, but how?

All she could do, she realized, was try to minimize the damage. "I know that Magni Bronzebeard is no longer truly a dwarf," she said. "But he once was. And I know that to you, High Chieftain, the thought of formally hosting a former leader of an Alliance race must be awkward, if not outright repellent. I will relieve you of the decision whether to welcome him. I am the warchief of the Horde. Anything he has to say, he can say to me alone."

Baine's nostrils flared. "I would think that you of all people would understand how a physical transformation can change one's views, Warchief. You once were a member of the Alliance. Now you lead the Horde. Magni is no longer even flesh."

It was not an insult in any way, yet somehow it stung. But she could not counter the logic. "Very well. If you think it is safe, High Chieftain."

The tauren and the trolls continued looking at her, and it took her a moment to realize that they were expecting her to offer the use of her mage. She pressed her lips together for a moment, then turned to Arandis. "Will you accompany Perith to where the Speaker is awaiting us?"

"Of course, Warchief," he said promptly. In the awkward minutes before all heard the hum of the portal, Sylvanas's brain was working on how best to handle the imminent conversation.

When Magni appeared, the myriad facets of his diamond body reflecting the firelight, Baine greeted him warmly.

"We are honored by your presence, Speaker."

"Yes, we are," Sylvanas said immediately. "I am told you asked to see me."

Magni nodded at Baine, accepting the welcome, before he squared his shoulders as he faced Sylvanas. He stabbed a diamond forefinger in her direction. "I did," he said, "an' there's much tae say. First, ye've got tae get rid o' yer little green men. They're just makin' a bad thing worse."

Sylvanas had expected that. "They are investigating the area," she said, keeping her voice calm and mild.

"Nae, they're not. They're pokin' and proddin', and Azeroth doesn't like it. She needs tae heal—or she's goin' tae die."

All present listened intently as the Speaker explained that Azeroth was in agony, racked by pain that was slowly destroying her. Her very essence was seeping to the surface, and this essence was powerful beyond imagining.

The last part, Sylvanas already knew. The first was troubling. "We've got tae help 'er," Magni said, his voice ragged, and this time she did not correct him.

"Of course we must," she said. This revelation could undo everything. "I assume you will speak to the Alliance."

"Already done," Magni said, clearly hoping to reassure her. "Young Anduin and th' Explorers' League, th' Cenarion Circle, and th' Earthen Ring are goin' tae be sending out teams tae Silithus soon." The Magni Bronzebeard who once had ruled Ironforge would never have revealed what this Speaker of Azeroth just had. This was valuable information.

"Good," said Baine. "We stand ready to do the same."

He should not have spoken before his warchief, but Sylvanas was starting to get an idea.

"High Chieftain Baine speaks for us all. What you have shared is grave news indeed, Speaker. Of course, we will do what we can to help. In fact," she continued, "I would like to ask the tauren to organize the Horde response."

Baine blinked twice but otherwise gave no indication of how surprised he doubtless was. "It will be an honor," he said, and brought his fist to his heart in a salute.

"Thank you for your warning, Speaker. We all exist on this precious world. And as recent events have brought home to all of us, there are not many places left for us to flee to should we destroy this one," Sylvanas said.

"That's . . . mighty enlightened o' ye," Magni allowed. "Right, then. Me task is far from over. I know th' members o' the Horde and the Alliance both have trouble imaginin' that they aren't the only people in the world. But there are many other races I must warn. As ye say, Warchief, we *all* exist on this precious world. Call off yer goblins. Or else we might be tryin' tae find an entirely new world tae call home."

Sylvanas did not promise she would, but she smiled. "Please let us save you some time as you execute this task. Where may Arandis send you next?"

"Desolace, I think," Magni mused. "Need tae tell th' centaur. Thank ye, lassie."

Sylvanas kept the pleasant smile on her face even as she seethed at the too-familiar, condescending term. All were quiet as Arandis conjured a portal that opened up onto the bare, ugly land, and Magni stepped through it and vanished.

Hamuul sighed deeply. "It is worse even than I feared," he said. "We must begin work as soon as we can. High Chieftain, we need all those who have worked with the Alliance before to—"

"No."

The warchief's voice cut off the conversation with the efficiency of a blade lopping off a head.

"Warchief," Baine said calmly, "we all heard the words of the Speaker. Azeroth is badly wounded. Have we forgotten the lessons of the Cataclysm already?"

Tails swished. Ears were lowered and flicked. The trolls looked down and shook their heads. Oh, yes, they all remembered the Cataclysm.

"Such a thing cannot be permitted to happen a second time."

I should have done this a long time ago, Sylvanas thought. She rose fluidly and went to the tauren leader. "I have words for your ears only, High Chieftain," she said, her voice a purr. "Walk with me."

Baine's ears flattened against his head for a moment, but he nodded and descended the steps that led from the tepee to the rise.

The rises of Thunder Bluff—Spirit Rise, Elder Rise, and Hunter Rise—were all connected to the center rise by rope bridges and planks. Sylvanas marveled quietly at the engineering. They seemed so rickety and precarious, yet they easily handled the weight of several tauren crossing at a time.

Sylvanas walked without hesitation to the middle of the bridge. It swayed slightly. From there she could see the faint glow of the cavern that housed the Pools of Vision. Before she left, she would have to pay a visit there; it was the only congregation of Forsaken in the tauren capital. She needed to return home, to the Undercity, too; to meet with the Desolate Council. To assess the threat—or lack thereof—for herself.

"What are these words you wish to share with me, Warchief?" Baine asked.

"Are my people happy here?"

The tauren cocked his head in puzzlement. "I believe so," he said. "They have all that they ask for and seem content."

"The tauren befriended the Forsaken when we were rejected by the Alliance. For that I will always be grateful."

Hamuul Runetotem, currently a thorn in her side, had argued successfully that the Forsaken were capable of redeeming themselves. With free will, they could choose to atone for what they had done after being murdered and enslaved to the Lich King's will. He had convinced the warchief Thrall, who knew a thing or two about people being seen as "monsters," to admit the Forsaken into the Horde.

Sylvanas would never forget that. She turned to Baine now, looking up at him. "And for that, I have looked the other way when you pursued a friendship with a certain human."

"My interaction with Jaina Proudmoore has long been known," Baine said. "It was made public knowledge at Garrosh Hellscream's trial. She aided me when the Grimtotem were in rebellion against the tauren. Why does this trouble you now?"

"That doesn't trouble me. What does trouble me is that you have continued to exchange correspondence with Anduin Wrynn. Do you deny it?"

He was silent, but his suddenly switching tail betrayed him. Tauren were terrible liars. At last he spoke. "I have never, by word or implication, advocated *anything* that would bring harm to the Horde."

"I believe you. That is why I have not interfered ere now. But Prince Anduin is now King Anduin. He's no longer an ineffectual, starry-eyed dreamer. He is the maker of policy. He can start a war. If you were me, would you condone secret messages sent to an Alliance king?"

"What will you do?" Baine asked with remarkable calmness.

"Nothing," she said, "as long as the connection is severed. And to show I do not hold a grudge at what some could understandably label treason, I stand by my offer to allow you to lead the response to help heal Azeroth. In fact"—she gestured to the cavern entrance below them—"I will speak with the Forsaken here and see if the Pools of Vision can be of any assistance. I will leave my ranger Cyndia behind. She will keep me advised of all developments."

She turned back to Baine. He stood as still as if he were a statue of a tauren. Even his tail had stopped twitching.

"Do we understand each other?"

"Perfectly, Warchief. Is that all?"

"It is. I hope this conversation marks the beginning of a new level of cooperation between the tauren and the Forsaken."

Baine followed her, a looming hulk of silence, as they returned to the tepee. She informed those who were waiting there of her suggestion that the Forsaken of the Pools of Vision work with the tauren as they sought to heal the world. When Hamuul spoke of a new Cenarion Hold in Silithus, one of the trolls spoke up.

"An' what of da goblins? Dey be dere thick as flies," the troll said. "Ya gonna pull dem out like da Speaker said?"

"The goblins," said Sylvanas, "know about the deep places of the world better than any other members of the Horde. I have spoken with Gallywix, and he assures me that they are exploring and investigating." When it appeared as though several were ready to object to this, she forestalled them by saying, "He reports directly to me. And when I am ready, I will share what I have learned with the Horde."

"But not the Alliance?" Runetotem said.

Sylvanas very carefully did not look at Baine as she replied. "Magni has already spoken to the Alliance. I am quite certain Anduin will not be sending couriers to Orgrimmar with their latest discoveries. Why should I?"

"Because this world belongs to all of us," Runetotem said quietly.

Sylvanas smiled. "Perhaps one day soon, 'all of us' will mean 'Horde.'" In the meantime, I put the interests and welfare of my people before the Alliance who destroyed Taurajo. I suggest all of *you* do as well."

"But—" the archdruid began.

She turned to him, her face cold, composed, but her eyes hot, angry fire. "Object again and I will not take it well. Vol'jin and his loa named me the warchief of the Horde. And *as* warchief of the Horde, I decide what is important to reveal—and when and to whom. Is that understood?"

Hamuul's ears flattened against his skull, but he spoke calmly enough. "Yes, Warchief."

THE UNDERCITY

Parqual Fintallas had been a historian when he still drew breath. He'd known all there was to know about Lordaeron and remembered, with a great deal of fondness, time spent with his wife, Mina, and his daughter, Philia, in his modest but comfortable chambers in Capital City. Even now, he could recall the smell of the ink and the parchment as he scribbled notes from various musty old tomes, and the golden, honey hue of the light that filtered in. The crackle of the fire, warm and comforting as he worked late into the night by the light of candles. Sometimes Mina would send in Philia to deliver his supper when he was too engrossed to come to the table. He'd pull her onto his lap when she was young and invite her to sit with him when she was older, encouraging her to browse through the massive library while he feasted on Mina's excellent cooking.

But there was no crackling fire here in the Undercity, no smells of parchment and ink and delicious food prepared with love by a warm and wise lifemate. No child to pester him with questions he'd loved to answer. Only coldness, dampness, the sickly smell of rot, and the eerie green glow of the tainted river that flowed throughout the subterranean necropolis.

Those memories were too fresh to be anything but painful, yet how sweet they still were. The Forsaken were strongly discouraged from revisiting places they had loved in life. Their home was no longer Lordaeron but the Undercity, a place that, like the inhabitants who no longer had need of sleep, didn't distinguish between day and night.

Once or twice, Parqual had sneaked into his former lodgings, smuggling books into the Undercity. But he had been caught once and admonished. His books had been confiscated. *There is no need to remember the human history of this place,* he had been told. *Only the history of the Undercity matters now.*

Over the years, he'd made use of adventurers to acquire more books, each one precious to him. But he could not use adventurers who sought gold or fame to bring back what had gone. Mina was either dead or a gibbering monstrosity. And Philia, his bright, beautiful girl, was still human, possibly still alive. But even so, she would be horrified at what had become of her beloved papa.

For the longest time, he had thought himself unique in his wistfulness. But then Vellcinda had founded the Desolate Council to take care of the city in the Dark Lady's absence. What had begun purely as necessity had, for Parqual at least, become something so much more. It had given him a sense of camaraderie and the knowledge that not everyone was content simply to serve without questioning. The Forsaken might not be living, but they had needs, desires, emotions that were not being met.

Vellcinda believed that Sylvanas would visit soon and would listen to what the council had to say.

Parqual sincerely hoped she was right, but he had his doubts. Sylvanas needed to stop forcing them to live again if they did not wish to; she needed to allow them to embrace their former lives as well as their undeath.

History taught that those who had power were generally loath to relinquish any of it unless they were forced to do so.

And in all his years of life and undeath, Parqual had seldom found history's lessons to be wrong.

CHAPTER THIRTEEN

Darnassus

The capital of the night elves was one of Anduin's favorite places, though he had seldom been able to travel there. The kaldorei were a beautiful people, and so was their city, nestled securely in the embrace of the massive World Tree, Teldrassil.

Anduin stood now beside High Priestess Tyrande Whisperwind and her beloved, the archdruid Malfurion Stormrage, in the Temple of the Moon. Serenity enveloped this place as the tenders of the temple went about their duties with grace and purpose. The rhythmic sound of softly splashing water was soothing, and the statue of Haidene, holding aloft the bowl from which the moonwell's radiant liquid flowed, was calming to behold.

His mind went back to the Netherlight Temple. *The Light finds us,* he thought. *All of us. It chooses the story, or the face, or the name, or the song that resonates the most with each of us. We may call it Elune, or An'she, or just the Light, but it doesn't matter. We can turn away from it if we desire, but it's always there.*

He caught Tyrande watching him, a slight smile curving her lips. She understood.

"I regret that I have not been a more frequent visitor to your beautiful city," he said aloud.

"War by its nature conspires to keep us all from places that nurture the spirit," Tyrande said.

With a sigh, Anduin turned away from the statue and faced the pair of leaders. "My letter outlined the nature of the current battle we face," he said. "A battle to heal our world. Has Magni come to you yet?"

"Not yet," Malfurion said. "It is a wide world, and Speaker for it he may be, but there is much ground to cover. We had already sent members of the Cenarion Circle back to Silithus after . . . after the tragedy. We wanted to assess the damage."

We have eyes on it, Shaw had told him earlier.

"Not for the first time, and I'm certain not for the last, I am grateful for the strong bonds between our peoples," Anduin said. "What did the Circle learn?"

The two exchanged a look. Then, "Come," said Malfurion. "Let us ride."

Anduin walked with them through the springy grass of the temple and out the arched doorway. Two Sentinels, the fierce female soldiers who guarded the city, awaited them with three nightsabers.

"Do you know how to ride one?" Tyrande asked with a smile.

"I've ridden gryphons, hippogryphs, and horses," Anduin said, "but not a nightsaber."

"They are similar to a gryphon, but with a smoother gait. I think you will enjoy it."

There was a spotted black one, one that had a soft gray coat, and a white one with black stripes that reminded the young king of the great White Tiger, Xuen, whom he had met in Pandaria. Too much so; he felt it would be almost disrespectful to ride it. He opted for the gray one, swinging himself into the saddle with ease. The big cat looked back at him, grunted, and shook its head before settling into a rhythmic lope that was as comfortable as Tyrande had promised.

"I believe it is as grim as the Speaker made it out to be," Malfurion said as the three made their way down the carpeted ramp and over the white marble stone, heading away from the temple. He kept his voice pitched softly. "Everyone in the Cenarion Hold and throughout the region was killed at once."

"I sent priestesses when I heard," Tyrande said, and left it at that. Anduin thought bleakly of the horrifying sight that must have greeted the gentle Sisters of Elune. More than the world was wounded by Sargeras. The only consolation was that the mad titan had, after so long cutting a swath of destruction and torment throughout the universe, finally been imprisoned.

"Our first thought was to send groups of druids and priestesses to create moonwells," Malfurion continued.

It made good sense. Moonwells contained sacred waters that could heal wounds and restore energy and vitality, and they often were put to use purifying corrupted areas. Or in this case, healing wounded ones.

"Did you meet with success?" Anduin asked.

"It is too early to tell. Most of our groups have not even had an opportunity to create one. The goblins are hard at work plundering Azeroth," Malfurion said, his normally pleasant, deep voice a rumble of wounded anger. "And there is plenty for them to exploit. As Magni told you, the essence of the world has come to the surface, and in great supply. We ourselves found a vein."

A vein. Anduin's mind went immediately to the intricate network of veins and arteries that went through a living body. Strange how so long ago, well before anyone understood that Azeroth was a sleeping nascent titan, the term "vein" had been used to describe the ribbons of various minerals that ran throughout the world.

Malfurion turned his black-striped nightsaber to the right, heading toward the Warrior's Terrace. As they passed the citizens of Darnassus, many turned to regard the sight of the young Stormwind king, bowing and waving to him. Anduin smiled and returned the waves, although the subject matter he was discussing with the Darnassian onlookers' leaders was a bleak one.

"We obtained some samples to study," Malfurion continued. "It is . . ." The archdruid, Anduin knew, was well over ten thousand years old. Yet this substance left him at a loss for words. For a moment, the night elf seemed almost overcome.

Riding closely beside and in perfect synchronization with her husband, Tyrande reached out to him, squeezing his arm briefly in silence.

Anduin regarded Malfurion with deep sympathy. "I have held it," he said quietly. "I know how it affected me. I cannot imagine how it must have moved those so deeply connected to nature and the land."

"I cannot deny the magnificence of it—or the power, for good or ill. And Tyrande and I—all the kaldorei—will do everything we can to prevent its misuse."

The Warrior's Terrace loomed up ahead. At the top, standing at attention, a unit of five Sentinels awaited them. Their leader was an elf with long dark blue hair pulled back in a ponytail. Her skin was pale reddish-purple, and the traditional markings on her face looked like claw marks. Like all her sisters, she was strong and lithe and fierce. But unlike many of the Sentinels Anduin had met before, she did not have a hardened expression. Tyrande slipped off her saber and greeted the Sentinel warmly. Anduin and Malfurion, too, dismounted.

One hand on the Sentinel's shoulder, Tyrande turned to her guest. "King Anduin Wrynn," she said, and Anduin realized that it would take a long time for him to grow used to that title, "may I present Captain Cordressa Briarbow."

The captain turned to Anduin and inclined her head. "I am honored," she said.

"A pleasure, Captain," Anduin said. "I remember you from the trial in Pandaria."

She smiled. "I am flattered you recall."

"We have been in communication with the Explorers' League," Tyrande said. "Ordinarily, they provide their own protection. But given the state of Silithus at this moment, I have offered them the aid of Cordressa's unit." Her eyes flashed. "Goblins are not to be trifled with, and with them present in so many numbers, the area is dangerous."

"A wise decision," Anduin said. "I am certain there will be several expeditions. I will assign some of my units to protective duty as well." Anduin was no lover of war, but he knew that others thrived on combat. This would allow them to utilize their training in a positive way.

"Druids and shaman can take care of themselves," Malfurion said, "but the members of the Explorers' League are generally archaeologists and scientists. And right now they are doing precious work."

Their attention was drawn by a soft swirl of white a few feet away, accompanied by the distinctive sound of a portal opening. A moment later, a gnome, all eyebrows and mustache, stepped through. Gold embroidery on his violet tabard depicted the all-seeing eye that was the symbol of the Kirin Tor.

What did the most powerful magi in Azeroth want with Tyrande and Malfurion? Anduin wondered. But when the gnome trundled directly up to him, the king realized it wasn't the leaders of Darnassus that the Kirin Tor had come to see.

"Greetings, High Priestess, Archdruid," the gnome said, nodding to the much bigger night elves. "King Anduin, this message is for you."

"Thank you." *Light, please let this not be more bad news. Our poor world cannot handle it.*

He broke the seal and read, feeling all eyes on him.

To Anduin Wrynn, King of Stormwind, Kalecgos of the Kirin Tor gives greetings.

Your Majesty, I hope this finds you well. I understand you embarked on a journey to thank your fellow Alliance members for their role in winning a terrible war. It is exactly the sort of thing I would expect of you, my friend, and I hope it goes well.

Our Mutual Friend paid me an unexpected visit just now. I believe we will not be seeing her again any time soon. But I have faith that she will return, and her mind will be the calmer and clearer for her retreat from this world. It is difficult to heal when a wound is constantly being reopened.

I know nothing about where she will be, but I felt you would wish to hear. —K

"Is all well, Your Majesty?" Malfurion asked quietly.

It was, overall, good news. At the same time, Anduin again regretted that Jaina still seemed to be lost. He hoped, as Kalec did, that she would find the answers, and the peace, she sought.

"Yes," he said. "An update on a personal matter. Nothing dire."

"Do you wish me to carry a response?" the gnome courier inquired.

"You may tell Kalecgos that I have received the message and I share his hopes. Thank you."

The gnome nodded. "Good day, then!" His small hands made motions that Anduin could not quite follow, and the air before the courier shimmered. Anduin caught a glimpse of the beautiful floating city of Dalaran for just an instant, then the gnome stepped through the portal. It faded behind him.

Anduin turned to Malfurion and Tyrande. "The letter concerned Jaina," he said. "She is safe, according to Kalecgos."

"That is good news," Tyrande said, "though it makes me wonder why she did not choose to fight alongside us against the Legion after the Broken Shore. Will she be returning?"

Anduin shook his head. "Not immediately, at any rate. Hopefully one day."

"And may that day be soon," Malfurion said. "The world needs all the champions it can find."

"It does," Anduin said slowly, thinking. His plan had been to rendezvous with Velen at the *Exodar*. He had spent much time there a few years earlier, and it was the closest thing he had to a second home. He yearned to walk its crystalline halls once more and to speak with the warm, friendly draenei.

But Velen already had enlightened the draenei about what Magni had revealed in Ironforge. Down to the littlest one, they were all probably hard at work already. The *Exodar* and Velen did not need him right now. His task was to spread the news to others and spur them on to action. And that was a task he could not do alone.

Anduin made a decision. He would not be traveling to the *Exodar*. He would return to Stormwind briefly, and then he would travel to the third place that, in his heart, he felt he could call home: the Netherlight Temple.

CHAPTER FOURTEEN

Stormwind

I t was very late when Anduin returned from Teldrassil. He used his hearthstone to avoid disturbing anyone. Wyll had been asleep for several hours, and Anduin didn't feel like getting into discussions with Genn Greymane just yet. There was, however, someone he did very much wish to speak with, and he wanted to give her a chance to report with news before he left for the Netherlight Temple.

He had materialized in the receiving room where he and his father had shared so many meals, arguments, and discussions. A ghost of a smile touched his lips, along with the ache of loss; then he turned and went to his private quarters, lit a candle, and placed it in the window. That task done, he tended to another one—filling his growling stomach. After descending into the kitchen, quiet at this hour, he heaped a plate with bread, Dalaran sharp, and goldenbark apples. When Anduin returned to his chambers, he closed the door behind him and said, "I'll feel silly if I'm talking to myself."

"You're not." Valeera was there. Anduin started to smile, then saw the expression on her face. All at once, he lost his appetite.

"Something's wrong," he said. When she didn't deny it, Anduin's heart sank. "Tell me."

She closed her eyes, then mutely handed him a letter. For a moment, Anduin didn't want to read it. He wanted to stay in this place of innocent ignorance. But that was not granted to a king, not one who wanted to be a good leader of his people, at any rate.

He swallowed hard. "Is he safe?"

"For the moment." Valeera jerked her head at the letter.

At least the worst hasn't happened, Anduin thought. But he suspected he knew what was in the letter now.

With a heavy heart, he unfolded the letter, which was written in the agreed-upon code. He translated it as he read.

> *For years, I have cherished our friendship.*
> *I cherish it still. But with great reluctance and*
> *for the sake of those who look to me for protection,*
> *I know the time has come when I must sever it.*

Anduin's stomach clenched. *She knows.* He continued reading.

> *I will not put my people nor you, friend, at*
> *further risk.*
> *I still believe that there will come a day when*
> *we can speak openly, with the support of all our people.*
> *But that day has not yet come.*
> *Earth Mother watch over you.*

Anduin had half expected this once Sylvanas had become leader of the Horde. But even so, it felt like a physical blow. Ever since the day he had accidentally materialized in the middle of a meeting between Baine Bloodhoof and Jaina Proudmoore, he had liked the tauren leader. Like Baine, Anduin had thought they were friends. But all at once he was besieged by doubt.

Baine had expressed his sympathies about Varian's death, reminding Anduin that he, too, had lost a father. The initial reports from Genn Greymane and others were that Sylvanas had betrayed them, abandoning Varian and presumably every other member of the Alliance, to die when she retreated with no warning from the Broken

Shore. Baine, who had been there, had told Anduin a different story. Another wave of demons had appeared, he said, and Sylvanas reported that a dying Vol'jin had ordered her to sound the retreat.

Had Baine lied to him?

No. Anduin's heart was sore, but there was no warning of danger or deceit from his once-shattered bones. Baine had told the truth as he knew it. Yet no one but Sylvanas, it seemed, had actually heard the order from Vol'jin.

I will not let Sylvanas tarnish my faith in Baine, he thought resolutely. With a deep sigh, he rose and tossed the letter into the fire, watching as the flames flared brightly and reduced the parchment to a blackened writhing ball and then to ashes.

"Did Perith accept my letter?" Anduin asked, forcing his voice to be calm and level.

"No," Valeera replied. Another gut punch. "He thought it would endanger his chieftain. There are eyes upon him."

"Perith is very wise," Anduin replied.

"But he said he would tell Baine what the letter said."

"I had so hoped that Baine would support my plan."

"He may yet."

"Or he may do nothing that smacks of disloyalty. I can't blame him. I'd do the same. A leader who jeopardizes his people is no leader at all." Anduin kept his gaze on the flames.

Valeera stepped beside him. "There is one thing more," she said. "Baine wanted you to have this."

She extended her hand. A small piece of what looked like bone, no larger than Anduin's fingernail, rested in her gloved palm. It took Anduin a few seconds to comprehend what he was looking at, and when he did, his breath caught.

This was a piece of Baine's horn, chipped off in an offering of respect and friendship.

His hand closed slowly around it.

"I'm sorry, Anduin. I know what a disappointment this is."

She did, too. He looked down at her, smiling sadly, recalling the days not so long ago when she was much taller than he was.

"I know," he said. "And I thank you for it. For everything. It seems each passing day reduces the number of people I can rely on."

"I hope you will always count me among that group," Valeera said.

"Never doubt that," Anduin assured her.

Her eyes searched his for a moment. "You are a kind person, Anduin. It's in your nature to think the best of people. But you're also a king," Valeera said quietly. "You cannot afford to trust unwisely."

"No," he agreed sadly. "I can't."

They stood by the fire in silence for a long time.

SILITHUS

The two moons were out tonight. Sapphronetta Flivvers, peering up at them after a long day of travel and setting up camp, said to her companion, "You know, they're really very beautiful."

The night elf Sentinel, Cordressa Briarbow, said, "Do you know their names?"

Heat came into the gnome's round face. "Um . . . one of them is the Blue . . . ah . . . something." At the night elf's soft chuckle, Saffy blushed even more deeply. Her former husband had always told her how cute she was when she blushed, which Saffy detested and which made her flush—*not blush!*—with anger whenever he said it. Which of course just made him happier.

"I'm sorry," she said. "I've spent almost my whole life underground or in a lab, you see. I'm afraid I don't get outside very much."

"You are well versed in so very many things I could never understand, Sapphronetta," Cordressa said gently. "No one can know everything."

"Try telling that to my ex-husband."

Again the soft chuckle. "The moons are named the Blue Child and the White Lady, the Child's mother. The White Lady has different names. My people call her Elune. The tauren call her Mu'sha. Once every 430 years, something truly marvelous occurs. The moons align with one another, and for a few precious, glorious moments it looks as though the Lady is holding her Child. Our world is bathed in a blue-white radiance, and time itself seems to stand still if you look upon it with an open heart."

Gazing at the beautiful orbs, Saffy let out a soft breath of awe. "When did it last happen?" she asked, wondering if she'd learned this interesting tidbit in time to witness the event.

"Five years ago."

Saffy's face fell. "Oh," she said. "Guess I probably won't be around to see it."

The long-lived elf, who probably *would* be around to see it, did not reply. "But you can see them both now in the beautiful, clear sky of the desert."

That was probably the first time Saffy had heard the word "beautiful" to describe anything concerning Silithus. Even before it had a gargantuan sword sticking out of it, by all accounts it was a hideous place. Her gaze traveled to the sword now. It was hard to miss. Not only was it humongous, but it was surrounded by a creepy aura of red light, so it was an eyesore at any time of day and night. The black monstrosity had been plunged halfway into the poor ground. Steaming fissures had been revealed, yielding the mysterious Azerite in its two forms—fluid and hardened blue-gold chunks. Saffy was more than a little frustrated that Mekkatorque and Brann Bronzebeard had sent her off on the expedition before she'd had a chance to actually touch the stuff. Their notes were useful, but she couldn't wait to see—and feel—the substance herself.

And the desert that surrounded the sword was hot, filled with insects of all shapes and sizes, cultists, mysterious things lurking in ruins . . . *that* was *beautiful*?

Well, all right, Saffy could agree that the sky was beautiful. She sneaked a glance upward at her companion, her face upturned and bathed with light as she smiled slightly. Other members of the Explorers' League, too, had paused to regard the pair of moons. Again Saffy looked up at them as well. How could they be so placid, the Blue Child and the White Lady? Just—sailing through the night sky, blissfully unaware that below them a *giant sword was sticking out of the world!*

That was when Saffy realized she'd spoken out loud. She clapped a hand over her mouth. Expecting laughter or chastisement for her outburst, she was surprised when Cordressa placed a gentle hand on her shoulder, having to stoop to do so.

"You but say what we all think," she said. "Their peace is enviable. But we know better. In a way, I envy the druids of the Cenarion Circle and the shaman of the Earthen Ring. They are looking at means to help Azeroth directly. That must be very gratifying."

Now it was Saffy's turn to reassure the night elf. "The Explorers' League has a role here, too. Last time things went bad in this place, it's because something very old got riled up."

She stabbed a finger in the direction of the sword. "Magni told us that Azeroth was hurting. But we also don't know how deep that thing goes; what Sargeras might have disturbed or awoken that's also contributing to her distress. And this time, we're walking right into an area that we know to be dangerous. High Priestess Tyrande and you are helping Azeroth by protecting us."

Us. It was Saffy's first expedition, though she'd been a consultant member back at the Hall of Explorers for a while. The whole thing was terribly exciting, though that was tempered by the proximity of so many goblins.

Cordressa smiled down at her. "I have not worked much with your people," she said. "But if you are a typical representative of the gnomes, I clearly need to rectify that."

Saffy blushed again. "We all just do what we can," she said. She had been tapped because she was a well-recognized geologist specializing in mineralogy. The archaeologists on the team would be looking for Old Gods, ancient doomsday technology—the usual sorts of things. Saffy had been brought into the mix specifically to study Azerite.

Provided they could actually get to any Azerite. The goblins—oh, how she hated goblins—were squatting on the visible seams of the stuff and conducting eye-hurtingly ugly mining forays. For the last two days, the league members had stayed safely away, observing with the telescopes and various contraptions with which Mekkatorque had furnished them.

Frustrating and crude as this method was, Saffy already had learned a great deal from her observation. For one thing, Azerite was liquid when it bled from the earth, turning solid only when it was exposed to air. Fascinating!

The other thing was that the ground near the sword was warm all the time, not just during daylight hours. Deserts had wildly fluctuating temperatures, from scorching in the day, to if not exactly chilly at least considerably colder at night. Not Silithus, not now.

Saffy was itching to get her hands on more of the material. She'd been added to the team after the Stormwind king had visited Ironforge, leaving with them only a small chunk to study. The next task would be to send out scouts to obtain more samples of Azerite, preferably from a variety of locales. Then Saffy would get to do what she loved to do: analyze, study, and understand.

It pained—physically *pained*—her to think about all those goblins messing around with this precious substance. The only value it had to them was how they could "transmute" gold liquid into gold coins. Goblins. How could anyone stand doing business with them? Filthy things. It was all about the boom and the flash and the noise, not the science of it all.

"Your thoughts are not happy ones, Sapphronetta," Cordressa said. Saffy realized that although her face was still turned up to the moons, she was scowling. "Come. Let us eat something. Then some of my sister Sentinels will stay and guard you while you sleep."

"Some?"

The night elf smiled, her eyes glowing in the darkness as brightly as the moons did. "Some. And some others will begin the first scouting mission."

That made sense. The kaldorei were called night elves for a reason other than the twilight hues of their skin and hair. They were used to hunting in the nighttime hours.

Saffy was thrilled. "Maybe you will return with some samples I can study!"

"Maybe, although I expect samples will come later. You must cultivate patience. More likely, we will return tonight with information on the enemy's numbers and locations. Maybe intel on their plans, too."

Smiling impishly, she tapped one long purple ear. "Not only do we see well, we hear well, too."

Saffy laughed.

Dinner, as was always the case whenever dwarves were involved, was hearty, stick-to-your-ribs fare washed down with plenty of beer. Saffy didn't want to think too hard about what was "beer basted" out here. She'd heard one of the Sentinels talking fondly about the gooey spider legs she'd grown up on, and that had been quite enough.

After the meal, two Sentinels, including Cordressa, slipped quietly out into the warm night. The leader of the expedition, Gavvin Stoutarm, gathered the five members of the league and addressed them.

"We're a tight-knit bunch," he said, "an' we're nae too accustomed tae night elves bein' part o' our number." Although the Explorers' League was open to all races of the Alliance, it seemed to appeal mostly to humans and dwarves, with the odd gnome or worgen showing up now and then. Night elves were a rare sight, as they were usually against disturbing the earth for the purpose of removing artifacts from where they lay hidden.

"I'm proud o' how ye all have interacted wi' 'em. We're all on this poor world together, an' we're all pullin' together. No offense tae other guards we've had, but I fer one will be sleepin' sounder than usual tonight."

"Och, Gavvin, ye'll be sleepin' sounder because ye drank about six pints o' brew!"

Guffaws filled the night air, with Gavvin Stoutarm, who certainly had indulged his thirst, laughing the loudest. "Off tae yer bedrolls wi' ye," he said.

Despite the reassuring words, Saffy found sleep elusive. She tossed and turned, first in her bedroll and then on it—it was so terribly hot—and then back in it because she realized that outside the bedroll meant *insects*. And *sand*.

She huddled, sweltering, listening to the loud nighttime sounds of four dwarves snoring loudly enough to wake the dead. It was a good thing there were Sentinels standing guard, she thought. Stoutarm's wheezing and snorting otherwise would have brought the goblins down on them in droves just to shut him up.

Saffy must have been more tired than she thought. Somewhere between the snores and the insects and the heat and the sand, she drifted off to sleep.

She awoke to the hideous sound of goblin bellowing, the crack of rifles, and the clang of steel against steel. Bolting upright, struggling to escape the confining swaths of fabric, Saffy went for the pistol she kept under her pillow and scrambled to her feet. Her heart thudded wildly in her chest as she glanced about frantically, barely able to take in the scene playing out before her.

The moons' light, so pleasant and calming earlier, now seemed cold and uncaring as it illuminated the bodies of two dead Sentinels. Their blood looked black in the pale blue light, and the glow had fled their eyes, leaving them dark pools of shadow. There was another body, too—a body Saffy didn't want to look at for fear the panic that was clawing at the back of her brain would swoop to the forefront and shut down her ability to *think, Saffy, think—*

Her former husband had insisted that she have a weapon. She told him she'd take a lab over an arsenal any day, but right now she wished she'd practiced with the thing. Why hadn't she taken her Lightning Blast 3000 with her? She'd actually gotten it working—

Saffy gripped the pistol with small, shaking hands, jerking it around toward the noise of each new horror that unfolded. Loud, fierce dwarven swearing brought a rush of joyful tears to her eyes. Gavvin Stoutarm, at least, was still alive and kicking—and punching, and biting, from the angry sound of a squealing goblin.

The gnome's soft mouth set in a hard line. She forced her hands to stop shaking and focused not on the awful, gut-wrenching sounds her friends made as they were fighting and—

—dying, Saffy, they're dying—

—and she pointed the pistol at a squat, large-eared shape that was blotting out the horizon's stars.

She squeezed the trigger. There was a gratifying shout of pain. The resulting boom had knocked her back, and she scrambled to her feet only to discover to her horror that the goblin hadn't been dispatched but was merely enraged.

"Why, you little—"

Saffy fired again, but this time the shot went wide as the dark shape reached out and seized her arm. He squeezed it hard, and with a gasp of fear and fury the mineralogist was forced to drop the gun.

"Hey! Kezzig, that's a gnome lady!"

"Yeah," Saffy's assailant said, making a fist and drawing back his arm, "and I'm gonna punch the living—oh." The fist paused in mid-motion. "Maybe she's not the right one."

"She fits the description perfectly. You know the rules."

"Yeah, yeah, stupid rules," the goblin named Kezzig muttered. He lowered his fist. Saffy took the opportunity to squirm, simultaneously attempting to twist free and bite the muscled arm.

Kezzig shrieked in pain but didn't release her. "Okay, you little spitfire, all bets are off."

The last thing Sapphronetta Flivvers saw was a huge, dark fist silhouetted against the too-calm, too-dispassionate night sky.

CHAPTER FIFTEEN

The Netherlight Temple

The sense of peace that stole over Anduin as he entered the Netherlight Temple was balm to a spirit still wounded from Valeera's news regarding Baine. It felt as if someone had tucked a thick, warm blanket around him while he lay cold and shivering. He smiled softly to himself and once again marveled at the Light's ability to comfort.

Archbishop Faol glanced up from an old tome he'd been perusing as Anduin approached. The glow in his dead eyes increased with pleasure, and his lips twisted in a smile.

"Anduin!" he exclaimed in that curiously warm voice, obviously remembering that the king of Stormwind had asked him not to use the formal title. "I had not expected to see you again quite so soon. Sit down, sit down!" He gestured to a chair beside him.

Anduin returned the Forsaken's smile with one of his own, accepting the offered seat. Even as he did so, he mentally shook his head. Sitting comfortably beside a Forsaken. It was something he'd never really thought would happen.

If only everyone could experience the peace of the Netherlight Temple, he thought. *Maybe then we'd stop trying to kill one another.*

Faol chuckled, that raspy sound, as of two pieces of parchment rubbing together. "Tell me all about your visit to Teldrassil."

A blood elf priest approached with a bottle of fruit nectar and a glass. Anduin thanked him. Pouring, he said, "The night elves can always be relied on to care for the world. By the time I visited Darnassus, they had already dispatched several groups of priestesses and druids into Silithus to create moonwells."

"Ah, moonwells. I never saw one while I lived, and, well, I try not to get wet these days. But I hear they are sights to behold."

"They are. If the kaldorei are successful, this could help Azeroth greatly. They are also sending Sentinels to accompany less militaristic organizations such as the Explorers' League."

"This all sounds quite positive," Faol said.

"It is," Anduin said. "But I think we can do more. I'm going to emulate the night elves and send along some of Stormwind's finest as well. What's happening to the world . . . we can't afford to lose those who might be able to find a solution to it. I thought I would come back and see how your priests were doing in spreading the word."

"Of course!" Faol said. "I'm proud to say that we've all stepped up to the challenge." He looked up and beckoned. "Calia, my dear, won't you come join us?"

As Calia approached them, Faol continued, "She wants so much to help. I've appointed her our liaison to the Alliance races, whereas I've been familiarizing myself with all kinds of new parts of Azeroth by visiting Horde members. It's been most enlightening!"

Calia now stood beside Anduin, looking from one to the other. "It's good to see you again, Anduin," she said.

"Our young friend has just returned from Teldrassil," said Faol. "He says the night elves are already hard at work, and I informed him that we've not been shirking our duties, either."

"I'm glad to hear it," Anduin said. "Actually, I came here hoping to speak with both of you on another topic as well, if we have time."

"Ha!" said Faol, delighted, as Calia slipped gracefully into the seat beside Anduin. "Saa'ra will be so jealous; usually everyone comes to see it. As for time, we have nothing but it in this place. It has done the

Conclave good not to stay cloistered here but to be out and about in the world again. Now, then. You've visited Ironforge and Teldrassil, and it sounds like both have already taken immediate steps."

For the next several minutes, Calia and Faol gave Anduin a run-down of where they had traveled and where they had sent others to travel. "We try to take into account whom we're talking to," Calia said. "For instance, if we are traveling to the Echo Isles, we send one of our trolls. To Tranquillien, a blood elf.

"Some have already heard," Calia said, "and I regret to tell you that some are still more interested in mining the Azerite than in helping Azeroth."

Anduin nodded. "Not unexpected, though it's extremely unfortunate." He sighed. "It does sound like we've done what we can. We just have to protect the Azerite as much as possible and attempt to ensure the Horde doesn't acquire much of it."

Even as he said the words, Anduin knew the idea was nothing but wishful thinking. For some reason, the goblins had figured things out first. They had descended on Silithus en masse and set up mines and ways to process the material before Shaw could even report back to Anduin. That battle might be lost already, and the thought pained him.

But there might be one way to fight back against the Horde without fighting at all. Anduin had hoped to have Baine quietly helping from the other side, but that was not to be. If this idea was to work, it would be up to Anduin.

He folded his hands in front of him and looked from Calia to Faol. "I wanted to discuss the Forsaken," he said. "And I apologize in advance if I sound ignorant or insulting."

Faol waved his words away. "No need at all to apologize. Asking questions is how we learn, and I happen to have some answers."

Despite the archbishop's assurance, Anduin was convinced he'd sound rude. He was beginning to think that discretion was the better part of valor and that he'd be best served by excusing himself now.

"I had seen Forsaken before now," he said. "And I was aware that they—you—were not mindless, raving Scourge. I also never thought you were inherently evil."

"But you thought us capable of doing evil things," Faol said. "Don't worry about that. That's nothing more than being observant. I'll be the first to admit the Forsaken have done terrible things. But so have humans. Even the tauren have a skeleton or two in their closet— metaphorically speaking, of course."

Anduin grinned, pleased that Faol understood him, and continued. "I found them . . . less relatable than the other Horde races, even though many used to be human. Perhaps *because* they used to be human. The Alliance turned them away. People that in life they knew. Maybe even had loved."

"Fear is a powerful emotion," Calia said quietly. Something in the tone of her voice, in the way she held her body, brought home to Anduin that her astounding journey of survival had to have been harrowing, perhaps beyond his ability to understand. She sat with her hands in her lap, tightly clasped, and he saw that they trembled.

"Calia," he said before he could stop himself, "how did you possibly survive?"

She lifted her sea-blue eyes to his. All over again he was reminded that she was Arthas's sister, familiar to him though he had never met her. Her smile was sad.

"By fate and by the Light's mercy," she said. "One day I will tell you. But it is still too . . . too close. Not just my journey, but . . . I lost people I loved, you see."

Anduin nodded. "Of course. Your father . . . and brother." It was a painful, ugly story. Arthas, corrupted by the sword Frostmourne and pulled step by step from the path of the Light by the whispers of the Lich King, had not simply turned the citizens of Lordaeron into monsters. He had used a public welcoming ceremony as a chance to murder his father as Terenas sat upon his throne. Anduin suddenly, sickly realized that it was possible—no, probable, a near certainty—that Calia Menethil had witnessed that murder. Again he marveled that she had been able to escape.

"Not just them," Calia said. "Others I loved as well." The king's eyes widened. Did she have a family of her own?

"I understand. I'm sorry if I caused you any distress." He bit his lip, wondering if he should continue. She seemed to sense his dilemma and straightened a little, giving him a wan smile.

"Go ahead. Ask me what you will. I can't promise I'll answer, but I will if I can."

"You had to have had a terrifying experience with the undead," he said quietly. "How is it that you are so close with the archbishop?"

Calia relaxed and smiled at her old friend. "He helped save me," she said. "I remembered him, you see. And in the midst of all that horror, when I was constantly fleeing so many I loved whose minds and wills had been stolen from them . . . to see the face of someone who was still who he had been—"

She shook her head, in awe of the moment even now, it would seem. "It was as if hope itself was a sword that stabbed clean through me. Except instead of wounding, it offered me the chance to move through my shock and pain to a place of healing. So you see, for me, the Forsaken weren't monsters. They were friends. It was the Scourge, the shambling, stumbling things that wore my friends' faces—*they* had become monsters."

Faol appeared genuinely moved by her words, and Anduin wondered if he'd ever heard them before. The archbishop took her hand, patting her healthy human flesh gently with his withered, almost mummified fingers.

"Dear child," he said. His voice was thick, as if with unshed tears. Could Forsaken weep? Anduin realized that he had no idea. There was so much about them that he didn't know. "Dear, dear child. The joy was mine at finding you alive."

Anduin was glad he had come. It had been, beyond a doubt, the right decision. "There's something I'd like to do," he said, "and I'd like the two of you to help me."

"Of course, if we can," Faol replied.

"A terrible war has come to an end. One that has harmed both Horde and Alliance. Tens of thousands of lives were lost, including those of Vol'jin and my father. Now we hear that our own world might be another casualty, with a precious substance that I cannot in good conscience allow to fall into hostile hands. The goblins certainly know about it, and Sylvanas is probably already plotting how to use it against us. But that's not happened yet. We have an opportunity here to come together—*truly* come together—and work on a large scale the way the Earthen Ring and the Cenarion Circle do. The way this temple does."

They were both listening. They did not scoff at his passion for peace as Greymane did or regard him with skeptical compassion as Valeera did. Encouraged, Anduin continued.

"Already, either Sylvanas or other factions have murdered innocent people who have done nothing but try to learn about the world's wound. I have an idea on how we can stop that. But I can't implement it directly. Not yet."

He paused. What he was about to say should have grown easier with time, but it had not. "Many believe Sylvanas deliberately betrayed my father and the Alliance at the Broken Shore. No one on our side is going to advocate extending an offer of peace without getting something in return."

Faol looked at him searchingly. "Do *you* believe she betrayed King Varian?" he asked calmly.

Anduin thought about Baine's report of the incident. "I don't know what to believe," he said finally. "But I do know how my advisers—and most of the Alliance—feel about her. She's the enemy. But she's not devoid of the ability to care about one thing, if nothing else."

Calia looked a bit confused, but Faol's eyes were bright with understanding. "I think I see where you're going with this, my boy."

"She cares about the Forsaken, people she views as her children. And the Alliance cares about *their* fallen loved ones."

Faol's glowing eyes widened, but it was Calia who spoke first. "You're saying that the Alliance was devastated after Lordaeron because so many of their loved ones were killed—or turned into the Scourge. It was personal loss." She paused. "Like mine."

Anduin nodded. "Yes," he said quietly. "And they've come to believe that the Forsaken are undead monsters. To most of my people, they're no better than the Scourge. But *you* know better. You found hope and help from a Forsaken who had been a friend in life and was still a friend in death."

But Faol was shaking his head. "You and Calia are remarkable individuals, Anduin," he said. "I'm not sure your average human would be able to make the leaps the two of you have."

"That's because they haven't had the chance to," Anduin insisted. "Calia was rescued by someone she knew and trusted, someone who didn't let her down. At Garrosh Hellscream's trial, the Vision of Time showed me another courageous Forsaken—Frandis Farley. There's a Fredrik Farley who's the innkeeper in Goldshire. They could be relatives. I wonder if Fredrik would like to know that Frandis died resisting a cruel and unfair leader. I'd like to think he would."

He leaned forward, speaking from his heart. "There have to be so many stories, Faol. So *many*. Lordaeron and Stormwind were more than political allies; they were friends. People traveled easily and freely throughout the kingdoms. There have to be relatives who mourn their loved ones as dead when in reality they're still—"

The king paused, realizing what he was about to say. Faol smiled sadly.

"Alive?" The archbishop shook his head. "It's probably a mercy they think them dead. Too many can't shake their prejudice to even try to see us as we really are."

"What if they did try?" Anduin leaned forward in his seat. "What if some of them were open to the idea? To meet their loved ones who've been . . . changed, yes, but still who they were? Isn't that better than their being truly dead?"

"Not for a great majority, it isn't."

"We don't need a majority to begin. Look at Calia. Look at me. We just need *some*. We need a spark of understanding, of acceptance. That's all. Just a single spark."

His voice trembled as he said it, and he felt the Light wash through him with its sweet, warm blessing. Anduin knew he was speaking a great truth. One that would require effort and nurturing, but one that could indeed catch fire and sweep through the world.

And when it did, nothing would be the same.

"I think he's right," Calia said. Her voice was stronger than it had been since the conversation had begun. There was color in her cheeks, enthusiasm in her face. She was lit from within, as he was, by the breathtakingly daring act of hope.

Calia turned to her friend. "I was lost, Alonsus. Emotionally and physically and mentally. You brought me back from a very dark place.

What other wonders could that again work? For both Forsaken and humanity?"

"I have seen much darkness," Faol said, and for once he was not warm and quietly mirthful. He was serious, and the lights in his eyes glowed a different shade as he spoke. "Much, much darkness. There is evil in this world, my young friends, and sometimes it does not require corruption from an outside source to thrive. Sometimes it is born in the hearts of the least likely seeming people. A tiny seed of resentment or fear finds fertile soil and blooms into something terrible."

"But isn't the reverse also true?" Anduin pressed. "Can't a tiny seed of hope or kindness find fertile soil as well?"

"Of course it can, but you are not talking about a tiny seed," Faol said. "First, the only Forsaken you know of who would support such a thing are myself and a few here in the Conclave. There may not be many others who would. And if there are, you then must work with the leader of the Horde—the Banshee Queen. She may not want her people thinking fondly of their time as living beings. And finally, are there any humans other than Calia who would even wish to meet their, er, still-existing relatives or friends?"

At Anduin's crestfallen expression, the Forsaken archbishop softened. "I'm sorry to discourage you. But a ruler—even a priestly one—must know all the obstacles in his path. You want what is right, Anduin Llane Wrynn. And it is my fervent hope that this idea of yours will come to fruition. But perhaps that hour is not now."

Anduin didn't quite slump, but he wanted to. He ran a hand through his hair and sighed. "You may be right. But it's a chance to reunite families. To get us all working together so that we're not focused on trying to kill each other. It's a chance to stop the harm to Azeroth. This is important on so many levels!"

"I didn't say I disagreed with that." Faol fell silent for a moment, thinking. "I'll tell you what. I'll talk with the rest of the Forsaken priests and get their opinions. We can begin to lay the groundwork for this."

The young king brightened somewhat. "Yes. That's probably the best way to proceed for now. But lulls in aggression between Alliance and Horde seem to be rare. I had hoped to make the most of—"

"Your Majesty?" Anduin turned to see High Priestess Laurena. Her normally friendly visage held an expression of concern, and her voice was somber.

Anduin went cold inside. "What's wrong?"

"It's Wyll. I think you'd better come back. Immediately."

CHAPTER SIXTEEN

Stormwind

G enn was there to meet Anduin and Laurena as they stepped through the portal. The look in the older man's eyes was like a cold hand around Anduin's heart.

"Your Majesty," he began.

"Is he . . . ?"

"No, no. Not yet. I'm no healer, but I think it won't be long now."

Anduin shook his head. No. There was still time. The Light was with him. "I won't accept that," he said, almost biting off the words as he raced toward the servants' wing.

"Anduin," Genn called after him. But the young king wouldn't listen. Aerin. Bolvar. His father. He'd lost too many he'd cared about. He wasn't going to lose Wyll. Not today.

As was proper for someone with so high a standing in the household, Wyll had a fairly large room. It was impeccably tidy, like the man himself. There was a washstand with a spotless basin, mirror, and shaving supplies along with a wardrobe, a clothing trunk, and a comfortable chair for reading. A mug of tea and a small bowl of now-cold cooked grains sat on a table next to it.

The only reason the bed wasn't perfectly made was that Wyll was in it. Anduin's heart lurched painfully. Wyll would never say how old he was, but Anduin knew that he'd tended the young Varian Wrynn and he'd hinted that he might even have served Llane Wrynn, Anduin's grandfather, when he, too, was young. But in Anduin's mind, Wyll was ageless.

He had been old ever since the king could remember, but he'd always had the energy to keep up with his young charge. Now, as Anduin regarded the figure lying in the bed, he felt as though all of Wyll's years had descended upon him at once. His normally ruddy face was pale, and his high cheekbones that had always made him look distinguished now only emphasized the sunken cheeks. He remembered noticing that Wyll had been losing weight even before they had traveled to Ironforge. He had thought nothing of it then. But it was as if the weight had simply melted off his tall frame. He looked diminished, smaller. Frail. Anduin felt a sudden, shameful flush of guilt.

"Wyll," he said, and his voice cracked.

The old man's eyelids, paper-thin and blue-veined, fluttered open. "Ah," he said, his voice reedy. "Your Majesty. Please forgive me if I don't rise. I told them not to disturb you."

Anduin grabbed the chair and pulled it over to Wyll's bedside, reaching for the gnarled hand. "Nonsense," he said. "I'm glad they did. You'll be fine in just a moment. Wyll, you've been there for me for as long as I can remember. Anticipating my wants and needs as if by magic. You've taken care of me all my life. Now let me take care of you." He took a deep breath and asked for the Light. At once his hand grew warm.

But to his shock, Wyll made a soft noise of protest and drew his hand back. "Please . . . no. That won't be necessary."

Anduin stared at him. "Wyll . . . I can heal you. The Light—"

"Is a lovely and beautiful thing. And it loves you, my boy. Just as your father did. Just as I do. But I think it's time I was on my way."

Anduin's stomach clenched. He knew he couldn't restore the old man's youth. Although he did not think that such was beyond the Light's power, if such a thing were possible, it was not granted to priests or others who used the Light to heal. But Anduin *could* cure whatever sickness was sucking the life out of his old friend. He could remove aches and pains and stiffness. Wyll had, albeit with reluctance, permitted him to do similar things in the past. Why was he refusing aid now, when it counted more than ever before?

"Please. I . . . need you, Wyll," Anduin said. It was selfish, but it was true.

"No, you don't, Your Majesty," Wyll said very gently. "You're all grown up now into a fine young man. You need a valet, not a child's servant. I've made a list over there of fellows I can recommend."

Wyll turned his white head and pointed with an unsteady finger. Sure enough, on the little table, there was a rolled-up scroll lying next to a book. Anduin noticed there was a bookmark inserted three-quarters of the way through. He seized on this and said, "But your book . . . you're not done with your story."

Wyll chuckled, wheezing. "Oh," he managed, "my story's finished, I'm afraid. And it's been a fine one, if I do say so myself. I've gotten to serve under three kings—good ones. Fair ones. One who needed a bit of guiding, to be sure. And don't worry, I'm not talking about you, my boy. I've had a purpose, and true love, and just enough danger to make things interesting."

He turned his watery eyes on Anduin. "But I'm tired, dear boy. I'm very, very tired. I've lived long enough, I think. The Light's got far better things to do with itself than to heal cranky old men who've lived long, full lives."

No, Anduin thought. *No, I don't think it does.*

"Please let me help you," he said, trying one last time. "I'm just starting my reign. And I've lost so much. So many."

"I've lost everyone," Wyll said almost conversationally. Anduin knew that the elderly man was not upbraiding him, but even so, he felt heat rise in his face. "Your grandparents. Your parents. My brothers and sisters and nieces and nephews. All my old friends. And my beloved Elsie. They're all waiting for me. Can't quite see them yet, but I will. It would be a grand thing to move with no aches and pains, I'll admit that. But it's going to be a grander thing to set all these burdens down and be with those I loved."

Anduin couldn't think of anything to say. He wondered what it was that was finally taking Wyll away. An illness? He could purge it. A weak heart or another failing organ? He could repair it.

He could, but had been forbidden to. His eyes stung.

Wyll gently laid a hand on Anduin's arm. "It's all right," he said. "You are going to be a wonderful king, Anduin Llane Wrynn. One for the history books."

Anduin covered the hand with his own. He did not call on the Light. He would respect the wishes of this good man who had served the royal family his whole life.

"I'd be a better one with you making sure my crown sat just right on my head," he said, recalling his trip to Ironforge a few years earlier, when Wyll had taken a good fifteen minutes arranging the prince's circlet.

"Oh, you'll figure that out," Wyll said.

"Wyll," Anduin said gently. "Will you let me ease your pain, at least?"

The old servant—the old friend—nodded. Grateful for even this little chance to help, to make at least some feeble attempt to repay Wyll for all he had done, Anduin asked the Light for that and only that. A soft radiance limned his hand. The illumination traveled quickly to Wyll's hand, then raced along his body for a few seconds, flaring brightly before it faded.

"Oh, yes, that's quite nice," Wyll said. He looked better. Not quite so pale, and breathing seemed to come easier to him as his chest rose and fell evenly. But Anduin's own chest was tight with grief.

"What else can I do? Something to eat, perhaps? I hear the chef has perfected some pastries." Wyll was as bad as any six-year-old child when it came to sweets.

"No, I don't think so," Wyll said. "I think I'm done with that now. Thank you, though, Your Maj—"

"Anduin." His voice broke. "I'm just Anduin."

"You're good to an old man, Anduin. I shouldn't keep you. Please don't berate yourself for this. Nothing is more natural than what I'll be doing shortly."

"I'd like to stay if you'll let me."

Wyll eyed him. "I'd not cause you any more pain than I have to, dear boy."

Anduin shook his head. "No. You won't." It wasn't a lie. Not quite. Losing Wyll would be devastating whether Anduin was present or not. But at least if he was here when the old man breathed his last, Anduin would know he had done all he could. He had been denied the chance to be with his father when Varian died. They had embraced when the king left, and their words to each other had been kind. But Varian had fallen alone save for the presence of demons and his killer, and not even his body could be recovered.

Wyll had earned the right to have someone with him at the end. He had earned it a thousand times over.

"How about I read you the rest of the book?" Anduin said.

"That would be very pleasant," Wyll said. "Do you remember that I taught you to read?"

Anduin did. The memory made him smile. "I used to get upset when you would correct my pronunciation," he recalled.

"No, not really. You were a very mild-tempered child. You just got frustrated. There's a difference."

A lump wedged itself in Anduin's throat. He hoped he could read past it. He owed Wyll that much, at least. "All right. We'll read. Let me get you some water."

He stepped outside to call for someone and found Genn pacing in the hall.

"How is he?" Greymane asked quietly.

Anduin couldn't speak and took a moment to compose himself. "He's dying," he replied. "He won't let me heal him."

"He told the same thing to High Priestess Laurena when I called her in to look at him," Genn said.

"What? Genn, why didn't you tell me?"

Genn looked at him levelly. "Would it have made any difference to you?"

Anduin sagged. "No," he said. "I'd have asked him to let me try regardless."

Genn reached out and squeezed Anduin's shoulder. "For what it's worth, I'm sorry. And it's his choice. You can't save everyone."

"It feels like I can't save *anyone*," Anduin said.

"I know that feeling, too," Greymane said. Anduin thought about what the other king had endured and knew it to be true. Only a few refugees had escaped Gilneas, and it was only through the night elves' kindness that they had survived at all.

The young king nodded, his heart as heavy as lead inside his chest. He took a deep breath. "I'm going to read to him for a while. Would you mind having someone bring some water and cups?"

Genn seemed about to speak, then nodded. "Of course. Would you like someone to stay with you?"

"No. I'm fine. I just . . . well. If there's an emergency, you know where to find me. I think it will be soon."

The older man nodded sympathetically. "I'll station someone outside just in case. You're doing a good thing, my boy."

"I wish I believed that."

"When you are Wyll's age or mine, you will."

The next few hours slipped by. Wyll had perked up for a bit and accepted some water, though he wouldn't allow Anduin to fuss too much over him. He listened to the book, which was a history about the Dragon Aspects, and initially made a comment or two. Then he spoke less and less, and finally Anduin realized the old man had drifted off to sleep.

Or had he—

As Anduin leaned forward to make sure Wyll's chest was still moving, Wyll's eyes flew open. Anduin realized at once that Wyll was looking at something the king couldn't see.

"Papa," Wyll murmured. "Mama . . ."

Anduin put the book down and took the old man's hand. How thin the skin was, how twisted the fingers, like a tree's roots. Yet up until his last few days, Wyll had completed his duties. Anduin's eyes stung again as he envisioned those hands performing with difficulty things he himself could do so easily.

How had he not noticed this? *I'm so sorry, Wyll. I didn't want to see.*

Then, suddenly, Wyll grew querulous. "But . . . where's my Elsie?

You had to have died, dearest. If you'd survived the Scourge, you'd have found a way to come to me. Elsie, where are you?" His arm extended, reaching for his phantom wife. "I can't find my way without you!"

Anduin's heart was breaking. Gently, he called the Light and placed his radiant hand on the old man's now clammy brow.

"Shh," he said softly. "Be at peace. You'll find each other, old friend. You will. When the time is right. But now rest."

Wyll blinked rapidly, frowning a little, and when he turned to Anduin, it looked as though he did recognize his charge. "Anduin? You're here, too?"

"Yes, it's me. I'm here. I won't leave you."

Wyll settled back down, closing his eyes. "You were such a good boy. It was a joy taking care of—" He broke off in midsentence. Anduin bit his lower lip.

Then the old man rallied. "Tell her I always loved only her. My little Elsie with the fire-red hair. If you see her. Tell her I'll wait for her."

Tears stung the king's eyes. "Of course I'll tell her. I promise." He swallowed hard. "You go on now."

"I think I will. It's really quite beautiful," Wyll sighed. "Thank you for not keeping me."

Anduin started to say something but then closed his mouth. He could feel the old man's pulse slowing . . . slowing . . . heard a soft sigh from the bed.

Slow . . . slow . . .

Stop.

CHAPTER SEVENTEEN

Stormwind

Genn was waiting for Anduin outside the door. When the king emerged, Genn looked at him with eyes that held far too many sorrows.

"I'm all right," Anduin said. It wasn't quite true, but he had a purpose now, and that helped. "I need you to do something for me."

"Of course. What do you need, my boy?"

"Please ask High Priestess Laurena to prepare Wyll's body for burial with all rites due to so close a friend of the Wrynn family. Then tell my advisers to meet me in the map room within two hours. Notify High Exarch Turalyon and Alleria Windrunner that I desire their attendance as well."

Genn's bushy eyebrows rose at that, but he stopped just short of asking why. Instead he said, "You don't need to do anything just yet, you know. Your head—"

"Is clear," Anduin replied. "But I thank you for your concern. I'll be in my quarters preparing for the meeting."

He turned and strode off before Genn could continue to press him. He had been alone with Wyll's body and his own pain for an hour before emerging, and the first wave of grief had crested and receded. Now he needed to focus.

Anduin spent the hours before the meeting writing furiously and consulting various tomes, then said a quick prayer to calm himself and went to meet his advisers in the map room.

Everyone he had requested was there: Genn Greymane, Mathias Shaw, Catherine Rogers, Alleria Windrunner, and Turalyon. Even Velen had traveled from the *Exodar* to be present. When Anduin informed them of his plans, only Velen stood with him.

Rogers, of course, was no surprise. "Have you been to Southshore recently?" she snapped rhetorically. "The very creature you're negotiating with deliberately unleashed the blight against an Alliance town! I had friends—*family*—there. Now there's only Forsaken."

"The Forsaken are not the Scourge," Anduin reminded her. "Some of them retain a sense of who they were, and they miss their living relatives."

"I can't believe them capable of such things," Catherine retorted.

Anduin turned to Shaw. "Spymaster?" he asked calmly.

Shaw nodded. "His Majesty is correct. A short while ago, he asked me to send extra agents to the Undercity. A governing body has sprung up in Sylvanas's absence. They call themselves the Desolate Council. I have reason to believe that the king's proposal of a gathering would be extremely well received among this number. But they do not represent the majority of the Forsaken."

Rogers looked stunned. Anduin took a step toward her, beseeching her. "Catherine . . . your family and friends . . . they could be among the council."

For a moment, he saw something soft flit across the sky admiral's face. Then her jaw tightened, and that face grew harder than he had ever seen it.

"They are *dead*." She all but spit the words. "Worse than dead— monsters. How can you possibly imagine I'd want to see them as they are now?"

"Remember, Sky Admiral," Anduin said, his voice still kind, "you speak to your king."

All the color that had fled her face rushed back. She bowed immediately. "My apologies, Your Majesty, if I've given offense. But the shambling wrecks of my loved ones are the *last* thing I would ever want to see. I'd prefer to remember them as they were. Alive, healthy, happy . . . and *human*."

"No offense was taken, Admiral," Anduin replied. "And your point is understandable. King Greymane?"

"You know my thoughts on Forsaken," Genn growled. His voice was so rough and deep, the older king might as well have been in his worgen form. "I agree with the admiral. They're monsters. If we care at all for our Forsaken relatives, we should be trying to give them true deaths, not embrace what they've become."

Anduin's heart sunk further with each opinion voiced. "Reunions can often be disappointing," Alleria said bluntly. "You may not know, but recently Vereesa and I met with Sylvanas. It . . . did not go well."

"No, I didn't know," Anduin said, strain creeping into his voice. He thought about his words to Valeera: *It seems each passing day reduces the number of people I can rely on.* "Perhaps you would care to enlighten me."

"We met only to see what was left of our family ties," she said. "I will tell you more if you wish. But suffice it to say that I would not put my faith in her, Anduin Wrynn. She has been too long in the darkness, and it has eaten away what is left of the sister I loved so dearly." Her voice was strong, yet it quivered slightly. Despite all that had happened to her, despite her worrisome familiarity with the Void, it was obvious to Anduin that she was still capable of deep love. She was still Alleria. And the failure of the reunion of the three sisters had wounded her. It did not bode well for his plan to convince this group of the power of familial bonds.

"Nor would I trust the rot-riddled brains of the Forsaken to be able to distinguish friend from foe if they came face to face with their erstwhile loved ones," Alleria continued. "I would advise against this path."

"As would I," said Turalyon, startling Anduin. More than most, the paladin understood the power of the Light and how it could change minds and hearts. He had even befriended and fought alongside a demon who had been infused with the Light. "I ask you as a tactician: Do you really wish to risk failure? You could start a war. If even one of the Forsaken snaps and kills an Alliance member—"

"Hell," boomed Genn, "if one of the Alliance members sneezes too loudly, we'd have war. It's too risky, Your Majesty." He calmed himself before continuing in a quieter voice. "Light knows your heart's in the right place. And it's a bigger, more generous heart than mine. But you have to be a good king as well as a good man."

Valeera had said something similar. Anduin knew the truth of the words, yet he also had to be true to himself.

Genn continued. "We have more than enough to keep us occupied and sleepless at night with goblins, Azerite, and a damaged world. Let's not start a conventional war over, what—a total of a few dozen individuals? We gain so little and stand to lose so much."

"We stand to gain peace," came Velen's quiet voice.

"The actions of a few dozen . . . *people*," and Rogers pronounced the last word in a slightly strangled tone, "don't determine peace."

"No," Anduin said. "Not in that moment, perhaps. But over time. If this goes well—"

"*If,*" Greymane emphasized.

Anduin shot him a sharp look. "If this goes well," he repeated, adding, "and I believe it will, this could plant a seed. If these few people can find common ground, why not a hundred, or a thousand, or ten thousand, or more?"

Aware that negative emotions were running high and threatening to overshadow other factors, he tried appealing to their tactical minds. "Why would Sylvanas openly start a war? She's got much to lose and little to gain. The Horde is preoccupied with the same concerns that face the Alliance: how to recover from the devastating war with the Legion. How to heal Azeroth and how to keep Azerite from falling into the hands of the opposition. Do you think she wants to fight another open war with all that going on?"

"There's always a plan with that banshee," Genn said. "She's always steps ahead of us."

"Then let us work out the same steps ourselves. In no scenario does open warfare work to either the advantage of the Horde or that of the Alliance."

"That we know of," Alleria said. "And there is much none of us knows about Sylvanas and how she thinks."

"Is there anyone present who thinks she would wish to see harm come to the Forsaken?" Anduin challenged.

There was silence.

"The Forsaken are her people. Her creations. Her *children* in a way. We've seen mountains of evidence that she is trying to save them, to find means to prolong their existences."

"As I've said before, she wants to make more of *them* by killing *us*," Genn said. "What if she thinks these humans might be amenable to becoming Forsaken themselves? They could be with their loved ones forever that way."

"So she could kill our people, recruit a couple dozen new Forsaken—and immediately enter a war. That's an *excellent* tactic." Anduin tried, but he couldn't quite keep the sarcasm out of his voice.

Genn fell unhappily silent. Anduin looked at them one by one. "I'm aware that this could backfire. The Forsaken could find themselves envious of the living, which could solidify a moderate attitude into a zealous one. The same could be said of the Alliance side. They may find themselves repulsed by people they once loved and become more determined than ever to destroy the Forsaken. But I believe they deserve the chance to find out. Both the humans and the Forsaken."

The hawks in the group stood with their arms folded and their lips pressed together. It was clear to them that Anduin's mind was made up. Even though they outnumbered him four to two—Shaw seemed to take no side—they knew this encounter would proceed.

Genn tried one final time. "I think the others need to know what I do," he said, not unkindly. "That you lost your oldest friend just a few hours ago. You told me Wyll had wanted to see his wife, who died at Lordaeron. You're doing this for him, and I understand why you want to. But you can't put innocent lives at risk just to make yourself feel better."

"You're partially right, Genn," Anduin said quietly. "I would be lying if I told you that I don't wish with all my heart that Wyll and Elsie had been able to see each other again. It's too late for Wyll, but it's not too late for others."

He placed his hands on the map table and leaned forward. "If Sylvanas responds with terms that are acceptable to me—terms that I believe will adequately protect Stormwind citizens—this meeting *will* take place. I expect all of you to accept that and turn your attention to following my orders to ensure that everything goes according to plan. Do I make myself clear?"

Nods and a few murmured "Yes, Your Majestys" went around the table. "Good. Now let's start our preparation."

CHAPTER EIGHTEEN

Tanaris

Sapphronetta Flivvers awoke to pain.

The gnome was bruised and battered, and her hands and feet were securely tied. She flexed them, noting that she still had good circulation, and began to assess her current situation.

It wasn't promising. She was lying facedown across something warm, and she could feel muscles tensing and contracting beneath her and hear the slow flap of wings. Gryphon? No; feathered wings sounded different when they beat. Wyvern.

She had known her team would be targeted. That was why they had beefed up the security. Saffy felt an awful pang for her friends and for the Sentinels who had been assigned to help them.

That an attack had come was hardly a shock. But why had she been allowed to survive? The Horde, of course, wasn't fond of any of the Alliance races, but they had little use in particular for gnomes. Yet here she was, not just spared but taken. Kidnapped!

She tried to recall the exact words she'd heard: *Kezzig, that's a gnome lady!*

Yeah, and I'm gonna punch the living—oh. Maybe she's not the right one.

She fits the description perfectly. You know the rules.

Yeah, yeah, stupid rules.

They had come to kill the Explorers' League members and their protectors; that much was obvious. They hadn't been looking for her but for someone who looked like her, and they wanted the "gnome lady" alive. If she could just figure out what they were after, she might be able to bluff her way to safety—and a chance to escape.

Saffy couldn't feel the comfortably familiar, pleasant weight of her massive tool belt. Obviously, they'd taken that. It was a shame they'd put ropes on her instead of locked chains, because she was pretty sure they hadn't removed her hairpins. There was nothing she could use as a weapon, and someone had to be sitting near her to make sure the gnome they'd gone to all this effort to abduct wouldn't fall off in mid-flight.

Urf. Now there was a thought. Saffy stopped even her slight squirming and lay still, thinking furiously. They'd have to land, and they'd have to take her out of the sack in which they'd thrown her. They must want something from her or whoever they thought she was, but she couldn't imagine . . .

Oh, wait. Yes, she could. She could imagine it all too well. They'd been in Silithus, and they knew there were goblins out in force. Goblin activity meant one of two things: profit or technology. Well, all right, three things: profit, technology, or mining. Well, no: profit, technology, mining, or pummeling people.

And goblins also meant . . .

Oh, come on, Saffy, she told herself. *There are a lot of goblins in the world. The odds of what you're thinking are approximately 5,233,482 to 1. Someone would have to know your location, and—*

Oh, dear. They didn't have to know her location. They were kidnapping every "gnome lady" they came across who fit the description.

The wyvern landed with a thump. Saffy started to slide off and couldn't suppress a gasp. Then the bag that encased her was abruptly dragged off the mount, and Saffy let out an *oof* as she was flung onto a bony shoulder.

She heard whirring, buzzing, beeping sounds and muffled conversation in, as expected, Goblin. A language she'd picked up long ago, when she had been young and innocent and—

Stupid. Come on, admit it, Saffy. Stupid.

She couldn't quite make out most of what they were saying, but she caught enough: . . . *dead . . . take her . . . better be worth . . . know what to do.*

Her heart sped up. No. It couldn't be. The odds were—

She was dropped unceremoniously on the floor.

"She better be okay," came a voice from Saffy's past. A voice attached to a goblin she despised with every fiber of her being. A goblin she had hoped to never have to lay eyes on for the rest of her life.

She should stay quiet. Not give him any gratification. Pretend to cooperate with whatever dastardly, despicable scheme he was plotting.

The bag was opened, and she blinked, momentarily blinded by the light. Rough hands grabbed her arms and held her down as a knife sawed through her ropes. Then she was hauled to her feet.

"Hey, hey, what did you do to her?" came the loathed voice. "Her face is all—"

With a roar of fury stoked by years of simmering resentment, Saffy managed to wrest free of the two bruisers on either side and launch herself like a mini-rocket, complete with fiery red hair, at her archenemy.

The symbol of misery, frustration, and rage.

She had the satisfaction of watching his tiny eyes widen in shocked horror and his big knobby hands come up toward his face.

"You lying, manipulative, lazy, horrible, no-good, filthy *wretch!*" Saffy shouted, her hands, fingers formed into claws, outstretched to scratch his eyes out.

Tragically, the bruisers got her just before she was able to scratch eight perfect furrows in that ugly green face. A rag coated with who knew what foul material was shoved into her mouth, and she was trussed up *again.* Could she ever learn to get her temper under control? Apparently not. Then again, this was Grizzek. He deserved everything she could throw at him. Just the thought made her squirm with impotent fury.

"You change your mind, we'll take care of her," the biggest, burliest one said.

"No need, Druz," the loathed coward said. "You guys scram. I got this."

Saffy continued to squirm as Grizzek showed the bruisers out.

"Hello, Saffy! Hello, Saffy!"

He couldn't have—but he had. There it was, the beautiful, exquisite parrot *she* had created. Oh, if she could just get free for two minutes—

"I'm sorry they hurt you. They weren't supposed to."

"Mmmphh mhphfmpp oo?" she repeated incredulously, and then launched into a string of beautiful but sadly unintelligible cursing.

"Funny thing is, that group wasn't even looking for you. They were after your friends. I—I'm sorry about that, too, kid."

But you're not sorry you had me kidnapped! she tried to say. All that emerged was more muffled noises.

"No, I'm not sorry about that. Besides," he said, shaking his head, those big ugly ears flapping slightly with the motion, "crazy as it sounds, I think by the time all this is over, you're not gonna be sorry either."

He winced at her denials this time. "You keep on like that, you're not gonna have any voice left." He paused. "Which, all things considered, might not be a bad idea."

She bit down on the terrible-tasting rag, her eyes shooting daggers at him. After her breathing calmed down a bit, Grizzek came over and untied the gag, keeping his big fingers away from Saffy's sharp little teeth.

They glared at each other. "Aw, Saffy. I gotta say, it's good to see you again."

"The pleasure is all yours," Saffy snapped.

"Miss me?"

"Yes. Repeatedly. As you recall, my Lightning Blast 3000 failed every time I took aim."

"I told you that piece of crap wouldn't work."

"Aww, honey, I hate you, too. Tell you what," the gnome said, "you untie me, give me food and water *and my parrot back,* and I'll head out and not report you to the authorities." Of course, she would. In a Gadgetzan minute, she would. Assuming there were any "authorities," wherever they were.

"Can't do that, Punkin," he said, shaking his head. "And it's not your parrot."

"It is *so* my parrot!"

"Nope, we made him together. C'mon," he said, almost looking hurt, "you gotta remember that. It was our first anniversary present to each other."

It had also been their last. Saffy didn't want to think how crazy in love she had been with the green mook. *Well*, she amended, *just plain crazy, at least.*

"Besides. Just hold on to your hat here for a minute and you'll understand."

"Your goons *took* my hat!" she shouted after him as he wandered out. Her beautiful pith helmet, given to her expressly for this mission.

"They're not my goons," he said. "They'd never have hurt ya if they'd been my goons. Or your pals. You know I don't work that way, Punkin."

"Don't call me that!" She strained against the ropes with all the strength in her small body, but the knots were good. Of course the knots were good. *We're in Tanaris, by the ocean. Everyone's a sailor. Even the goons.*

She was thirsty, hungry, overheated, sunburned, and exhausted, and she slumped against her bonds.

"Here," Grizzek said almost gently, and took one of the hands that were bound behind her back. Saffy twitched angrily, but he pressed something into her palm and closed her fingers over it.

She gasped once. The pain on her sunburned, bruised face eased. Her mouth was no longer dry nor did her stomach rumble for food. She felt alert, strong, sharp. Her gaze fell on the parrot.

"There's about five different things I can do to improve Feathers if you'll just give me an arclight spanner, three sets of nuts and bolts, and a good screwdriver," she announced. And then blinked.

How had she known that?

Grizzek released her hand. She kept her fist tightly closed around . . . whatever it was he had pressed against her palm.

He moved around behind her, sitting in the single chair, watching her reaction. "It's something, ain't it?" he said, his voice soft and filled with reverence.

"Yeah," she breathed, as awestruck as he was.

Silence stretched between them. Then, finally, Saffy asked, "What is it?"

"Boss says it's called Azerite," Grizzek said.

Azerite! The very substance she'd been brought into that awful desert to analyze. Now Saffy understood why. Her brain was on fire but calm, not frantic. This stuff was amazing.

"Actually, what the boss really calls it is 'My Path to Ruling Azeroth with Lots of Statues to Glorious Me.'"

Saffy abruptly recalled one of the things he'd said to her while she was shouting and struggling to escape. *They're not my goons,* he had said. Which meant that they were someone else's goons. Which meant . . .

"Oh, Grizzek," she said, horrified. "Please tell me you aren't working with that ugly green monster with the terrible fashion sense!" She paused. "That could apply to lots of goblins, actually. What I meant to ask was—"

"I know what you meant," he said, lowering his head and not meeting her eyes. "Or, rather, who you meant. And yeah."

"Jastor Gallywix?"

He nodded miserably.

"I don't think I've ever been more disappointed in you. And that's saying something."

"Look. He came to me with this stuff. You got a taste of what it can do. He's agreed to let me decide what I do, what I make, and most important, how it's used. And he's given me everything I've asked for supply-wise in order to understand it, refine it, and make amazing, fantastical inventions with it."

"Everything, huh? I guess that explains why you had me kidnapped."

"Punkin, I—"

She shook her head. "No. I get it. I . . ." She gulped. Swallowing her pride was hard. "I might have done the same. Might have. Probably not. But I *might* have."

His eyes widened in an expression of gratitude, and his ears drooped ever so slightly with relief. "So . . . you'll help me?"

"I'll help you."

"Aw, Punkin, we made a hell of a team back when," he said.

She smiled. "Yeah. We did. Too bad we got married and ruined all that."

"Well, we ain't married now, so I say, let's get to work."

"You have to untie me first."

"Oh? Yeah, right, sure." He slipped off the chair, reaching for a knife with one hand, and hurried behind her. Her bonds were cut free for the second time that morning.

Belatedly, he paused. "You . . . you mean it, right? You're not going to clonk me with something and run off with Feathers?"

The thought had occurred to her, but Saffy didn't volunteer that bit of information. No, she was in this for the long haul. Anything that could do what this Azerite could do was something she wanted a part in developing. What vehicles, what gadgets and trinkets, what contraptions they could create!

"No. I won't do that." She got to her feet as easily as if she hadn't spent far too long in a burlap sack being shunted across a continent. "But I do have one condition."

"Anything!"

"When we're done, I get Feathers."

He winced, then stuck out his hand. She opened up her tiny pink one, seeing the soft golden-blue gleam of Azerite, and then it was nestled between their two hands as they shook on it.

CHAPTER NINETEEN

The Undercity

Vellcinda didn't miss sleep.

She had not realized until after her death just how much time had been wasted with her eyes closed and her body still. There was an old saying, "Plenty of time for sleep in the grave," but she had found the reality to be exactly the opposite. She'd slept far too much when she lived: an entire third of that life, how remarkable. Now that she was a Forsaken, she had done all she could to make the most of what she, with what remained of the incorrigible optimism she'd had in life, firmly viewed as a second chance.

She'd been a servant when she died. So of course, when Vellcinda "awoke" as a Forsaken, the first thing she did, as her mind gradually became accustomed to her new reality, was serve. It was what she knew best. She'd been kind and patient with those who had awoken terrified and disoriented and had helped to rebury those who had refused Lady Sylvanas's dark gift.

Part of her understood the refusal. Who among them hadn't been confused and frightened to awaken to the sight of their own skin decaying? No one with half a brain left, that was who. And of course, some of the poor things didn't have even half a brain.

Vellcinda seemed to have been one of the fortunate ones who'd awoken with their minds completely intact, thank you very much, and had firmly resolved to put it to good use.

She missed her husband, and upon awakening, she had wanted to seek him out. He had been in Stormwind, and Vellcinda had been in Lordaeron, visiting family, when she died. She had been in the castle when Arthas had returned. She'd hoped to catch a glimpse of the beloved paladin and his triumphant homecoming but had been stuck working in the kitchens as he marched through a rain of rose petals into the throne room. But she had been well within range of what unfolded immediately after Arthas committed both patricide and regicide with one thrust of an unhallowed sword.

Her beloved had been spared that, and she was glad of it. Others told her that attempts to contact him would only lead to heartbreak for them both. He believed her dead, and in the end, Vellcinda had decided that it was better that way. He was a good, kind man. He deserved to find a living woman to love.

Many other Forsaken, such as her friend and fellow Governor Parqual, seemed to miss their loved ones as much as she did. Others seemed lukewarm, and still others didn't care at all. Some were even . . . evil. What had happened, to her, to them, to have such differing personalities and mind-sets? It was one of the mysteries about being Forsaken.

She had no memory of her time as a mindless creature, and that was a good thing.

As the years unfolded, though, Vellcinda grew tired of serving. But her brain was almost as sharp as it had ever been, and Vellcinda began to want to learn, to achieve, rather than simply do for others.

She directed her genuinely caring nature toward how best to take care of the, ah, *unique* challenges of being an active, sentient corpse. Injuries, for example.

"Come now," she would say to the wounded, "Forsaken flesh won't heal itself, you know!" Stitching; grafting on new muscle, sinew, and skin; and magical potions were the options open to her people instead of simply cleaning a wound, bandaging it, and trusting in the body's innate ability to repair itself.

Time spent physically mending undead flesh eventually led to a desire to study with the apothecaries. Although Sylvanas put most of them to work on poisons, Vellcinda studied ways to keep the Forsaken active and healthy, mentally and physically.

She noticed that some of the wounded appeared to be more afraid of dying now than they had been when they lived. As she inspected the fit of a new hand onto the right arm of a blacksmith—an accident with molten steel had made short work of his original one—he had said to her, "Always makes me nervous to come in here."

"Why is that, dear?" Vellcinda hadn't been terribly old when she had died. A young sixty, she had always said. "I'm far less frightening than Doctor Halsey."

The blacksmith, Tevan Whitfield, had chuckled, a raspy, hollow sound. "That's certainly true. No, I mean . . . when I was alive, I felt immortal. I didn't take care of myself, and I was a bit reckless. Now I *am* immortal, technically. But because injury is the only thing that can threaten that, I'm suddenly aware of how fragile flesh is."

"Flesh has always been fragile." She inspected the hand. She'd sewn it on well. She noticed again that it didn't have calluses, nor were the muscles strong. The previous owner of the hand the blacksmith Tevan now wore probably had been some sort of artist or entertainer.

She tapped the fleshy palm of the hand gently with her forefinger bones. "Can you feel that?"

"Yes," he said.

"Excellent." She regarded him levelly. "I must let you know that this hand won't be as strong as you're used to."

"A few weeks of hammering will take care of that."

Vellcinda gave him a compassionate look. "No, dear," she said gently, "it won't. You can't grow muscle anymore."

His face fell. Not literally. His face hadn't decayed much at all. He was, in fact, rather handsome for a Forsaken.

"Come back if you can't use it properly," she said. "We'll see if we can't find a better one for you." She patted the hand gently.

"You see?" Tevan had said. "This is what I'm talking about. In time, we'll just . . . wear ourselves away."

"That's what happens in life, too," Vellcinda reminded him briskly.

"We can't all be pretty, nigh-immortal things like elves. The proper attitude is that we must accept what we have and be grateful for it. You and I and the others are here. And that's a lovely thing. Nothing lasts forever, and if we die and can't come back, well, we've had a second chance, and that's more than many have had."

Tevan smiled. With his intact face, it was a pleasant expression. Vellcinda had no false modesty about her own face, which was somewhat the worse for wear from being a lazy layabout in her grave for so long. She'd been plain even as a living, breathing human. Her husband had always said she was beautiful to him, though, and she believed him.

That was what love was, wasn't it? Seeing with the heart and not the eyes and finding beauty there.

"You're right," the blacksmith said. "I don't think I ever thought about it like that. I chose to receive the Gift. I know others didn't. At the time, I thought them fools. But now I wonder. I know Lady Sylvanas is trying to find ways that we can continue our existence. But what if we weren't meant to?" He gestured to his fine new noncallused hand. "How much should we do, how far should we go, just to keep existing?"

Vellcinda had smiled. "Goodness, for a blacksmith, your thoughts are quite philosophical."

"Maybe it's my new hand."

Tevan had been the first with whom Vellcinda had conducted such discussion, but he would not be the last. Once the idea had come into her head, Vellcinda found she couldn't stop thinking about it.

Now, months after that conversation, the leader of the Desolate Council stood in the throne room of the Undercity, in the spot where Sylvanas Windrunner had stood for so long until she had left to lead the Horde. Beside Vellcinda on the top dais were the other four leading members of the governing council, who were called, simply and logically, the Governors. On the second step, just below them, were the seven known as the Ministers, who would implement the policies the Governors created. At the bottom were those who Vellcinda thought were actually the most important members of the council: the ten Listeners. Every day, they would meet and speak with those among the Forsaken who had questions, comments, or complaints about how the leadership governed. They reported directly to the Governors. Although any citizen of the Undercity was free to flag down any member of the council—including the Prime Governor, Vellcinda herself—the Listeners were more readily available.

Thus far, things seemed to be going swimmingly. Vellcinda looked out over the calm crowd that filled the room to overflowing and continued outside. She was so very pleased. Today, more than ever, they needed to stand together, work together, for the betterment of everyone until their Dark Lady returned.

Today they were holding a service for those Forsaken who had experienced their Last Death, fighting against the terrifying evil of the Burning Legion. Vellcinda had spoken with the Dark Lady's champion, Nathanos Blightcaller, on his recent visit to the Undercity and had implored him to persuade Sylvanas to return.

"I know she has many responsibilities," she had told him. "But surely she can spend a few hours with us. Please, tell her to come for the ceremony we will be holding for those who willingly accepted death on behalf of the Horde. She doesn't have to stay long if her duties call her, but it would mean so much."

Nathanos had said he would carry the message. But there had been no sign that Sylvanas would come.

She waited a few moments longer just in case. The Forsaken in the crowd waited patiently, as they always did. Finally, their leader sighed.

"I suppose you all want me to speak," Vellcinda said. "So I'll try to say a little something. Forgive me if I clear my throat a few times; we're all too familiar with that tickling of the ichor!"

That brought some laughter, raspy and guttural. Vellcinda continued. "I want to first acknowledge our friends who made the journey to be here today. I see blood elves, and trolls, and orcs, and even a few goblins and pandaren. Thank you for standing with us to honor those who fell from among our dwindling numbers. I'm particularly grateful for all the tauren out there. If not for you, we might all be extinct."

There were representatives of all the Horde races there, but she saw more tauren than any other. It was thanks to the tauren that the Forsaken had been admitted into the Horde. Vellcinda shuddered to think about what would have happened to her people without that protection.

"Even so, with the exception of our kind friends who stand here with us, I fear it is, sadly, accurate to say that many of the living still don't accept us. And these individuals seem to think that because we've already been dead, we don't really care about life, or whatever you choose to call our existence. They seem to think that we should suffer less when those of our numbers perish. Well, they're flat-out wrong. We *do* care. We *do* grieve.

"Our queen is hunting for a way to increase our numbers by bringing back the fallen from the dead. Making more Forsaken. But what those of us assembled here today really wish from her is to know that she values the Forsaken she already has. Not just us as her people— which of course we are—but as individuals. To accept that some of us are content with just a second chance and might not want a third or a fourth but the Last Death instead.

"We stand here today, thinking of those who did experience their Last Deaths. They are gone, utterly. Their blood doesn't flow in the veins of their children and on to generations—at least not generations who will ever live here and interact with us. Those Forsaken are lost, but they are also at peace. Reunited at last with those they loved in life. Let us honor their loss by never forgetting their names. Who they were. What they did."

Vellcinda steeled herself. "I'll go first. On this day, I remember Tevan Whitfield. He was a blacksmith, and he once told me that he was more afraid of death as a Forsaken than he had been as a living man. And yet when he was asked to serve, he did so. He made weapons that enabled others to fight the foe. He mended armor when it was damaged as we mend bodies when they are damaged. He faced his greatest fear and lost that gamble. I'll remember you always, Tevan. You were a good friend."

She nodded to Parqual Fintallas, who stood beside her. He cleared his throat and began to speak of a woman who had been a warrior in life and in her undeath, until her body had been hacked to pieces by a fel reaver. The remembrances spread out like ripples from a pond. First from those who stood on the dais, then the Ministers, and then the Listeners. Then, one by one, members of the crowd, too, began to speak.

So many of them had lost their families on that long-ago awful day, when Arthas had returned, that it was rare to see an intact one. Most Forsaken had made new families—unions made with those whom they had never known in life but who were just as important.

As Vellcinda listened, holding her friend Tevan in her thoughts, she was sad, but she was content. All mourned, but no one wept. No one railed against injustice. But more important to her was that no one was angry. She had come to believe that anger wasn't good for the Forsaken. Many already weren't thinking too clearly, with their brains usually being rotten to some degree or other. As far as Vellcinda was concerned, rage just muddied the waters until no one could see where he or she was trying to swim.

There were some in the Undercity who resented the role the Desolate Council had created for itself, but Vellcinda had been firm that it was only a stopgap measure. Supplies needed to be brought in. Replacement limbs had to be attached.

"Gracious," Vellcinda had said once at a public meeting, "if our dear Sylvanas should step through that door, I'd be more than happy to say, 'Hello, Dark Lady, we've missed you terribly. Please do take over running this great city. It's a very wearying thing!'"

As a servant, she had prepared meals, tended the sick, scrubbed bathtubs, and emptied chamber pots. She'd done what needed doing, and as far as she was concerned, she'd much rather step back and let others who were better at leadership step up. She couldn't recall the last time she'd just sat and enjoyed watching the calming flow of the green canals.

She returned to the present, chiding herself for woolgathering. When the last person had finished talking, she looked at the gathered crowd. "My, I'm so proud of all of you. And of those who gave all they had for the Horde. Thank you for coming."

And that was it. The crowd dispersed, and she watched them go. She was disappointed that Sylvanas hadn't accepted the invitation to attend but it was not unexpected.

"Prime Governor Vellcinda," came a calm voice. She turned, surprised and delighted.

"Why, Champion Blightcaller," she said. "How good of you to come. I . . . don't suppose . . . ?"

He shook his head. "No. Our queen has urgent business to attend to. But," he added, "she has sent me to learn more about what is happening in her absence and to let you know that she does intend to visit shortly. She regrets that she was unable to be here today."

"Oh, that is so kind of her! I'm pleased to hear that." She patted his arm. "I'm old enough to read between the lines, young man. Lady Sylvanas is afraid she has another Putress on her hands. But don't fret. We're just a group of concerned citizens, caretakers of a sort, minding the house while the mistress is gone. Why don't you come around for a visit this afternoon? We'll be happy to discuss what we're trying to do. Perhaps you would care for some tea?" Vellcinda liked to brew tea, to smell it, to hold the warm cup in her hands, even if she did not drink the beverage.

He looked slightly baffled and opened his mouth to reply. But before he could do so, Vellcinda heard another voice. "Ah, precisely the fellow I have come here to meet. Well, not quite, but close enough."

Vellcinda and Nathanos both turned to see a rather short Forsaken dressed in priest's robes. She didn't recognize him, but that wasn't surprising. The Undercity wasn't vast, but there were still a lot of people here, not to mention all those who were simply passing through.

"I've not had the pleasure," she said.

The newcomer bowed. "Archbishop Alonsus Faol," he said. Vellcinda was surprised. It had been a well-known name not so long ago. She was pleased he had not perished with so many others.

"Oh, my," she said. "It's an honor."

Even Nathanos Blightcaller bowed to the archbishop. "Indeed it is. What is it you wish of me, sir?"

"I have a letter. Actually, two. The first one is for your warchief. The second one is for someone named Elsie Benton."

Vellcinda swayed slightly. Nathanos caught her arm, looking at her with concern, but she smiled and waved him off. "It's been a long time since I heard that name. Only my family and closest friends called me that."

The archbishop's expression softened. "Then . . . here. Your letters."

He handed each of them a tightly rolled scroll, and Vellcinda took hers with a trembling hand. Her eyes flew wide as she saw the wax stamp, which was blue, with the imprint of the lion of Stormwind.

And she knew at once what it was.

So did Nathanos. "This is from the king of Stormwind," he snapped, his red eyes blazing with anger as he turned to Faol. "What are you doing, fraternizing with an enemy of the Horde?"

"But as I'm not a member of the Horde, the king is not my enemy," the archbishop said pleasantly. "I serve the Light. I'm a priest, and so is King Anduin. The letter is for your queen, and it's important. You should make sure that she sees it. But," he added, "it's not immediately dire. I suggest that you do as you had intended. Spend some time here in the Undercity. Take your thoughts and this missive back to the warchief. And you, dear lady . . ."

Faol laid a gentle hand on her arm. "This missive, I am sorry to say, does contain bad news. I'm so very sorry."

Vellcinda was glad of the warning as she broke the seal, opened the scroll, and read:

To Elsie Benton,

I do not even know if you still exist. But I feel compelled to ask Archbishop Faol to search for you while he is in the Undercity. If you are reading this, I assume his quest was successful.

It is with the deepest sorrow that I must inform you that your husband, Wyll Benton, passed away peacefully this afternoon. I hope it comforts you to know he did not die alone; I was with him.

Wyll served my father and me devotedly for many years. He did not speak to me of his family; I suspect it was too painful for him to recall those times and what he thought was your fate. He called out for you before he died and hoped to see you again.

I follow the path of a priest, as you may know, and I pleaded with him to allow me to heal him. He refused, and I respected his wish.

I have resolved to do all I can so that those who are Forsaken can reunite with their human friends and families, if only briefly. There are some things, I believe, that transcend the politics of kings and queens and generals. Family is one of them. To this end, I have sent a missive to your warchief. I hope she agrees with me.

I close by fulfilling a promise asked of me by my friend Wyll: telling you that he always loved only you and that he will wait for you.

Again, please accept my sincerest condolences.

And a signature in an elegant, educated hand: King Anduin Llane Wrynn.

"My poor Wyll," Vellcinda said, her voice trembling. "Archbishop, please thank King Anduin for me. I'm grateful my husband didn't die alone. No one should die alone. You tell the king that I think this is a fine plan. I hope our warchief does, too. I'd have been so glad to have seen Wyll one more time."

"What plan?" Nathanos demanded, looking from Vellcinda to Faol suspiciously.

"This," Vellcinda said, handing him the scroll. As Nathanos read, Faol said, "The outline for the king of Stormwind's proposition is clarified further in the scroll to be given to Warchief Sylvanas. I will be here for a few days, and I am happy to answer any questions you or Vellcinda might have."

Looking displeased, Nathanos returned the missive. Clutching the precious scroll, the Prime Governor of the Desolate Council corrected Faol.

"Elsie," she said. "I think it's time I went by Elsie again."

CHAPTER TWENTY

The Netherlight Temple

Lu, la lu, my dearest child,
Lu, la lu, lu la lay,
Lordaeron says, "Go to sleep."
Azeroth says, "Dream you deep."
Lu, la lu, la lu, la lay,
Safe in my arms you'll stay.

Calia sang softly to the dreaming child she held. This precious little one would one day be heir to the throne of Lordaeron.

No. No, there was no Lordaeron, not anymore. There was only the Undercity, inhabited by the dead. Her father's crown had been broken and bloodied and now was lost to time. Calia would never wear it now. This drowsing, dreaming infant would never wear it, either. And that pained her. A single tear trickled down her face to land on the rosiest, softest cheek in the world.

The child who was by all rights the trueborn heir to the throne blinked, the small mouth forming a pout. Calia lifted the bundle and kissed the tear away, tasting salt on her lips.

And the baby laughed as her mother began once again to sing the old, old lullaby, glancing up as her husband came in to kiss the top of his wife's head. He placed his hand on her shoulder, giving it a gentle squeeze—

—the bony claw digging deep and—

Calia screamed. She bolted upright, her heart slamming against her chest, gasping for breath. For an interminable, horrible instant, she could feel the pain of the undead hand that grabbed her. Then she blinked, and the horror retreated into memory.

She buried her face in her hands, realizing it was wet with tears, and tried to still her shaking.

It was only a memory. It wasn't real.

But it had been, once.

She slipped off the bed, reached for a robe, and then padded barefoot to Saa'ra.

No matter what the hour, there was usually someone about in the Netherlight Temple. Someone was always coming in or heading out. Those who made this place their home knew of Calia's night terrors and had made it clear they were available at any time if she needed company or to talk. But she only ever wanted to speak to Saa'ra.

The naaru was expecting her, as it always did. It hovered over her, a crystalline entity limned with luminous purple, and emitted a faint, ceaseless exquisite music. Saa'ra spoke sometimes in words that all could hear and sometimes directly and privately to someone's heart and head, as it did now.

Dear one. I am so sorry the dream has troubled you once more.

Calia nodded, sinking down in front of Saa'ra and twisting her fingers awkwardly. "I keep thinking that they will stop at some point."

They will, the gentle being assured her. *Once you are ready for them to stop.*

"So you've said. But why can't I be ready *now*?" She laughed a little, hearing the petulance in her own voice.

There are things you must do before that peace will be granted to you. Things that you must understand, that you must integrate into yourself. People who need your help. What one needs in order to heal will always come one's way, but sometimes it is hard to recognize it. Sometimes the most beautiful and important gifts come wrapped in pain and blood.

"That's not making me feel better," Calia said.

It might when you realize that all that has happened to you hides a gift within it.

Calia closed her eyes. "Forgive me, but it's hard to think that way." The corruption of her beloved brother and the murder of her father, of so many of the people of Lordaeron . . . her flight, her terror . . . the loss of her husband and child, the loss of everything—

No. Not everything. What we participate in, we can benefit from. For every fever you have cured, bone you have mended, life you have improved . . . that, and the joy that has come from that, is now as much a part of you as your pain. Honor them both, dear child of the Light. I would say trust that there is a purpose, but you already know there is. You have seen the fruits of your labor. Do not ignore them or belittle them. Taste them. Savor them. They are yours as much as anyone else's.

Her tight chest eased as peace stole into her heart. Calia realized she'd been clenching her hands, and as she unfolded them, she saw small red crescents where her nails had dug into the flesh of her palm. She took a deep breath and closed her eyes.

This time she did not see the horrors of her escape. Or, more difficult to endure, the sight of her daughter at play. She saw only darkness, tender and soft. It gentled what was too harsh to bear in the full radiance of light. It provided safety for wild creatures and privacy for those who wanted to create, just for a time, a world with only two.

Calia felt Saa'ra's warmth brush her like the stroke of a feather.

Sleep now, brave one. No more battles, no more horrors for you. Only peace and rest.

"Thank you," Calia said, bowing her head. And as she padded back to her room, a hand on her arm, its flesh cool and unnaturally soft, made her pause. It was Elinor, one of the Forsaken priestesses. "Calia?" she said.

Calia wanted nothing more than to sleep. But she had vowed to always be there for those who needed her, and Elinor looked troubled. Her glowing eyes darted about, and her voice was pitched low.

"What is it, Elinor? Is something wrong?"

Elinor shook her head. "No. In fact, something might be going *right* for the first time in a long, long while. May we speak in private?"

"Of course," Calia responded. She brought Elinor into her little alcove, and the two sat down on the bed. Once they were alone, Elinor needed no further urging to speak. The words tumbled from her leathery lips so quickly that Calia had to ask more than once for the Forsaken priestess to repeat herself.

Calia's eyes widened as she listened, and her mind went back to what the naaru had told her: *There are things you must do before that peace will be granted to you. Things that you must understand, that you must integrate into yourself. People who need your help. What one needs in order to heal will always come one's way, but sometimes it is hard to recognize it.*

Calia's eyes filled with tears, and she hugged her friend gently. Her heart felt full and hopeful for the first time since Lordaeron fell. She now had a purpose.

Healing had come her way.

GALLYWIX PLEASURE PALACE, AZSHARA

There were many places in Azeroth where Sylvanas Windrunner would prefer not to be. Gallywix's disgustingly named Pleasure Palace was not at the top of the list, but it was close.

Once Azshara had been a beautiful land, full of open spaces and autumnal hues and opening out to the ocean. Then the goblins had joined the Horde under Garrosh, and they had defaced the region with their trademark garishness. The "palace" where she now sat in an overstuffed chair next to Jastor Gallywix had been hewn from a mountainside. The escarpment of the mountain had been turned into a literal "face" so that Gallywix's grotesque mien leered over the wreckage of the land below.

The palace itself was even uglier, in Sylvanas's opinion. Outside was a vast green lawn with a course for some sort of game involving a small white ball, a huge pool with a heated area, and bartenders and waitresses currently standing idle save for those who attended to Gallywix.

Inside was not much better. Tables groaned with food, much of which would never be eaten, and huge barrels served for decor. Upstairs was the trade prince's bedroom. Sylvanas heard it said that he slept on piles of money, and she was in no hurry to find out if those rumors were true.

He'd been pleased to receive her message and kept offering drinks. She declined each time. While he indulged, she told him of the meeting at Thunder Bluff, omitting the delicate threat she had given Baine, of course. She would give Gallywix only the information he needed to know.

"I trust that their efforts to heal the world will not damage your efforts to gather Azerite," she finished.

Gallywix laughed, ginormous belly jiggling, and sipped his frothy, fruity beverage. "Nah, nah," he assured her, waving a big green hand. "They can have their little ceremonies. My operation is far too vast at this point to be impacted. And hey, if it keeps them happy, that's the point, am I right?"

Sylvanas ignored the comment. "Your operation thus far has not yielded much that I can use," she reminded him.

"Relax," he said, "I got—"

"People on it. Yes, I know."

"No, seriously. I got the best minds I know of in a little place in Tanaris. Gave them a generous dollop of the golden goop. Told 'em to go nuts." He took another swig and smacked his lips.

"And?"

"And they're working on it." His gaze slid to the side.

"What exactly are they working on?"

"I, ah . . . told 'em they could do whatever they want. But you know scientists. They'll think of things you and I could never imagine. Best way to operate."

"I want weapons, Gallywix."

He downed his drink and waved for another. "Sure, sure, they'll have weapons for us."

"I want them to *focus* on weapons. Or else I will send in every Forsaken, blood elf, tauren, troll, orc, and pandaren I can find and take over your 'operation.' Are we clear?"

Sullenly, the trade prince nodded. Doubtless he knew she'd send her own people around to take the weapons that were made, whereas his scientists could craft other items he could sell on the side to make a tidy profit.

A distraction for Gallywix came in the form of a hobgoblin who lumbered into the room and babbled something only his boss understood. "Of course, idiot," the goblin said. "Show Champion Blightcaller in at once!"

Sylvanas thought she was almost as relieved as Gallywix at the interruption. Nathanos entered, gave Gallywix the barest minimum of a nod, and bowed to his queen.

"My lady," he said, "forgive the intrusion, but I thought it best to bring you this missive immediately." He knelt before her and held out a scroll. It was sealed with blue wax and stamped with the head of a lion.

"Oho! I know that seal!" Gallywix exclaimed, then sipped his banana cocktail. Sylvanas knew it, too. She tore her gaze from the scroll and impaled the goblin with a cold stare.

"You will excuse us," she said.

He waited for a moment. When she continued to sit, raising a pale blonde eyebrow, Gallywix made a face and heaved himself out of his chair. "Take your time," he said. "I'll be in the hot tub if you want to join me when you're done with this fella." He waggled his eyebrows, then trundled out. "Heya, honeybunny, bring me a pineapple punch, will ya?"

"Sure, boss!" a squeaky goblin female voice replied.

Nathanos's red eyes were fixed on the trade prince's retreating form. "I will kill him," he said.

"Oh, no. That pleasure will be all mine."

Sylvanas got to her feet and gazed down at the scroll he held. "So. This is from Varian's whelp? Given to you at the Undercity?"

Nathanos's face was unreadable. "Yes. Hand delivered to me by Archbishop Faol. He's now a Forsaken."

Sylvanas let out a short, sharp bark of laughter at that. "His Light works in strange ways."

"So it would seem."

Sylvanas broke the seal and read.

Unto Queen Sylvanas Windrunner, Dark Lady of the Forsaken and Warchief of the Horde, King Anduin Llane Wrynn gives respectful greetings.

I write to you with a proposition that has nothing to do with armies, territories, or goods, but it is one that I believe will serve both the Horde and the Alliance.

I will cut directly to the heart of the matter. When you approached the Alliance, seeking a home for your people, you were refused. We were still reeling in terror from what Arthas had done to Lordaeron and couldn't understand that your Forsaken were truly different.

I have spoken recently with a Forsaken who was greatly respected in life and have learned that despite all he has endured, he still follows the Light. His name is Alonsus Faol, and he was once archbishop of Lordaeron. He has agreed to be a go-between in the interest of helping both the living and the undead.

This missive is about families. Families that were torn apart not by Horde and Alliance but by Arthas, who rained despair and devastation upon all of us. Spouses, children, parents—so many separated, divided first by death, then by fear and anger. Perhaps, if we can work together, those driven apart can at last be reunited.

Sylvanas stiffened. Oh, yes. She, more than anyone, understood about divided families. Slain loved ones. She had lost everything because of Arthas: her friends, her family, her beloved Quel'Thalas. Her *life*. Her ability to care, truly care, truly feel any emotion save hate and anger about those things.

And she had attempted a reunion. Had accepted her older sister's offer to call what Arthas Menethil had left of her family together, to reclaim Windrunner Spire and purge it of the dark things that dwelled in it. And perhaps to purge themselves of their own darknesses by harking back to a time when there were no shadows within them.

But it had been a futile endeavor. Suns and moons they had been when they were young. Bright Alleria, with her gleaming golden tresses, and laughing young Lirath. Sylvanas had been Lady Moon, and Vereesa, the youngest of the three sisters, had been Little Moon.

Vereesa was bowed and sullied with grief for a lost love. The death of her husband, Rhonin, in Theramore, one of so many victims of Garrosh Hellscream's mana bomb, had shattered her. Shattered her so completely that for one lost, lonely, lovely moment, she had turned to her shadow sister, Sylvanas, and they had plotted together. Vereesa had come so close to joining Sylvanas in the Undercity.

So close to joining her in undeath.

But at the last minute, love for her living children had eclipsed Little Moon's grief for her dead husband. And so Vereesa had stayed with the Alliance. And Alleria, thought lost for so long and then miraculously returned, had invited the unfathomable darkness of the Void within her. It granted her powers and strength. But it changed what she looked like as well as who she was—who she was becoming. Sylvanas knew enough of what such powers could do to recognize the mark of cold fingers on Alleria.

As for her own shadows and darkness, Sylvanas knew them well enough not to examine them now.

The boy king's plan was a foolish one. He still believed that people could change. Oh, they certainly could. Alleria, Sylvanas, and Vereesa were all proof.

But it was not change for the better; at least, Anduin would not see it that way.

Why was she so angry? The pup got under her skin so much more than the Wolf had.

She returned her attention to the letter.

We are not currently at war. But I am not so naive as to believe that means hostilities do not still linger. We have experienced recent tumultuous change to our very world in the form of Azerite—a manifestation of the pain Azeroth herself is feeling. With unity, we could direct our exploration of this substance in ways that can save her. Let us therefore focus on a smaller but no less important gesture of unity as a first step toward a potential future that benefits both the Horde and the Alliance.

I propose what amounts to a single day of a cease-fire. On this day, those families who have been divided by war and death will have a chance to meet with the ones they lost. Participation will be strictly voluntary. All those on the Alliance side will be thoroughly vetted, and no one who I believe would be a danger to the Forsaken will be allowed. I would ask the same of you. We will determine a limited number of participants.

A site suitable for this event is the Arathi Highlands. I will have my people assemble at the ancient fortress of Stromgarde Keep. Thoradin's Wall is close to a Horde outpost. There, in the open field, with sufficient protection as agreed upon by the two of us as leaders of human and Forsaken, these ruptured families will meet. It will last from dawn until dusk. With your agreement, Archbishop Faol and other priests will facilitate, assist, and offer comfort as needed.

Should any harm befall my people, be certain I will not hesitate to retaliate in kind.

I also understand that should my people harm any Forsaken, you will do likewise.

As a priest, as king of Stormwind, and as the son of Varian Wrynn, I will guarantee safe passage to the Forsaken who choose to be involved. If this cease-fire is successful, it could be repeated.

Do not mistake this for an offer of peace. It is only an offer of a single day's compassion for people who were cruelly torn apart by a force that was neither the Horde nor the Alliance.

You and I have both lost family, Warchief. Let us not force that upon others who, like us, did not choose it.

Done this day by my hand,

KING ANDUIN LLANE WRYNN

"He is even more foolish than I thought if he believes I do not see right through his trap," Sylvanas said, crumpling the letter into a ball. "What do you think of this Archbishop Faol who gave you the letter?"

"He is indeed Forsaken. He seems genuine, though when I suggested he pledge fealty to you and the Horde, he demurred. He said he preferred to serve the Light rather than kings or queens."

"Ha!" Sylvanas said without humor. "I liberated him to be a Forsaken so that he could have free will, and thus am I repaid. No matter. I take it you believe he is harmless."

"He is powerful, Dark Lady. But he is no enemy. He also brought a letter for the head of the Desolate Council."

Sylvanas tensed. "I see that the king's spies are hard at work if Wrynn knows of the council." Wrynn. For so long it had meant Varian. Strange.

"Possibly. We must remember that many of our number move freely in the Netherlight Temple. Besides, the letter he sent to her did not even mention the council. It turns out that until very recently, Elsie herself was among the number of Forsaken who had living family. Her husband, Wyll Benton, served both Varian and Anduin Wrynn."

"Elsie?"

"It was the name Wyll had for Vellcinda, and she's reclaimed it now," Nathanos explained.

The majority of Forsaken had taken new given names or surnames for themselves. They did so to mark their rebirth as Forsaken, to cast aside their old identities and bind themselves together as a unified group. Sylvanas was surprised to find that her chest ached to hear that Vellcinda had rejected her Forsaken name. "Vellcinda" was a name with dignity, gravitas. "Elsie" was ... well, evocative of what the woman had been in life, most likely. Common and ordinary. And *human.*

Sylvanas focused on the other piece of information her champion had given her. This plan of Anduin's seemed suddenly much less strategic than personal if he had lost a devoted servant. Which made it much less threatening. Even so—

"Vellcinda likely served the royal family as well." Sylvanas would not dignify the Prime Governor's new, offensive name by utilizing it.

"Yes. She worked in the kitchens," Nathanos continued. "She was saddened to hear of her husband's passing. This proposition meets with her approval, as she believes that she is far from alone in retaining fond memories of family members."

Sylvanas shook her head. "This cease-fire is a mistake. It will only lead to pain for my people. They *cannot* be human, and to dangle this temptation of reunion with loved ones will result in them growing discontented with who they really are—Forsaken. They will deteriorate to heartbroken shells, wanting something they can never have. I have no wish to see them suffer so." Again, she thought of her own attempt at connection with the living and how all it had done was stir up old ghosts best left resting in peace.

"You could use this to your advantage," Nathanos said. "Vellcinda said that many Forsaken wish their next death to be their Last Death. They do not wish to keep existing. And one reason commonly cited is that they want to be with those they loved while they lived."

Sylvanas turned her head to him slowly, considering his words.

"If you authorize this experience—this reconnection with people they loved in life—and present it to them as something that *you* have generously granted them, perhaps they will be more amenable to accepting your solution: finding ways to keep the Forsaken as a race from going extinct."

"It is fraternizing with the enemy," Sylvanas said. "Letting them interact with life and the living."

"Perhaps. But even so, it is only for a single day. Give them this hope, this moment with people they thought they'd never see again. Then—"

"Then I hold the power to their happiness, at least in this aspect," she finished. "Or they might decide they hate the living and be all the more devoted to their Dark Lady." Either way Sylvanas would win.

He nodded. "At the very least, it will demonstrate to them that you are listening to their concerns. I truly believe the Desolate Council to be ultimately harmless. They're not radical traitors. Give them this chance, once. If you see benefits, you can determine if you wish to repeat it."

"You make a good argument." She unfolded the crumpled missive and read it again. "It will be difficult for my archers to stay their hands with so many humans in front of them."

"They will obey you, my queen," Nathanos said. It was the truth. Her dark rangers would never loose an arrow without her orders. And Sylvanas was not ready for a war with the Alliance, not over this, at least.

She made her decision. "I will accept this invitation on behalf of the Forsaken. Return to the Undercity. Inform Vellcinda Benton that her queen is sympathetic toward her desire and will be visiting her to discuss this gathering in more detail. Have her begin compiling a list of those members of the council who have living relatives in Storm-wind. Get their names and information. I will give that list to Anduin so that he can locate them and determine if they, too, wish to partici-pate."

"There are more than just the council members who would like to be involved," Nathanos said. "A great many attended the memorial service and are sympathetic to them."

But Sylvanas shook her head. "No. This needs to be a small number so I can control the situation. Council members only."

"As my queen wishes. If I may speak freely, I believe you have made a wise decision. From all that I have seen, I believe this will quell any rumblings of discontent."

"One way or another it will." She smiled coldly. "It could also pave the way for claiming Stormwind. I had thought that an attack would be the only means to take it. But if the young king trusts us, we could one day soon pass through those magnificent gates to a friendly wel-come."

Her thoughts once again went to the astonishing substance that was Azerite. What it could do. What it could create.

What it could destroy.

CHAPTER TWENTY-ONE

Tanaris

Shortly after Saffy had agreed ("of your own free will, now," Grizzek had emphasized) to assist him in plumbing the potential of the magical, marvelous, miraculous Azerite, Gallywix had sent them a single large vat of the stuff along with a note: *You two creative kids go crazy!*

The first experiments had covered the basic steps: identifying the material's properties, testing it under various conditions. Exposed to sunlight and moonlight. Sealed away, exposed to air. Immersed in various liquids, including acid and other highly dangerous chemicals. That had been Grizzek's favorite part so far.

During one such experiment, Saffy noticed that the thick, tarlike substance of a deadly poison they'd smeared on a sample chunk had changed color.

"Will you look at that," she said. Quickly she grabbed a vial of the antidote and set it down within easy reach. Then, before Grizzek could even yelp in surprise, she'd extended a hand and touched the discolored poison.

"Saffy, no!" He surged forward and grabbed her arm with one hand and the antidote with the other.

"Hang on a minute," Saffy said. "This stuff should be eating my skin away by now. But look. I'm fine."

They both stared at the poison on her hand, then at each other. "Nothing ventured, nothing gained," Saffy muttered. And she licked the stuff off her fingers.

Grizzek uttered a strangled cry. Saffy smacked her lips. "Astounding! This highly poisonous, corrosive substance now tastes like sunfruit and cherries," she said.

"Maybe it always tasted like that," Grizzek offered. His voice trembled a little.

"No, it's supposed to be completely tasteless."

"Yeah, whatever, just . . . just don't *do* stuff like that, Saffy, okay?" She looked at him and saw that he had gone pale. He had been worried about her. Not just worried as in *oh, I'm going to lose my lab partner* worried but worried as in . . .

Saffy couldn't let herself think about that. They had work to do. Bringing old feelings back would only be a distraction. They'd always done better as lab partners, anyway.

She returned her attention to her hand. "This is . . . important, Grizzy. Really important. Long term, who knows what this stuff can do? We've just seen that it can neutralize poison. Bet it can heal wounds, too. Maybe it can extend life." She shook her head in disbelief. "What a gift! Come on, back at it! There's so much else we need to know!"

After they'd done everything they could to test Azerite in liquid form, next up were tests to determine if, once it had hardened, anything could break it.

Nothing could.

Not a sword, or a hammer, or a goblin shredder, or even a device Grizzek had named the Crunchola, which he demonstrated to Saffy. It was a modified shredder, but one of its mechanically operated limbs was outfitted with a grasping hand augmented by an energy beam.

"The idea," Grizzek explained, "is that the energy pulse increases the pressure, so it's seven times as strong as the usual hand."

"That's an odd number," Saffy observed, perplexed.

"It is!"

It took her a second, then she said flatly, "I meant odd as in unusual. Why not ten or fifteen?"

He shrugged. "Seven is supposed to be lucky."

She rolled her eyes. They scooped out a pail of liquid Azerite from the tightly sealed vat Gallywix had provided and placed it to harden in the open air. The substance slipped out easily once it set and was surprisingly light. The Crunchola, or "Crunchy," as Grizzek, who seemed inexplicably fond of the thing, dubbed it, grasped the chunk of Azerite in its Lucky Seven energy-enhanced hand. Grizzek threw the switch. The Crunchola squeezed—tight—tighter—

And then Grizzek shrieked in dismay as its four digits snapped. "Your hand!" he cried. "Crunchy, I'm so sorry!"

Saffy looked at her notes and crossed off "TEST NUMBER 345: Crunchola" and wrote down "Azerite 1, Crunchola 0."

"One resource we do lack is a mage," Saffy commented, peering at the unharmed, pail-shaped Azerite. "It would be fascinating to see how this is affected by magic!"

"If you really want one to join us, I can ask Gallywix." Grizzek didn't sound so keen on it, and Saffy stiffened at the thought.

"Maybe later. Right now we have a good rhythm going with just the two of us." She was surprised that she was saying it, but it was undeniably true. The thought of a third party entering their lab felt wrong somehow.

Grizzek seemed to brighten at her words. "Yeah, we do," he said. He climbed out of the Crunchola, patting its arm sadly. "I'll fix you up, buddy," he promised. Then he took a deep breath and turned to Saffy.

"Magic can be phase two," Grizzek said. "Let's exhaust our own resources and imagination first. Give Gally-boy a baseline for what we can do with pure science."

Saffy giggled. "Gally-boy?"

Grizzek scratched his enormous nose and chuckled a little bit. "Yeah," he said. "Silly, but the guy bugs me so bad."

"I think it's perfect," Saffy announced. Their eyes met, and Grizzek's expression was unguarded.

"Ya do?" he asked, surprised.

"Yep," she replied. "Pompous airbags sometimes need the occasional sharp poke. Deflation is better than exploding."

"For him or for us?"

"Oh, for him, definitely. I don't care if he explodes."

They laughed together, just as they had in the old days, in that narrow band where everything had been perfect and they'd been crazy *about* each other instead of being driven crazy *by* each other.

Watch out, Saffy, the gnome reminded herself. *Don't jinx this. It's all going too well for things to turn bad.*

"We've gathered a good baseline on the nature of the substance in isolation," she said. "I'll compile my notes, and then we can move on to see what happens when we try to shape it, or manipulate it, or combine it with other items."

"Oooh! We should do wearable items."

"Like rings or necklaces?"

"Yeah! Gally-boy inadvertently gave me the idea. He used the first known chunk of this stuff as an ornament for his cane. We can experiment with it and figure out how to make amulets, rings, and other trinkets with it. Think we can mix it with other metals?"

"We'll find out!" That was her specialty. "But first I better compile these notes."

But Grizzek was shaking his head. "Nope. Those can wait. Go outside, clear your head."

"I never go outside."

"I know. But you oughta. Moons'll be out here soon. Go on, scram. I'll handle dinner." It was not said unkindly.

"Do you still burn things down when you cook?" she asked.

"Not so much these days." He made a shooing motion. With a shrug, Saffy ambled out to the beach. She was not alone, of course; Gallywix's goons were stationed all around the enclave and even patrolled the beaches. But they kept their distance and didn't bother her or Grizzek too much.

He'd put out a chair, and there was a table. An umbrella was up as well, not that one needed it at this hour. As Saffy settled into the chair, she had to admit that the sky was absolutely glorious and the moonslight on the ocean was astonishingly soothing.

Saffy usually took a while to wind down when her brain was percolating briskly. She heard the noise of something clattering behind her and turned to see Grizzek balancing a tray in one hand and lugging a chair with the other. He didn't say anything as he plunked the tray down on the table and pulled up the chair.

"Wine," Saffy said, startled. "You poured wine."

"Yeah," he grunted. "Had a bottle somewhere. Knew you liked the stuff."

He hadn't really cooked, which was probably why the place was still standing. He'd just reheated some seafood stew she'd made for lunch and grabbed some bread. They ate in silence, listening to the sound of the sea. Saffy was thinking very, very hard, and not about Azerite, though that did want to sneak in around the corners of her pondering.

"Grizzek," she said.

"Yeah?"

"When I first came here, you called me by my nickname." One of them, at least; they'd had several of them over the sliver of time when things were going well.

Their marriage had been, well, as short as they were. They had been lab partners first, and that had gone well, but then they'd been stupid enough to fall in love with each other. The first month had been glorious, the very epitome of a great love story. And then it had fallen apart just like one of Grizzek's faulty and poorly designed contraptions. Suddenly everything one did irritated the other beyond tolerance. Many things got thrown or broken, and once Saffy had found herself shouting so loudly that she lost her voice. That had been a horrible day. Grizzek had felt free to taunt her, and she couldn't shoot back a pithy retort.

But not even the unpleasantness of that dreadful time seemed to encroach on their collaboration now. They worked together almost seamlessly, listening to what the other said, offering suggestions, forming a true partnership. Saffy was loath to admit it, but the last few weeks working alongside Grizzek had been pretty good. Wonderful, actually. That in itself was almost as unbelievable as the strange material she and her former husband had been working with.

She heard him sniffing and clearing his throat. "Yeah," he said. "I guess I did call you Punkin. Sorry, I guess."

Saffy sipped her wine and thought some more. "It's been good, these past few weeks."

"Yeah, it has."

"It reminds me of old times," she said cautiously.

"Me, too," he said quietly.

She wanted to ask a thousand questions. *Do you still miss me? Why do you think we don't hate each other anymore? Is the Azerite affecting how we feel about each other? Can we only be all right when we're working? Would it be a mistake to try again?*

Instead, she said, "This Azerite . . . it's pretty amazing. Could help a lot of people."

"You're a genius, Saffy. An absolute genius. You're going to make such things—"

"And you, Grizzy," Saffy said enthusiastically. "Your robots, and your launchers, and those little one-person airships—the Azerite's going to help with all that, too!"

"Ya think so?"

"I *know* so!"

"Saffy, we're going to make this world sit up and take notice, you and me. The sky's the limit."

Slowly, her heart beating as fast as a rabbit's, Sapphronetta Flivvers slid her hand across the table. And felt Grizzek's big green callused paw close around it. Gently, protectively, as if it was the most precious thing in the world.

And Saffy smiled.

In between kisses and canoodling, the reunited, reinvolved pair got a staggering amount of research done. They mixed the Azerite with a variety of different metals and even used it as paint. They made pendants, rings, bracelets, and earrings. And they made armor. It was ugly, goblin-designed stuff, but it wasn't meant to be pretty. It survived three solid minutes of bombardment from the reconstructed Lightning Blast 3000. The only damage was a slight melting of the metal.

All of this had required only a small amount of Azerite.

Then Saffy decided to go full gnomish alchemist. She began to experiment with potions. With a single drop of one on Grizzy's completely smooth green pate, he grew a luxurious mane of thick, glossy black hair that flowed down his back.

"Aaaah!" he yelped. "Cut it off, cut it off!"

When a drop of poison was mixed with heated Azerite, a result similar to the earlier experiment in which Saffy had licked off poison was achieved. When she poured the mixture on a struggling plant, the palm tree doubled in size.

"That's a high ratio of Azerite to poison," she mused. "Let's see what happens when we switch the proportions."

"Careful there, Punkin," Grizzek said worriedly. "I only just found ya again."

Saffy's heart warmed, turned over in her chest, and turned to mush. Figuratively, of course. She went over and kissed him soundly. "I'll take every precaution and then some."

He hovered anxiously as she prepared the poison, then offered to be the one to mix it with the Azerite. "Oh, Grizzy, you're so sweet! But you don't know exactly how much I used."

Sticking out her tongue in order to concentrate better, Saffy poured the precise amount of Azerite into the beaker of poison. There was no visible change to the substance as she swirled it gently to mix the contents. Then she took a deep breath and poured a single drop on the plant.

The reaction was immediate.

The plant went from the almost absurdly healthy, vibrant emerald green color to first sickly yellow, then black. It drooped, completely dead.

They stared at it, then at each other. They said nothing. Saffy tried it on another plant. But this time, before the poison's effects had visually manifested, she clipped a segment. The pair of scientists pressed their heads close together as they watched the section rot right before their eyes, as if every fragment that made up the plant had been targeted instantly.

Saffy spoke first. "Let's increase the amount of Azerite."

As she was doing so, Feathers flew into the room and circled their heads. "Big ugly guests! Big ugly guests!" it squawked.

They looked at each other, wide-eyed. "I hope it's not Gallywix," Grizzek muttered. "Hopefully it's just the goons. I'll get rid of 'em. Be right back."

Saffy's eyes followed him as he left. She had never before regarded "just the goons" as a hopeful phrase, but the alternative would be far worse. They weren't prepared to demonstrate anything to the leader of the Bilgewater Cartel goblins yet, and to say that what they'd just witnessed made her uneasy was as much of an understatement as saying the Sword of Sargeras was a knife stuck in the ground.

She took a moment to jot down her notes, cataloging the precise ratios, then doubled the amount of Azerite in the deadly mixture. She'd just poured a dollop onto another plant with almost identical results when Grizzek returned. His normally healthy emerald green coloring had paled to a sickly chartreuse.

"You don't look good, Grizzy," Saffy murmured.

"Well," he said heavily, "I got good news, and I got bad news. The good news is that that was indeed just the goons."

Saffy let out a breath she hadn't realized she'd been holding. "Thank goodness for small favors," she said.

"Bad news is Gallywix wants a demonstration in two weeks. And," Grizzek added heavily, "he wants us to focus on weapons."

CHAPTER TWENTY-TWO

The Undercity

Parqual Fintallas stood with the other members of the Desolate Council for what, he hoped, would be its most productive meeting yet. This time, he stood a step lower than he usually did, as did all the members.

The Prime Governor herself stood not on the topmost stair but one step below it. This time, someone else—someone who should have been at every single meeting of the council—would finally be present and occupying that place. Archbishop Faol, who had become a regular at the Undercity over the last few weeks, stood beside Elsie. They put their heads together and talked quietly.

The room was filled to capacity. Those who drew breath doubtless would have difficulty doing so in this room; Parqual was well aware that although some of the Forsaken had dried out rather than decayed, most of their number had been raised while they rotted, and the smell could not be a pleasant one.

Elsie was smiling. So were most of those assembled. They were excited to be present for this meeting. Parqual was glad, too, but was not as hopeful as they were about the end results. He and a few others wanted to move much faster than patient, forgiving Elsie did. He did not expect Sylvanas to move at a rapid pace, but he was willing to listen to what she had to say.

All at once, the room went quiet. Parqual turned and saw the figure of Nathanos Blightcaller standing in the doorway at the end of the long corridor that led into the large room.

Nathanos waited for a moment, then announced: "Queen Sylvanas Windrunner, warchief of the Horde and beloved Dark Lady of the Forsaken, has arrived."

A cheer arose. Not as lively as an orc's bellow or as sweet as a hurrah from a blood elf, but as genuine as it could possibly be coming from dead throats. And then *she* was there.

Even here, in the safest place in the world for her, Sylvanas Windrunner had chosen not to shed her armor, Parqual mused. Did she simply never remove it?

She stood straight and tall, unlike so many of those who adored her. Beautiful still, whereas they had been ravaged by death and rebirth. Then she inclined her head in acceptance of their adoration and strode with a smooth, elegant gait toward her place as queen of the Forsaken.

"I have missed this place," she said as she looked around fondly, nodding to a few individuals she recognized. "And I have missed you, my people. The orcs, blood elves, trolls, tauren, goblins, and pandaren are worthy and loyal members of the Horde, but they do not have the unique bond that you, the Forsaken, and I do."

There was a rumble of appreciation for the acknowledgment. With other races, it would be applause and stamping of feet. The Forsaken, however, had learned it wasn't wise to unduly wear out their appendages prematurely with such gestures. Clapping was terrible for the hands.

Sylvanas looked down at Elsie. "Prime Governor. I hear from my loyal Nathanos that you have taken good care of my realm in my absence."

Elsie inclined her head and bowed as deeply as she could. "Only because you were absent, my queen. We are dearly glad that you have come back."

"Only for a few hours, unfortunately," Sylvanas said. The regret in her voice sounded sincere. "But in that time, I hope I will be able to settle some things that will please everyone here." She looked out again at all of them.

"I understand that the Prime Governor has also received a letter from the king of Stormwind. He proposes a day's cease-fire in the Arathi Highlands in order to hold a gathering of Forsaken and humans. Families or friends who have been separated by the slaughter that took place in this city only a few years past."

Sylvanas turned her crimson gaze to Archbishop Faol. "Archbishop Faol has been speaking both to him and to the Desolate Council. What are your thoughts on this, Archbishop?"

Faol didn't reply at once. He looked out at the gathered crowd, then back at Sylvanas. "You can trust King Anduin, Your Majesty. He means no ill. I know from my conversations with the Prime Governor and others in the Undercity that all those here today—and more than a few Forsaken who could not be present—are in favor of this gathering. It remains to be seen if the human half of this plan is also amenable. If they are, I and another priest from the Conclave would be honored to supervise the event."

Excited murmuring swept through the hall. The Dark Lady paced back and forth for a moment, considering. *Or pretending to consider,* Parqual thought. *She already knows what she will do. This moment is for our benefit.*

Finally, she stopped and faced the throng. "I will permit this."

A cheer went up. Not a murmuring of approval but a genuine cheer, even louder than the one that had greeted the Dark Lady. Sylvanas let her lips curve in a faint smile, then lifted her hand, calling for silence.

"But I must above all ensure the safety of my beloved Forsaken," she said. "So here is what I will say to the king when I reply. Each member of the Desolate Council will submit five names, in order of preference, of people in Stormwind they would like to meet. If these individuals are still alive, they will be contacted and asked if they wish to participate. The king and a priest selected by the good archbishop will permit only those whom they deem sincere to attend. I will tell him that his people may assemble at Stromgarde Keep. On the selected date, we will fly to Thoradin's Wall before dawn. Champion

Blightcaller, I, and two hundred of my finest archers will be there . . . in case the human king decides to betray our trust."

It was possible. It was unlikely from this king if half the things Parqual had heard about him were true, but it was indeed possible. And he had to admit Sylvanas's words were a comfort.

"Twenty-five priests will be mounted on bats and actively patrolling the field. In case of an open attack, teams of my dark rangers and others will be sent to defend you. I will allow the king to field a similar number of priest defenders, although I do not expect any member of the council to initiate hostilities."

It was a lot to protect twenty-two Forsaken. But Parqual was highly aware of the significance of this meeting, as, clearly, were Anduin and Sylvanas.

"At sunrise, you will walk forward to a halfway point that will be marked by Horde and Alliance banners. Archbishop Faol and his assistant will meet you there. As will your Alliance counterparts."

Parqual had thought he had passed beyond the ability of such things to cause deep emotion, but apparently not.

Philia. Would they be able to find her? Would she want to come? What would she think if she did? He was suddenly acutely aware of how bent and twisted his body was, of flesh that stank, hanging off exposed bones. Would she be horrified?

No. Now that the possibility was manifesting, he realized he had wronged her by fearing her revulsion. Not his Philia. He was quietly certain of that. If his heart could still beat, it would be racing with excitement. He felt a gentle touch on his right shoulder and turned to Elsie. She was smiling for him. *Oh, Elsie, if only your Wyll had lived just a little bit longer.*

But Sylvanas, apparently unaware of how profoundly her words had affected him and others, continued. "All participants will be allowed to remain on the field until dusk. At that time, you will return to the wall, and the humans to Stromgarde Keep."

She paused, again scanning the crowd. "Obviously, what I have just said assumes that everything goes smoothly. There is a chance that it will not. If I perceive any kind of danger to you, my people, I shall *immediately* order a retreat. A Forsaken flag—not a Horde one—will fly on the ramparts of the wall, and the horn will sound. If the Alliance decides to order a retreat, the same thing will happen, except they will fly the Stormwind flag on Stromgarde Keep and sound their own horn. If either horn is sounded, you must turn around and *return to the wall at once*."

Her voice cracked like a whip and echoed in the vast chamber. The effect was chilling, and the crowd was utterly silent.

"Now, then. Are there any questions?"

Parqual steadied himself and raised his hand. The glowing red gaze fell upon him. "Speak," Sylvanas said.

"Will we be allowed to exchange anything?"

"Exchanges of trinkets will be permitted in the following manner," Sylvanas said. "Prior to the event, anything you wish to give to your counterparts will be examined. There will be areas on the field where they may be placed on tables when you reach the meeting site. The Alliance will do the same. Do not touch anything they have left on the tables while you are on the field. At the end of the day, these items will be collected and gone through to ensure they are safe and contain nothing seditious. They will be distributed to you at a later date. The Alliance will, I hope, do the same with your gifts."

"Our Dark Lady is most generous," Parqual said.

Sylvanas inclined her head. "I take it you have an item you wish to share."

"I do." He thought fondly of a toy Philia once had loved. She had left it behind when—

"Then it is my sincere hope that the Alliance does not decide to throw it away," Sylvanas said in that soft, purring voice. It was a cruel thought, and Parqual did not like to entertain it.

"Any other questions?"

Another hand was raised. "May we touch them? Our loved ones?"

"You may," Sylvanas replied. "Although I cannot guarantee that such a touch would be welcome."

Again, an unkind thought. Doubt stirred in Parqual's mind, but he forced it back. Not his Philia. He had hoped hearing from his leader would make him feel better, but instead, he felt unsettled and un-happy. Others seemed to feel that way, too. And then he understood.

Sylvanas didn't want them to do this, but she couldn't come out and simply forbid it. There were too many of them. Their ideas were spreading. Even people like Elsie, who were completely loyal to the Dark Lady, who loved her . . . even Elsie wanted to take the Forsaken in a different direction. So Sylvanas was doing what she could to rob them of any little pleasure in the planning.

Suddenly he saw his "queen" in a new light. He saw many, many things in a new light.

As if reading his mind, Sylvanas said, "I realize I do not sound optimistic. That is because I am not. I confess to you now, I wish you would not do this. Not because I would deny you any joy but because I would not see you hurt. You are ready to embrace your living relatives. But do they feel the same? What will you do if they do not wish to see you? If they think you abominations, monstrosities instead of the remarkable, courageous Forsaken that you are? If I am cruel, it is only to be compassionate."

"Everyone knows that, my lady!" Elsie exclaimed.

"Thank you, Prime Governor," Sylvanas said. "Are there any more questions?"

There had to be. But no one was daring to ask them, and Parqual thought he had drawn enough attention to himself.

"If there are not, Prime Governor, I have some for you. Will you join me later to discuss them?"

"As my queen wishes," Elsie said. She turned to the crowd. "Everyone, I hope you share my pleasure and anticipation of the coming reunion with our loved ones. I would like to thank Warchief Sylvanas again for permitting this to happen. It is my fondest wish in the world that this goes smoothly so that we may see our friends and families more in our future. For the Dark Lady!"

Another cheer went up, and Sylvanas smiled fleetingly, then stepped down off the dais. The crowd of Forsaken parted for her. The cheering continued until Sylvanas, flanked by two dark rangers, disappeared into the corridor.

Parqual turned to Elsie. "You seem a little melancholy," he said. "I thought you would be happy."

"Oh! Oh, yes, I am. I do admit I'm feeling just a bit sorry for myself, though. I wish I'd been able to see my Wyll. To show him that after all this time I still have my wedding ring."

Surprised, Parqual glanced down at her hand. She chuckled. "Oh, no, of course it doesn't fit on my finger anymore. My hands are too bony, and I wouldn't want to risk losing it. But it's safe and sound in my room at the inn nonetheless."

He thought of Philia. "Elsie, I'm so sorry," he said.

She waved a hand. "Don't you worry about me. I've had more luck and love than most. Wyll's legacy will be that many others are going to be able to experience something wonderful thanks to him. It's all right if we two didn't get to have it. One can't have everything."

She leaned in conspiratorially to Parqual and whispered, "Even so, I'm going to loop the ring on a chain and wear it to the gathering."

"Somehow I think he'll know," Parqual said, and meant it.

CHAPTER TWENTY-THREE

Stormwind

Anduin had frankly expected either an immediate refusal from Sylvanas or a dragged-out back-and-forth communication chain. To his pleasure—and surprise—the Horde leader had replied promptly that she was indeed interested in supporting his proposal. *But*, Sylvanas had written, *we will start with a small, well-vetted group. I will not risk tempting the less noble among your people to assassination.*

There was a second letter, too. This one had cemented the rightness of his decision in his mind—and touched his heart as well.

Dear King Anduin,

> *Thank you for taking the time to write so kind a note informing me of my dear Wyll's passing. He was terribly fond of your family, and it pleases me to know that the boy he took care of became the man who comforted him as he left this world.*

> *We all will die eventually, even we Forsaken. It moves me more than you might imagine to know his last thoughts were of me. He has never been far from mine.*

> *Archbishop Faol has been a very kind presence here, and I write*

today not only to thank you but to let you know that all twenty-two members of the Desolate Council gladly accept your offer to meet with our loved ones who yet breathe—if they want to meet with us.

Our beloved Dark Lady has asked each member of the council for five names to submit to you. This way, if one person is no longer living or doesn't wish to attend, there are other options for reunions.

As for me, I've no one left that I know of to meet during this gathering of the living and the undead. Wyll and I weren't young when death parted us, and most of our connections were with the royal families and servants.

If pressed, I would say I should very much like to meet you to express my gratitude in person, but I would understand that such a thing would be far too risky for you. Even suggesting this gathering shows much courage, and I commend you.

Know that your letter is now one of my most cherished belongings, such as they are, second only to the wedding ring Wyll gave me so long ago, when we were both young and happy and the world was full of hope.

Thank you for making it full of hope once again, if only for a single day.

With respect,

ELSIE BENTON

Anduin felt himself smiling. It faded as he mentally acknowledged that there were others who, though they would certainly be surprised by the pair of responses, would not be at all pleased.

A knock on the door brought him out of his reverie. "Come in," he called. He braced himself for another scolding from one of his advisers but was surprised when the guard opened the door and Calia Menethil entered.

He rose and went to her. "Calia," he exclaimed, "it's good to see you. To what do I owe this unexpected pleasure?" He had been working at a table and now pulled up a second chair for his guest.

She slipped into the proffered seat. "I reached out to Laurena. I was worried about your friend. I'm so sorry, Anduin." Her eyes, the same sea-blue that Anduin had seen in old paintings of Arthas, were filled with sympathy. "I understand that Wyll asked you not to heal him. As a priest, I know how hard a request that is to honor. Especially when it's someone you love."

"Thank you. Wyll was such a constant presence in my life—and in my father's, too. I'm ashamed I knew so little about him personally. To me, he was just . . . Wyll." Anduin paused. "You've been with the dying, Calia. You know that sometimes when people pass, they believe they see their loved ones."

She nodded her golden head. "Yes. It happens frequently."

"In his last moments, Wyll was searching for his wife, Elsie." He looked at her intensely. "She was at Lordaeron."

Calia inhaled swiftly. "Oh," she said. "And now you're even more determined to make this gathering happen."

"I'm absolutely committed to it. My advisers were . . . not exactly happy with the idea, but it's going to happen." He held up both letters. "Two letters. One is from the warchief herself. She's accepted."

Calia's face melted into a smile. "Oh, Anduin, I'm so glad! And the second?"

"From Elsie Benton. The head of the Undercity's Desolate Council. She was Wyll's wife. And she wants this meeting, too."

Suddenly Calia was up out of the chair and throwing her arms around him, laughing delightedly. He laughed a little, too, the first laughter that had passed his lips since Wyll's death. He hugged her back. Calia was close to Jaina's age, a little bit older. He had missed his "aunt," and was glad to have found someone similar in Calia.

She drew back, suddenly realizing what she'd done. "My apologies, Your Majesty. I was just so pleased—"

"No apology needed. It's good to have someone who . . . well, who's similar to me in some ways. We both grew up royal children, and we both were called by the Light to become priests. If Moira were to drop in now, we could form a club."

Anduin regretted mentioning Calia's former life almost at once. She stiffened and looked down. It was clearly still something she didn't wish to discuss. Before the moment grew awkward, he spoke again, changing the subject.

"Sylvanas sent along a list of names gathered from all the members of the Desolate Council. I'm wondering: Would you like to assist me when I interview these people?"

They both knew, but Anduin did not say, that she would be of particular help because she might remember some of the Desolate Council from their time as living beings. And she also might recognize some of the names on the council's list.

She nodded. "Of course. I'll be happy to."

"Before we get started on the interviews, there's someone I think we should meet," he told Calia. "He'll be here this afternoon."

"Oh? Who?"

"Someone who, I hope, will give us a feel for how the others might respond. Let's call it testing the waters."

Fredrik Farley was used to providing food, beverages, and entertainment for a crowded inn. He also was used to subsequently breaking up the brawls that often resulted from the combination. He'd cleaned up blood a time or two and had had to expel a few too-rowdy individuals from the Lion's Pride Inn, but mostly he simply made people happy. His patrons, be they locals or those just passing through, came to sing songs, tell tales, or sit by the fire with a mug of ale. Sometimes they poured their hearts out to him or his wife, Verina, as they offered a sympathetic ear.

What Fredrik Farley was *not* used to was appearing before the king of Stormwind.

His first reaction when presented with the summons was terror. He and his wife took pains to run an aboveboard inn at the Lion's Pride. It had been in the Farley family for years and had offered brews to thirsty visitors since King Llane's time. Had someone lodged a complaint because of a recent scuffle? Accused them of watering the beer?

"Young King Anduin has a kind reputation," Verina had said, trying to bolster them both. "I can't imagine him throwing you in the stocks or closing our public house. Maybe he wants to talk to you about a private party."

Fredrik loved Verina, had since they were both in their early twenties. And now he loved her more than ever. "I think if King Anduin Wrynn wanted to host a party, he's got a lovely keep to do it in," he said, kissing her forehead lightly. "But who knows, right?"

The letter the courier presented to him referenced "a personal matter" and asked for him to come "at his earliest convenience." That, of course, meant reaching for his coat and hat after the quick conversation with his wife and accompanying the courier back to Stormwind Keep.

He was escorted to the Petitioner's Chamber. It was a large, austere room. Lit by lamps and candles, it included an area with a thick, richly embroidered rug and a few benches as well as a small table with four chairs in the center. A nobleman with an elegantly trimmed beard and two long, graying braids of hair greeted him, introducing himself as Count Remington Ridgewell. Fredrik was invited to take a seat.

"No, thank you, my lord—er—Count," he stammered. How did one address a count, anyway? "I prefer to stand if it please you," he said.

"It matters not at all to me," the count said. He stepped back a few paces and clasped his hands behind his back, waiting.

Fredrik removed his cap and held it, now and then nervously running a hand over his bald pate. He expected to be kept waiting for a while. Kings, he supposed, had quite a lot of things they needed to do in a day. He looked about the great chamber. *So big! I could fit the entirety of the Lion's Pride in here with room to spare,* he mused.

"Am I addressing the innkeeper Fredrik Farley?" came a pleasant, youthful-sounding voice.

Fredrik turned, expecting to see a squire, and instead found himself face to face with King Anduin Wrynn. But the ruler of Stormwind was not alone. An older woman stood beside the king, dressed in a flowing white robe. And slightly behind him was a muscular older man with white hair, a neatly trimmed beard, and piercing blue eyes.

"Your Majesty!" Fredrik said, his voice climbing with surprise. "Your pardon—I wasn't—"

He's so young, Fredrik thought. *My Anna is older than he is. I hadn't realized that . . .*

The startlingly young king smiled easily and indicated a chair. "Please, do sit. Thank you for coming."

Fredrik edged toward the chair and sank down, still holding his hat. The king sat down across from him, and the priestess and the older man who had accompanied him did likewise. King Anduin folded his hands and regarded Fredrik steadily but kindly. The older man crossed his arms and leaned back in his seat. In contrast to the king and the priestess, he looked almost angry. Fredrik thought him familiar-looking but couldn't place him.

"I'm sorry for the mystery of all this, but it's a bit of a delicate matter, and I wanted to speak with you myself."

Fredrik knew his eyes were as big as eggs at that point, but he was utterly unable to do anything about it. He gulped. Anduin waved to the attendant nobleman. "Wine for Mr. Farley, please, Count Ridgewell. Or would you prefer a beer?"

The king of Stormwind is asking me if I want wine or beer, Fredrik thought. The world had gone mad.

"W-whatever you're having, Your Majesty."

"A bottle of Peaked Dalaran Red," he said, and the count nodded and left. The king returned his gaze to Fredrik. "You're an innkeeper. I'm sure you'll be familiar with my selection."

Fredrik was indeed familiar with the vintage, but it wasn't something there was much call for in the Lion's Pride, as the price was exorbitant. "I'm offering you a glass now because we're going to toast a very brave man," the king continued. "And then I'm going to ask you if you yourself would, if it were possible, be inclined to do a very brave thing."

Fredrik nodded. "Of course, sir. It's as you wish."

The priestess placed a gentle hand on his arm. "I know it's hard not to be nervous, but I promise you, you're free to leave at any time. His Majesty's request is just that, not an order."

Fredrik felt some of the trepidation abate, and his heart, which had been pounding fiercely ever since the courier had arrived at the inn, finally started to slow down despite the older man's glower.

"Thank you, Priestess."

Anduin continued. "It's my understanding you lost your brother to the plague. I want you to know that I am truly sorry for your loss."

This wasn't at all what Fredrik had been expecting. He felt like he'd been gut punched. But the young king's blue eyes remained friendly and sympathetic, and Fredrik found himself speaking freely.

"Aye," Fredrik said. "We was close as boys. Frandis always liked to play with swords. He was good at it—ever so much better'n me. Got a job guarding supply caravans from ruffians. He would go from here to Ironforge or wherever the caravans went. That day, they went to Lordaeron."

The boy—*no, Fredrik, the king!*—looked down for a minute. "And you thought Frandis died, didn't you?"

Sudden hope seized the innkeeper. "He's not—is he alive?"

The king shook his blond head sadly. "No. But he eventually became a Forsaken. And it was as a Forsaken that he became a hero. He was killed because he defied a tyrant—the warchief of the Horde, Garrosh Hellscream. He died because he wouldn't follow orders he knew were wrong and cruel."

Count Ridgewell returned, bearing a tray with four glasses and the promised wine. The king nodded his thanks and filled the glasses. Fredrik reached for his, careful not to hold the fragile blown glass too tightly. It was not the heavy mugs he was accustomed to at his tavern, that was for certain.

Frandis—his brother—had been a Forsaken. Abruptly Fredrik started to tremble, and the wine sloshed around in the beautiful goblet. He took a gulp to steady his nerves, then kicked himself for not savoring the rare vintage.

"A hero," Fredrik said, repeating King Anduin's words. "That don't sound like a Forsaken," he added cautiously, wondering if this was some kind of game.

"Not like what we think of as Forsaken, no," the woman said. Beside her, the gray-haired man was looking increasingly irritated.

"But does it sound like Frandis?" the king asked.

Tears shimmered in Fredrik's eyes. "It do," he said. "He were a good man, Your Majesty."

"I know," the king said. "And he was a good man even after he died.

There are other Forsaken who also retain themselves even after . . . their transition. Not all of them, certainly. But some."

"It . . . don't seem possible," Fredrik murmured.

"Let me ask you a question," the king said. "Let's suppose, by some chance, Frandis was still with us. As a Forsaken. Knowing that he was still largely himself, still the good man who was your brother, would you have liked to meet with him?"

Fredrik dropped his gaze to his lap. He saw that his large, strong hands had been clutching and twisting his hat until it had completely lost its shape.

What a question! *Would* he want that?

"Bear in mind as you answer, this may be your brother—but he would also be a Forsaken." For the first time, the older man had spoken. His voice was deep and had almost a growl to it. "He wouldn't be alive. He might be rotting. Bones would likely be jutting through his skin. He would have done terrible things as a member of the Scourge. And he would serve the Banshee Queen. Would you still be interested in meeting your 'brother'?"

King Anduin did not look pleased with the older man's words, but he did not silence him, either. Fredrik felt cold, reeling from the graphic picture that had been painted. It would be terrifying to come face to face with—

With what? Or, more important, with who? With a monster? Or with his brother?

Fredrik would have to find that out for himself, wouldn't he?

The innkeeper swallowed hard and looked squarely first at the boyish face of his king, then at the gentle one of the priestess, then, less willingly, at the almost angry older man.

His answer was for his king.

"Yes, Your Majesty," he stated. "I'd have wanted to see him. And if he was as you say he was—someone who tried to stop something evil—then he'd still be my brother."

The king and the priestess exchanged pleased glances, and the king refilled Fredrik's glass while the older man shook his head and sighed in frustration.

CHAPTER TWENTY-FOUR

Stormwind

Over the next few days, Anduin and Calia took the list of human names Sylvanas had given them and dispatched letters to all those mentioned. Anduin himself wrote them rather than having a scribe do so. He made it clear that participation in the Gathering, as he and Calia found themselves calling it, was completely voluntary.

No harm will come to you or your family if you refuse, he said in the missive. *This is not an order but rather an invitation, a chance to see your loved ones again, although they are different from the ones you recall.*

The couriers delivering the letters had been instructed not to leave without a reply. Some of those on the list were literate and wrote their own responses; others dictated them to the courier. Anduin looked at the pile of responses and sighed. "Counting today's batch, there are more refusals than acceptances," he said.

Calia smiled sadly but kindly. "That shouldn't surprise you," she replied.

"No. It doesn't." *And that's why it's painful*, he thought but did not say.

"But there were some who accepted right away," she reminded him.

"And every member of the council submitted five names, anticipating that some might not want to be involved."

"True." It was good for him to remember that. Their task was still just beginning; all the people who did respond positively would have to be interviewed to ensure that their desire to reunite with family or friends stemmed from love and concern rather than vengeance. Others of his advisers had offered to aid Calia and Anduin in the process, but the young king had refused them. It was a bitter thing, but he didn't trust them to be unbiased. He'd seen how unhappy Genn had been with Fredrik Farley. People needed to understand what they might encounter, but they didn't need to be bullied into refusing.

Anduin had been informed that negative sentiment was not limited to his advisers. Guards and Shaw's people had reported that there was muttering in some of the taverns and on the streets. The guards had been instructed to interrupt such conversations if they verged on sedition or grew violent. So far, nothing untoward had happened; the hatred expressed, the guards reported, was toward Sylvanas and the Horde for what they had done to their loved ones. Some still believed that death was better than becoming "monsters."

Communication between himself and the Banshee Queen continued to go surprisingly well. They had hammered out a set of rules that each agreed to adhere to and that had even passed muster among his advisers for safety purposes. Everyone was, if not exactly happy, approving of the spot selected, the numbers chosen, and the steps that would be followed from the arrival of each faction's forces to the time and manner of their departure.

At one point, Genn had confronted Anduin and asked him point blank: "How can you work so easily with the creature who betrayed your father? There's more blood on her hands than there is water in the ocean!"

"It's not easy," Anduin had replied. "And she does have blood on her hands. We all do. No, Genn. I can't change the past. But if this goes well, then I can change the future: one person, one mind, one heart at a time. And maybe that will be enough so that a fresh outbreak of war fueled by Azerite won't wipe out every one of us."

The days passed. Anduin and Calia continued to meet with those whose names were on the provided list. Some were like Fredrik: individuals who struggled with the concept of a Forsaken as a "person" but yearned for connection. Others, though they might have expressed a willingness to meet with their Forsaken kin in the letter, were deemed unsuitable. Calia was a keen observer, and Anduin trusted the old injuries he had received from the Divine Bell to guide his decisions. And sometimes, sadly, it was quite obvious that the "reunion" would have resulted in violence.

There was an undercurrent of hostility, an unvoiced desire to punish the Forsaken simply for the act of having died and been reborn. Others, usually with more than sufficient reason, were openly angry at Sylvanas. They were given coin and refreshment for their time and dismissed.

"Hate," Anduin said once to Calia, "always surprises me. It shouldn't. But it does."

She nodded her golden head sadly. "As priests, we cannot harden our hearts and still do what the Light would have us do. Vulnerability is our strength and our weakness both. But I would have it no other way."

The candles had burned low in the chamber on the final day as the last person settled into the chair. Her name was Philia Fintallas, and the person who had asked for her was her father, Parqual.

Philia looked to be about fifteen years old, if that. She had large, expressive eyes and a small button nose. With the vibrancy of her demeanor, she seemed as far removed from a Forsaken as the summer from the winter.

"My father was a historian in Lordaeron, and I was born there," she said. "But we had family here—aunts, uncles, cousins—and I had come back for a visit. I was supposed to have gone home the day after—" She broke off, and tears welled in her eyes. Anduin fished out a handkerchief and handed it to her. She accepted it with a trembling smile of thanks and sipped at the water Calia had poured for her.

"After Arthas came," Anduin finished for her. He sneaked a glance at Calia. He couldn't count the number of times her brother's name had been mentioned during these meetings with survivors. And every one had cursed him heartily. On some level, it had to wound that man's sister. Anduin never identified Calia by name, and she never reacted to the vile things that were said about the slain Lich King. He admired her strength, particularly given what she had said about not hardening her heart.

Philia nodded miserably, then took a deep breath and continued. "We never heard anything from Mama or Papa, so we assumed they were dead. *Hoped* they were dead, given all we had heard about the Scourge. Oh, isn't that horrible now that I know—I have to tell you that my uncle didn't want me to come when I got your letter, Your Majesty. But I had to. If by some miracle it's still him, I have to see him. I have to see my papa!"

Her voice caught as the tears she had tried so hard to contain spilled down her cheeks.

Calia had unfailingly been kind and comforting to all she and Anduin had spoken with, but this girl's obvious love clearly struck her powerfully. She rose and went to Philia, holding her tightly, letting her sob against her shoulder. Anduin thought he glimpsed tears in the priestess's eyes as the two women clung to each other, and a thought struck him. It was a delicate subject but one he needed to broach with Calia once their task here was completed.

"It's true, I promise you," he said to Philia. "I haven't met your father, but I have encountered many Forsaken who remember who they were and who would be very happy to be reunited with those who have thought them dead or destroyed beyond recognition."

Calia stood back a step from the girl, placing her hands on her shoulders. "Philia? Look at me."

The girl did so, gulping, her eyes red and swollen. "I have heard of your father from someone who knows him as he is now. He speaks very highly of him and tells me he is still kind and intelligent. I believe it will be a joyful reunion for you both."

"Thank you! Thank you so much! When will this happen?"

"We will send a courier with instructions," Anduin promised her. "Hopefully, not too long."

When the girl left, beaming with joy, Calia gave Anduin a smile even though her face was still flushed from the empathetic tears she had shed.

"I hope you see now what good you do, Anduin Wrynn."

He gave her a lopsided grin. "I hope it *will* be good," he said. "I'll relax when it's all over. I couldn't have done this without you, Calia. You have a gift for reading people."

"That was something I learned from an early age as a royal child, as I'm sure you did. Working so closely with so many fellow priests has only helped to hone that skill and temper it with compassion."

There was a pause. Calia herself had just provided him a segue into the conversation he wished to have with her, but even so, Anduin steeled himself.

"Calia," he began carefully, "you have been a tremendous help. And you aren't a Stormwind citizen. If this plan does lead eventually to peace, you'll be a hero of the Alliance."

She smiled a touch ruefully. "Thank you, but I don't consider myself a member of the Alliance. I'm a citizen of nowhere now except perhaps the Netherlight Temple," she said. "I go where the Light wills me. I truly believe this is the right path toward mending other, greater rifts."

Anduin couldn't let it go without making absolutely certain. Too much was at stake. "The kingdom of Lordaeron is your birthright. Few would be willing to let go of such a title and the power it would grant them," he pressed. "I understand your reasoning, but many do not. You may have some nationalist champions rising, ready to take the city in your name."

Suddenly her expression grew thoughtful, and she searched his eyes. "Would you be among them, Anduin? Is that why you ask? Would the king of Stormwind make war on the Horde, scour the Undercity, to grant the queen of Lordaeron her empty kingdom?"

The throne *was* hers by every right. Yet was it worth war should she express a desire to claim it? She saw the struggle on his face and put a hand on his.

"I understand. Don't worry. Those who currently inhabit Lordaeron lived there in life. The Forsaken are the true heirs. It belongs to them now. The best I can do for those whom I would have ruled is exactly what I'm doing. I've found peace and a calling where I can really matter. That's more important than a bloodied crown."

"Sacrificing peace and a calling is usually the *price* of a crown," Anduin said.

"You have not let it be so. Stormwind is fortunate to have you. But if you truly wish to thank me, I have a favor to ask. Of both you and the archbishop. I'd like to participate in the Gathering."

Anduin frowned slightly. "I don't think that is wise," he said. "There may be those who recognize you. It could be dangerous. It could be . . . misconstrued." It could, in fact, lead to war.

"If any of the Forsaken do recognize me, it will give me the chance to show that I bear them no ill will," she countered. "That I have no desire to run them out of the place that's been their home for so long. I want them to stay there. I want them to be safe."

Anduin watched her carefully, taking a breath and centering himself. *Light—let me know if she means them harm.* He felt no responding ache in his bones, no hint that Calia Menethil was planning some kind of murderous coup. Her intentions were in alignment with the Light they both served.

"I've already established a bond of trust with these people we've interviewed," she continued. "And no one knows the archbishop better than I do."

This was true. And no one knew her better than Faol. "I will speak with the archbishop," Anduin said at last. "If he is agreeable, then I am, too."

Calia beamed at him. "Thank you," she said. "It means more than you know."

There was one last thing he felt compelled to say. "I have a question, and it's important that I know the answer."

Her golden hair, as golden as that of Arthas, as golden as his own, fell in a bright sheet to hide her face as she looked down. Her voice was small when she spoke.

"I trust you, Anduin," she said. "If you feel you must know the answer, then ask it."

He took a deep breath.

"Calia . . . Is there a child? Do you have an heir?"

CHAPTER TWENTY-FIVE

Stormwind

T he unspoken words hung between them, heavy and sad, and
Anduin knew the answer before she gave it.

"There was a child," Calia Menethil said so softly that he had to
strain to hear her. It was enough, but Anduin waited to see if she was
ready to tell her story. Just as he drew breath to change the subject, she
began to speak.

"You must understand . . . my father was ordinarily a kind and understanding man, but on this one thing he was firm. He was to choose
the man I was to marry, and I was to agree to it."

Her sorrowful sea-green eyes lifted from the clasped hands in her
lap. "I have made many mistakes and poor choices in my life. Everyone has, but as royalty, our decisions matter more than those of others
because they affect so many more people. You may feel that you have
to find a queen, have an heir. Your advisers will want you to make a
good political match. Others might be able to live with such things.
But not people like us. Promise me this, Anduin: whatever anyone
tells you to do, don't marry if your heart doesn't tell you to."

Her face was fierce but still beautiful and haunted, and her words struck him with the power of truth. Even so, Anduin knew that in the end he would have to do what was best for his kingdom.

"I cannot make a promise I may not be able to keep," he said, "but for what it's worth, I share your feelings on this matter."

"We all do what we must," Calia said. "I was not the direct heir. I don't have your responsibilities. If I had, I might have agreed without protest. But Arthas was the heir, the firstborn son, and as he grew up, Papa began to focus more on him. It seemed as though he and Jaina would be a perfect couple—a love match as well as a sound political one. At least until Arthas somehow decided that it wasn't perfect."

She paused, then looked up at him. "Jaina . . . I've been afraid to ask you. Is she . . ."

"She's alive," Anduin hastened to reassure her. "We don't know where she is, but she can take care of herself." He did not tell her of Jaina's struggles or of her apparent abandonment of the Alliance. Calia had enough sorrows on her heart. Anduin had no desire to add to them unless she inquired.

His words seemed to be enough for her. She smiled, her eyes distant, and said, "I'm glad. She was dear to me when we were younger. When the world was less cruel than now. And with what Arthas . . . became . . . I am deeply glad she was not wed to him.

"But while Father's eye was on my brother, I conducted my own quiet rebellion. I fell in love with someone Father never would have approved of: one of the footmen. We stole what moments we could, and once, in the dark of night, we slipped away and begged a priestess to marry us. She refused at first, but we persisted. We came to her again and again, my sweet love and I, and at last, with the Light's blessing, we were wed."

Her hand fell to her belly, flat now but once rounded with child. "When I was certain that I was carrying, I confided in Mother. Oh, she was furious with me! But she could tell by my face that this was a true love, and I assured her my child would be legitimate. Father was too caught up in Arthas to make much objection when my mother and I went on a 'long rest' to more remote parts of the kingdom."

Calia's hand ceased to move on her abdomen, and both hands

curled into fists. "I got to hold my beautiful little girl and tend to her for a few weeks before it was decided that my husband would raise her, away from Lordaeron and ignorant of her birthright. Mother promised that when the time was right—when Arthas had finally married and produced an heir—we could acknowledge my daughter and perhaps elevate my husband to a nobleman's status so that her name would be unsullied.

"That day never came. But the Scourge did."

Anduin listened, his heart full of sympathy. Calia was describing being sold off like livestock to the highest bidder. She'd rebelled, fallen in love, and conceived a child. A daughter. For a brief moment, Anduin wondered what a daughter or a son of his would look like. Regardless of appearance or gender, that babe would rule one day . . . and until then would be deeply loved.

"I don't remember much of that time. I remember lying in a ditch while the Scourge passed above me. I believe to this day it was thanks to the Light that they never found me. I made my way to Southshore, where my husband and child had been hidden away. We all three wept when we were reunited. But it was not to last."

No. Not a second time. Anduin reached for one of her fisted hands. For a moment, it was tense beneath his, and then, slowly, the fist unclenched as Calia allowed her fingers to entwine with his.

"You don't have to say anything else, Calia. I'm sorry I troubled you."

"It's all right," she said. "I've started now. I think I want to finish."

"Only if you wish," he assured her.

She gave him a faint smile. "Maybe if I tell someone, the nightmares will stop."

Inwardly, he winced; he had no response to that. She continued. "No one recognized me. Everyone assumed I was dead. We were happy for a time. And then came the blight. We ran. I wasn't about to leave my family again, but in the crowd we were separated. I stood in the middle of the street, screaming for them. Someone took pity on me, pulling me onto his horse and galloping past the limits of the town barely in time.

"There was a cluster of refugees in the forest. So many of us waited, desperate for word of our loved ones. Sometimes prayers were answered, and there were reunions that were . . ." Calia bit her lip. "I prayed that my family, too, would be spared. But . . ." Her voice trailed off. "I never saw them again."

And then, with a realization that stopped his breathing with shock, Anduin understood why Calia had decided to befriend the Forsaken. Why, instead of seeing them as the destroyers of her city, her way of life, and all her family, she had chosen to identify with them.

"You're hoping that your husband and child, too, became Forsaken instead of dying as Scourge," he said softly. "You're hoping you'll get word of them at the Gathering."

Calia nodded, wiping at the tears on her face with one hand. The other remained clasped with the young king's. "Yes," she said. "It wasn't until I met the archbishop that I started to understand that the Forsaken weren't monsters. They were just . . . *us.* The same people you and I would be if we had been killed and given a different sort of life."

"You don't know if your family would have been like that," Anduin cautioned. "They could have been driven mad or turned cruel. It might be devastating for you to see them." Genn's words to Fredrik came back to him now even as he spoke.

"I know. But I have to hold out for the chance. Isn't that what the Light is all about, Anduin? Hope?"

Anduin's mind went back to the trial of Garrosh Hellscream. When that orc had executed his escape, he had done so thanks to the chaos sown by an unexpected attack on the temple. In that battle, Jaina had been severely wounded.

No, he corrected himself. She had been dying.

So many tried to heal her, both Alliance and Horde. But the wound was too much. Anduin remembered kneeling on the cold stone floor of the temple, watching Jaina's labored breathing and seeing red bubbles form on her lips, his hands on her bloodied robe. *Please, please,* he had prayed, and the Light had come. But he, like the others, was exhausted. And the Light he had called would not be enough to save her.

He remembered others telling him to come away, that he'd done all he could. But he stayed there in those bleak, impotent moments before the death of this woman he'd loved as an aunt. *No,* he had told those who wanted him to walk away. *I can't.*

And then the voice of his teacher—Chi-Ji, the Red Crane. *And so, the student remembers the lessons of my temple.*

Anduin quoted Chi-Ji's words to Calia now. "Hope is what you have when all other things have failed you," he said. "Where there is hope, you make room for healing, for all things that are possible—and some that are not."

Her eyes shone, and she gave him a tremulous smile. "You understand," she said.

"I do," he said. "And I know that having you participate in the Gathering is the right thing to do." As he spoke, he felt warmth and calmness steal through him. That warmth passed through their clasped hands to Calia, and he saw the lines around her eyes and mouth lessen, her body relax.

Whatever betided, this act of kindness was the right thing. Anduin had to hope that they would not pay too dear a price for it.

TANARIS

The team of goblin engineer and gnome mineralogist picked up their pace. Saffy grilled Grizzek on everything he knew about his "boss," and it killed him to watch her face, normally so bright and cheerful—especially recently—grow darker and more withdrawn. Sometimes Grizzek bridled at how his people were regarded or, more accurately, reviled. Not all goblins were out to sell dangerous things at ludicrous prices. There were some who were even well regarded: Gazlowe, who operated out of Ratchet, south of Orgrimmar, came to mind.

But Jastor Gallywix epitomized the worst that could possibly be said about goblins. He was cunning, selfish, arrogant, completely ruthless, and unburdened by remorse. He'd even sold his own people into slavery right after the Cataclysm hit, for crying out loud. Grizzek and his darling Punkin had become so engrossed in the breathtaking magnificence of Azerite that they'd lost sight of what surely was at the heart of Gallywix's desire to learn about it: its ability to kill anyone that goblin chose.

"This is all my fault," Grizzek said at one point, more miserable than he'd ever been in his life. "I should never have trusted Gallywix to keep his promise. Should have known he'd want me to make weapons. And worst of all, I should *never* have dragged you into this. I'm so sorry."

"Hey," Saffy said, slipping into his arms and snuggling against his sunken green chest. "While I cannot approve of your methods, I'm glad we're working together on this. You were right. You knew I'd want to be involved. I may have come here kicking and screaming—literally—but I stayed because I wanted to. And because—"

Grizzek caught his breath. Was she going to say—

"Because I'm glad that we found each other again. This Azerite is powerful stuff. Its natural state is toward growth and healing. Maybe even Gallywix will understand that it's much better to put it to those kinds of uses."

"Pookie," he said, "he's a goblin. We like to blow things up."

She was, of course, unable to deny the truth in this. "Well," she hemmed, "building and healing are just as important as destroying and killing."

Sapphronetta was so naive. And he loved her so much for it.

By the time Gallywix showed up, all big belly, big attitude, and big smiles, they were ready.

"Trade Prince," Grizzek said, "please allow me to introduce my lab partner: Sapphronetta Flivvers."

Saffy dropped a curtsy, which looked ridiculous but endearing as she was wearing overalls and clunky boots. Gallywix appeared charmed.

"Delighted, delighted," he boomed in his abrasive, raspy voice, taking her hand and pressing his lips on it. Saffy turned pale but did not pull away. "You were worth every copper to kidnap, my dear, and I haven't even seen your work yet."

"Uh . . . thanks," she said. Her eyes narrowed, and it was obvious she wanted nothing more than to deck him, but again she refrained from actions that probably would result in their imprisonment and/or execution.

"We've been working on a variety of things," Grizzek began, but Gallywix cut him off.

"Lots of weapons, I hope," Gallywix said as he trundled through the door into the courtyard. "Our warchief is extremely interested in things that go boom. And I told her, 'Warchief,' I says, 'don't you worry, honey. I got the best guy who makes things go boom.'"

"Actually," Saffy said, forcing a smile, "goblins already excel at making things go boom. What we've been working on is much more valuable."

They led him inside to the lab. Arranged with an eye to impress were all their labors of love. They proceeded to put the items through their paces as Gallywix watched, his tiny eyes fixed hungrily on the Azerite.

First they shared the wearable items: the jewelry and trinkets. "We got our inspiration from you," Grizzek said. "Your cane was the very first adornment made of Azerite!" Gallywix beamed and petted the glowing golden orb under discussion. Saffy discussed the properties of the various trinkets, and Grizzek brought out the armor they'd crafted.

"Holy smokes," Gallywix exclaimed as he watched the armor take minute after minute of direct fire from the Lightning Blast 3000. Next up was Crunchy's demonstration. Grizzek had rebuilt the damaged hand and winced afresh as yet again it was destroyed when the modified shredder tried to crush a lump of Azerite.

"My, my!" Gallywix said. "That's tough stuff."

"Think of the building material you could make from it," Saffy said. "It would withstand fires, earthquakes—"

"Think of the shredders we could make!"

"Er . . . yes. Let's move on." Next, Saffy demonstrated what Grizzek referred to as her "best parlor trick" of neutralizing poison and licking it off her hand.

"You won't need to craft specific antidotes," she said. "Just carry around some of this and keep it liquid, and no matter the poison, it's no longer a problem!"

"Ha ha! When *we* use it, poison is *never* a problem!" All of Gally-wix's chins and his belly, too, jiggled with his guffaws.

Grizzek was starting to feel sick to his stomach. His poor Saffy was looking as if she felt the same way.

By the end of the demonstrations, Gallywix was not looking very happy. "I asked you for weapons," he said. "Specifically. By name."

"Ah, yeah," Grizzek said. "About that. We, ah—"

"Some things could be modified into weapons," Saffy said, startling Grizzek. "But I highly urge you not to do so. What we've shown you could save lives. Horde lives." That admission was hard for her, but she persevered. "You can build structures that the Alliance can't attack. You can extend lives, heal wounds, save people who otherwise might have died. This helps the Horde. You don't need weapons."

Gallywix sighed and looked at Saffy with an expression that was almost kind and nearly respectful.

"You're a cutie and a smarty," he said, "so I'll tell you nicely. We're in a world that's always going to be at war, sweet cheeks, and the only ones who survive it are the ones with the biggest weapons. Grizzek here understands. You gnomes seem to have problems with that concept. Sure, sure, this Azerite does all the things you say it's gonna do. We *will* make buildings, and cure sickness, and save lives. But we are also going to grind the Alliance down beneath our heels, and, Miss Smarty-Pants, you need to decide if you're gonna be on the winning side when that all goes down. Believe me when I say I hope so."

He looked at Grizzek, stabbing a finger at him to punctuate the words. "Weapons. Pronto."

Then he tipped his hideous hat to Saffy and waddled out.

For several long moments, neither Grizzek nor Saffy spoke. Then, quietly, Saffy said, "What he's going to do with the Azerite . . . those will be crimes against gnomanity. And humanity, and goblins, and orcs, and everyone. *Everyone*, Grizzy."

"I know," he said just as quietly.

"And we will have made it possible for him to do it."

Grizzek was silent. He knew that, too.

She turned to him, her eyes wide and shimmering with tears. "Azerite is part of Azeroth. We can't let him do that to her. We can't let him do that to *us*. Somehow we've got to stop him."

"We can't stop him, Saffy," Grizzek replied. His eyes roamed the magnificent things the two of them had made out of their passion for science and tinkering—and for each other. All of them made his heart swell with pride and then ache with terror for how they would be used.

She came to him and started weeping softly. He put his arms around her, trying to hold her tight enough to shut out the pain of their complicity.

Then a thought occurred to him. "We can't stop him," he repeated, "but I think I have a plan on how we can stop *something*."

CHAPTER TWENTY-SIX

Stormwind

"Thank you for coming," Anduin said to his guests. "I know the hour is late, but it is important."

"So your letter said," Turalyon replied. It was indeed late, well past midnight, but the young king suspected that neither Greymane nor Turalyon had yet seen his bed. Too much was going on.

The king had requested their presences in the Cathedral of Light. A few acolytes and novices moved about even at this hour, but most of the priests were gone. He awaited them at the narthex of the cathedral and indicated that they should join him as he walked down the aisle toward the altar.

"I wanted to give you an update on where we stand for the Gathering," Anduin said.

They frowned, exchanging glances. "Your Majesty," Genn said, "we have already given you our opinion on this."

"We have," Turalyon said. "With respect, Your Majesty, we have a fundamental disagreement on the Light's intentions and purpose." He hesitated. "I do not condemn you for your feelings. It would not be the first time a devotee has misunderstood the Light. I know I have. I don't claim to be perfect or to have a true comprehension of it. No one can."

"But you both do feel that this is wrong?" Anduin pressed. "That there is nothing to be gained by having Forsaken and humans meeting when a prior bond had existed between them?"

"We have made that clear, Your Majesty," Turalyon stated. "If you have bidden us to come here at this hour simply to rehash this argument with you—"

"No," Anduin said. "Not with me."

"With me," came a rich, warm, oddly echoing voice.

They turned around.

Archbishop Alonsus Faol stood on the blue steps leading up to the altar.

He was clad in a miter and robe that bespoke his stature in life. Anduin had looked diligently for the garments. It was, he had realized, easier for humans to recognize the outer trappings of an archbishop than what remained of the man himself.

Both Greymane and Turalyon seemed stunned. Anduin waited but did not speak. This had to unfold between Faol and his oldest, dearest friends without interference from outsiders. Anduin said a silent prayer that everyone in this room would look with eyes of remembered friendship and see truly.

"I'm quite aware that I don't look as you remember me," Faol continued. "But I think you recognize my voice. And my face is mostly intact, though it lacks that bushy white beard I was so fond of."

Turalyon went as still as if he were the statue that stood at the entrance to Stormwind. The only thing that proved he was not was the rapid fall and rise of his chest. The expression on his face was one of utter loathing, but he did not speak or move.

If Turalyon's reaction was cold, Genn's was pure fire. He whirled on Anduin, his face contorted in fury. Not for the first time, the young king was aware of the sheer power of the man even when he wasn't in his worgen form. He needed no claws and teeth, not even a sword, to kill. And right now, he looked as though he was about to rip Anduin apart with his bare hands.

"You've gone too far, Anduin Wrynn," Greymane snarled. "How

dare you bring this *thing* into the Cathedral of Light! You're chasing this distorted ideal of what peace really is. And now you've brought that here."

His voice shook. "Alonsus Faol was my friend. He was Turalyon's friend. We'd accepted that he was gone. He was buried at Faol's Rest. Why are you *doing* this to us?"

Anduin didn't flinch. He had been expecting this reaction. When he got no response, Greymane turned on the source of his loathing.

"Have you got the boy under some sort of spell, wretch?" he bellowed. "I know that there are priests who can do that sort of thing. Let Anduin go, get out of here, and I will not rip that putrid corpse of yours to shreds.

"You chose this . . . this shambling existence. You chose to be this creature of nightmares. And you *have* to know what's happened to me. To my people. What yours did to me and how much I loathe what you've become. If you had any decency, any respect for those you once called friends, you'd have hurled yourself into the fire during your first Hallow's End and spared us all this!"

Anduin closed his eyes in pain at the vitriol Greymane was hurling at a man he'd loved in life. He had known this would be difficult, but he had not expected Genn to be so malicious in his anger.

Faol, though, seemed completely unsurprised by the reaction and looked at Genn sadly. "You stand there, a few strides away from an old friend, and you attack me with words chosen for their power to wound," Faol said. "And I know why you do so."

"I do so because you are a monstrosity! Because your people are an abomination and should *never* have been created!"

Faol shook his head. His voice remained calm, tinged with a hint of sorrow. "No, my old friend. You do this because you are afraid."

Anduin blinked, shocked. Genn Greymane was many things, but he was no coward. Anduin did not want to interfere, but if it looked like Faol was in danger, he would do so. Although Faol was probably a more powerful priest, even in his present state, than Anduin could ever be.

Greymane stood absolutely still. "I've killed for lesser insults than that." The words were pitched low, a growl.

"I know that," Faol continued. "And yet I say again: you are afraid.

Oh, not of me personally." He put a withered hand on his bony chest. "I'm certain you believe you can take me in one of your heartbeats. You may be right at that, but I'd just as soon not find out."

He shook his head sadly. "No, Genn Greymane. You're afraid because you believe that if you acknowledge here, now, with me, that Forsaken aren't irredeemable monsters—if you show any hint of understanding, or kindness, or compassion, or friendship—then that will mean your son died for nothing."

A human cry of rage and pain turned into a wolf's howl as the Gilnean king arched his back. His form shifted, wreathed in mystical smoke as gray as the wolf's pelt. Taller, much more massive, he crouched on his lupine haunches and prepared to spring at Faol. Turalyon seized the worgen by the arm, shaking his head.

"No bloodshed in this place," he said.

"The creature doesn't even *have* blood," Genn snarled, his voice deep and ragged. "He's tied together like a stick puppet with ichor and magic!"

"I know something about loss," the archbishop continued. Anduin marveled at Faol's calmness. "And I know something about you, too. You've held fast to that pain. It's served you well. It's enabled you to fight with unbridled ferocity. But like any edged weapon, it can cut both ways. And right now, it's coming between you and an understanding that could change your world."

"I *can't* change my world!" Genn cried in a broken voice. The words were still blazing with fury, but shot through them was a deep thread of pain that made Anduin's heart ache. "I want my son back, but that banshee murdered him! She and her kind—*your* kind—nearly destroyed my people!"

"Yet here you are," Faol continued almost placidly. "Many of you are still healthy. Strong. Alive." For the first time since this confrontation began, the undead priest stepped forward. "Answer me this, old friend. If I had not come alone—if I had brought Liam with me, raised, as I was, and still himself, as I am—would your answer be different?"

The worgen jerked back at words that pierced him more than any blade. He panted, his ears flattened to the back of his skull, his tail lashing the air. Anduin, himself reeling from the shock of the archbishop's words, lifted his hands, cupping them in preparation for the Light. But before he could act, Greymane howled in fury, dropped to all fours—and raced from the room.

Anduin started to go after him, but Faol stopped him. "Let him go, Anduin. Genn Greymane ever had a temper, and now he's been forced to look at something sad and ugly within himself. He'll either come around in his own time or he won't. But now, whatever he says, he has realized he cannot tar us all with the same brush. It's a small victory, but I will accept it."

"Victory."

The single word was laced with more icy abhorrence than Anduin had ever heard, so filled with disgust that it physically hurt him. In the tense moments with Genn, he had almost forgotten the silent paladin. The two men had reacted differently but with the same repellence.

Turalyon had no sword and wore no armor. Yet he still loomed large and powerful in the cathedral as he straightened to his full height. If Genn had been racked by anguished fury, Turalyon, one of the first paladins of the Silver Hand, was brimming with righteous rage.

"You blaspheme what was once a good man," he snapped. "You have stolen his form and parade him about, wearing him as if he were a suit of clothing. Your broken mouth is good for nothing save spewing filthy lies. The undead are unholy. Whatever priestly powers they have come from the shadows of the Light, not the Light itself. If there is *anything* left in you of that good, kindly man I loved so much, you capering piece of carnage, come to me, and I will blast him into merciful oblivion."

How could Turalyon not see what Anduin saw? The high exarch had embraced a redeemed dreadlord as a companion and fellow soldier! The young king, too, had been initially horrified. But although the legendary paladin doubtless had encountered more dark things, including truly evil Forsaken, than Anduin ever would, Varian's son had seen courage displayed by one of Sylvanas's creations. He held fast to the memory of witnessing Frandis Farley murdered for daring to oppose unnecessary cruelty and violence. He recalled Elsie's letter, how it had nearly broken his heart. He had seen things Turalyon, in his thousand years of war against the Legion, had never witnessed.

And now Turalyon was refusing to see something—someone—who stood right in front of him.

"I created the Order of the Silver Hand," Faol admonished him, his voice growing stronger. "I saw in you something that no one else had. You were a fine priest, but that wasn't what the Light wanted you to be. The Light needed champions who could fight with both the weapons of humanity and the love and power of the Light. The others were strongest with the first and came to the Light later. You were the opposite. They were good, fine men. They were noble paladins. But they are all gone, and you have become the high exarch of the Light. You are too wise, Turalyon, to deny the truth. Deny that and you deny the Light itself."

To Anduin's horror, Faol closed the distance between himself and the paladin. He spread his arms open wide. Turalyon trembled and his fists clenched, but he did not strike.

"Look for the Light in me," Faol instructed. "You will find it. And if you do not, then I do beg of you to strike me down, for I would not wish to exist as a broken corpse the Light had abandoned."

Anduin looked down to see that Calia had stepped beside him. She looked up at him, and he saw that she was afraid for her friend. He was, too, even though he had met the archbishop only recently.

All will be as the Light wills it, he thought.

For a moment, Anduin thought the paladin so enraged that he wouldn't even try. But then Turalyon lifted an arm. A ray of what looked like pure golden sunlight, impossible at this hour of night when that orb hid its head, shone down upon both forms.

Turalyon's face was hard as stone. It was the unforgiving expression of the righteous doing what they deemed to be the right thing. But then, as Anduin watched, transfixed by the silent struggle going on between belief and faith, that granite visage softened. Turalyon's eyes widened; then the radiant, golden glow that enveloped both the living and the dead caught the glitter of unshed tears. Joy spread across his face, and then, as Anduin watched, moved beyond the ability to speak, Turalyon, paladin of the Silver Hand, high exarch of the Army of the Light, dropped to his knees.

"Your Excellency," he breathed. "Forgive me, my old friend. My arrogance blinded me to what was clear all along had I looked with the right eyes."

And he bent his head for the archbishop's blessing.

Faol, too, was struggling with emotion. "Dear boy," he said in a voice that shook, "dear boy. There is nothing to forgive. There was a time when I would have agreed with you. You are the sole living member of the original order, the last of the only sons I would ever have. I am grateful that I have not lost you, too, not to death, or the Void, or to your own limitations."

He placed his hand, decaying and lifeless, upon the paladin's gray-gold head. Turalyon closed his eyes in quiet joy.

"My blessing, such as it is, is upon you. There is no one, living, dead, or anywhere in the mysterious shades in between, who cannot benefit from always looking with eyes, heart, and mind wide open. Rise, my dear boy, and lead even better now that you have greater understanding of the ways of the Light."

Turalyon did so, appearing clumsy for a moment before straightening. He looked over at Anduin. "I owe you an apology as well," he said. "I thought of you as someone who hoped for the best at the cost of wisdom. I could not have been more wrong."

Anduin heard Calia sigh deeply with relief. "There is no need," he replied. "We are taught to fear the Forsaken. And even the archbishop understands that there are many whose rebirth turned them cold and cruel. But not all."

"No," Turalyon agreed. "Not all. I am overjoyed to have my old friend and mentor back."

"We will work together," Faol assured him.

"If only Greymane could have witnessed this," Calia said.

"Like all people, he will see when he is ready," Turalyon said. "I will certainly reassure him as best I can. But for now, let me do what I can to aid you. Others should be able to have the gift that the archbishop and I have received this night."

Anduin smiled. He could not see the future. But he could see this moment, and his heart was full. "I will accept your aid most gladly."

CHAPTER TWENTY-SEVEN

Tanaris

"Ya know," Grizzek observed as he and Saffy prepared their escape, "life with you is never dull."

"We do keep hopping, don't we?" she replied, and gave him a look that turned his heart all gooey-melty.

Grizzek, not being a complete idiot, had anticipated that at some point, someone who did not wish him sunshine and rainbows and a long happy life might come knocking. He had prepared for the eventuality by digging out—well, by modifying a second shredder to dig out, actually—a tunnel that opened up into a random spot in Tanaris. After Gallywix had departed, they'd decided to make a run for it. They packed up what they could take with them in the little mining cart, including a few airtight casks of Azerite, and everything else . . . well, some of it couldn't be destroyed, but they'd dismantled what they could.

The bomb set to detonate an hour after they left also would help.

All their notes were coming with them. They'd programmed Feathers to fly to Teldrassil with a warning about what had happened and a plea for rescue at a specific location. They would offer the Alliance what they had discovered on the stipulation that they would be creating only things that could help, not harm.

It was a risk. A crazy, glorious one, but it was the only option they had. Neither, they had decided, could live with knowing their discoveries were going to be used to kill so effectively.

Just before they left, Grizzek took a long last look around. "I'm gonna miss this place," he admitted.

"I know, Grizzy," Saffy said, her big eyes filled with sympathy. "But we'll find another lab. One where we can create to our hearts' content."

He turned to her. "Anywhere in the world. Just so long as it's with you." Then, as her eyes widened with shock, he knelt in front of her. "Sapphronetta Flivvers . . . will you marry me? Again?"

In his large green hand, he held one of the Azerite rings they had created. The base was rough because neither of them was a jeweler, and the Azerite was an imperfect drop that had been allowed to harden. But when Saffy said, "Oh! Grizzy, yes!" and he slipped it on her teeny tiny finger, he thought it was the most beautiful ring in the world.

He embraced her tightly. "I am one happy goblin," he said, kissing the top of her head. "Come on, Punkin. Let's head out on our next adventure."

They descended into the tunnel. "I hope it hasn't caved in," Grizzek said. "Haven't checked in a couple of years."

"I guess we'll find out," Sapphronetta said grimly.

It was a long underground trek from Grizzek's lab to the hills that separated Tanaris from Thousand Needles, where Grizzek promised Saffy they would emerge. Along the way, they talked openly for the first time. About how much they cared about each other and always had. About what they'd done wrong and how they felt they'd been wronged. Over meals, they analyzed what had worked this time that hadn't worked the last time. And when they slept, they did so snuggled close together.

There were no cave-ins, fortunately. And finally, the pair reached the end of this phase of their journey. "According to my calculations, it's about midnight," Saffy said. Grizzek believed her.

"Perfect," Grizzek said. "It's a pretty remote location, but even so,

I'd like to not pop out of this hole in broad daylight. How did you gnomes ever stand living underground, Saffy? I'm going bonkers without sunshine."

"There's sunshine out there," Saffy assured him.

"But we'll be living with night elves."

"They get sunshine in Teldrassil, too; they just prefer to sleep through it."

"You Alliance people are very strange." He kissed her. "But cute. Definitely cute."

Grizzek had left a ladder at the end, and he climbed up first and undid the latch. "Look out below," he called down.

"Huh?" Then: "Hey!"

"I covered it with sand," he explained as the yellow grains poured down over them. He didn't mind. Freedom and a life with the gnome he'd given his heart to years ago awaited him above. He wiped off his face and clambered up the rest of the way, sticking his head up and blinking even in the faint light of the moons and the stars.

Nothing looked out of the ordinary. Grizzek cocked his head, listening. He heard nothing. "Okay, I think we're good," he said, and hoisted himself up onto the ground. He extended a hand to help Saffy out. They stood, stretched, and grinned at each other.

"Phase one complete," he said. "I'll go back down and bring up the rest of our stuff."

"Actually," came a voice, "that won't be necessary."

They whirled. A large goblin was silhouetted against the star-studded sky. Grizzek knew that voice. He reached out for Saffy's hand and clutched it tightly.

"Druz, you and I always got along okay. Tell you what. I'll come back and work for Gallywix. No more tricks. I'll do whatever he wants. You can take everything we got. Just let Saffy have some food and water and let her go."

"Grizzy—"

"I ain't letting you die, Saffy," Grizzek said. "We got a deal, Druz?"

Druz climbed down, followed by no fewer than three other large, irritated-looking goblins. "Sorry, pal. We've been on to you this whole time. Within five minutes of you hopping down into your hole, we'd deactivated the bomb you set to go off in your lab. And as for your parrot, we shot it out of the sky. We just need what you took, and then . . ." He shrugged.

"You're not just going to kill us? In cold blood?" Saffy stammered.

Druz looked at her and sighed. "Little lady, your sweetheart here knew what he was getting you into. This comes directly from the boss. It's outta my hands."

The other goblins leaped forward, grabbing both Grizzek and Saffy roughly. Grizzek made a fist and slammed it into the belly of the nearest one. He heard a yelp and a growl from Saffy and figured she'd gotten in a good blow of some sort, too. But any resistance on their part was but a gesture. Within a handful of minutes, the goblin and the gnome had been searched, slapped around a bit, and then tied up back to back. Even their feet were bound.

"Hey, Druz! I got some notes off the gnome," one said.

"Good job, Kezzig," Druz said.

"This is dumb, Druz," Grizzek muttered through a mouthful of blood and broken teeth. "And you ain't dumb. I'm worth a lot more to you alive than dead."

"Not really," Druz said. "We got all the things you made back in the lab. We got all the things you tried to steal. And now we got the gnome's notes. We can take it from here. You're too great a risk."

"Hold me hostage," Saffy piped up. "You'll guarantee he won't escape."

"Saffy, shut up!" Grizzek hissed angrily. "Tryin' to save you here!"

"I got my orders," Druz said, sounding almost apologetic. "You ticked off the boss, and this is what we've been told to do with you." He nodded to Kezzig. "Set the bomb."

"Wh-what?" Back to back with Saffy as he was, Grizzek couldn't see her. But she sounded pale.

"You try to blow up our stuff, we blow you up. Smaller bomb, though." Kezzig approached and shoved something cold and hard between the bound pair. "Sorry it didn't work out, Grizz. Look at it this way: it'll be fast. It didn't have to be."

And they walked away, laughing and talking.

Grizzek analyzed the situation. It was not good. He and Saffy were sitting back to back, tied together tightly with what felt like sturdy rope. Their hands were bound, presumably so that they would not be able to work them free and thus untie themselves.

"Think maybe if we wriggle, we can scoot away from it?"

Saffy. Always thinking. Despite the awfulness of the situation, Grizzek felt himself smiling.

"Worth a shot," he said, though he didn't add that it might cause the bomb to go off immediately. She probably knew that anyway. "Count of three, scoot to the left. Ready?"

"Yeah."

"One . . . two . . . three . . . scoot!" They moved about six inches to the left along the uneven surface of the narrow trail. The bomb was still wedged solidly between them. "That's not going to work. Punkin, can you get to your feet?"

"I—I think so," she said.

On the count of three, they tried that. They toppled over to the right the first time. They attempted it a second time once they'd straightened up. Grizzek's foot turned on a loose stone, and they went down again.

"One, two, three!" Grizzek said again, and then, with a grunt, they were standing.

The bomb was still wedged tightly between them. "Okay, Pookie, it's not gonna drop out on its own. We gotta shake it loose."

"You're the explosives expert, but I cannot *imagine* that would be productive to keeping a bomb unexploded."

"I think it's the only chance we got."

"Me, too."

Again, on the count of three, they began jumping up and down. Disbelieving, Grizzek felt the bomb shift. It had been pressing, silently threatening, against his lower back. Now it was at his tailbone.

"It's working!" Saffy squeaked.

"I think it is," Grizzek replied, trying not to be too hopeful. They kept jumping. The bomb slipped lower, lower . . .

And then Grizzek no longer felt the pressure. He braced himself for what he secretly thought was inevitable: detonation on contact with the ground.

But their luck seemed to be holding. He heard it plop on the sand but nothing else. "We did it!" Saffy cried happily. "Grizzy, we—"

"Quiet for a sec," Grizzek said. Saffy obeyed. Grizzek closed his eyes sickly.

In the silence of the desert night, he could hear the tick-tick. The bomb was on a timer.

"We ain't out of this yet," he said. "Hop to the right and keep hopping."

"For how long?"

"Till we reach Gadgetzan."

They hopped. Even as he believed the bomb was ticking away their lives second by second, Grizzek marveled at what they had done together. Even now, they were working together in perfect coordination. The clichéd well-oiled machine.

"Grizzy?"

"Yeah?" Hop. Hop. Hop.

"I have a confession."

"What's that, Pookie?"

"I didn't tell you something I did because I thought you'd be angry with me." Hop. Hop. They were three yards away from it now. If only they both had longer legs—

"Can't be angry with you for anything now, Punkin."

"I burned the notes."

Grizzek was so shocked that he almost stumbled, but he managed to keep their rhythm.

"You . . . what?"

"I tore out all our notes and burned them." Hop. Hop. "There's no way Gallywix can re-create our experiments. He has a few prototypes and a couple of already-mixed potions, but that's it. Whatever awful thing he intends to do with Azerite, it won't be on us."

Hop. Hop.

"Saffy . . . aw, you're a genius!"

At that moment, Grizzek's left foot turned on a slippery sand-covered stone, and he heard something snap. They toppled over, and this time, he knew with sick horror that he was not going to be able to get back up. Lying facedown in the sand, he couldn't determine how much distance they'd put between them and the bomb, and in the darkness, he hadn't been able to identify the kind of explosive Druz had wedged between them. Were they far enough away to survive if it went off?

He gritted his teeth against the pain as he said, "Saffy, my ankle's snapped. We gotta crawl, okay?"

He heard her gulp. "Okay," she said bravely, though her voice quavered.

"Roll over so we're both on our left sides; that way I can push with my good leg."

They did and started squirming away. "Grizzy!" Saffy gasped as she panted, "I still have the ring! My engagement ring!"

The ring, made of commonplace ugly metal. And adorned with a small golden, glowing drop of Azerite.

"It might be enough to protect us!" she said.

"It might at that," Grizzek said. Hope, dizzying and wonderful, flowed through him, and he began squirming in earnest. "I got a confession to make too, Punkin."

"Whatever it is, I forgive you."

He licked his lips. All these years, he'd never said it. Wasted, stupid years. But all that was gonna change, starting now.

"Sapphronetta Flivvers . . . I lo—"

The bomb exploded.

CHAPTER TWENTY-EIGHT

Arathi Highlands, Stromgarde Keep

Anduin stood atop the ruined ramparts of Stromgarde Keep. The wind that stirred his fair hair was damp and cool, and the overcast sky did little to dispel the sense of sorrow that permeated this place.

The Arathi Highlands were a part of Azeroth rich in both human and Forsaken history. Here, the mighty city of Strom once had stood, and before it, the empire of Arathor, which had given birth to humanity. The ancient Arathi had been a race of conquerors, but they had recognized the wisdom in extending cooperation, peace, and equality to the vanquished tribes. Those qualities had made humanity strong. Those ancient tribes of the Eastern Kingdoms had joined together, succeeding in carving out a nation that had changed the world.

Here, too, was the birthplace of magic for humanity, a gift from the beleaguered high elves of Quel'Thalas in exchange for the aid of Strom's mighty army against their common foe, the trolls. All the major human nations had been settled by those who left Arathor: Dalaran, founded by the first magi instructed by the elves, as well as Lordaeron, Gilneas, and later Kul Tiras and Alterac. Those who stayed behind had built the fortress on which the king of Stormwind now stood.

He heard the sound of boots on stone and turned to regard Genn. The older man stepped beside him, his eyes roaming thoughtfully over the landscape of pine trees and rolling green hills.

"The last time I stood here," Genn said, "Gilneas was a powerful nation and Stromgarde's star was waning. Now both kingdoms lie in ruins. This one's home only to criminals, ogres, and trolls. And mine is home to *them*."

He pointed across the rolling fields to the gray stone of what was known as Thoradin's Wall. Anduin, Greymane, Turalyon, Velen, Faol, and Calia, along with exactly two hundred of Stormwind's finest, had arrived a few hours earlier from Stormwind Harbor. It had been sobering to see these ruins appear out of the mists, their stone as gray as the sky itself; more so, to stand where they stood now.

Thoradin's Wall and the small Forsaken encampment outside it marked the farthest point of the Horde's reach in this land that was the birthplace of humanity. Gilneas was not too far, wreathed in blight, invaded by the Forsaken who had driven Genn's people to become refugees and had slain the king's son.

Genn lifted a spyglass, made a soft growling sound, and handed the instrument to Anduin. Anduin emulated him. Through the gnomish tool, he could see armed figures patrolling the ancient wall. Just as his people did the walls of Stromgarde Keep.

They were all Forsaken.

Tomorrow, at first light, the Desolate Council would gather at the arch of Thoradin's Wall. They would march out to a halfway point marked by a fork in the simple dirt road. At the same time, the nineteen humans selected to meet with their friends or relatives would approach them. Calia and Faol would conduct the meetings. There would be no other Horde or Alliance interference, though each side had agreed to allow a group of priests to fly overhead just in case.

Anduin returned the spyglass to Genn. "I know this must be difficult for you."

"You know little about this," Genn snapped.

"I understand more than you think," Anduin continued. "I have

Turalyon and Velen to assist me." Kindly, he added, "You didn't need to put yourself through this."

"Of course I did," Genn said. "Your father's ghost would haunt me if I hadn't come."

As Liam's haunts you, because you did, Anduin thought sadly. "It will all be over soon," he said. "Thus far, Sylvanas appears to have kept her word. Scouts report that everything seems to be in order on the terms we discussed."

"If she *did* honor a promise, it would be a first," Genn said.

"Whatever we may think of her, we must be aware that she is a master strategist and that she therefore believes agreeing to this will somehow benefit her and the Horde."

"That's what I'm afraid of," Genn replied.

"She's worried about losing her grip on the Undercity because of the Desolate Council, but she's smart enough to know that they're no real threat. So she agrees to one day where members of the council only are permitted to meet their loved ones. The council is satisfied. Plus, it's an honorable thing to do, and that placates any orcs, trolls, or tauren. It's shrewd politics."

"She could very easily double-cross us and murder us all."

"She could. But that would be a terrible idea. Going to war over this right when the Horde is recovering from a brutal one? When she could be focusing on Silithus and Azerite?" He shook his head. "A terrible waste of resources. I don't trust her to keep her word for honor's sake. I *do* trust her not to be stupid. Don't you?"

Genn had no response to that.

"Your Majesties," came Turalyon's deep voice. "I've put the priests into position. Per your agreement, twenty-five of them will mount their gryphons tomorrow and be our eyes on the battlefield."

"It's not a battlefield, Turalyon," Anduin reminded him. "This is a peaceful gathering site. If all goes according to plan, it never *will* be a battlefield."

"My apologies. I misspoke."

"Words have power, as I know you know. Make sure the soldiers under you refrain from using that term."

Turalyon nodded. "We've seen nothing to indicate deception on the Horde's part. They appear to be keeping to the proper numbers and holding their positions."

Anduin felt a flutter inside his chest that he quickly quelled with a deep breath. For all his insistence that this would not provoke a war, he shared the worries of his advisers. Sylvanas was indeed a good strategist, and she almost certainly had plans in place that even SI:7 had been unable to ferret out.

For the moment, though, he would put aside his apprehension. Archbishop Faol and Calia would be conducting a service shortly, and after that he would move among those who had been brave enough—and who loved enough—to accept the chance to be reunited with people who would not be as they were in memory but who would be present. Would be, as much as the Forsaken could be, alive.

There was still something left of the old sanctum of the keep. It was more than sufficient to house the nineteen civilians who had come to be part of the meeting, the priests, and any soldiers who wished to join them. There were a few missing timbers in the roof, and drops of drizzly rain fell on some of those who had assembled. No one seemed to mind. Hope shone on their faces on a gray day, and Anduin took heart in those expressions. *This,* he mused, *is how you combat fear and long-held grudges. With hope and with open hearts.*

Calia and Faol waited until everyone was assembled, and then Faol spoke.

"First, I want to reassure you that few people enjoy sitting through a religious service for long even at the best of times. And today," he continued, glancing up at the gray clouds, "suffice it to say I'll spare you a lengthy session spent standing in a drafty old building."

There were some chuckles and smiles. Turalyon stood next to Anduin and said quietly, "They are still getting used to the idea of a Forsaken priest."

Anduin nodded. "It's to be expected. That's why I asked Calia to participate, too. Seeing the two of them side by side, priests of the Light, so obviously comfortable with each other, is a good introduction to what they're going to encounter shortly."

"Has anyone recognized her yet?"

Calia had donned a nondescript, practical dress and a heavy cloak with a hood. Most everyone had their hoods up in the light rain, so she did not stand out. Valeera had once told him that the best disguises were simple ones; appropriate clothes, behaving as if one belonged. No one was looking for a queen long thought dead today.

"Not that I've heard. To them, she's just a fair-haired priestess."

Turalyon nodded but still looked concerned.

Faol continued. "Your king has already told you what we expect will transpire, and he has advised you about what to do if a banner is raised either at Thoradin's Wall or here at the keep. I wish to avoid tedious repetition, so I'll just say be alert and move quickly.

"But I truly hope that doesn't happen. I and my fellow priestess will be out there with you. Others will be standing by to lend aid if needed. You may be shopkeepers, or blacksmiths, or farmers. But today you are my brothers and sisters. Today we are all servants of the Light. If you're afraid, don't be ashamed of it. You're doing something no one has ever done before, and that can always hold fear. But do know that you are doing the work of the Light. And now, accept its blessings."

He and Calia lifted their arms, turning their faces skyward. The sun might be hidden behind clouds, but that did not mean it wasn't there, sending its life-giving rays to those who dwelled on the face of this world. It was the same with the Light, Anduin thought. It was always present even when it seemed to be far beyond one's reach.

A golden glow filled the area: no explosion of blinding illumination but a gentle radiance that made Anduin's tight chest loosen as he inhaled deeply. He had been awake all night, both unable and unwilling to sleep, but as he closed his eyes and opened to the healing energy, he felt renewed, refreshed, and calm.

He stepped outside just as the clouds cleared for a moment and a few lone, beautiful rays of sunshine fell upon the group as they made their way out of the sanctum. This, too, was a blessing of the Light, though simple and mundane if something as magnificent as the sun itself could ever be called such things.

Many of those present—including Anduin himself—had never been to this historic site. They were allowed to roam within the confines of the fortress, though not outside it. Anduin would put no one unnecessarily at risk by allowing them to venture too far. He believed that Sylvanas would keep her word, but neither of them had said any-thing about spies. He had SI:7 to observe and report; she had her Deathstalkers to do the same. Their presence was yet another reason to be concerned about Calia, and she was under strict instructions to keep her cloak's hood up every time she ventured outside an enclosed space.

Most would return to the ships to sleep, though some had asked to remain inside Stromgarde Keep. Plenty of food, clean water, tents, and dry firewood had been provided for their comfort. Anduin watched them as they departed the chapel, some in groups of newly found friends, others in solitude. Some stayed behind to talk to Calia and Faol, and that made Anduin smile. Among them he noticed the pas-sionate and headstrong young Philia, who seemed to almost palpably radiate joy at Emma, an elderly woman who had lost so many to Arthas's war against the living—a sister and her family and, even more tragically, Emma's own three sons. "Ol' Emma," as Anduin had learned some called her, was not the hardiest of women, and her mind had a tendency to wander. But she seemed alert and her color was good as she spoke first to Calia and then, cautiously, to Faol.

"I have, in some ways, learned more lessons in the past several months than in a thousand years," Turalyon said, following Anduin's gaze. "There's much I have been wrong about."

"Genn still thinks this is a bad idea."

"He's right to worry. Sylvanas is . . . slippery. But no one can truly know another's heart. You have to make the best call with the infor-mation you have—and your own instincts. Genn is fueled by anger and hatred—not all the time, but often. You and I are fueled by other things."

"The Light," Anduin said quietly.

"The Light, yes," Turalyon agreed. "But we should let it guide us, not command us. We also have our own minds and hearts. We should make use of those as well."

Anduin said nothing. He had heard of the battles that Turalyon and Alleria had been fighting for a millennium. He knew they had been devotees of a naaru called Xe'ra, who, they thought, had epitomized what they loved best about the Light. Instead, Xe'ra had revealed herself to be stern and implacable—dangerously so.

"One day soon," Anduin said at last, "I would talk to you about your experiences with the Light. But for now, I understand your words and agree with them."

Turalyon nodded. "I will share what I can in the hope that it will help you be the ruler your grandfather and father were. And I will ask my son, Arator, to come to Stormwind soon. You two are very similar."

"From what I hear, he's the better swordsman." Anduin grinned.

"Nearly every swordsman I know says the same thing, so you're in good company." Turalyon looked up at the sky. "Still late afternoon. What are your plans?"

"I'll walk with Genn. Have him tell me what he remembers of this place. It will help distract us both. Then . . ." He shrugged. "I don't think I'll be getting much sleep tonight."

"Nor I. I seldom sleep before battle."

"This isn't a battle," Anduin said, not for the first time. Turalyon regarded him kindly with warm brown eyes, a hint of a smile on his scarred visage.

"Tomorrow, you, the forty-one people on the field, and everyone watching will be engaging in a battle not for property or riches but for the hearts and minds of the future," Turalyon said. "I would call that a battle, Your Majesty, and one well worth fighting."

That night, torches were lit along the ramparts of the old fortress, something the walls had not seen in many years. The warm, dancing light chased away darkness but coexisted with the flickering shadows of its own creation. The night was oddly clear, and the moonlight was kind to the area.

Anduin had wrapped himself in a cape and now stood looking out over the rolling landscape. Thoradin's Wall was only a slight smudge of pale stone in the distance. Anduin saw nothing moving there or in the field that stretched between the two outposts.

He closed his eyes for a moment, breathing the cool, moist air.

Light, you've guided and shaped me for most of my life. And since my father died, I've woken up every morning with the fate of tens of thousands of people resting on my shoulders. You have helped me bear this burden, and I have been blessed to have many wise people to rely upon. But this one's on me. It feels like the right thing to do. The bones that were shattered by the bell are easy tonight. My heart is clear, but my mind . . .

He shook his head and said aloud, "Father, you always seemed so certain. And you acted so swiftly. I wonder if you ever doubted as I do."

"No one save a madman or a child is completely free from doubt."

Anduin turned, laughing a little in embarrassment. "My apologies," he said to Calia. "You stumbled upon my ramblings."

"*I* apologize for intruding," she said. "I thought you might want company."

He considered declining her offer, then said, "Stay if you like. I might not be the best companion, though."

"Nor I," she admitted. "We'll be awkward together, then."

Anduin chuckled. He was growing fond of Calia. At nearly forty, she was much older than he was, but she felt less like a parent figure, as Jaina had been, and more like a big sister. Was it the Light in her that made him feel so easy in her presence? Or was it simply who she was? She *had* been a big sister once.

"Would it pain you to talk of Arthas?" he asked. "Before things . . . before."

"No. I loved my little brother, but few people seem to grasp that. He was not always a monster. And that little boy is how I'll always remember him."

A sudden smile crossed her features. "Did you know," she said, "he was once terrible at swordplay?"

CHAPTER TWENTY-NINE

Arathi Highlands, Thoradin's Wall

Elsie hoped that the Alliance participants in the Gathering had had a pleasant journey. It was a much longer trip for them than it was for the Forsaken. The Arathi Highlands were comparatively close, only a short flight via bat.

Of course, a short flight via bat was still exciting, as she so seldom traveled anywhere other than Brill to visit some friends. She could hardly believe that the day had finally come, that this meeting was actually happening, as her bat landed and she slipped off onto the soft grass at a site named Galen's Fall.

It was an apt name, as the human prince Galen Trollbane, onetime heir to the once-great kingdom of Stromgarde, had been slain on this spot years earlier by the Forsaken. Lady Sylvanas's apothecaries had raised him from death's grasp, and for a time he had served her. Then he rebelled, taking his men and declaring that he owed no allegiance to anyone other than himself and that he would restore Stromgarde to its former glory.

Stromgarde Keep lay to the south; one could see it from here. It was still in ruins, and Galen had fallen twice—once as a human, once as a Forsaken. *Such*, mused Elsie, *is the fate of those who would defy the Banshee Queen.*

A Forsaken handler took the reins and fed the bat a large dead insect, which it chomped happily as it was led away.

Parqual was waiting for her, his gray-green lips turned up in a smile. In his arms he held a ratty old teddy bear. "I'm glad you came," he said, "even though you don't have anyone waiting for you."

"Of course I had to come," she said. "I had to see you reunite with that daughter you keep going on and on about." She nodded at the toy. "You must remember, Philia is going to be a big girl now. She might be a little old for a teddy bear. Quite a few years have passed."

He chuckled. "I know, I know. I'm just so pleased she wanted to see me." He indicated the stuffed animal. "Brownie Bear here was the first toy I gave her when she was born. She was afraid she'd forget it on her trip to Stormwind, so she left it behind. It's . . . one of the few things of my old life that I have. And I wanted to share that with her."

Elsie beamed at her friend, letting his pleasure and anticipation be hers just a little bit. She looked around contentedly. Although many on the council had met with rejection on their first—or sometimes second or third—attempts to contact the living, every member finally did find someone who would agree to come. It was going to be a memorable day.

"She's not here yet," Parqual continued. "I wonder if she had second thoughts about coming."

"I don't see why she would tell us she would come and then not," Elsie said. As she looked around, she noticed that Annie Lansing had a basket of sachets, flowers in full bloom, and scarves and she was allowing council members to make a selection. Annie had no jawbone, and she currently had a pretty green scarf wrapped around the lower part of her face.

"Oh, that's such a nice thing Annie is doing," Elsie exclaimed. "It's going to be difficult for our loved ones to see what's happened to us. A scarf or a sachet will help." Some Forsaken had survived their time with death better than others; a gentling of their decomposition would assist the Alliance members in seeing past the body, which had endured so much, so they could focus instead on the person.

"That's a fine idea!" Parqual's face was not too disfigured, and carefully chosen trousers and a jacket covered his exposed bones. But he was aware that to the living, he might not smell particularly pleasant. "I think I'll get myself a sachet."

"You'd better hurry; they look very popular!" Elsie smiled as Parqual, clutching Brownie Bear, shuffled off quickly toward the thronged Annie.

Elsie turned her attention to the ramparts of the great wall and the line of archers atop them. When one of them turned around, Elsie started as she realized that these women, strong and lithe and still beautiful even in their undeath, could only be Sylvanas's elite dark rangers. They stood as still as if carved from stone, their quivers full of arrows, their bows held in one hand. Only their cloaks and their long hair moved in the breeze.

Nathanos Blightcaller was atop the wall as well, talking quietly to them. He met Elsie's gaze and nodded to her. She nodded back.

"There she is!" someone called, and Elsie turned.

The Dark Lady was coming.

Sylvanas rode atop one of the bats, her white-gold hair and glowing red eyes marking her as unmistakably as her bearing. The bat came in for a landing, and Sylvanas leaped gracefully from its back. No stiff movement of bone or sloughing skin for her. Her face was smooth, with high cheekbones, and her movements were as lithe as they had been when she yet breathed. Elsie felt an overwhelming sense of gratitude that her leader was here to support them even though Sylvanas had concerns.

The fire-red gaze swept the small crowd and alighted on Elsie.

"Ah, Prime Governor," Sylvanas said. "It is good to see you again. I trust that no one has forgotten the procedure I outlined for what is to come."

Forgotten? Elsie had it emblazoned on her mind, and she was certain everyone else did, too. No one wanted to jeopardize future meetings by causing anything to go wrong at today's.

Sylvanas turned and pointed at the figures on the wall. "A few reminders, just in case. These archers are here for your protection. Anduin has the same number along the ramparts of Stromgarde Keep.

You already know Archbishop Alonsus Faol. He and another priest will be accompanying the Alliance humans as they head toward the meeting site, which will be halfway between the fortresses. They will be moving about with you to facilitate conversations—and to monitor them."

Her gaze roamed over the assembled council members. "When you engage with your Alliance counterparts, you will speak of nothing other than your past history with them. You will not discuss your existence with me in the Undercity. They will not discuss their current lives, either. Faol and the other priest have agreed that if they happen upon anyone, Forsaken or human, indulging in such conversations—or indeed anything that could smack of treason or disrespect to the other side—those parties will receive a reminder. A second time, and they will be escorted off the field. Treat the archbishop and the priest with appropriate courtesy and obey them. Dawn is almost here. Once day breaks, if we are prepared, I will sound the horn once, and you may take the field. You will have until dusk. If for any reason I deem it necessary to call a halt to the meeting, I will sound the horn again three times and erect the Forsaken banner. Should this happen, return *immediately*."

Elsie wanted to know how immediate "immediately" was. Surely, if one wanted to express a final word of caring, or perhaps even an embrace if the Alliance member was brave enough, that was not a treasonous action. But one did not question the Dark Lady.

"When the meeting has concluded, the horn will alert you that it is time to come home," Sylvanas finished. "Is that understood?"

One obeyed, especially in this situation, in which misconduct or even a simple misunderstanding on either side could mean a fresh outbreak of a war that—well, no one needed that right now, certainly.

So Elsie stayed silent. When the horn blew, her people would say farewell and return right away. It was clear-cut and brooked no disagreement.

There was the soft thudding of hooves on grass as one of Sylvanas's dark rangers led a bony horse to the Dark Lady. She nodded and took the reins, then returned her glowing gaze to her subjects.

"I ride now to meet with the young human king. I do this for you.

Because you are Forsaken. I will not be long. And then you may go forth and meet the humans who had once been part of your former life. You will see if they still have a place in your current existence."

She paused, and when she spoke again, Elsie thought she heard threads of regret lacing the words.

"You should prepare for great disappointment. Though they may try, the living cannot truly understand us. Only we can. Only we know. But you have asked this of me, and so I give it to you. I will return shortly."

Without another word, she swung herself into the saddle and turned the skeletal horse's head.

Alone, weaponless, Sylvanas Windrunner, the Dark Lady of the Forsaken, the Banshee Queen, rode to meet the king of Stormwind.

Elsie had never felt prouder to be a Forsaken.

CHAPTER THIRTY

Arathi Highlands

Anduin had seen Lady Sylvanas Windrunner before, of course. All the major political figures in Azeroth had assembled in the Temple of the White Tiger to witness judgment passed on Garrosh Hellscream. He suspected but did not know for certain that she had been involved with the plot against Hellscream's life. Certainly he wouldn't put it past her. Sylvanas, she who was dead and yet "lived," had no compunctions about ending the lives of others.

There was no question in Anduin's mind that forbidding Genn to accompany him to this meeting had been the right thing. Greymane had proved a worthy and valuable ally, and he had been open about his affection toward Anduin. But there were some positions you just didn't put someone in. So close to the person Genn hated more than anyone in the world was one such. Anduin trusted Genn and was fond of him, but he knew that here, but a few paces away from his enemy, Genn probably would have attacked. And whether Genn died or Sylvanas did, war would have broken out at the worst possible time.

Anduin did not need Shalamayne or even the more familiar mace, Fearbreaker. His weapon was the Light. And of course, Sylvanas was deadly enough without a bow. All she needed to do was open her mouth and utter a wail, and he would perish.

As he rode the white-coated Reverence along the soft earthen road toward the meeting site, a small hill midway between their respective fortresses, he saw a still-tiny shape approaching.

Sylvanas was mounted on one of her unnerving skeletal steeds. Reverence's nostrils flared as he caught the scent of death and decay, but true to his name, the horse didn't falter. He was a trained war mount. Ordinary horses would be unsettled by the scent of blood or bodies. They would avoid stepping on other creatures if possible. Not warhorses. In battle, Reverence would be an extension of Anduin and an additional weapon, running down enemies and trampling them underfoot. The horse was trained to act counter to his instincts.

As I have been, Anduin thought. *We are both prepared to go against our natures if we must.*

He continued to draw closer to the Banshee Queen. He could see her more clearly now. Sylvanas had come unarmed, as he had demanded they both be. He could see her red eyes glowing beneath the hood she wore, her skin a muted blue-green not at all out of place in the somber, drizzly land, the marks under her eyes looking oddly like tear stains. She was beautiful and deadly, as beautiful and deadly as the flowers of the toxic herb Maiden's Anguish.

Emotions tumbled within him at the sight: Apprehension. Hope. And at the foremost, anger. Baine had told him that Vol'jin had ordered the retreat; Sylvanas had carried it out. But had Vol'jin done so, really? Had there truly been no alternative? Had Sylvanas betrayed his father and left him and everyone on that airship to die? And if she had . . . should Anduin even be talking peace with her now?

The words he had said so recently about Varian Wrynn, to the gathered crowd at Lion's Rest, came back to him. *He knew that no one—not even a king—is more important than the Alliance.* Anduin did, too. If all went well today, the Alliance could soon be safer than it ever had been. Whatever Sylvanas had or had not done, Anduin was certain that this was the right path. And sometimes the right path was a painful and dangerous one.

They came within ten feet of each other and brought their mounts to a halt. For a long moment, they simply took each other's measure. The only sounds were the soft sigh of the wind that stirred both gold and silvery hair, the stamp of Reverence's hooves, and the creak of the saddle as the great horse shifted. Sylvanas and her undead mount stayed perfectly, unnaturally still.

Then, impulsively, Anduin swung himself down and took a few steps toward Sylvanas. She raised a brow. After a pause, she emulated him, walking almost languidly until they were less than a yard apart.

Anduin broke the silence. "Warchief," he said, and nodded acknowledgment. "Thank you for honoring my request."

"Little Lion," she said in that throaty, strangely echoing tone that the Forsaken had.

The term stung more than it ought to. Aerin, the brave dwarf who had died trying to save lives, had called him that with warmth. He did not like Sylvanas twisting that memory to an insult.

"King Anduin Wrynn," he said, "and not so little anymore. You would do well not to underestimate me."

She smirked slightly. "You are still small enough."

"I'm sure we have better use of our time than to stand here flinging insults."

"I do not." She was enjoying this. He imagined that to her, he did appear small. After all, by her actions at the Broken Shore, ordered or not, she had sealed Varian's death. What was the son to her but a speck, a flea, a minor inconvenience?

"Yes, you do," he said, not allowing himself to be baited. "You are the warchief of the Horde. Its members fought bravely against the Legion. And the people closest to you—the Forsaken—have asked something of you that means much to them, and you have listened."

She met his gaze implacably. He had no idea if he was getting through to her. *Most likely not,* he thought ruefully. But that was not why he had come here today.

"This is not an offer of peace," he continued. "Merely a cease-fire for a twelve-hour period."

"So you said in your letter. And I responded that I agreed to your terms. Why are we having this conversation?"

"Because I wanted to see you in person," the king replied. "I want to hear from your own lips that no member of the Alliance will be harmed."

She rolled her eyes. "Does your precious Light tell you if someone is lying?"

"I'll know," he said simply. That wasn't exactly true. He thought he would know. He *believed* he would know. But he wasn't certain. The Light was not a sword. A sharp blade could always be relied on to cut flesh if the blow was struck a certain way. The Light was more nebulous. It responded to faith, not just skill. And oddly, it was because of that that he trusted it even more than Shalamayne.

Something flickered on her face and then was gone. She lifted her chin slightly as she replied, "Do you not trust me to keep my word, then?"

He shrugged. "You've gone back on it before."

There it was. Varian's death. Sylvanas didn't reply at once. Then, almost courteously, she said, "I give you my word. As the Dark Lady of the Forsaken and as warchief of the Horde. No member of the Alliance will come to harm by any member of the Horde today. Including me. Does that satisfy you, Your Majesty?"

There was an extra emphasis on the last two words. She was not showing respect by using them. She was using his new position as a not-so-subtle knife between the ribs. Because they both knew that in a better world it would have been Varian Wrynn speaking with her. And this meeting would have been less fraught with tension, resentment, and mistrust.

Anduin spoke before he could stop himself.

"Did you betray my father?"

Sylvanas stiffened.

Anduin's heart sped up, slamming against his chest. It was not a question he had intended to ask. But it was the one he needed to. He had to know. Had to know if Genn Greymane was right—if Sylvanas had set up his father and the Alliance army to die.

The words were out there.

Sylvanas stood motionless as a stone, her face expressionless. Her chest did not rise and fall with breath. Her heart did not pump blood. But even so, she was shocked that the boy had the courage to confront her so bluntly—and so quickly.

She had not given much thought to the events of the Broken Shore. There had been so much else to seize her attention, and she was not one for rumination. But now her thoughts flew back to that bloody, chaotic moment as if she again stood on that rise, with the Alliance army below her, fighting fiercely, while the Horde gave all its mighty heart to the attack.

We make our stand here, she had told the archers. And so they had, firing arrow after arrow, like a deadly rain, a storm, upon the loathed, fel-fueled enemy. And it was working. The Legion came, wave after wave of demonic monstrosities, each more horrible and horrifying than the last. But Varian's people were good. As were her own.

The bellow of surprise and warning had caused her to whirl. Sylvanas had watched, stunned, as a flood of demons poured through the gap behind her. She beheld Thrall, mighty warrior and shaman, the founder of the current Horde—on his knees, his green body trembling with the simple effort of trying to get on his feet. Baine stood over him, savagely defending his friend. Shock paralyzed her for a moment.

And then her warchief's words: *Dey're comin' from behind! Cover da flank!*

The spear. That awful spear, piercing Vol'jin's torso as he shouted out his order. It should have killed him immediately, but Vol'jin was not ready to die. Not yet. Purpose fueled him. He slew his killer and continued to fight, growing weaker before her eyes. Before Sylvanas knew it, she was on her horse, riding toward her leader, scooping him up to get him off the battlefield to safety.

In what must have been an agonizing effort, the troll turned and looked up at her. He whispered the order to her, his voice too weak for others to hear over the din of furious battle.

Do not let da Horde die dis day.

It was a direct command from her warchief. And it was the right one. The Alliance effort below, valiant as it was, was dependent on Horde assistance. If the Horde retreated now, Varian's army would fall.

But if the Horde stayed and fought, then *both* armies would fall.

Sylvanas had closed her eyes, each option unacceptable to her, but she made the only choice she could: obeying the will of the warchief, who later would die from the poisoned spear and, to everyone's astonishment, appoint Sylvanas Windrunner as leader of the Horde.

She lifted the horn to her lips and sounded the retreat. She had told no one of the regret she had felt when, standing on the stern of her ship, she beheld the green smoke of the explosion below, where Varian had fallen, and wondered if she was watching the final, excruciating moments of a mighty warrior.

Sylvanas would tell no one of that now, either. But as she stood before the young king, she could see traces of his father in him that had come with the last few years. Not just physically, in Anduin's increased height and more muscled physique, or even in the strong line of a determined jaw. She saw Varian in his bearing.

Did you betray my father?

Later, she would question her choice in responding. But in this moment she had no desire to offer falsehood.

"Varian Wrynn's destiny was set in stone, Little Lion. The Legion's numbers would have seen to that whatever choice I made that day."

His blue eyes searched hers for the lie. He found none. Something about him relaxed ever so slightly. He nodded.

"What happens here today benefits both the Horde and the Alliance. I am glad you have agreed to honor this cease-fire. I hereby swear to you that I, too, will abide by it, and no member of the Horde will come to harm by any Alliance hand this day." He inclined his head in acknowledgment as he mirrored her words, adding, "Including mine."

"Then we have nothing more to say."

He shook his golden head. "No, we don't. And I regret that. Perhaps another day we will meet again and speak of other things that could help both our peoples."

Sylvanas allowed herself a small smile. "I doubt that very much."

Without another word, Sylvanas turned, offering him a clear shot at her back, leaped into the saddle of her undead steed, and galloped down the path the way she had come.

CHAPTER THIRTY-ONE

Arathi Highlands, Stromgarde Keep

Despite the harsh words from the Horde leader as she left, Anduin felt hopeful. He believed her . . . Legion forces had been appearing everywhere, Genn had told him. If Horde soldiers had been surprised on that ridge, and Anduin believed Baine's report that they had, it was not unreasonable to suppose that remaining there would have doomed them—*and* the Alliance.

He had thought he would never know the real, full story. But if things went well today and in future such encounters, then perhaps many questions could be answered—and not just his.

A squire stepped forward and took Reverence's reins as the king slipped from the horse's back. "You're back in one piece," Genn observed.

"Don't sound so disappointed," Anduin joked.

"It went well, then," Turalyon said.

Anduin sobered as he regarded the paladin. He was as much a personal hero to the young king as Faol was. Turalyon loved a woman who skirted the line between the Void and the Light, whose sister was the one with whom he had just met.

"Yes," he said. "It did." He made a decision on the spot. "I asked her about Father," he told Genn. "She said there was nothing she could have done to save him. And I believe her."

"Of course she would say that," Genn scoffed. "Anduin . . ." He shook his head. "Sometimes you are simply too naive. I fear that something is going to come along and beat that out of you one of these days."

"I'm not naive. This . . . *felt* true."

Genn continued to scowl, but Turalyon nodded. "I understand."

Anduin stepped between them, clapping each of them on a shoulder. "Let's begin. There are people anxious to be with their families."

"I'll tell the priests to stand ready by the gryphons," Turalyon said.

May they be needed only for blessings, Anduin thought but did not say. Aloud, he said only, "Thank you, Turalyon."

He moved forward, looking at the nineteen people who stood waiting. On their faces were expressions of apprehension and excitement. Their king understood both emotions completely.

"It is time," he said. "May today be a day of change. Of connection. Of hope and looking forward to a day where reuniting with loved ones becomes a commonplace occurrence rather than a historic one. You'll be watched and will be protected."

They had been blessed by two priests already, but this benediction would be from their king. He lifted his hands and called down the Light upon those gathered. Eyes closed. Lips turned up in soft smiles, and he could feel calmness settle on those present. Including himself.

"Light be with you," Anduin said. He looked first at Archbishop Faol, who put a hand on his unbeating heart and bowed, and then at Calia, who had stayed up with him all night distracting him with stories. She smiled, her eyes shining. This moment was as much for them as it was for the active participants.

He nodded to Turalyon, who bowed his head, and waved to Genn Greymane. Anduin's chief adviser's glower had not lifted since their arrival, but he nodded now and shouted orders.

What remained of the enormous wooden doors creaked and shuddered open. Anduin recalled his conversation with Turalyon. The paladin had said that they would all be battling "not for property or riches but for the hearts and minds of the future."

For a moment, the group simply stood. Then one of them—Philia—shouldered her way through the crowd and began striding forward boldly, her body straight, her jaw set, her booted feet traveling swiftly over the green sward.

As if it was a signal the others had been awaiting, they started moving, too, some with quicker paces than others. No one was allowed to break into a run lest someone mistake haste for danger. But they flowed out of the gate and toward the cluster of shapes that were now coming out of Thoradin's Wall.

Over the sounds of conversation, a happy laugh rang out, sounding kind and strangely hollow. It was Archbishop Faol. And suddenly Anduin found joyful tears stinging his eyes.

You led the Army of the Light, Turalyon, Anduin thought, and his heart lifted. *But this is the army of hope.*

Ol' Emma kept wondering if this was truly happening or if it was just one of her daydreams. She decided that the pain in her joints as she walked across the soft grass, at a much more rapid pace than usual, proved that it was indeed a reality. Emma walked a great deal on a daily basis, carrying water back from the well to her small, tidy home, so endurance was not the problem. Speed was. She wanted so badly to be like Philia and all but run toward the center of the field, but her age would not permit her. She told herself that Jem, Jack, and Jake doubtless had learned patience in their time as undead. They could wait a few more moments to see her.

She was the one who didn't want to wait.

Someone fell in step beside her. He carried a beautifully crafted helm and introduced himself as Osric Strang.

"I'm Emma Felstone," Emma said. "That looks mighty heavy."

Osric, a powerfully muscled man with red hair and a beard, laughed. "Heavy enough to do its job. I made this for the—the person I'm going to see today. Tomas was like a brother to me. We used to argue over who made the best armor, when we served as guards—him in Lordaeron, me in Stormwind. I thought him lost forever that horrible day."

Osric gestured to the helm. "I thought if he'd survived being turned into a Forsaken with his brain intact, I'd better do what I could to keep it that way." He smiled down at her. "Who are you going to see?"

"My boys," Emma replied. She could hear the smile in her voice. "All three of them. They were in Lordaeron when . . ." She couldn't finish.

Osric regarded her with deep sympathy. "I'm . . . I'm so sorry you lost them. But I'm very glad they joined the council so you can see them again."

"Oh, I am, too," Emma said. "You have to focus on what you have, don't you?"

"That you do." The armorer shifted the helm to the crook of one arm and extended the other to Emma. "It can be a bit tricky walking over this terrain. Hang on to me."

Such a good boy, she thought as she gratefully did so. *Just like mine.*

The meeting site—exactly midway between Stromgarde Keep and Thoradin's Wall—had been prepared for the event. There were two tables, one on each side. One was where the Horde could put gifts for the Alliance, and the other was where the Alliance could place their own gifts. Osric walked up to the Alliance table and set down the helm, then rejoined Emma. The priestess who had interviewed them smiled winningly beneath her hood at the assembled participants, then asked them to form a long line facing their Horde counterparts.

Earlier, the weather had been damp and cold, the sky overcast. Now, though, the clouds were disappearing and sunlight peeked out. As everyone moved into position, Emma looked about anxiously for her sons. With a pang of worry, she wondered if she would even be able to recognize them. Although she had met Archbishop Faol, Emma wasn't fully prepared for how bad some of the Forsaken looked.

No one would mistake them for living beings, and the sunlight was not kind to them. Bones jutted through gray-green skin. Their eyes glowed eerily, and they hunched and shuffled as they walked.

Well, she told herself. *My skin is all wrinkled, and I sometimes hunch and shuffle, too.*

There was a long silence. Archbishop Faol moved forward. "If you wish to leave now, you may do so," he said in that strange but pleasant voice. At first no one moved, but then Emma saw about four or five humans, their faces shocked and almost as gray as those of the Forsaken, turn and hasten back toward the keep. One of those who had been rebuffed cried out after a departing figure in a hollow voice that held a world of sorrow. The others stood for a moment, then turned and began the long walk the way they had come, their heads bowed. *Oh, those poor things*, Emma thought.

"Anyone else?" Faol inquired. There were none. "Excellent. When I call your name, please step forward to me. You'll be joined by your loved one, and you may then roam the field together freely."

He unrolled a parchment and read.

"Emma Felstone!"

Emma's heart surged. To Osric, she queried in a shaking voice, "Is it time for me to see them now? After so long?"

"If you like," said the priestess. "If you don't, you can return to the keep."

Emma shook her head. "Oh, no. No, no. I won't disappoint them like those other folks." Osric patted her hand reassuringly; and Emma pulled away, straightened, and made her way unaided to where Faol stood.

"Jem, Jack, and Jake Felstone," the archbishop called.

Three tall Forsaken stepped forward from their own line, advancing hesitantly. Emma stared at them as they approached. They had all been so large and fit in life. Such strong young men. How confident they had been, how proud to serve Lordaeron. Now they were but skin and bones and limp clotted hair. It took her a moment to read their expressions.

Her sons, once laughing and confident, looked . . . frightened.

They are more afraid here, in front of me, than on a battlefield, Emma realized. And then all the differences between her and them suddenly didn't matter.

She started to weep even though she felt her mouth curve in an enormous smile.

"My boys," she said. "Oh, my boys!"

"Mama!" Jack said, lurching toward her.

"We've missed you so much!" Jem said. And Jake simply bowed his head, overcome with the moment. Then, all three of the Forsaken bent to embrace their mother.

Thank you, Calia said to the Light as she watched the matriarch of the reunited family shed tears of joy. *Thank you for this.*

She listened, smiling, as other names were called. They stepped forward, hesitant or joyful. Some simply shook their heads and, unable to take the final steps now that the moment had come, returned in silence, leaving their Forsaken loved ones standing alone until they, too, turned away and went back to the wall. Calia prayed for them: the ones who had refused and the ones who had been rebuffed. All were hurting. All needed the Light's blessing.

But there were surprisingly few of them. Most of the reunions were cautious at first: stilted, awkward. But that was all right, too.

"Philia Fintallas," read the archbishop. Philia was in the very forefront, and she had spotted her father, Parqual, already. At the sound of her name, she ran right up to him, shouting, "Papa!"

These two needed no urging or mediating. They hastened to each other, stopping just short of touching, and both wore smiles as large as Calia's heart felt. "It's really *you,*" Philia said, putting so much into the single word.

After the first few reintroductions, things flowed much more smoothly and swiftly. Not all the reunions were as joyful and easy as others, but they were talking. Forsaken and human were talking. Who could ever have believed this moment would happen? One man—one king—had.

And if this could happen, perhaps more could, too. More events that should have happened but that Arthas had so tragically destroyed.

There is such a thing as a new beginning, she thought. *For all of us.*

Faol stepped beside her. "These eyes have seen so much pain. How delightful, after everything that has happened, that they can still behold this."

"Do you think there will be another gathering?" Calia asked.

"I hope so, but that rests entirely with Sylvanas. Perhaps even she will find she still has a heart, just as these people have."

"We can hope," Calia said.

"Yes, indeed," Faol replied. "We can always hope."

CHAPTER THIRTY-TWO

Arathi Highlands, Thoradin's Wall

Sylvanas Windrunner stood on the top of the ancient wall. Nathanos, as always, was beside her. Her gaze was fixed on the scene unfolding in the distance.

"It seems to be going without incident," Sylvanas said. "Any reason to believe it is not?"

"None that I have learned, my queen," Nathanos said.

"Although I see that some of the humans have scorned interaction with those whose hopes they had raised," she said. "That was cruel of them."

"It was," Nathanos agreed. He offered nothing more.

"I was reluctant to agree to this gathering, but perhaps this is a good thing. Now my Forsaken begin to understand how they are perceived even by those who once claimed to love them."

"You were wise to have permitted it, my queen. Let them see for themselves what the situation is. If it is painful to them, they will not wish to repeat the experience. If it is joyful to them, you have something to hold over them to keep them obedient. Not," he added, "that there was ever much to fear from this group."

"It was good for me to witness this. I have learned much from it."

"Will you repeat it?"

Sylvanas squinted up at the sun. "The day is young yet. I am not done observing. Nor will I relax my vigilance. Varian's whelp likes to appear as though he is utterly without guile, but he may be shrewder than we give him credit for. He could have planned an attack on his own people with an eye to blaming us for it. Then he would be seen as a strong leader to declare war on us. The ultimate protector of the helpless."

"It is possible, my queen."

She gave him one of her rare, wry smiles. "But you think otherwise."

"With respect, such a thing sounds more like a strategy you would employ," he said.

"It does," she said. "But not today. We are not prepared for a war." She glanced at the rangers she had positioned atop the wall. Their quivers were full, their bows strapped to their backs within easy reach.

They would attack the instant she told them to.

Sylvanas smiled.

Arathi Highlands Field

Parqual and Philia had wandered over to the Forsaken exchange table. Elsie watched them happily as Parqual pointed at an old, tattered teddy bear, and tears streamed down the girl's face.

"I want to hold Brownie," Elsie heard her say. "I want to hold *you*, Papa."

"Oh, my little one, or not so little one," he chuckled, "Brownie is off limits till your king says it's safe. And as for me, my skin can't handle those bear hugs I remember."

Philia wiped her face. "Can I hold your hand if I do it gently?"

People thought that because Forsaken flesh was dead, it was limited in what it could communicate. Nothing could be further from the truth. A myriad of expressions crossed Parqual's face: joy, love, fear, hope.

"If you like, child," he said.

Forsaken came in all stages of death: freshly slain, partially rotting, almost mummified. Parqual was the last of these even though he'd been so determined to have a sachet tucked in his pocket, and Elsie wanted to hug them both as he extended his withered, parchment-fragile hand and placed it in his daughter's smooth, living one.

Elsie wanted to linger with Parqual and Philia to savor the reunion of parent and child. But there were others, who found themselves at a loss for words or didn't know how to react and might appreciate someone to help. These two would be all right. They had come with love and trepidation in their hearts. But they also had come with something else: hope.

"Mother?" The voice belonged to Jem, the oldest of the Felstone boys. He sounded upset. Elsie looked around for him. She found him with Jack and Jake, forming a ring around their tiny mother; then one of them stepped aside, looking around for aid.

Elsie saw that their mother, Emma, was ashen and seemed to be having difficulty breathing. "Priestess!" one of them cried, his sepulchral voice tinged with fear. "Please, help her!"

The cloaked woman hastened over and lifted a hand. The Light came to her, called down as if from the sun itself, and she sent it toward the mother. The older woman gasped softly. Her pale face warmed to a humanly healthy pink hue, and she blinked, looking around for the woman who had healed her. Their eyes met, and the priestess smiled.

"Thank you so much," Elsie said.

"It's an honor to be here," the priestess replied. "Pardon me, I couldn't help but notice that you're standing alone. Did your meeting not go well?" Her face was largely in shadow, but Elsie saw that her smile was kind.

"Oh, my dear, you're so sweet," Elsie said. "I'm fine. I'm just here to share my council's joy."

The priestess gasped softly, and she moved toward Elsie. "You must be Prime Governor Benton," she said. She reached for the Forsaken woman's hands. "I heard about Wyll. I'm so sorry."

Elsie started to draw back, then paused. Surely someone Faol trusted to assist him would not find Elsie's leathery, cold appendages horrifying. The priestess took them in hers very carefully, already aware, as brave young Philia was just discovering, that one had to be gentle with the Forsaken. Their flesh was so very fragile. And yet, as Elsie had observed, most of them seemed starved for physical contact.

The priestess's hands were soft and warm. The touch felt so pleasant. Then she released Elsie's hands but stayed near.

"Thank you," Elsie said. "The archbishop has been so kind to us. We're grateful that you and he are here with all of us today."

"I am happier to be here than you know," the human woman assured her. "I wanted to make sure I found you to thank *you* for being so willing to work with us. Know that King Anduin deeply regrets that he can't thank you in person."

Elsie waved a dismissive hand. "This isn't a safe place for a human king to be. He's got to think about his people. I owe him a debt I can never repay. He was with my Wyll as he passed, when I couldn't be. And I will tell you, Wyll loved those Wrynn boys like they were his own."

The two women stood together, watching the event continue to unfold. Here and there they heard the sound of laughter. They smiled at each other.

"This is a good thing," Elsie said. "A very good thing."

"His Majesty hopes that if all goes well today, your warchief might be agreeable to another such meeting at a later time."

Elsie's smile faded slightly. "I do not believe that will happen," the Prime Governor said. "But then again, I never believed it would happen at all. So it shows you what I know, I suppose." She chuckled.

"If there is a second Gathering," the priestess continued, "King Anduin wants to meet you."

"Oh, my, wouldn't that be lovely!" Elsie glanced back toward the keep. It was far enough away that she couldn't distinguish faces, but it would appear that the young king was not shy about letting himself be seen. He stood wearing his distinctive armor draped with a blue tabard bearing the golden lion of Stormwind. The bright shafts of sunlight seemed to seek him out, to catch the gleam of his armor and his golden hair.

"Queen Tiffin was such a beauty. And so kind," Elsie mused. "Anduin has her hair. 'A boy of sunshine,' Wyll called him. No one knew then, back when I still breathed, that the boy of sunshine would one day be a king of the Light!"

As they watched, another stepped up beside the king of Storm-wind: tall, powerfully built, with white hair. "Who's that gentleman?" Elsie asked.

For a moment, a deeper shadow passed over the priestess's face. "That's King Genn Greymane of Gilneas," she said.

"Oh, dear," Elsie said. "I imagine he's not too happy about all this."

"He may not be," the priestess replied. "But he's standing beside his king, and he's watching us."

She lifted her arm. "You might not be able to meet King Anduin, but you can wave to him," she told Elsie.

Hesitantly, Elsie imitated her. At first, her movements were small and shy, but when Anduin saw them and returned the gesture, pleasure rushed through her and she waved more vigorously. Unsurprisingly, Greymane did not join in. But that was all right. He was there. Perhaps he would see something today that would move him.

"Imagine me, Elsie Benton, waving hello to a king!" she murmured. And when Anduin bowed to her, the Prime Governor of the Desolate Council laughed brightly in surprise.

ARATHI HIGHLANDS, THORADIN'S WALL

Sylvanas made a point of speaking with each of the council members who had returned, angry and disillusioned, to the wall. She was both sorrowful and satisfied as she spoke to them. "I feared this very thing would happen," she told them. "You understand now, do you not?"

They did. The gulf between human and Forsaken could not be bridged. Sylvanas felt particularly vindicated when Annie Lansing, who had labored to create sachets and scarves to make the Forsaken more appealing to the humans, trudged slowly back.

"You went to so much effort to please them," Sylvanas said.

"I thought if they weren't distracted by what we looked like . . . what we smelled like . . . they could truly see us," Annie replied sadly. "Truly see *me*."

"Who was it?"

There was a pause. "My mother."

"A mother's love is supposed to be unconditional," Sylvanas said.

"Apparently it isn't," Annie said bitterly. She unwound the scarf, and Sylvanas gazed unflinchingly into her maimed face. "We should have listened to you, Dark Lady. We were terribly wrong."

The words were sweet as honey. Sweet as victory. The council would be divided, and the conflict among its members would destroy it. And Sylvanas hadn't had to do a thing.

Sylvanas ascended the wall with quick, lithe steps and pulled out her spyglass. With any luck, she would see more newly enlightened Forsaken returning back where they belonged. Where was the Prime Governor in the midst of all this? Was she shaken by the attrition?

Sylvanas found her. And all her satisfaction evaporated.

Vellcinda stood easily and comfortably next to the cloaked and hooded priestess Faol had brought with him. The Prime Governor looked toward the keep, upward, to someone atop it. And then she waved.

Quickly Sylvanas moved the spyglass, the images it revealed to her veering about madly until they lit upon the figure of Stormwind's king.

Anduin, smiling, was waving back. As Sylvanas watched, fury boiling inside her, he put his hand on his heart and bowed.

Bowed.

To Vellcinda Benton, the Prime Governor of the Desolate Council.

Sylvanas opened her mouth to order the retreat. But no. Not yet. This was not enough to convict Vellcinda in the eyes of the council. Sylvanas needed to tread carefully.

To Nathanos she said, "I want someone watching Vellcinda at all times. And," she added, "I want that priestess watched, too."

ARATHI HIGHLANDS FIELD

She laughs like a little girl.
  Almost like a living thing.
Calia's heart was full, so full. She tried to burn this moment into her mind so that she would remember it when she woke with achingly

empty arms from the nightmares that still haunted her dreams. When she would hear ugly words uttered by both sides of Azeroth's seemingly endless war between Horde and Alliance. She would remember standing in this field while the grown boy of sunshine waved to the woman whose husband had tended him his whole life. She would remember this day and all its gifts, as the day when everything began to change.

"I did bring something for him to give to Wyll wherever they buried him."

Elsie patted her chest, touching a simple golden ring that hung from a chain around her neck. "I want to wear it until the last possible moment, and then I'll put it on the table. It's my wedding ring. I wore it till the day I died . . . and after, too, until I just couldn't." She indicated her bony fingers. "It becomes hard to keep rings on. Or fingers, for that matter. But I kept this. I'd be so grateful if you made sure it reaches the king."

The priestess stared at the ring and thought of her family. Of her child, whom she imagined as having grown up to be like Philia: brave and loyal and kind. Of her own husband, who had kept her secret and loved her for who she was. Of all the people of Lordaeron, who didn't deserve what had happened to them and who had struggled on bravely. Of every one of those on the field today, brave enough to look past outer ugliness to an inner beauty, or, conversely, brave enough to overcome their fear of rejection and see loved ones again as such, not as the enemy. Of Philia, who wanted to hug her father. Of Emma and her sons, reunited in a mother's twilight years. Of the untold numbers of people just like them, on both sides, yearning to be united.

Of her brother, who was responsible for all the pain, all the loss.

A Menethil had done this.

A Menethil would have to fix it.

CHAPTER THIRTY-THREE

Arathi Highlands, Stromgarde Keep

For several long moments Anduin stood watching, a smile playing about his lips. He recalled his first experience with the Conclave, how it felt to be walking into a place of complete safety, to see races that might otherwise be slitting one another's throats laughing together, or discussing philosophies, or researching, or simply sitting side by side in quiet, joyful coexistence.

And now similar scenes were unfolding beneath him, but ones of possibly even greater import to the future of Azeroth. He watched Calia, who had hidden in a ditch for two days while enraged mindless creatures swarmed and searched above her, move about the crowd, speaking to small groups and blessing them. He'd watched her heal Emma, whose reunion with not one but all three of her sons had been almost more than she could handle. He'd watched Parqual and Philia respond joyfully and freely to each other, as if death had not separated them at all.

Calia was too far away for Anduin to make out her expression, but she lifted her arm and waved. Standing beside the priestess was a Forsaken woman who appeared not to have an Alliance family member. Glancing at Calia, she, too, lifted her arm and waved to the king of Stormwind. This had to be the Prime Governor, Elsie Benton. Anduin couldn't suppress a grin as he waved back and impulsively gave a quick bow.

"That's not how you pat yourself on the back."

Anduin laughed and turned to Genn, clapping the older man on the shoulder. "I confess, I might want to do a little back patting. But I think the congratulations belongs to them. Those down there. The courage it had to have taken for any of them to be willing to do this . . . it's almost unfathomable."

He expected an irritated retort. Instead, Genn Greymane was silent, as if seriously considering Anduin's words. And that, Anduin thought, was a victory right there.

ARATHI HIGHLANDS FIELD

Philia had believed that her father as he was now would not be too different from the man she'd loved so much. She was discovering as they spoke and ambled around the field together that she was both wrong and right.

Parqual's appearance, especially up close, had shocked her initially. For a brief moment, though she would never tell him, horror and disgust had closed her throat and urged her body to flee. But then he had smiled. And it was her papa's smile.

Different—oh, yes. Changed beyond imagining. But he was still himself. Some things he had forgotten, and that pained her. But in many ways, he was still so much himself that she could scarcely believe it.

At one point, they were chatting happily about history, a topic about which they were both passionate. Without thinking, Philia blurted out, "Oh, Papa, you should write about Arthas and what happened that day!"

Horrified, she put a hand to her mouth as her father turned very still. "I'm so sorry," she said. "I shouldn't have—"

"No, it's all right," Parqual replied quickly. "It's something that I've thought about. A firsthand account. Primary sources are the most important, you know."

Philia did know, and she smiled slightly.

"I never did, because everyone who would read it already has their own firsthand account. But now . . ."

The possibilities. "Papa—you could write it, and we could share it with the Alliance! We only know rumors and whispers. You could let us all know what really happened!"

He looked at her sadly. "I don't think our Dark Lady will permit a second meeting, my dear."

Philia felt as though her heart had plunged to her toes. "Is . . . is this our only chance to see each other?"

"It may well be."

She shook her head. "No. No, I won't accept that. I've only just found you again, Papa. I won't lose you a second time. There has to be a way!"

Philia expected more sad denials, but instead her father was silent. His lambent gaze was not on her but on the woman who had been pointed out as the leader of the Desolate Council. Elsie Benton stood now with the human priestess who had been so kind to the Forsaken. As if feeling his gaze, the priestess turned her head and looked at Parqual.

"I think we may have found that way," Parqual murmured. Gently, he placed a hand on his daughter's back. "Come. There are people I would like you to meet."

Calia continued to keep her eyes on the field as she spoke with Elsie. It looked as though all those who remained were having positive conversations with their loved ones. She heard laughter and saw smiles. *This is how it should be. The people of Lordaeron haven't been free to be who or what they wish to be. For this moment, they are.*

There was Osric, talking to his friend Tomas. Over there, two sisters were reunited. There was Ol' Emma, whom Calia had healed, looking ten years younger as she smiled at her children. And Parqual and Philia were coming to join them. They spoke for a few moments; Calia was too far away to hear what they said.

Parqual said something to his daughter, then headed alone toward

Calia. She felt a flicker of concern; he shouldn't be approaching her like this. No one was supposed to know that she and Parqual knew each other. Loudly, he said, "Priestess . . . may this Forsaken have your blessing?"

"Of course," she replied.

He bent his head, whispering to her, "We need you now. It's time."

"Wh-what?"

"You'll see. Be ready."

Calia steadied herself and called for the Light's blessing. It came, bathing him in its warm, gold-white glow. Parqual grimaced; the Holy Light healed Forsaken, but it was not pleasant for them. With a nod of appreciation, he turned and rejoined the group. She watched them, alert now. For a while, they simply chatted. And then, too casually, Philia and Parqual walked away from the Felstones. After a moment, the Felstone family, too, began to walk. Slowly and indirectly, so as not to attract too much attention, they were moving from the center of the field toward Stromgarde Keep.

Saa'ra's words rushed back to Calia so swiftly that she staggered.

There are things you must do before that peace will be granted to you. Things that you must understand, that you must integrate into yourself. People who need your help. What one needs in order to heal will always come one's way, but sometimes it is hard to recognize it. Sometimes, the most beautiful and important gifts come wrapped in pain and blood.

Was this the moment she had been thinking of ever since she had found her way to the Netherlight Temple and Archbishop Faol? So much had fallen into place so perfectly: the Desolate Council, Anduin's noble call for this gathering. And now, spontaneously, human and Forsaken had taken a step so courageous that Calia felt both inspired and ashamed.

Yes. Parqual was right.

It was time.

She whirled toward Elsie, her hood falling off with her movement. "Elsie, there's something you must know. And I pray to the Light that has sent me here this day that you will understand—and support it." She swallowed hard. "Support . . . me."

ARATHI HIGHLANDS, THORADIN'S WALL

"Something is wrong," Sylvanas murmured. "But I cannot put my finger on precisely what."

The priestess had said something to Vellcinda that had the Prime Governor agitated. No one else on the field seemed to notice. They were too busy taking strolls with their loved ones.

And that was it.

"They're defecting," Sylvanas snapped.

Nathanos was instantly alert, scanning the field with his spyglass. "Several of them are moving in the direction of Stromgarde Keep," he confirmed, "but that may not be intentional."

"Let's find out," Sylvanas said. She lifted the horn to her lips and blew three long, clear notes.

Now to see who comes when called—and who breaks and runs.

At that moment, one of the priests returned, urging her bat to go as quickly as it could. She looked shocked and sickened.

"My lady!" she gasped. "The priestess—I didn't recognize her until her hood fell off—I can scarce believe it—"

"Spit it out," Sylvanas snarled, her body taut as a bowstring.

"My lady—it's Calia Menethil!"

Menethil.

The name was laden, heavy with meaning and portent. It was the name of the monster who had made her. Who had slaughtered and destroyed. It was the name of the king who had ruled Lordaeron. And it was the name of that king's daughter—his heir.

And to think she had thought the king of Stormwind an ingenuous fool. He played politics better than she could possibly have imagined.

Anduin Wrynn had brought a usurper with him. And now, that girl, that damned human *child* who ought to be long dead, was taking Sylvanas's own people to join the Alliance.

"My lady, what are your orders?"

ARATHI HIGHLANDS FIELD

In the center of the field, Elsie stared at the queen of Lordaeron. "It's not possible," she said. But she knew it was true. Calia had taken care to keep her face hidden in the shadow of her hood. But now the hood was gone and she had turned to look directly at Elsie, and Elsie could not look away.

"You are my people, and I want to help you," Calia pleaded. "I only came to observe, to begin to get to know the Forsaken of Lordaeron."

"Undercity," Elsie said. "We live in the Undercity."

"You didn't once. You won't have to live in the shadows anymore. Just—please. Come walk with me. Parqual, the Felstones, all the others—see them? They're defecting. Anduin will shelter and protect you all; I know he will!"

"But—the Dark Lady—"

As if in response, the horn sounded three sharp blasts. Elsie turned her gray-green face back toward the wall and the Forsaken banner that had been unfurled.

"I'm sorry, Your Majesty," Elsie said. "I can't betray my queen. Not even for you." She turned and shouted, "Retreat! *Retreat!*"

ARATHI HIGHLANDS, STROMGARDE KEEP

Anduin heard the sound of the horn. Baffled, he looked down, trying to ascertain what had caused it. As far as he could see, nothing had changed from a moment—

He pressed his lips closed to prevent a groan from escaping. There was sudden deep, dull pain inside him.

"What's wrong, son?" Genn asked sharply.

"It is the bell," Velen said somberly, sadly. Turalyon looked confused, but Greymane's face went hard. He knew about the bell. About the warning it meant to his young king.

"The retreat," Anduin managed, grimacing as the pain increased. "It's dangerous." A second pain struck Anduin, different but even

260 . CHRISTIE GOLDEN

more devastating to him. For this was not the bone-hurting ache of the Divine Bell's handiwork but the knife-sharp pain of a dream shattering before his eyes. With a sick jolt, Anduin saw that the tiny figures who had stood at attention on Thoradin's Wall were now mounted on bats and flying toward the field.

Dark rangers.

"It's over," he whispered, and leaned on the parapet. "Get them to safety before it's too late!"

On the field below, spread out like markers in the map room, were other tiny figures. Some of them were heading back toward Thoradin's Wall. Some were returning to the keep.

And some still stood in the field as if paralyzed.

The pain wasn't abating, and Anduin clenched his jaw against it as he looked back at the wall. He forced his fisted hands to open and lifted the spyglass.

His mind saw things with a strange, swift clarity, and he immediately picked out Archbishop Faol and Calia. The former was close to the wall, urging his charges to rush through the gates to safety. But Calia stayed in the field, arguing with Elsie Benton. The priestess's hood was down.

Calia . . . what are you doing?

Calia turned away from the Prime Governor, ran forward a few paces, cupped her hands around her mouth, and shouted, "Forsaken! I am Calia Menethil! Head for the keep!"

"What is that girl *doing?*" shouted Genn.

But Anduin was not listening. His gaze was riveted on the pair of women in the field, one human, one Forsaken, and at that moment Elsie Benton dropped like a stone with a black-fletched arrow protruding from her chest.

Calia turned back toward Elsie, but she was too late. A look of horror was on her face, but there was nothing she could do now for the murdered Prime Governor. Calia shouted again, "To the keep! Run!"

Anduin jerked back, his mind reeling. Now he saw that everyone, humans and Forsaken both, had broken into a run.

Sylvanas had moved to the offensive, just like that. Right under their watchful eyes.

And he, Anduin Wrynn, had put innocent unarmed civilians directly in her path. The only way to correct his terrible mistake was to do everything he could to save them, even if it meant starting a war.

But even with that thought, the pain did not ebb. Everyone was shouting at him, asking for orders, telling him one thing while someone else was screaming another. But Anduin couldn't hear any of them. He knew that he needed to listen to what this strange, contradictory gift of the Divine Bell had to say to him. He squeezed his eyes shut and pleaded silently, *Light, what is happening? What can I do?*

The answer came. It was swift, blunt, and brutal.

Protect.

And mourn.

"No," he whispered, protesting even as he accepted the words. His eyes snapped open.

Genn was raging at him. "—got to get our soldiers out there and—"

"—stand ready to defend our people by—" It was Turalyon, radiant with the Light. Anduin couldn't speak, but he nodded to Turalyon that he should proceed.

Bats swooped and darted over the field, their riders showering it with black lines.

Each one struck its target. And Anduin understood.

"Genn," he said, his voice a harsh rasp. "Genn—she's killing them. She's killing them *all.*"

Sylvanas Windrunner had kept her word. Her rangers were not attacking humans.

They were attacking Forsaken. Even those who were returning to the wall.

This is wrong, he thought. *And I am wrong for standing here.*

He made his decision, and the pain ebbed at once. "Whatever happens"—he called over his shoulder, racing toward the one remaining gryphon left—"do not attack the rangers unless they attack us. Is that clear? I need your word!"

"You have it," Turalyon stated. Anduin wondered if the paladin had some inkling of what he was about to do or if he was simply being a good soldier. Genn, however, could never be counted on simply to obey without protest.

"What are you planning?" he demanded. "These aren't your people. They're hers! She'll *kill* you, boy!"

Anduin was about to find out.

CHAPTER THIRTY-FOUR

Arathi Highlands Field

For a ghastly moment, the slaughter around Calia Menethil overlapped and blended with the memory of those two terrifying days years ago when she had lain motionless in a ditch while crazed undead rampaged only a few feet away. She was frozen and could only watch in horror as the dark rangers of Sylvanas Windrunner loosed arrows upon the members of the Desolate Council.

They had come with no hatred in their hearts for Sylvanas. These were only people who wanted to see friends and family they thought were forever beyond their reach. But their warchief, their own Dark Lady, she who had made them and above all others should be safeguarding their well-being, had ordered her rangers to shoot into their midst.

They aren't even armed, Calia's mind said stupidly, as if that were the most important thing in this horrifying betrayal. They had brought only rings and love letters and toys onto this field. They wanted nothing other than kindness and connection.

I didn't mean for this to happen, she thought. But that didn't matter. Nor did it matter that the initial idea to seek sanctuary with the Alliance had come from Parqual. They would have been her people had they lived, and they were her people in undeath, too. And she would *not* scurry to safety like a coward while her people were being butchered by a jealous usurper queen for daring to race toward what they believed to be a sanctuary.

She was Calia Menethil. Heir to the throne of Lordaeron. And she would fight—and die—to defend her people. She just had to get them safely to Stromgarde Keep and maintain a barrier of Light between them and the arrows that continued to claim them.

"To the keep!" she shouted. "Run!"

And she hastened to do whatever she could to shield her people from the false queen's rage.

ARATHI HIGHLANDS, THORADIN'S WALL

"My queen, what are you *doing*?"

Sylvanas heard the shock in her normally calm champion's voice. She chose to overlook it. On the surface, what was unfolding below—the firing of arrows, the screams and pleas of the Desolate Council as they tasted their Last Deaths could seem perplexing and disturbing.

"The only thing I can do and still hang on to my kingdom as it is," she said. "They were defecting."

"Some were running back here, to safety," he replied.

"They were," she agreed. "But how much of that was fear? How tempted were they until that point?" She shook her head. "No, Nathanos. I cannot take the risk. The only Desolate Council members I trust are the ones who returned to me early on, broken and bitter. Truly *Desolate*. All the others . . . I cannot allow that sentiment, that hope, to grow. It is an infection ready to spread. I have to cut it out."

Slowly, accepting her words, he nodded. "You are letting the humans go."

"I have no wish to fight a war when I'm not ready to do so." She gazed at the growing number of motionless Forsaken corpses on the field. So many had opted for death. "I don't think the boy king arranged this. It was stupid. He is naive, but he is not stupid. He would not risk war for a handful of Forsaken merchants and laborers." Her initial suspicion had evaporated quickly. If he had intended this defection, he would have planned better for it. No, Sylvanas placed the blame on the Menethil girl, as reckless and deceitful as her loathed brother. She had gulled both the king of Stormwind and the warchief of the Horde.

And she was about to die for it.

"I grow tired of the game," Sylvanas said. "I will kill the usurper myself. And then the Forsaken will return home, where they belong. With me."

She gave her champion a cold smile. "One of the Desolate Council's desires was not to be reborn again and again. So I have given them two gifts today. A reunion with their loved ones and their final deaths.

"And now," she said, grasping her bow and leaping lightly atop a waiting bat, "I am about to consign Calia Menethil to the annals of history's dead royalty."

Arathi Highlands Field

Anduin prayed to the Light as he never had before. These people—both human and Forsaken—had done nothing but try to see past their old hatred, their fear. They had reached out in love and in trust—

—*trust in me*—

—to do what was right, and good, and kind.

Even as he urged the gryphon on to his greatest speed, he realized with a sick, sinking horror that he would be too late.

Up ahead, Osric Strang ran beside his friend Tomas. The young king reached for the Light, but before he could release it upon the running Forsaken, an arrow sang past his ear and implanted itself in Tomas's bony chest. It went clear through, piercing the spine with inhuman precision.

No . . .

Anduin glanced around wildly. There was Philia, with her father, Parqual, running with her arm around him protectively, as if she were the parent, not he. But the arrows of the dark rangers were as merciless as those who fired them. They struck true, and Parqual tumbled in midstride. Philia fell to her knees, her arms going around the decaying body and her sobs ripping Anduin to shreds.

He could reach none of them in time. Not even any of the Felstone boys, who were running toward the keep as fast as their long legs could go. One of them cradled the frightened, elderly Emma in his arms, trying to shield her with his own body, not understanding that he and his undead brothers were the ones in danger, not their mother.

Three arrows sang. Three arrows reached their targets. Three bodies toppled to the ground, their mother hitting the earth hard and crying out their names.

The other Forsaken on this lethal field were much too far away. Anduin knew he could not save them. But he could save Emma.

He brought the gryphon down and jumped off his back, gathering up the weeping woman and calling to the Light. *She has lost them all, now. Please, give her hope as well as healing. Her boys would want her to live.*

Emma's eyelids fluttered. She opened them and gazed up at him. Her eyes were swollen with tears. "All of them," she said.

"I know," Anduin said. "And you must live for all of them, since they cannot." He lifted her—she was so light, so frail—and eased her atop the gryphon. "He'll take you back safely."

She nodded, summoning her courage, and held on tightly as the beast gathered himself and ascended into a sky crowded with bats and gryphons bearing dark rangers and priests. Despite the provocation, Anduin's priests had not attacked, for which Anduin was grateful.

Sylvanas Windrunner had killed her own people. But she had ordered restraint when it came to humans. At least thus far. Anduin's gaze swept the field. There were a few more Stormwind residents running toward the keep, but they drew no fire from the dark rangers.

But a warning began to sound in the back of his mind. If they were done with the slaughter of their own kind and they did not want to attack the humans who had participated in the Gathering, why were they here?

And the answer slammed into his head. He frantically began to scan the field for the one person, living or undead, who could possibly pose a threat to Sylvanas Windrunner: Calia Menethil.

She was running as fast as she could. A warm golden field enveloped her: the Light, shielding her from harm. For now. Anduin cast a

spell on himself as he raced after her, trying to close the distance between them.

A shadow passed overhead. Anduin looked up, and his heart surged
as a single bat flew over him, low and close, an intimidation and a
taunt. He caught a glimpse of glowing red eyes, and then the bat was
gone, moving forward more swiftly than he could ever run toward the
Light-shielded uncrowned queen of Lordaeron.

Sylvanas was running her down like a hawk would a rabbit. The
shield would protect Calia, but it would not last forever, and then
there would be a few heartbeats during which she would be completely vulnerable. If he could just reach her in time, he could call
down another shield for her. But his decision to send the elderly
Emma back to safety on his gryphon meant that he was relying on his
own two feet. He called on the Light for strength and speed and a
shield of his own.

He knew that he had made himself the perfect target. So be it. If
Sylvanas wanted war, let her start one.

But even as he closed the distance, he knew it would not be enough.
The cry of denial scraped Anduin's throat raw as he uttered it. The
world around him seemed to shatter like glass; all its bright shards of
hope and idealism and joy were rendered jagged and sharp.

The glowing aura of protection around the true queen of Lordaeron shimmered, then vanished.

He watched, only a few yards too far away to save Calia, as Sylvanas Windrunner drew back a black arrow, slowly, languidly, savoring
the moment, and then let it fly.

Violet tendrils of smoke twined around the weapon as it flew un-
erringly toward its target. Time seemed to slow as Calia, her hood
down and her blond hair flying, was struck in the center of the back—
directly through the heart. She arched and fell forward, hitting the
ground hard, arms and legs akimbo, making her last movements
clumsy and graceless.

Anduin called on the Light, but he was too far, too slow, and there
was no response.

Calia Menethil, heir to the throne of Lordaeron, was dead.

Now, past all ability to help, to heal, he reached her and dropped to his knees beside her. Once more, a shadow fell over his body as well as his heart, and he looked up, devastated and furious, to see Sylvanas Windrunner smirking down at him, another arrow nocked to the bowstring.

The air was filled with the sound of beating membranous wings as she was joined by a host of her rangers. They, too, had arrows nocked, all aimed at him.

A spurt of fear raced through him, then absolute white-hot fury. The shield of Light still glimmered around him, but it would not last. He had a choice. He could save himself and immediately run to the keep, protected by the Light, or he could gather Calia's limp frame and, vulnerable to even a single ordinary arrow, bear her from the field.

Turalyon kept calling this a battlefield. I kept telling him he was wrong.

Silently, Anduin gathered Calia's still-warm body in his arms and rose. He looked up at the dark rangers, at their dark mistress, and gazed evenly into those glowing red orbs.

"You don't want a war," he said calmly.

"Don't I?" She drew back on the string farther. Anduin could hear the bone bow creak. "If I kill you today, too, I'll have a matched set of dead royals: a queen *and* a king."

He shook his head. "If you wanted war, we wouldn't be having this conversation. But I have a right to declare it. You promised not to kill any of my people." He lifted Calia's body, letting her still frame say all that needed to be said.

"Ah, but she is not one of yours, is she?" Sylvanas's voice had a cold but angry edge to it, and the hair along Anduin's arms lifted. "She is—was—a citizen of Lordaeron. Its queen. You brought a usurper onto the field, Anduin Wrynn. I would be well within my rights to consider that a hostile action. Who violated the treaty first?"

"She came as a healer!"

"She leaves as a corpse. Did you think I would not discover what you had done?"

"I swear to you by the Light, I acted in good faith. I gave no orders to your people to defect. You can believe that or not. But if you strike me down, my people and all of Stormwind's allies will retaliate. And they will do so holding nothing back."

Her eyes narrowed. Anduin knew she understood the lesson of this day's tragic events. She was not universally loved among her people. He was. She ruled with an iron fist. He ruled with compassion. Neither of them was ready for a war. Anduin said a silent prayer that Sylvanas would not start one.

The silence stretched on. "I grieve for the fallen today," Anduin said. "But they did not die by my hand. Calia Menethil was indeed not my subject. As for what she thought she could accomplish . . . I truly do not know. Whatever it was, she paid the price for it. I am going to take her body back to the Netherlight Temple and the Conclave she so loved. If you want a war, you can start it now."

He turned, feeling a phantom tingle in his exposed back as he began to walk calmly, without rushing, toward Stromgarde Keep. The shield around him faded and disappeared.

Nothing happened. Then he heard the bats utter their unnerving, high-pitched sounds and a rapid, loud flapping of leathery wings. And then they were gone.

There would be no war between the Alliance and the Horde today.

CHAPTER THIRTY-FIVE

Arathi Highlands, Stromgarde Keep

The next few days were a blur of regret, pain, and soul-searching for Anduin Wrynn.

Genn, predictably, had been furious, but to Anduin's surprise, he had bitten his tongue when the young king walked through the gates of Stromgarde carrying the body of Calia Menethil. Faol was heartbroken, receiving the corpse of his beloved friend humbly from Anduin's arms, as stunned as Anduin had been at Calia's turn and riddled with remorse for not anticipating it.

"I would never have brought her today if I'd had the slightest idea," he said.

"I know," Anduin said. "Take her home. And I will do the same for my people. I'll come to the temple as soon as I can."

It tore at him to see the people who once had been so full of hope look so shocked and devastated as they boarded the ships that had borne them to the Arathi Highlands and its ghosts. Even those who had not parted well from their Forsaken counterparts looked shaken. Anduin usually was able to find the right words at the right time, but now he found none.

What could he tell them, really? How could he possibly comfort them? There was no easy, obvious road back from this, and so he retired to his cabin, deep in prayer for guidance.

It came in the form of a knock on the door and the appearance of an old friend. "I do not wish to disturb," Velen said.

Anduin smiled wearily. "You never could," he said, and invited the draenei inside. He offered some refreshment, but Velen declined gracefully.

"I will not stay long," Velen said. "But I felt I should come. You are king now, not the youth I guided only a few short years ago back on the *Exodar*, but I will always be there if you ever wish what wisdom the Light sees fit for me to give you."

Velen doubtless thought the reminder of Anduin's time among the draenei would be comforting. But all Anduin could think of was how much he longed for those days. For that peace. And before he knew what was happening, he had blurted out, "I feel helpless, Velen. I promised my people a reunion with their loved ones. Instead, they watched them be slaughtered. I want to comfort them, but I have no words. I miss my time learning from you. I miss the *Exodar*. I miss O'ros."

Velen smiled sadly. "We all do," he said, "but we cannot go back to happier times. We can only live in the present, and right now that present is painful. But we do have a way to be with a naaru. We are priests, Anduin, but we cannot heal others until we are steady and calm within ourselves. Go to the Netherlight Temple now. Share your grief with Faol and in so doing, help each other. Speak with Saa'ra. See what it has to say to you. There is time. Then you can greet your people on the docks and, Light willing, know what to say to help their wounded hearts."

Anduin smiled. "I'll never be as wise as you, old friend."

Velen chuckled and shook his head ruefully. "My only wisdom is to understand that I am not."

THE NETHERLIGHT TEMPLE

When Anduin entered the temple, he saw at once that something was happening. It seemed as though everyone in the temple had clustered around the entrance to Saa'ra's chamber, which was marked by its constant radiance. Anduin, frowning, hastened toward the crowd, making his way through the priests who stood or knelt, silent, reverent. Up ahead, Anduin could see the radiant lilac form of Saa'ra, and despite his heartache and confusion, he felt the naaru's comforting brush upon his spirit.

Calia Menethil's body hovered in front of Saa'ra. She lay in the air as if she were sleeping, her hands folded on her breast. Her blond hair gleamed almost as brightly as the naaru itself, falling softly, her gold and white robes draping her slender frame.

Faol knelt in front of the crystalline entity, his head bowed in prayer. High Priestess Ishanah stepped beside Anduin and said quietly, "Something is happening to Calia. Her flesh has not begun to decompose. Faol has been with her since he brought her here." The draenei turned, looking down at Anduin as she said, "Saa'ra told him to wait for *you*, my young king."

A shiver ran down Anduin's spine, and he swallowed. He took a deep breath and stepped toward the archbishop. "I'm here, Your Grace," he said quietly. "What would you have me do?"

Faol turned his face up to Anduin's. "I'm not quite sure," he said. "But Saa'ra was insistent that you were to be part of this."

And then Saa'ra, who had been silent, spoke in their minds.

Calia would come to me when the dreams of what was past were too painful to endure, Saa'ra said. *I cautioned her to have patience. There were things she had to do before the dreams would cease, things she must understand. People who would need her help.*

And I assured her of this seemingly strange truth: that sometimes the most beautiful and important gifts come wrapped in pain and blood.

The truth of those words hit Anduin's heart. Those were the gifts that no one ever wanted, that one would do anything not to have bestowed. But they were also indeed as Saa'ra said: beautiful and important.

There will be no more of those battles for her now. Calia Menethil will be freed from the pains of the living, from the nightmares that once rent her heart.

She understood that those on that field were her people. And she accepted that responsibility by giving her life to try to save them. Not human, as they were when she was young, but Forsaken, as they were in that moment.

Light and dark. Forsaken priest and human priest. Together you shall bring her back as the Light and she herself would have her be.

Anduin's mouth was dry, and he trembled. He looked at Faol, but the priest only nodded. They moved wordlessly to Calia's side, standing as she hovered in midair, and each of them took one of her small, pale hands.

Bring her back as the Light and she herself would have her be, Saa'ra had said. He didn't know what the naaru had meant by the words, and he suspected that Faol didn't either.

But somehow, he knew, Calia did.

Anduin felt the Light come to him, warm and calming. It seeped through his body, soothing his spirit and his tumultuous mind. It was a familiar sensation, yet there was something different. He usually experienced the Light's power flowing through him like a river. But now it seemed like a whole ocean was utilizing him as a vessel. Anduin felt a quick flicker of fear. Would he be able to contain and direct something this powerful?

He anticipated that he would feel overwhelmed, stretched to his limit, but the tide of Light that swept through him now was one that reinvigorated him even as it asked him to be fully present, to give all of himself to the task ahead.

Yes, he said in his heart. *I will.*

The Light limned him in its warm hue, and it chased around the still yet completely intact body of the queen of Lordaeron and whirled about the Forsaken archbishop. Anduin felt it swell like a wave, then crest and break, emptying him but not depleting him.

The cold hand in his squeezed.

Anduin gasped as Calia opened her eyes. They glowed a soft, gentle white, not the eerie yellow hue of a Forsaken's. A smile curved a face that had no flush of life to it. Slowly her body tilted from horizontal to vertical, and her feet settled onto the stone floor.

Calia Menethil was dead, but she lived. She was no mindless undead, but she was not Forsaken, either. She had been raised by a human and a Forsaken both using the power of the Light, bathed in the radiance of a naaru.

"Calia," said Faol, and his voice trembled. "Welcome back, dear girl. I didn't dare hope that you would return to us!"

"Someone once told me that hope is what you have when all other things have failed you," Calia said to him. Her voice was echoing, sepulchral, but like Faol's, it was warm and kind. Her white gaze went to Anduin. She smiled gently. "Where there is hope, you make room for healing, for all things that are possible—and some that are not."

Anduin watched as everyone responded to Calia's—what? Resurrection? No, she was still dead. Dark gift? That wouldn't be accurate either, because it was the Light that had been present today. There was nothing of darkness in this undead woman.

After a short time, though, she turned to Anduin and gave him a rueful smile. "Thank you," she said, "for helping the archbishop bring me back."

"The Light didn't need my help," he said.

"Well, then, for not abandoning me on the field."

"I couldn't do that." He frowned and asked quietly, "Was that your plan all along? To use my work on the Gathering as a chance to reclaim your throne?"

Sorrow flitted across her pale face. "No. Not really. Come sit with me."

They found a small table, and everyone gave them privacy. "Ever since I met Archbishop Faol, I had believed that one day, if I had the chance, I could show that even though I was not Forsaken, I could treat them as my people and rule them well. My brother had tried to destroy them. I wanted to help them."

"So when you heard about the Gathering, you wanted to participate."

She nodded. "Yes. I wanted to meet more Forsaken who were not priests. I wanted to see how they would react to meeting their families. But that was all I intended for the Gathering. I swear it."

"I believe you," he said, and he saw her visibly relax.

"I don't deserve that, but thank you."

He folded his hands on the table and looked at her piercingly. "So what changed your mind?"

"Parqual Fintallas approached me and said that they—they needed me now. That it was time. I didn't know what he meant at first, but then I realized they were defecting. I had a choice: support them, reveal who I was, and get them and others to safety, or disavow them and get them killed." She looked away. "But I got them killed anyway."

"You also almost started a war," Anduin said, his voice hard. "You could have been responsible for the deaths of hundreds of thousands. Do you understand that?"

She looked chagrined. "I do now," she said. "I was never taught how to rule, Anduin, because no one expected me to. I never formally studied politics or strategy. So when I got out there . . ."

"You just followed your heart," Anduin said, his anger turning to sorrow. "I understand that. But a ruler doesn't always have that luxury."

"No. I am not yet ready to rule. But I wish to serve the people of Lordaeron. They are my people, and now I am like them. It feels . . . right." She smiled. "I'll learn. And from the archbishop, I'll learn what it's like to be . . . this. To be undead yet walk in the Light."

It should have been harrowing. It should have been ghoulish. But as Calia Menethil, changed but still herself, gazed at the king of Stormwind, all Anduin could think of were the naaru's words: Calia was freed forever from the nightmares that had haunted her.

And he was glad.

It was the only comfort on one of the bleakest days he had ever known.

The Arathi Highlands

Velen had advised Anduin to go to the Netherlight Temple, speak with Saa'ra, and listen to what the naaru said. Then, Velen had suggested that Anduin would be able to greet his people on the docks and "Light willing, know what to say to help their wounded hearts."

The draenei had been right.

When the ships had come into Stormwind Harbor, Anduin was there to meet them but not to welcome them home. He was there to take them back to the Arathi Highlands.

He brought with them the carvers of tombstones and the diggers of graves. The people of Lordaeron—of the Undercity—would not be left to rot, forgotten in a damp green field. Anduin had invited those who wished to return to stay on the ship; others were welcome to go back to their homes.

Most stayed.

Now he walked among them, watched but undisturbed by the Forsaken who manned Galen's Fall near Thoradin's Wall, as they identified, spoke words over, and buried those who had been brave enough to try to move past prejudice and fear. Anduin listened as humans told their stories about the fallen as the Forsaken were, at last, laid to rest.

Velen might deflect compliments about his wisdom, but Anduin knew better. This was healing. This was respect. When they buried Jem, Jack, and Jake—Anduin did not think he would ever forget their names—Emma broke down. Philia was there, slipping an arm around her to support the older woman, her own eyes red with weeping.

"They're gone now, every one of them," Emma said. "I'm all alone."

"No, you're not," Philia said. "We'll help each other."

Genn had returned to the Arathi Highlands with Anduin. He still hadn't had a chance to talk to the boy, and he wasn't about to let him return without accompanying him. Now he listened as Philia and Emma comforted each other, and watched as Anduin, clearly deeply moved, strode a few paces away.

Genn stepped up beside him.

"I knew cats were quiet, but you wolves are almost as stealthy," Anduin said.

Genn shrugged. "We know how to move to suit the task," he said.

"So I am discovering . . . repeatedly."

"I've gotten to know you rather well over the last few years," Genn said, ignoring the jab. "I've watched you grow up—a harder task for you than it ought to have been. But nothing is easy in this world, it seems."

"No," Anduin agreed. His blue eyes roamed the field. "Not even keeping peace for a single day."

"You should know by now that peace is one of the hardest things in this or any world to keep, my boy," Genn said, not unkindly.

Anduin shook his head in sorrow and disbelief. "I can't blot out the images of the Desolate Council running as fast as they could to what they thought was a future with their loved ones. I feel responsible. For them. And for them," he said, gesturing to the living still moving on the field.

"Sylvanas killed her own people, Anduin," Genn reminded him. "Not you."

"Rationally, of course I know that. But it doesn't matter. Not in my bones. And not here." Anduin placed a hand on his chest for a moment, then let it fall. "Those who fell on this field did so because King Anduin Wrynn of Stormwind had promised them they would be safe as they reunited with their loved ones. And they died because of that promise. Because of me."

The bitterness in his voice was like acid. Genn, who had never heard it from him before, fell silent. After a time, Anduin spoke.

"You've come to lecture me, obviously. Go ahead. I deserve every word."

Genn sniffed and rubbed his beard for a moment, his eyes on the horizon. "Actually, I've come to apologize."

Anduin's head whipped around, and he didn't bother to hide his shock. "Apologize? What for? All you did was warn me against this."

"You told me to watch. So I did. I listened, too." He pointed at an ear. "Wolves have excellent hearing. I watched the interactions. I saw tears. I heard laughter. I saw fear give way to joy."

He kept his gaze on the people of Stormwind honoring their dead as he continued to speak.

"I saw other things, too. I saw a Stormwind guard head out onto this field. He spoke with a Forsaken woman—his wife or his sister, perhaps. But finally he shook his head and walked away from her, back to the keep."

Anduin's brow furrowed in puzzlement, but he remained quiet.

"The Forsaken lowered her head and stood for a moment. Just . . . stood there. And then, very slowly, she walked back to Thoradin's Wall."

Now Genn faced Anduin. "There was no violence. No . . . anger, or hate. Not even hard words, it seemed. And while those happy reunions were remarkable, extraordinary, it struck me that this was even more important. Because if humans and Forsaken could meet, with so much emotion involved, and disagree—dislike or even be repelled by one another—and simply walk away . . ."

Greymane shook his head. "All I'd seen from the Forsaken was treachery, deceit, and a hunger to end life." *I watched my boy die in my arms, giving his life to save mine,* he thought but did not say. "I saw ghastly, shambling monstrosities descend upon living beings with no desire other than to snuff out that light of life. I'd *never* seen what I saw that day. I never thought I could."

Anduin listened.

"I believe in the Light," Genn stated. "I've seen it, benefited from it, so I have to. But I've never really *felt* it. I couldn't feel it from Faol. I just saw what I viewed as a gut-wrenching travesty—an old friend, dead, animated like some sort of joke. Spouting things that couldn't possibly be true.

"And then he said something that *was* true. Too true. It cut like a blade, and I couldn't bear that."

Genn took a deep breath. "But he was right. *You* were right. I still think what was done to the Forsaken against their will was horrifying. But it's clear to me now that some of them haven't been broken by it. Some of them are still the people they once were. So I was wrong, and I apologize."

Anduin nodded. A smile crossed his face fleetingly, then was gone. It was clear he was still burdened with guilt and stubbornly wouldn't relinquish the pain of it. Not yet.

"You were right about Sylvanas," Anduin said, that cold bitterness lingering in his voice. "Light knows, I wish I'd listened."

"I wasn't right about her, either," Genn said, startling Anduin for the second time in as many minutes. "Not entirely. I knew she couldn't let this go by without doing something. I thought she'd attack *us*. Not her own people."

Anduin winced and turned away. "She may have killed them, but I promised the Desolate Council safe passage. Those deaths are on my conscience. They will haunt me."

"No, they won't," Genn said. "Because you kept your end of the bargain. No one realized how poorly Sylvanas Windrunner could deal with anything that wasn't complete and utter obeisance. If you ask me, the Desolate Council signed their own death warrants simply by existing as a governing body. She'd have done something to them sooner or later. Their ghosts, if Forsaken can have ghosts, won't haunt you, my boy. You did something wonderful for them."

Now Anduin did turn to Greymane, looking him full in the eye.

"Answer me this: Would it have been enough for you, Genn? To see your son one more time and pay for that one encounter with your life?"

The question was utterly unexpected, and for a moment Genn was taken aback. Old pain shot through him, and he tightened his jaw. He didn't want to answer, but there was something in the youth's face that would not let the older man refuse.

"Yes," he said at last. "Yes. It would have."

And it was true.

Anduin took a deep, shuddering breath and nodded at Genn.

"Nonetheless, it is a tragedy, and it's done any chance of peace great harm. It's destroyed the prospect of working together with the Horde to heal the world. Azerite will continue to threaten the balance of power. It's hurt the Alliance, too. Sylvanas used a moment that could have been a true turning point as a chance to eliminate people whom she viewed as her enemies. And she did it so smoothly, so *well*, that I can't even call her on it. She didn't break her word. Calia was a would-be usurper. I can't ask Stormwind to go to war because the warchief of the Horde chose to execute individuals she will now paint as traitors. So she gets away with it. She's won. She eliminated the opposition, killed the rightful heir to Lordaeron, and did it all while looking like a noble leader for not attacking the Alliance and starting a war."

Genn said nothing. He didn't need to. He simply stood next to Anduin and let the young king sort it out on his own.

The minutes passed, and then, finally, Anduin spoke.

"I will never, *ever* stop hoping for peace," he said. His voice trembled with leashed emotion. "I have seen too much good in too many people to paint them all as evil and worthy of slaughter. And I will also *never* stop believing that people can change. But I realize now that I've been like a farmer expecting to harvest crops from a poisoned field. It's simply not possible."

Greymane tensed. The boy was leading to something.

"People can change," Anduin repeated. "But some people will never—*never*—desire to do so. Sylvanas Windrunner is one of those."

He took a deep breath. Sorrow and grim resolve made him look older. Genn had seen similar expressions on the faces of those who had been tasked with a heartbreaking duty.

When the boy spoke, Genn was glad of the words but saddened by his need to say them.

"I believe," said Anduin Llane Wrynn, "that Sylvanas Windrunner is well and truly lost."

ACKNOWLEDGMENTS

This is the first Blizzard novel I have started and finished as a formal employee. My experience of being able to instantly ask any question and have it answered, sitting in on meetings that determined the far-flung future of Azeroth, and being surrounded by the energy of creation and its amazingly talented creators permeates this book.

Shout-out to some of the remarkable people I work with regularly and who help make "going to work" more like "coming home": Lydia Bottegoni, Robert Brooks, Matt Burns, Sean Copeland, Steve Danuser, Cate Gary, Terran Gregory, George Krstic, Christi Kugler, Brianne Loftis, Timothy Loughran, Marc Messenger, Allison Monahan, Justin Parker, Andrew Robinson, Derek Rosenberg, Ralph Sanchez, and Robert Simpson.

ABOUT THE AUTHOR

CHRISTIE GOLDEN is the award-winning *New York Times* bestselling author of fifty-four novels and more than a dozen short stories in the fields of fantasy, science fiction, and horror. Her media tie-in works include launching the Ravenloft line in 1991 with *Vampire of the Mists,* more than a dozen *Star Trek* novels, several movie novelizations, the Warcraft and World of Warcraft novels *Rise of the Horde, Lord of the Clans, Arthas: Rise of the Lich King,* and *War Crimes, Assassin's Creed: Heresy,* as well as *Star Wars Battlefront II: Inferno Squad, Star Wars: Dark Disciple,* and the *Star Wars: Fate of the Jedi* novels *Omen, Allies,* and *Ascension.* In 2017, she was awarded the International Association of Media Tie-in Writers' Faust Award and named a Grandmaster in recognition of over a quarter century of writing. She currently works full-time for Blizzard Entertainment, where she gets to hang out in Azeroth to her heart's content.

christiegolden.com
Twitter: @ChristieGolden
Find Christie Golden on Facebook

ABOUT THE TYPE

This book was set in Caslon, a typeface first designed in 1722 by William Caslon (1692–1766). Its widespread use by most English printers in the early eighteenth century soon supplanted the Dutch typefaces that had formerly prevailed. The roman is considered a "workhorse" typeface due to its pleasant, open appearance, while the italic is exceedingly decorative.